Shieldmaiden

by

Marianne Whiting

Published by Accent Press – 2016
ISBN 9781786153012
Copyright © Marianne Whiting 2016

The stories contained within this book are works of
fiction. Names and characters are the product of the
authors' imagination and any resemblance to actual
persons, living or dead, is entirely coincidental.

For my husband, Jon,
who has learnt quite a lot about Vikings.

Part One:

Loyalty

1.

On the day I was born, my father saw the fylgia. Our family's guardian spirit appeared to him holding a distaff in one hand and a sword in the other. He thought it meant twins, a girl and a boy. Then he was called into the hall and presented with me, his first daughter. He already had sons, so there was probably no disappointment. I like to think that he smiled as he put me in his helmet to show that he accepted this child as his own. Later, when he thought about the fylgia again, he wondered about her message. This is the way with gods and spirits. They show you signs but you have to interpret their meaning for yourself.

I had seen eight summers when it became clear to my father that it was not his sons but his daughter who had an aptitude for swordplay. He called me to him and handed me a short scabbard. My heart beat like thunder in my chest as I drew a blade from the fleece-lined bed. I turned it so it caught the sunlight. The grip had a pattern of trefoils. The top of the hilt had broken off and in its place our blacksmith had forged a disc with a picture of an eye on each side. My father pointed to it.

'She can see in both directions and your enemies won't take you by surprise,' he said.

I nodded. It made sense.

'Is it really mine? To keep?'

He smiled and I knew a dream had come true – *my*

very own sword. No more playing with sharpened sticks or pestering my brothers to let me use their blades. I swung it a couple of times from side to side. It lay smooth and balanced in my hand. It was a wonderful feeling.

'What's she called?'

'That's for you to decide.'

'I shall call her *Snakebite*.'

'That's a good name. Remember you will be judged by how you use her so think before you act and make sure you bring honour to both your names.'

* * *

Becklund, my father's farm, was set among the Cumbrian fells. There I rode my small mare Whitefoot and hunted deer and hare with bow and arrows. I swam in Loweswater and tickled trout in the small beck. When unable to escape, I also helped with the work on the farm and in the house. It seemed a perfect life and I saw no reason for it ever to end. But in the year we now call 933, it did. I was twelve years old when my whole world changed with the arrival of a stranger who had violence etched in the lines of his face.

Late one evening at the time when summer begins to fade, Jarl Swein Hjaltebrand of Manx arrived alone and unannounced. He had to stoop even lower than my father to get through the door and he stumbled with fatigue as he put his shield down and stepped forward to be embraced. His long, woollen cloak concealed a saerk – the short mail shirt, worn by warriors. A place was made for him next to my father and he unbuckled his belt with the heavy sword and left that, and an ornate battleaxe, by the door. My father, unsmiling, greeted the Jarl.

'You are welcome, Swein. It's been a long time since we had news of you.' He led him to the seat next to his own and nodded to me to bring mead, while the thrall-girls went to fetch meat from the cookhouse. The flickering light of the tallow showed the deep furrows on Jarl Swein's brow and the stubble on his chin. I had never met him before, nor had I heard anyone speak of him and yet my father treated him like an honoured friend.

Jarl Swein ignored the food but emptied the gilded horn in one draught and held it out to be refilled. My father said no more. Nobody else dared speak and silence grew like a black mould on the smoke-filled air. Then the Jarl spoke in a hoarse voice.

'Kveldulf, we have seen many things and faced many perils together. Often we survived by watching out for treacherous knives and bloodthirsty swords. We have mixed our blood and become brothers, is this not so?'

'You speak the truth, Swein.' My father sounded calm but my mother's breath came in shallow gasps.

'Things have gone badly for me, Kveldulf. I grow old, my warriors die and my allies turn to the plough and the net. No ...' he held up his hand when my father made to reply, 'no, I mean no reproach, Kveldulf, you are a man of honour.' It sounded almost like a question. They stared at each other, the Jarl gradually straightening his back, my father's eyes dark under his heavy brow. All along the table, spoons and knives were held still, men stopped chewing and the wenches froze with serving-plates and bowls held aloft, as we listened to the unsaid words that made the air between the two masters vibrate with suppressed anger. My two elder

3

brothers leaned against each other, Steinar's eyes wide open, tears beginning to well up, Thorstein chewing his lips and clasping his wife's hand.

I was ashamed of my feeble brothers, unable to hide their fear, their cowardliness bringing shame on the family. I straightened my shoulders and took two trembling steps up to the Jarl.

'Your horn stands empty, Jarl Hjaltebrand, shall I pour you some mead?' My voice fluttered through the air. Both men turned to me. I didn't dare meet my father's eye so looked the Jarl full in the face. His mouth opened in surprise and I noticed he had most of his teeth but they were yellow and rotting, and when he breathed out, I had to steady myself not to turn away. Then he shook his head, laughed and turned to my mother.

'So, Gudrun Haraldsdaughter, I see your girl takes after you, ever ready to interrupt the deliberations of men.'

'You have paid slight attention to my offerings, Swein. The meat is untouched, does it not please you? Don't be in a hurry. You can't travel this evening. We are all eager to listen to tales of your exploits.' After that reproach, the Jarl seemed to relax and remember his manners. He began eating and the rest of the household took the opportunity to help themselves. That is with the exception of my brothers, who still sat close together, watching our guest, fear lingering on their faces.

The tales of awesome perils and mighty deeds never materialised. The Jarl wished to speak to my father in private and they withdrew to a corner of the hall. The rest of us had to make do with one of my mother's stories about giants and trolls. I heard none of it, since I sat at the back straining my ears, trying to listen in on the conversation between my father and his guest. I couldn't hear them either so ended up with nothing but an angry feeling of being left out.

Jarl Hjaltebrand left early the next morning. He would return with his household for a visit before continuing inland in search of a place to settle. My mother seemed agitated and she was impatient with the thralls during the preparations for our guests. My father went silent and brooding around the farm. I had my own preoccupations; one was to keep out of my mother's way before I was drafted in to help; the other was the riddle of my father and the mysterious Jarl Swein.

* * *

A few days later, I returned from a lonely ramble, having picked a few cranberries to account for my absence. Passing the bathhouse I could hear my parents' voices. There was no smoke, so the small stone hut was not in use. I crept up and put my ear close to the cool, moss-covered wall.

My father's voice came through. He sounded tired and he spoke slowly, as if he was trying to be patient.

'… side by side, our blood mingled with that of our enemies. I cannot forsake him now.'

'You were Harald's sworn man, you accepted his ring and now you'll give shelter to his enemy.' Mother sounded like she'd been crying.

'We both fought for King Harald Finehair.'

'And now, Swein has turned against the king and brought this terrible danger to his family. I think he lies when he says he didn't know who owned the island. He must have known it belongs to King Harald and yet he still raided there. Harald may be old now but he has sons. His revenge on Swein, his household and anyone who helps him will be bloody and without mercy. We have a good life here, Kveldulf. Don't allow this misplaced loyalty to put us all in danger.'

'He saved my life, I owe him.'

'But you saved his too – he told me so, when we first met in my father's house in Norway. You owe him nothing, a life for a life, your debt is cancelled.'

'You don't understand the bond between warriors.'

Mother's voice became an impatient cry: 'Oh but I do, and I …'

'Be still, Gudrun!'

Father rarely interrupted my mother. He was slow to anger but when it came over him, strong men stood aside. The way he sounded now made me crouch deeper behind the piles of firewood. I could hear movement in the hut and father shouting.

'Get out of my way, woman!'

The door crashed open and my father stormed out. He strode across the copse, kicking at the ground. My mother emerged shortly afterwards and walked with a heavy tread towards the farm. As she came within view of the buildings, she straightened her shoulders and raised her head, always the composed, proud mistress of the house.

Relieved not to have been discovered, I was left with my own thoughts. So, my father had been King Harald of Norway's man. That's why the neighbours, the tradesmen in the towns and farmers in the villages, karls and thralls alike, showed respect for him and did his bidding. It wasn't because he was rich; he wasn't particularly, it wasn't because of his wisdom; there were others wiser than him, but because he was a great warrior. And now he would stand by his blood-brother in the face of danger. I felt a surge of pride because I was still too young to understand the dilemma of divided loyalty and the difference between respect and fear.

* * *

For days on end, we brewed and baked and slaughtered and cooked. The floor in the longhouse was covered with fresh rushes and the bathhouse fired up so our guests could cleanse themselves after their journey. It was almost like preparing for the midwinter sacrifice. I was happy and excited with the thought of so many new people to meet and, of course, I thought that among the warriors there was bound to be one who was taller, handsomer and braver than all the rest, a young hero meant for me.

The Jarl's household arrived. They came with cattle and sheep and dozens of packhorses laden with sacks, chests and bundles. Our guests pitched their tents in the meadow behind the main house and sent their animals to graze on the hillside. People and animals all looked tired and dejected. The women were a miserable lot, grumbling and complaining about having to leave their homes. They spent most of the time hunched around the hearth with their spinning, telling my mother about the splendid houses and bulging storerooms they'd left behind. The men soon recovered their good humour and went hunting or amused themselves with sword games and riding competitions. I kept making excuses to leave the women and walk past the men without seeming to pay them too much attention.

My efforts were wasted. The men were either old or

ugly or, in most cases, both. They were also rather coarse and took a delight in rough wordplay of the kind I had heard in town and which my father would stop with a look and a sharp turn of his head. But here, in my own home, I was now prey to uncouth pestering while my father was too occupied with his old friend to notice. After a troll-ugly housekarl tried to fondle me I decided to deal with the problem in my own way.

On the second evening, as the company settled down to roast meat, curly kale and rich, steaming broth, I strapped my dagger to my belt under the pinafore. I poured ale with one hand while the other rested on the handle of my dagger. When hairy fingers reached inside my pinafore I was ready.

'Thor and his goats!' the scar-faced fighter swore and wiped his bleeding hand on his tunic. His neighbours sniggered.

'What is it, Thorfinn?' asked the Jarl. Thorfinn cleared his throat, thought a minute and replied with a *drapa*.

'Salt-stained warrior suddenly savaged
Meek-looking maiden carries the teeth
of a wild-running wolverine
Time now to tame her
by marriage to manly master.'

The guests all laughed and clapped their hands. My father looked thoughtful and my mother glared at me but I had no more trouble from any of the men.

Towards the end of the meal one of the Jarl's daughters was called upon to recite a story. She was very good and we all laughed as the god Thor wrestled with an old woman, who was really old age, which, as I know now, *nobody* can defeat. Then my brother

8

Thorstein fetched his lyre and played. The women closed their eyes and swayed like saplings in the breeze. Ruffians, who had made fun of him earlier, listened slack-mouthed, their calloused hands wiping tears from weather-beaten cheeks.

A serf stirred by the door, the music died and all turned to listen. A horse could be heard entering the yard. The door crashed open. Women grabbed their children. All round the hall men got up reaching for their weapons. A dark, bulky figure entered without putting down his weapons or uttering a word of peace. My father stood up and drew his sword.

The tall figure staggered, his legs buckled under him and he fell, face down, to the floor. The shaft of an arrow protruded from his back. I rushed up to him and stood looking at the dark stain on his cloak. Although I didn't know it then, my hero had arrived and lay bleeding in my father's hall.

2.

I stood as still as a stone, clutching the jug to my chest and staring at the blood soaking into the floor-rushes. Jarl Swein pushed past me and knelt by the body.

'Ragnar,' he said and his voice was hoarse.

My mother ordered a table to be cleared and the wounded youth was placed on it, face down. Jarl Swein's wife cried and called to the gods.

'Oh, my son, my son! Baldur, Frigga look to your servant the …'

'Hold your tongue, woman, or leave!' the Jarl made a threatening gesture and she stopped. He then bent over his unconscious son and with a swift movement broke off the feathered shaft of the arrow. 'Keep still,' he muttered as Ragnar came to and groaned. Ragnar fell silent but his nails dug into the boards he was lying on. I dug my nails into the palms of my hands, willing him to be brave. The Jarl then removed the thick woollen cloak and cut the blood-soaked tunic open. My mother was ready with hot water and clean rags. The Jarl looked at her and nodded.

'You always had your wits about you, Gudrun,' he said, 'noble blood, it shows.' He handed her the rag he'd used to clean around the wound.

'We don't speak of that here, Swein.' Mother wrung the used rag in the water and gave it back to him. She turned and, with a hard look, handed me the bowl. I snapped my mouth closed, took the bowl and went to change the water.

When I returned, Jarl Swein was removing the arrow. It had hit Ragnar at an angle, glanced off a rib and lodged in the flesh below the shoulder blade. The bruising had yet to come out and a wound, the size of a baby's fist, glowed, red against pale skin. Having established that no bone was in the way, Jarl Swein made a small incision in Ragnar's side to allow the arrow to be pushed right through. The boy had seen no more than fifteen summers but he stifled his groans and earned the respect of all the men present. The wound was washed with salty water and covered with clean cobwebs. Ingefried, my mother's Norwegian servant, prepared a poultice of crushed comfrey leaves and tied it in place. Ragnar was supported to sit up and given strong mead to drink.

The arrow had been fired by an angry trader, after Ragnar had killed his serf, whom he accused of cheating. The men found this quite in order and praised Ragnar. His mother, at last allowed to get close, stroked his sweat soaked hair and kissed his pale cheeks. Over her shoulder, Ragnar's eyes met mine and my heart beat so hard I could feel my whole body singing. My cheeks burnt. I wanted to look away but my eyes wouldn't leave his and I couldn't stop myself smiling.

* * *

When Jarl Swein and his household departed, Ragnar was still too weak to travel and stayed behind to be nursed by Ingefried. It was regarded as a good opportunity for me to learn more about wounds and healing. Under Ingefried's watchful eye, Ragnar and I had to be careful what we said but there are so many ways young people can convey their feelings. When I put ointment on his wound, Ragnar put his hand on mine and moved it to where I could feel his heart beating.

'Over here. This is where it hurts.'

Ingefried cleared her throat and he let go, but our eyes stayed locked together and I felt my heartbeat quicken.

As he grew stronger, Ragnar was supposed to spend time with my brothers practising weapons skills but they avoided him – Thorstein because he had perfected the skill of avoiding anything to do with sword and axe and Steinar because he took such a thrashing on their first encounter, he was frightened to try again. So I offered to help.

'It's not swordplay I want with you, pretty Sigrid.' Ragnar laughed and looked at me in such a way I felt both angry and happy at the same time.

'She's good,' said Steinar. 'She's better than me.'

'That doesn't take much.'

'Don't be discourteous to my brother,' I said. Ragnar laughed and, feeling only a little remorse for being disloyal, I joined in. Steinar muttered something under his breath. But when I drew my sword and picked up a shield, Ragnar lowered his.

'I can't fight you, Sigrid.'

'Why not?'

'This isn't play. It's serious practice for warriors. You're a woman. Women aren't warriors.'

My smile faded as I realised he was not teasing.

'Well, *this* woman is, so defend yourself!' I went towards him, sword raised. He took a step back.

'Coward!' I hissed and slashed a blade of grass at his feet. He leaped aside and I followed.

'Get him, Sigrid!' called Steinar. Ragnar raised his sword and shield.

He was good, a real swordsman. We practised together the rest of the afternoon. He always won but he taught me much about how to parry a blow with my shield and how to confuse the enemy by looking behind them or by shouting out. There is more skill involved in fighting without causing injury than there is in killing and maiming. It was many years before I realised how I had courted danger with that attack. My father realised however and, when he found out, he spoke to me with an anger I had rarely seen in him. But worse than that, he took my beautiful sword Snakebite from me. I loved that sword but now my father took it back.

The next day he had calmed down. He came and sat next to me and took my hand.

'Ragnar has taken the blame for this but I know you too well, Sigrid. One thing I have failed to teach you is to choose your opponents and to keep a cool head. Fighting Steinar and the untried boys at the Allthing is different. Oh yes, I know about that. Did you think nobody would tell me? I had to pay compensation to Mord Lambason when you made his son lame.' He sounded amused and a bit proud rather than angry, and I cheered up. But then he cleared his throat and with a stern face continued: 'Look, Sigrid, you shall marry and have sons, who will be brave like you. But that will not happen if you are scarred or maimed.'

'But, Father, you say yourself I have learnt well. May I not have Snakebite back? I will take more care, I promise. Maybe we could find a helmet for me as well.'

At this point my mother joined us.

'So that's where you are. Did I not warn you, Kveldulf, the girl will become impossible to marry. Who shall want a wife better at swordplay than weaving? Will you finally put a stop to this folly and get rid of that sword?'

I squeezed my father's hand and held my breath. He stayed silent.

'Kveldulf?' my mother's voice was full of angry impatience. My father released his hand from mine, stood up to face my mother with his arms crossed in front of his chest.

'I have thought this through, Gudrun. Sigrid has the heart of a warrior. She is of my blood and of your father's. Our roots are in Norway and in the way of the Norse. So I shall not get rid of it. But she shall only have it back when she shows more sense in how to use it.' He held up a hand to stop my mother saying anything more and turned to me. 'It is not a plaything. Wielded by a hand that's not guided by the head, it is a dangerous and destructive thing. Now, there's the end of it. And, Sigrid, you need to apologise to Ragnar for attacking him. Steinar tells me you were defending his honour but Ragnar is our guest.'

As I left them, I heard my mother complaining: 'I don't want her spending time with Ragnar. The less we have to do with the family of Jarl Swein, the better.'

I found Ragnar grooming his horse. He smiled and put down the bunch of teasels.

'You know, Sigrid, your father is almost as frightening as you are.'

I burst out laughing. When I got my breath back I tried to apologise, as my father had told me to, but

Ragnar shook his head.

'You are not to blame. I was arrogant and should not have offended Steinar. Is Kveldulf Arnvidson very angry still?'

'He took Snakebite from me.' I choked on the words. 'He says I can have it back when my head guides my hand. It's so unfair.'

'Well ...' Ragnar didn't continue and I looked at him. He chewed his lip. Then he sighed. 'Your father may have a point. You're not going to deny you have a temper, are you? That's why I won all the time. You rush ... oh, Sigrid, don't cry. You are a good swordsm ... woman, I mean. Your father will give you Snakebite back, surely.'

'I don't know.'

'If he doesn't, I shall give you a sword so magnificent it has no equal in all of Cumbria.' He had a way of screwing up his eyes so they looked full of laughter. I wiped my tears. It was impossible to be sad around Ragnar. 'I understand now, you're no ordinary girl. I think maybe you'll be a shieldmaiden, like in the stories.' I felt my cheeks burn but couldn't help smiling. He laughed and took my hand.

'Thorstein tells me there are trout in the beck,' he said. 'Race you there.'

Full of young happiness, we ran through the meadow, down to the water. It was the most perfect day and, when we heard Ingefried calling me, we crossed the stream and walked along the lake-shore until we were well out of earshot. We talked the way young people do about all and everything and, although I think we must have disagreed about some things, we forged such strong bonds, I felt they were for life.

Five glorious days we rode, swam, hunted and laughed together. We climbed Raven Crag and White Crag and up to the ridge of Mellbreak. From the tallest peak we looked across Crummockwater to the looming bulk of Grasmoor wondering whether there were giants there. We tickled trout and cooked it over an open fire. We sneaked away early in the mornings and had no need to return until the light failed. We fed on berries and fish and wild fowl we snared by the lake. The world was ours. Avoiding my mother's and Ingefried's demands that I carry out my duties on the farm became an amusing game. Many times afterwards I wished I had not been so reckless about that. But I was happy and gloried in Ragnar's friendship.

One day we rode up onto Burnbank Fell where we had spotted a small herd of roe-deer a couple of days before. We tethered our horses to track on foot. I wore breeches and a tunic and my bare feet moved silently on the soft grass. Ragnar nodded and we split up to approach the heard from different directions. He disappeared round a low knoll and I continued to move at an angle to his path. When I saw him about sixty ells away I waved. We got down and began creeping up on the deer. I got so close, so very close. I saw the strong, yellow teeth biting off the grass, the small, pointed horns and the delicate hooves. I reached for an arrow.

But we had mistaken the direction of the wind. One of the does sniffed the air and then they were all moving away from us. We ran with them, keeping them in our sight. After a while they stopped and resumed their grazing. Ragnar crouched next to me. We were both breathing hard with the effort of running. I looked at his hand where it rested on the ground. It was tanned and covered in fine golden hairs that glistened in the sun. I could smell the sweat and feel the heat from his body and it made my insides go soft and warm. I felt excited and confused and drew aside. He didn't seem to notice. He pointed to a doe that had been separated from the rest of the bevy. We crawled through the bracken to get downwind of her. As we came within range we both pulled our bows. Two arrows pierced her neck. The doe ran, staggered, fell. We raised a victory-cry putting the rest of the heard to flight.

'You're splendid, Sigrid,' said Ragnar. 'I sometimes feel we could conquer the world together.' He laughed and put his arms around me. 'You're both my friend and my ...' He stopped. His arms tightened around my body and I gasped. My heart beat so hard, he surely must have felt it through our clothing, just as I felt his.

There was a call from the distance.

'Whoa, you two!' Steinar had been sent to look for us. He seemed to take pleasure in relaying just how angry my parents were about my behaviour. We rode home in silence. After we released our horses into the meadow, Ragnar took my hand and whispered, 'You're my shieldmaiden, Sigrid.'

The next morning Ingefried declared Ragnar well enough to travel. He was handed gifts for his family and my father sent a servant to show him the way to Buttermere.   My mother looked pleased. I still remember Ragnar's farewell to me.

'We'll meet again before long. Sigrid, don't forget me.' He kissed my hand as I gave him the drinking horn. His sea-green eyes held mine and we both trembled and spilt some of the farewell ale.

Jarl Swein's farm by Buttermere was but half a day's ride away and every day I watched out for Ragnar, expecting to see him arrive on horseback. I knew better than to ask my mother about him. My father's reply the time I mentioned Ragnar was curt. 'Put that boy out of your mind, daughter.'

Two summers went by with no word from Ragnar or from the rest of the household at Buttermere. I suffered the doubts and the longing, and also the teasing of those who found it amusing.

3.

Autumn on Becklund farm was always busy with
preparations for winter. The storehouses were filled
with grain, fruit and nuts. The animals we couldn't feed
through the cold season were slaughtered. I spent days
on end with my mother and the serf girls in the
cookhouse making sausages, brawn and black pudding.
We needed salt to cure hams and preserve herring. To
pay for that and other essentials my father took pigs and
heifers, or whatever animals we could spare, to the
market in Cockermouth. I sometimes accompanied my
father on these trips.

I was fair of face, strong in body and of a good
family. Becklund was a prosperous farm and I began to
attract the attention of marriageable men in the area. I
turned down three proposals in rapid succession. My
mother was vexed, especially when I returned Hauk of
Swanhill's elaborately carved love-spoon. Hauk's
messenger was barely out of earshot before she cried,
'This just won't do, Sigrid. Hauk may only have one
eye but he has the best farmland in the area and he
returns with the largest catches of herring. You'd be
well provided for. You can't keep turning your suitors
down like this, you'll end up an old maid, a burden to
your brothers.' She talked about it for days but always
out of my father's hearing. She'd already lost that
argument.

'She's still young, there's no hurry,' he'd said. 'Let her find somebody she likes, no harm in that is there, wife?' The way he looked at my mother made her cheeks blush and the corners of her mouth stretch into a reluctant smile. 'Oh, Kveldulf, really,' she'd say and then father grinned and winked at me.

But as the year passed my father, too, became concerned about my lack of interest in the local young men. He put a stop to my sword practice and insisted that I should help my mother in the running of the house. Only when I had made progress in carrying out a woman's duties would he consider returning Snakebite to me.

One day he came to sit with me when I was salting herring.

'I'm getting old.' he began. I thought I knew what he was leading up to but couldn't think what to answer, so I continued sprinkling salt on the layer of cleaned herrings in the barrel.

'Your brothers,' he paused to clear his throat, 'they have no children.'

'I know,' I said and slit the next herring open.

'I need heirs. The farm, someone has to take over when I'm too old.'

'Yes.' I bent over the barrel spreading another layer of fish as evenly as I could on top of the salt.

'This is your problem too.' I straightened up and turned to him. He sat with his elbows resting on his knees and his head bowed as if searching the ground for an answer. 'Thorstein will inherit the farm and you can stay on, as will Steinar, but when you are all old and weak there will be nobody to defend the farm, to work the land and keep you alive. You will be attacked and killed or starve in your old age and I will have built all this in vain.'

I hadn't thought of it like that before. Becklund without my father, with Thorstein and Freydis in place of my parents. And what if Thorstein died? Steinar and I trying to run the farm, perhaps with Freydis. We would be easy prey to the Scottish raiders who ventured ever further into Cumbria rustling cattle, robbing farmsteads and killing anyone in their way.

I was almost past the age when a girl would expect to marry. The suitors I had turned down had taken other brides and, after two years without a word, I had to accept that Ragnar had forgotten about me. With many bitter thoughts about his betrayal, I decided that, if I couldn't have Ragnar and if I must take a husband, it didn't matter who I got. So I agreed that my father should approach Hauk of Swanhill. He had not married and he still sought me out at the gatherings of the Allthing to praise me and offer gifts. He could probably be persuaded to disregard my earlier rejection.

My mother was happy. She sang her Norwegian songs as she washed and braided my hair. She smiled as she pinned two new brooches to my pinafore.

'I'm so proud of you, Sigrid.' She kissed me and I saw tears gather in her eyes. 'So proud, my beautiful daughter. Hauk is a good man. He will be a good husband.' I was determined to make the best of my situation and tried to smile back. Hauk was a prosperous farmer. As his wife I would have thralls and servants to do the heavy, tedious work. Maybe it wouldn't be so bad.

As we stepped outside for the gathered household to admire my bridal gear, my father stepped forward. He handed me the best present I could ever have wished for and I gave a triumphant shout as I once again held my beloved Snakebite. My mother was not so pleased.

'Kveldulf! Oh, husband how can you be so foolish?' she hissed so the servants wouldn't hear.

'The fylgia, I have seen her. Sigrid shall need her sword. There's no getting away from it.' My mother's eyes widened and drew her breath through open mouth.

'The fylgia,' she whispered. 'What did she show you?'

'Just the sword.'

'What does it mean?'

'She who guards our family does not speak or explain. I have to follow her meaning as best I can.'

I paid scant attention apart from that I understood the Norns had woven me a future where I would use my sword. I felt a rush of excitement as I turned Snakebite so her blade reflected the sunlight. Then I looked at my mother. Tears rolled down her face.

'You don't understand,' she whispered to me. 'You don't know what it's like. All that killing, it's …' She was interrupted by the sound of a horn announcing the arrival of my husband-to-be.

Hauk arrived, dressed in an embroidered tunic and a fur-lined cloak, riding a grey stallion and accompanied by his brother, two karls, two servants and a thrall. As he drew close he flicked open his cloak so the gold around his neck and the silver on his buckles and weapons would catch the light. He was an impressive sight but all his finery could not hide the fact that one eye was closed by an ugly, red scar.

'He has a proud bearing and looks are not everything.' My mother wiped her tears and regained her composure. She took my hand and led me forward to show off my new pleated linen dress and the rich brooches holding my red pinafore together. She seemed proud to show me to Hauk and his retinue.

As Hauk dismounted, the wounded side of his face was turned to me. The damaged eye had a dead, unwavering stare. I recoiled. My mother put a steadying hand on my elbow.

'There now, allow him time,' she whispered.

Hauk came across to exchange greetings with my parents. He had the habit of turning his good eye to the person he spoke to so he could see them more clearly. I had never really looked at the undamaged side of his face, a straight nose, a strong chin and his mouth smiled with white teeth. I realised he must have been a handsome man before a Scottish raider slashed his face.

'Sigrid Kveldulfsdaughter, I wish to marry you. May I speak to your father on this matter?' His good eye seemed to bore inside my clothing and touch my bare skin. It made me uneasy but, at the same time, I felt a little excited. I knew he liked me. Maybe my mother was right and I would learn to like him, given time. It would serve Ragnar right for his lack of faith. I gave Hauk my hand and managed to keep my voice steady as I spoke my consent. Then Hauk turned aside to greet Thorstein and Steinar. I saw the ugly side of his face again and shuddered.

Hauk and my father went inside to discuss terms. I knew the negotiations would follow the traditional pattern.

'I shall lose a good pair of hands,' my father would say, 'someone else will need to cook and weave and tend the fields.' Hauk would argue about the cost to keep me and any children we might have. But even I realised there couldn't be much to haggle about, since my children would inherit Becklund as well as Swanhill.

So the bride-price was decided. I was to be replaced by a thrall-girl, ten fleeces of best quality wool and twenty silver pennies. My dowry consisted of linen, wool and furs, my jewellery, a set of drinking horns inlaid with silver, a tapestry measuring three ells with pictures of men and horses. It was all mine to use as I pleased for myself and my children. More important to me, but not mentioned in the agreement, was that I also brought Snakebite, a shield and a helmet.

* * *

We drank the bride-ale and I was delivered to Swanhill by my father and Steinar. They led me to Hauk's bed and left me there behind the thick curtain. My mother had prepared me and I had resolved to accept my situation and be a wife to Hauk. I tried thinking of his handsome side and his smile but, as I lay there listening to the voices from outside, the image of Ragnar floated into my mind. I remembered the way he'd held me close, the way he looked at me and his teasing smile. I wondered whether he had really forgotten me or whether something had happened to keep him away. Perhaps he would one day come asking for me at Becklund. But it was too late. I had given my word and I must be Hauk's wife.

I heard the door open to let in a shower of excited voices. Then it closed again and I heard a rustle of clothes being removed, a thump as first one then another boot was kicked off. I gritted my teeth and closed my eyes. The drapes were pulled open. I looked up to see

Hauk climbing in beside me, panting and leering. His face was flushed and his manhood erect. His scar throbbed purple and ugly.

'At last, Sigrid! You kept me waiting long enough.' He tore at my shift to uncover me. Twin talons of fear and revulsion gripped me. My mind went blank. Out of control, I screamed and fought. My nails dug into his cheeks. My knee caught him in the chest. My teeth sank into his arm. He pulled back, swore and slapped me across the face.

'You shall pay dearly for this!' he roared as he struggled into his trousers and boots and stormed off. I was left to sob and listen to the commotion outside. At first everything went quiet then there was a great roar of voices, anger but also mirth and mockery. It dawned on me what I had done. I crawled under the bedclothes and cried and cried.

After a while Steinar came in. 'Sigrid, you have offended everyone. Your father is crushed by the shame you have brought on the family. You must dress and come outside.'

My father sat on a bench with his back to the wall. A small distance away stood Hauk and his household. His mother cried into her apron. His half-brother and some menservants stood talking together with their hands on their swords. Some of the servants and thralls sniggered behind their hands. A black-haired woman with tanned skin stood to one side cradling a baby while two young children clung to her skirt. She looked at me and laughed.

My eyes were still watering as I faced my father. He looked pale and his voice trembled.

'How could you bring such shame on me, Sigrid?

We will be the laughing stock of the whole of Cumbria. How can we go trading with our heads held high? How can I demand respect from our neighbours after this?' He clasped his hands and I noticed the swollen knuckles and misshapen fingers. He looked very old to me then. 'Listen, Sigrid, Hauk is a proud man. His humiliation has cost me dear. I have agreed to send the bride-price back. In return, Hauk will give you three full moons to get used to him. In that time, you will share his bed but he will not force himself on you. Daughter, this is the best offer you'll get. News of your behaviour will spread faster than rings on water and no other man will want you. Hauk is no worse than any other man but don't try his patience any further – or mine.' I made to answer but he rose and left me there. His shoulders slumped as he and Steinar rode off.

Hauk was true to his word. We slept side by side. I would retire first and he joined me later, sometimes much later. I ached for Becklund and my former life but tried to settle down to life as the mistress of the house. My mother-in-law, the quiet Thorgunn, handed over the keys to the storehouse and the chests. She seemed relieved. She never questioned any of my decisions but rather submitted to my rule as if she were just another servant. There were five free men and three women in servitude, eight male and five female thralls. They did my bidding but were surly and disrespectful. Then came the day when one of them defied me.

It was my second week at Swanhill when Lydia, the dark slave-woman from the lands in the South, refused to clean out the privy.

'Not my work,' she said in her rolling accent, 'I weave and cook and ...' The smack as the flat of my hand landed on her mouth silenced all those who witnessed the event but not her. She slipped past me and from a safe distance she screamed.

'I, Princess de Galicia. You no hit! You bad wife! I real wife. Hauk soon make you go, leave!' She ran towards the lake, where Hauk and a servant were mending nets. I chased after her and we reached them together, panting and shaking. The serving man left after a quick glance at Hauk's face. Hauk didn't look up from his work. His scar glowed red under his knitted eyebrows, his movements were jerky and his voice a hoarse growl.

'Lydia, return to the farm.' She made to speak but changed her mind and walked slowly with many backward glances.

'Who is that thrall? She dared disobey me. Unless the insolent creature mends her ways, you'll have to …'

Hauk threw the net down, took one long stride towards me and shook his fist in my face. I ducked, side-stepped him and reached for my knife.

'Don't even think of hitting me, Hauk! I have a right to know if the wretched woman is more than a thrall on this farm.'

He breathed hard but lowered his hand. His face was contorted and he choked on his anger as he said, 'Lydia is my special woman and until you become a proper wife to me, she will remain so. She will not do hard work and you will treat her well. As it stands, she has more right to be the mistress of Swanhill than you have.'

I ran then. I ran as if it were possible to leave time and place behind, up through the copse, across the newly harvested fields and onto the wooded hillside. I tore past the grasping branches and weaved between the rough trunks. My headscarf caught on the thorns of a dog-rose and I left it hanging on the bush. As the slope grew steeper, I slowed down and walked but all the time I headed towards Loweswater and Becklund.

I followed the course of a small beck snaking its way down the hillside. Higher up the ground became stony and at times I had to climb over steep rocks. The trees disappeared and on the open fell heather scratched my ankles and bracken snared my feet. Beads of sweat hung on my forehead and my under-dress stuck to my back. Out of breath and with my heart racing, I reached the path on the flat, boggy area flanked by steep, rocky hillsides. Straight on would take me to Crummockwater but before then there was Mosedale, which led north to Becklund. I thought of the reception I would get at home and my steps became heavy. I had the right to divorce Hauk but, by running away instead of taking my case to the Lawmen at the Allthing in the approved manner, I had again brought shame on myself and my family. I thought of my father and how old and tired he had looked and I felt ashamed to let him down.

My shadow was still short. It was not long past midday, not too late to return to Swanhill. I could either try again or get a proper divorce. I stopped to give myself time to think. I longed to return to Becklund and my parents, but I knew that was impossible. My mouth felt dry and I descended to Mosedale Beck. As I knelt down to drink, the bundle of keys, which marked my status as mistress of Swanhill, tumbled with a clatter down on the grass. Fear hit me like a blow from a raven's wing. I crouched on the ground and moaned. Odin and Freya would be offended by my disregard for honour and duty. I would be punished for breaking my oath, for running away like a thief with the keys to Swanhill. Trembling I prayed and promised I would return there and act with humility and honour. I pledged a sacrifice, a brooch or an armlet, if they would only overlook my rash behaviour.

I washed my face in the cold water. I wished I'd stopped to pick up my head-scarf. My hair had worked loose of the pins and hung in heavy tresses down my back. I looked at my muddy shoes sticking out from under the torn, soiled hem of my dress. But for my jewellery, I must look like a runaway thrall. I twisted my hair into a bun and returned up to the path the way I had come. Then I heard voices from further up the valley. Men on horseback, never a good sign to a woman alone. I climbed as fast as I could up the slope. My body trembled and my breath caught in my throat. I scanned the hillside, searching for shelter, but no rock was large enough and no plant grew tall enough to hide me. I was alone, unarmed and exposed. Was this punishment from the gods already?

There were five of them. The horses struggled on the boggy ground and the riders steered them up towards the drier slopes, where I had taken refuge. I squatted among the sparse tufts of grass to make myself small. The riders had to concentrate on their balance as the horses slipped and stumbled on the loose, stony ground. They were coming ever higher, ever closer. They carried full armour, swords at their sides, spears in hand and shields on their backs, axes, bows and arrows tied to their saddles.

One of the horses lost its footing and the rider was thrown forwards in the saddle. He swore, dismounted and bent down to check the front legs of the horse. As he stood up he looked straight at me. A grin spread across his leathery face and his eyes glinted like cold iron. I leaped up, gathered my skirts and ran. The men below roared their pleasure at the unexpected entertainment. The man following me was heavy but his sturdy boots gave a firm grip on the treacherous ground. My soft leather shoes slid on the damp grass but I was light and fear gave me speed. The slope became steeper and it was hard to keep upright. I needed one hand to steady myself as the run became a scramble. One foot caught in the hem of my dress. That was all it took. My scream echoed round the valley. I fell, rolled down the slope into the arms of my assailant. He laughed and his companions cheered.

'What have you there, Thorfinn?'

'A wench, fit for some sport.'

'Bring her here, let's have a look.'

He dragged me down to where the others were waiting. He twisted my arm up my back and forced me to bend forwards. I struggled but couldn't look up at the faces around me.

'Get her shift off and let's see what we've got.' A young voice breathless with excitement.

'What *I've* got. you mean.' Thorfinn's voice rumbled in my ear. 'Mine to keep or to trade, as I please.'

'To share with your brothers!' The young voice became agitated and there was a murmur among some others. I thought of Snakebite, left behind in my temper. I closed my eyes. I would die and I must be brave.

'I claim the girl for what you owe me in gambling debts, Thorfinn.'

'So do I, he owes me more than you.'

Several of the riders were now dismounting. Thorfinn had stopped laughing.

His grip on my wrist hardened. More horses arrived. A new voice interrupted the growing discord, a cold voice which I recognised but couldn't place. I tried to turn my head to see who it was but he had come up behind us.

'What are you doing? We need to make haste. Your lives are in danger and you quarrel over a wench. Get back on your horses.'

'She's mine, I found her and I caught her.' Thorfinn sounded a lot less sure of himself. The rest were already mounting. 'I'll catch up with you.'

'That's up to you. We call in at Becklund but not for long.'

That's when I recognised the voice. 'Jarl Swein,' I called but too late. The horses and men made too much noise, nobody heard me. Thorfinn remained standing for a while but his grip became less firm and I could sense him relaxing.

'Let me go, Thorfinn,' I said, 'and there will be a reward for you from my father, Kveldulf Arnvidson of Becklund.' He let go of one of my arms so I could straighten up. I turned my head to look at him. I recognised his squashed nose and heavy jowls. He was the ugly poet I had knifed when he tried to fondle me at the table. He didn't recognise me but became interested when he noticed my jewellery, which marked me out as a woman from a prosperous family.

'I give you my word. If you take me to my father, you will be richly rewarded.'

I could almost see the thoughts tumbling round inside his greasy head. I twisted and did a sideways kick at his knee. As my foot made contact, his leg buckled and he toppled over. He swore and lost his grip on my arm. Before he could struggle up from the soft, muddy ground, I was by his horse grappling to free his bow. He limped towards me, his face contorted in fury and pain. I moved round so the horse was between us. I grabbed an arrow from the quiver and ran uphill. He followed me but now I had him in my sight. If he had stood still, as I told him to, he may have lived. But he lunged at me and I was too good a shot to miss his large, lumbering frame. He fell backwards and hit the ground with one of his own arrows through his neck. There was much blood but I didn't wait to witness his death-throes. I grabbed the horse by its bridle and moved away as quickly as I could. I forgot all about my promises to the gods that I would return to Swanhill. I had one thought only: if Jarl Swein was at Becklund, so would Ragnar be and that's where I had to go.

The horse was lame and unwilling to move. I had to pull hard on its bridle to get it to walk. I struggled on the boggy ground, exhausted and trembling after my ordeal. I waited till I had put some distance between myself and Thorfinn before I stopped to catch my breath. I checked over his weapons, the shield was too heavy for me but the axe I could just about manage for a brief fight. I already knew his bow was well balanced and his arrows straight. As I hurried down Mosedale I kept looking behind me, thinking I could hear pursuers. I felt sick and my limbs were shaking so much I found it hard to continue. It was well after noontide and I'd had enough. By a clump of trees I put a halter on the horse and removed Thorfinn's axe and his thick woollen cloak from behind the saddle. Then, thinking that people look down on the uneven path rather than up the side of the slope, I climbed a short way up. There, wrapped in Thorfinn's cloak and with his axe next to me, I lay down to rest.

I was woken by an angry voice and a foot in my back. 'Thorfinn, you ugly goblin! Get up!'

4.

I rolled over and grabbed the axe. As I leapt up, I trod on the long cloak and was pulled down again. I struggled to get out of the heavy garment but it seemed Thorfinn's cloak was intent on his revenge, for it wrapped itself ever tighter around my legs. As I toppled over, I heard my assailant laugh and draw his sword. I cried out and the cry gave me strength. I rolled down the slope and, as I did so, managed to fight free of the cloak. I got to my feet and, trembling with fear, needed both hands to raise the heavy axe. I looked up. Above me hulked a tall, broad-shouldered figure with a halo of blond hair. It was Ragnar.

The relief was so great I lost my speech and burst out crying. Deep, rasping sobs forced their way from the very core of my body. The axe fell from my hands and I staggered towards my lost love to embrace him. He stood, sword in one hand, the other shielding his eyes against the setting sun.

'Odin's beard! What's this? Where is Thorfinn?'

Still speechless, I buried my face in the folds of his tunic and clung to the safety of his presence.

'What's happened?'

I tried to answer but was silenced by a fresh lot of tears. Ragnar put his arms around me and rocked me like a child. I felt the taught muscles in his chest and my body began to relax. My crying abated and I blew my

34

nose on my apron and took a deep breath. The scent of sweat and leather from Ragnar's body made me giddy and the remnants of fear were driven out by new and different feelings. My heart began to beat faster. Ragnar's arms tightened around me. The stubble on his chin scratched my cheek as he bent down to kiss me. Then he looked at me.

'You're quite pretty under all that dirt, do you know that?' His smile was mocking and I laughed. He kissed me again. I pressed my mouth against his. My nipples went hard and a warm moistness spread inside the cleft between my thighs. I began to enjoy this rush of emotion. But then I caught my breath. Ragnar was pulling up my dress and his rough hand stroked my legs and my stomach.

'No, don't, we must wait!'

'What for?' He laughed and pulled me down on the ground. His mouth was hard on mine and smothered any attempt to protest. I tried to push him away but his heavy body pinned me to the ground. I felt his fingers guiding him inside me. There was a brief moment of sharp pain and then the urgent movement of his body. A muffled cry, then he relaxed on top of me and sighed. This was not how I had imagined it to be. My lust turned to disappointment and then to red-hot anger. The man who had filled my waking and sleeping mind for two long years had helped himself to my body as if I were a common thrall-woman. I pushed at him. He rolled on to his side and yawned.

'That was good, my little wench.' He'd hardly finished his sentence before my fists drummed against his face. I hit blindly, growling with my teeth bared. He sat up and grabbed my wrists.

'Too late to change your mind, wench!' he said and laughed.

'There was no need for that, Ragnar! I have waited for you all this time and now ...' He stopped laughing and his eyes clouded over.

'You know my name? Who are you?'

'Ragnar, don't you know me? I'm Sigrid!' He let go of me and stared at my brooches and my necklace. The colour left his face and his voice shrunk to a whisper.

'Sigrid ... Sigrid ... Odin's eye! How ... I ...'

I collapsed back on the grass and covered my eyes with my fists. He stood up, pulled at his trousers and tunic. Then he sat down again but at a distance. He was silent for a long time while his eyes travelled between the sky, the ground and me. Then he knelt beside me.

'Sigrid Kveldulfsdaughter, my little shieldmaiden, how was I to recognise you in that state? I would never have treated you with anything but respect if I'd known. Why didn't you tell me?' I sat up and tried to push my tangled hair from my face.

'I was sure you'd recognise me. But then ...'

He put his arms around me.

'I'm sorry. Did I hurt you? Sigrid, I wish I could undo what I have done but the way you clung to me like a ...'

Again, the force of my furious fist silenced him. Humiliated, angry and disappointed I screamed at him.

'And you don't even do it properly. It wasn't nice at all. It's supposed to feel all ...' Realising what I had said, I fell silent. Ragnar stared at me with open mouth. In my embarrassment, I started crying again. He stroked the tears from my cheeks with gentle fingers.

'So you want it done properly, do you, Sigrid? Well,

the damage is done, so …'

His eyes were as green as the sea in a storm and his hair reflected the last of the sunlight. For a moment I thought he was a young god come down from Asgard to take a mortal woman for his bride. He pulled me close and, this time, his touch was as light as a moonbeam. His hand set my skin tingling and made me sigh and tremble. He entered me slowly and lay almost still on top of me until my womb responded, my mind took flight and my body, arched against his, began to move without restraint or shame. I heard, as from a distance, my moans and cries and my whole being shimmered and shook with delicious pleasure.

When I came out of my ecstasy, dusk was closing around us and the reality of my situation chilled me. Ragnar was asleep but I shook him and said, 'We must decide what to do, Ragnar. I am married to Hauk.' He sat up with a cry of horror. Then his body sagged and he put his head in his hands.

'Sigrid, what are you doing to me? I must have broken every pledge of honour this day. I have spoiled a woman from a good family, I have broken a sacred oath of friendship and gratitude to her father, I have taken another man's wife. Your father and your husband will both seek my blood. My name will be dragged through the dirt, my family dishonoured and I …' He fell silent, thought awhile then with narrowed eyes he leaned towards me. 'Married? Since when? You didn't feel like a married woman to me.'

'I'm married in name only. I can't stand Hauk to come near me.' He smiled a bitter little smile.

'That's understandable but why did you marry him then?'

'I had to marry someone. Ragnar, you said we'd meet again and then never a word. I waited and waited. I thought you'd forgotten me. Where have you been?'

'On the run. We were outlawed by King Harald. His arm is as long as his memory and it wasn't safe for us to stay here. I tried to get word to you. I sent a thrall with a message. Didn't you get it?' I thought of my mother and her servant Ingefried. They would have made very sure no message from the son of Swein Hjaltebrand got to me. I shook my head.

'We spent some time raiding then we joined King Olaf of Dublin against King Æthelstan. My father is unlucky in his choice of allies. It's not wise for us to remain in Æthelstan's realm either.'

I threw my arms round him and pressed my face to his.

'I'll divorce Hauk and we can get married. My father, at least, won't object. You are the son of his blood-brother.'

'Sigrid, I cannot marry. I am an outlaw – any children I sire will be outlaws. I have no home, nor anything else to offer you.' He shook his head and got up. 'It's getting dark. I'll see to the horses. We'll stay here tonight.' He returned carrying a small bundle of food. We shared cheese, bread and apples. No chieftain's feast could have tasted better than that meal.

I spread Thorfinn's cloak over us. The stars were coming out and a crescent moon dipped in and out of the scattered clouds. I lay with my head on Ragnar's shoulder listening to the sounds of the night, a horse shifting its stance, the hoot of an owl, the churring of a nightjar. I was happy, convinced Odin had tried me and found me worthy. He had brought me my love and, outlaw or not, all would be well. We'd think of something.

We woke and our bodies craved each other and found each other again. The horses had wandered off in search of grazing but we felt neither hunger nor thirst and the sun was above the crest of the nearest hill before we dressed and faced our situation. We sat hand in hand trying to decide what to do.

'Sigrid, I can't stay. My father and I have pledged our loyalty to William Longsword in Neustria and we must go. Oh. Sigrid, I wish it weren't so.'

'I want to come with you, Ragnar.'

'You can't. Believe me, my love, where we're headed is no place for a woman.' He looked at me with a sad little smile. 'Not even a brave shieldmaiden.'

'It's all your father's fault, isn't it?'

'He is my father, Sigrid, don't speak ill of him.'

I thought again of my own father. He would not refuse to take Ragnar as his foster-son and offer him sanctuary at Becklund. Ragnar was doubtful but agreed we should speak to him.

We retrieved the horses. Thorfinn's steed was still lame, so Ragnar pulled me up to sit in front of him on his stallion. We rode towards Becklund and I told Ragnar how it came I had Thorfinn's weapons and his horse. As I spoke, I felt Ragnar's close embrace melt away and he became quiet. The silence frightened me. I tried to turn and look at him but couldn't.

'Ragnar, it was self-defence! What was I supposed to do?'

'My father won't see it like that. He has lost one of his men and will want compensation.'

'But he saw Thorfinn holding me down. He knows it

was a fair fight.'

'That is what you would have to argue in front of the Allthing and my father is not in a position to go there.'

'I shall hide the weapons and let the horse go. Nobody needs to find out – ever.'

'And we'll leave the warrior's body to the crows and the foxes?'

'What do you want, Ragnar? I confess I killed him. One of your father's warriors was killed by an unarmed woman. He'll be ridiculed rather than honoured. I'll see to it that he's buried but I'll do him the favour to have it done in secret.'

I held my breath waiting for his response. It was a long time coming. His shoulders seemed to shake and I wondered if he was crying. But when he spoke his arms were firm around me again and there was laughter in his voice.

'Maybe Thorfinn got what was coming to him and perhaps it would be kinder to his memory if we kept the manner of his death a secret. But please don't kill any more of my father's warriors, it doesn't help our situation at all.'

Thorfinn's weapons found a resting place beneath a rock and I took an oath to reunite them with Thorfinn in his grave. We kept the horse with us; it could be tethered somewhere closer to Becklund until the Jarl had left. Then we continued down the valley towards Loweswater. We walked in single file, each leading a horse down the steep slope towards the river and the lake. Soon I could see the trees down in the valley and I knew I was close to home.

The ground levelled out and we entered the wooded area. The sudden noise of dry twigs snapping and leaves rustling startled the horses and made us reach for our weapons. A small boy tumbled out of the shrubbery and landed on all fours in front of us. He was dirty, his clothes were torn and his face streaked with tears. He got up, gave me a confused look and turned to Ragnar. His words fought each other to get out.

'Ragnar Sweinson, your father sends word. He says ... um, he says you must go to Buttermere ... swiftly ... ah, and ... and warn your mother to seek safety wherever she can.' His eyes darted between us as he continued, 'And then you're to join Jarl Hjaltebrand where the ship is waiting. He says you know the place.' Having delivered his message, the urchin stood aside and stared at us with round eyes and open mouth.

'Sigrid, I must go.' For a moment Ragnar held me close. 'Whatever happens, I'll be back. I promise I'll be back.' His voice choked. Then he got on his horse and I watched him ride off.

My breath was like a knife in my throat. I tried to blink away my tears but they fell heavy from my eyes. I turned my back to the boy so he wouldn't see. He pulled at my sleeve.

'Sigrid Kveldulfsdaughter, terrible things are happening.'

I told the boy to lead Thorfinn's horse and set off ahead of him. I heard the noise long before I got to Becklund and, as I drew closer, I distinguished the clanking of weapons, the angry shouts of fighting men, the agonised cries of the wounded and the fearful screams of women and children. A roundabout route took me unseen to the farm. Strangers in full armour stood guard outside the enclosure behind the hall. I crept

41

up behind the drystone wall above the meadow. I saw two of our free men bleeding on the ground, their weapons still in their hands. A girl, undetected by the marauders, cowered behind a shed, another crawled slowly towards the fence. Over by the barn a small group of women and children were kept under guard by a shaggy-looking fighter. Blood stained their clothes but whether their own or that of others was impossible to say. The women tried to shush their crying infants. I heard more shouting and the clashing of swords, axes and shields but I couldn't see beyond the other buildings.

My legs trembled as I continued to crawl along the wall. On the other side of the farm I saw horses, more than a score of them, guarded by a couple of young boys. This was no ordinary raid by Scottish clansmen rustling cattle, nor was it lawless Vikings looking for slaves and gold or a vengeful neighbour in search of retribution. All those horses. Armed warriors against my father's eight karls. Had there even been time to summon the karls? The twelve thralls were not fighting men and, although both they and the women would help defend the farm, they had no hope against these attackers.

I moved from tree to tree, staying out of sight. The noise was abating and it became possible to separate out individual sounds. My mother's voice, strong and commanding soared above the grunts of men pushed to their limits. I could not hear my father anywhere. As I came closer to the farm I came across dead and wounded. Old Ulf, the storyteller, lay sprawled on the ground, his eyes dull below half-closed lids. An armed stranger lay draped across a tree stump, his blood running thick and red into the grass. Ketil, the brown-eyed thrall I had played with as a child, was choking on his own blood, his chest cut open, his fingers digging furrows in the soil. Next to him lay his enemy, pinned to the ground with Ketil's pitchfork. I took it all in, the smell of torn human flesh, the sight of life ebbing away. All the time I kept moving towards where those alive were still fighting. I crawled under the fence and slid underneath the floor of the grain store. Hidden behind one of the props I could, at last, see the yard.

With his back to me, my father knelt on the ground, a deep wound in his right shoulder, the arm lifeless and his open hand resting on the ground next to his battleaxe. A warrior stood on either side of him. One of them rested his sword on my father's neck. I pressed my hands over my face. My stomach heaved and bitter bile gushed into my throat. I forced myself to look again. My mother, bloodstained and dishevelled, was pushed forward and a warrior wrenched a sword from her hand. She was led up to a tall, blond man who wore a fine mail shirt and an ornate helmet with a pattern glinting of gold. She said something to him. He looked closely at her face and then he bowed. Her captor let go of her arm and stepped back. She remained standing by the chieftain but her eyes were fixed on my father.

There were dead and injured scattered across the yard. Inside a circle of onlookers two men were fighting. One of them was Jarl Swein Hjaltebrand. His mail shirt had been slashed open in several places and he was bleeding from many wounds. He struggled for breath and staggered with fatigue. His shield lay discarded on the ground and he used both hands to swing his sword. His opponent, a much younger man, sidestepped. The Jarl stumbled and had to put the tip of his sword on the ground to steady himself. The other man laughed. Onlookers shouted out, some in terror, some in triumph as the uneven fight came to an end and the Jarl was pinned to the ground by his grinning enemy.

The chieftain left my mother's side and went up to the Jarl.

'Hjaltebrand, you are a traitor and will meet with a traitor's death. Tell me where your son is hiding and I will make your end swift and painless.'

I couldn't hear the Jarl's reply over the moans and cries of the injured and bereaved. The chieftain nodded to two of his men and they carried the Jarl across the yard to the water trough. The Jarl cried out.

'My sword! Hakon, in Odin's name let me die with my sword in my hand!' The men looked at the chieftain who shook his head. They immersed Jarl Swein's head in the water and held him down until his legs stopped kicking and his arms hung limp. The lifeless body was dumped at the feet of the chieftain. The horde of invaders cheered. My mother didn't flinch even though the Jarl's hand came to rest on her foot. Her face was as pale as moonlight, her eyes were still on my father and her lips moved as if she were whispering to him.

The chieftain then turned to my father, who was pulled into a standing position by his two guards. I saw his trousers were soaked in blood and he didn't put any weight on his left leg. Someone gave him his axe and he used it to lean on.

'You harboured a traitor, Kveldulf Arnvidson. You met the son of your king with force. What happened to your sworn loyalty, brother-in-law?' The chieftain's voice was both angry and mocking when he said 'brother-in-law'. Then my father's voice cut through.

'You do me an injustice, Hakon. Swein was my brother-in-arms. He made a mistake. He never meant treachery to your father or to you. I asked for parley but you attacked without hearing our pleas.'

'There's no negotiating with traitors. Your duty is to your king first, did you forget that? You still wear his ring on your arm. Do you mock him, Kveldulf, as well as betray him?'

The chieftain nodded to his housekarl. My father was still shaking his head when the long sword made a mighty arch through the air and cut it from his body. I saw my father's head roll across the dirt and come to rest on its side against the wooden walkway. I saw the jet of blood pulsating from his neck. I saw the legs buckle and the twitching body fall to the ground his hand still holding his battleaxe. There was a hush, then a wave of muffled voices and, amidst them, a scream; a long, wailing noise rising and rising, higher and higher. Someone pulled me out from my hiding place and slapped my face. The screaming stopped, everything stopped.

Part Two:

Shieldmaiden

5

I still hurt when I remember the day my father was killed, my brothers disappeared and my mother disowned me, leaving me without the protection of the family I had taken for granted would be there for me always.

I was the youngest of my parents' children and I was my father's favourite. He encouraged the wild, even violent, nature I displayed early on. Girls, in those days, were still taught to use a bow and arrows and to wield a knife to defend themselves. I could ride and swim by the time I was three. Today it's different. It's the influence of the English and of their religion, Christianity. Their God doesn't favour women. My father was baptised when serving under Christian kings and chieftains but it was accepted by all that such baptisms did not count once the warrior left the service of his godfather. So he lived by the Old Religion and followed the Norse way of life. He stopped going on raids soon after I was born. He made more profit from trading than raiding and adventure didn't appeal to him as in his youth. He would perhaps have continued if his three sons had been able to follow him.

The eldest of my siblings was a boy. He was killed by Scottish cattle rustlers. I don't remember him. I had seen but two summers when it happened. My mother never spoke of him but my father told me once that Rolf would have grown up to be a great warrior. He sounded sad as he spoke of the youth, in charge of the cattle over on Burnbank Fell. His body was found many days after, when one of the calves wandered into the farm enclosure on its own.

'I rode up onto the fell in a great anger,' my father said, 'thinking the boy had neglected the animals. When I found him he was lying on his front. I thought he was asleep. Then I saw the wounds and the blood and I knew he had died a warrior's death. I carried him home and we drank the funeral ale and the smoke from a large funeral pyre took him to Valhalla. I made a sacrifice to Odin and raised a stone where Rolf fell.'

It was true. I have seen it many times. The runes inside the body of the snake of Midgard wind their way round the face of the stone. At the top is the large snake head with the tail in its mouth. The inscription says: "Kveldulf Arnvidson of Becklund raised the stone for his son Rolf who fell in battle with many wounds". The stone is still there but in the soft ground it is not stable and the last time I went there it was tilting.

There were two other children. A stillborn girl then a boy rejected as deficient and put out to die. This, too, my mother never spoke of and neither did my father. It does no good to dwell on what fortune the Norns weave into the fabric of your life.

Then there were my brothers Thorstein and Steinar. Thorstein took ill as a child and it was his musical talent that saved him. He was three summers when a burn went bad and he was struck down with a fever. He was put in the sick-tent with water and some food. On the second day he was heard singing with a weak but pitch-perfect voice. One of the servants swore by the golden hair of Baldur that he'd heard the sound of a lyre accompanying the singing infant. Be that as it may, he overcame the dread of sickness and helped the child to eat. He remained attached to Thorstein and it was he who persuaded my father to pay ten silver coins for a lyre. Those coins were well spent. Thorstein's music didn't just entertain; it cheered and comforted and had the power to make men and women laugh and weep. But he was no replacement for Rolf, for he remained weak and sickly all his life. He was never able to help with the heavy work and he never learnt to handle weapons. He named his lyre Enchanter and, many years later, it saved his life better than any sword or shield.

My other brother, Steinar, had a big, strong body but was slow-witted. It didn't much matter in the day-to-day work on the farm but he was a poor hunter, unable to figure out where the swift hare or the graceful deer would run to and an even worse fisherman, since he never learnt to tell the weather or judge where the shoals of herring would gather.

Then there was me. I was a healthy, sturdy child, inquisitive and headstrong. My father found me amusing and took me with him when he went hunting and fishing. I had a good eye and was soon useful with my bow and arrow. The first time I shot a hare, my father gave a loud shout of triumph and all the way home he couldn't stop laughing and praising me. That's when he gave me my first hunting dog, Swift. For years he would tell the story of how I stalked my first deer and brought it down with a shot through the eye. My mother was displeased and accused him of spoiling me. She was right, of course. She had only the one daughter and I should have spent more time learning women's pursuits: my weaving was uneven, part of the cloth tight and stiff, part of it loose and thin; the patterns in the ribbons I made were full of knots; and I only paid attention to cooking after my mother made me eat my mistakes.

When they were six and seven, my father began teaching my brothers to use proper weapons. Thorstein was a lost cause and was soon set to help with the animals instead. I watched as my father showed Steinar how to use the shield.

'If you raise the axe you must move the shield towards that side or the enemy will be able to stab you.' They tried again and again. Every time he raised his axe, Steinar moved the shield out of the way and my father tapped him on the unprotected shoulder with his sword.

'You've just lost your right arm,' he would say.

Father got increasingly impatient and after several failures, threw his sword on the ground and walked away. Steinar stayed and tried to practise on his own. I could see tears running down his cheeks. Thinking I would help, I slid down from my vantage point on the dry stone wall. I picked up my father's sword with both hands and managed to lift it and let it fall on Steinar's exposed shoulder. It sliced through his tunic and cut into his flesh. He dropped his axe and shield, I lost my grip on the sword and it hit the ground with a dull thud. We stood together in stunned silence and watched as thick, red blood welled out of the wound and soaked the sleeve of Steinar's tunic before trickling down his hand and onto the grass.

'You should have moved the shield.' I said.

Steinar didn't answer but, with the full force of his

uninjured arm, he planted his fist in my face. We were both bleeding, he from his arm and I from my nose. We hugged each other and cried in unison so loudly the servants in the outlying fields heard us and came running, thinking there had been an attack on the farm. We were both punished. This created a special bond between us and, believe me, I never wanted any ill to befall my brother and to this day I am haunted by the memory of his death and the part I played in that event.

* * *

When my brothers turned twelve and thirteen, my father decided it was time to start searching for wives for them.

'My mind is not set on marriage,' said Thorstein. He stroked his lyre Enchanter and it sang a sorrowful note.

'Put that down,' said my father. 'Don't play your magic on me. I know what you're trying to do.'

Thorstein sighed and put Enchanter on the bench next to him. 'Father, you know I'm not a farmer. Nor am I a fighter. I will never be a Viking but I still want to see the world outside this valley. I want to make poetry and music about great events. Kings and chieftains pay for entertainment in their halls and for songs about their battles. I can't steer a plough but with Enchanter I can make a living as a minstrel.'

'A minstrel! As Odin is my witness, no son of mine will be a minstrel.' My father's raised voice prompted my mother to speak.

'Nobody denies you play well and people are sometimes greatly affected by your tunes but, while you run the farm, take decisions and give orders to the thralls and freemen, you can still play and give pleasure to your family and visitors. You are the heir to Becklund, Thorstein. Others will steer the plough for you.'

'I can plough,' said Steinar, 'and I'd like to marry.' He was ignored. My father continued to speak to Thorstein.

'The farm prospers. You will take over and after you, your sons and ...'

I sidled out through the door at this point. I had heard it all before and none of it seemed to have anything to do with me. Becklund was the most perfect place and I couldn't understand why Thorstein didn't want to stay. It was true he didn't like to swim in the lake or race horses across the meadow but he was good at tickling trout in the beck and he loved playing with the young animals in spring. No one could calm a frightened mare or train the dogs better than he and yet he wanted to leave. I felt sorry for him because I knew our parents would have their way.

Thorstein's bride, Freydis, only needed to listen to Enchanter once before agreeing to the match and she remained loving and faithful to him for the rest of her life.

Finding a girl willing to marry Steinar was not as easy. He was a tall, good-looking youth but it never took long for his intended brides and their fathers to discover that he had the mind of a child half his age. It was Thorstein and Enchanter who seduced Eahlswith and made her agree to the marriage. Young as I was, I thought it a bad idea for Thorstein to use his music to woo a woman on behalf of his brother. I was not surprised when, after less than a year, Eahlswith left Steinar and returned to her parents. Many excuses were made for why the marriage failed.

'It's never good to marry among the Anglians,' said my mother. 'They have different ways of doing things. The cloth she wove was full of snags almost as bad as Sigrid's.'

'She used too much salt on the herring, wasteful,' father grumbled. 'And her religion. Being baptised doesn't mean you can just forget about the old gods. I was baptised a couple of times, once when I fought with Rollo along the river Seine and ...' mother cleared her throat and father stopped mid-sentence.

Steinar didn't listen to them anyway. He got his message from the giggles and taunts of the serving wenches and the sneers of the thrall girls and he knew there was no prospect of another bride.

This may not have mattered much, if Thorstein and Freydis had delivered the grandsons my father so longed for. In the end, of course, that didn't matter either since Becklund was burnt to the ground, my father beheaded and my mother led away by a Viking, called Hakon, who wore a helmet inlaid with gold and who called my father brother-in-law and then ordered him killed.

It all happened a long time ago and I have seen many deaths since then but sometimes I have dreams when I see my father's grey hair in the brown mud, his cheek resting against the wooden walkway, while blood flows from his severed neck. And in my dream I hear myself scream like I did then, until someone struck me and allowed me to find brief solace in oblivion.

* * *

I woke up cradled in a pair of soft arms. A voice made soothing noises in my ear. There was a strong smell of burning. I looked up to see the red, swollen eyes of

53

Ingefried, my mother's serving woman. I tried to turn towards where my father's mutilated body lay but Ingefried held my head and made me look the other way.

She whispered, 'You must not say anything, Sigrid. Just stay quiet. Whatever happens, be quiet.'

My mother's face was the colour of wood-ash. I wanted to run to her, to embrace her, to comfort and be comforted by her. But she didn't look at me. With her back straight and her head held high, she spoke to the chieftain.

'I don't know what her errand is, Hakon,' she said, 'this is the wife of one of our neighbours, Hauk of Swanhill. Hauk is not part of your quarrel with Swein, you must let his wife go. I shall send Ingefried with her to keep her company.' Her words twisted like a dagger in my breast. I was Hauk's wife and no longer a daughter to her. Was my disobedience so bad, my shame so deep I had to be denied?

I was helped to my feet and began the long, sorrowful walk back to Swanhill. Ingefried led me by the hand, slowly, coaxing me along. I closed my mind and put one trembling foot in front of the other. We came across the boy Olvir guarding Thorfinn's horse. He turned and followed us without a word. That night we huddled together like frightened animals. I kept dropping off to sleep and then waking up, my screams smothered by Ingefried's apron. The boy sobbed quietly on and off. The morning arrived heavy with dew and we got up and continued trudging along the track leading up through Mosedale.

The sun hid behind heavy clouds and a drizzling rain soaked through my clothes. The acrid smell of burning buildings followed me like a ghost of loss and despair. The moment of my father's death appeared like an evil vision at every turn on that heavy journey. I was shaking. One moment hot and soaked in sweat, I threw off my shawl, turned my face to the sky and let my tears mingle with the rain. Then I shivered with cold and tried to hug some warmth from my wet clothes. I thought I saw blood everywhere: blood from my father; from Jarl Swein; and from the dead friends and servants I had seen – but also blood from the mortal wound I had dealt Thorfinn. My mother's words of rejection throbbed inside my aching head and I began hearing other voices too: father telling me I had brought disgrace on the family; the chieftain calling him a traitor; Ragnar making me promise to bury Thorfinn; and, through them all, Ingefried whispering to me to keep going.

At the head of the valley I realised we would soon pass the place where I had felled Thorfinn. I thought of Ragnar. He would trust me to do the right thing. I had promised. My head buzzed. What *is* the right thing? How can I bury him? There's no ale to serve … and I'm so tired … my legs … shaking … the heat … I have nothing to dig with … is a grave the right thing? But how can I light a funeral pyre on the wet muddy ground … I can't go on … where will I find dry fire wood? And he's so large … masses and masses of logs needed for that large body … he's so large … so …

'Sigrid, hush, child! Stop mumbling. Sit and rest a moment.'

'But we must bury him!'

'Your father will be buried. My mistress will make sure her husband gets the funeral he is entitled to. Hakon Haraldson will not refuse her that.' My legs gave way and I sat down on the muddy path. 'Not my father, not him, not him …'

From far away, I heard Ingefried tell the boy to take the horse to Floutern Tarn and wait for us there. I tried to speak, I tried to move but I was floating in a dark cloud, which filled my mouth with ash and tied my limbs to the ground.

I came to with Ingefried rubbing my gums with a bitter herb.

'Uuugh!' I sat up spitting to get rid of the vile taste. She handed me a twig.

'Here, chew this. It will get rid of the taste of the wormwood. The tarn isn't far now. You can drink there.'

Still spitting, I let Ingefried lead me by the hand. We emerged from Mosedale and the ground became soft and boggy. The hoof marks left by Jarl Swein and his warriors had filled up with water but were still visible. They led to the place where I had killed Thorfinn. There was no doubt about where it was. The blood had washed away but I knew it was the right place. I ran in circles. I looked behind rocks and among the tufts of grass. Ingefried shouted at me to stop. I tried to make her understand that I must find the body.

'Sigrid, there's no body here. Your father's body is at Becklund. Calm yourself.' She forced some more wormwood between my lips and dragged me away. We rested by the little tarn and I regained enough of my senses to realise I must not speak of Thorfinn. Somehow this seemed to make all talk unnecessary and I found I couldn't say anything at all.

* * *

We arrived at Swanhill as the shadows were

56

lengthening. A group of thralls, ploughing the outlying fields, spotted us and supported our exhausted bodies the last furlongs. The karl leading the ploughing-party spoke with Ingefried before sending a man running ahead to warn the household of our arrival.

Hauk was in the yard and came towards us. When he saw the state we were in, he picked me up and carried me the last steps to the hall.

'Sigrid,' he whispered, 'Sigrid, this is a terrible day. Rest and then we shall speak.' He placed me on the bed and covered me with blankets and soft cured skins. Someone brought warm ale and my mind escaped to a dark, soothing place of dreamless safety.

The sun rose and set on my sleep many times. When I awoke I was insensible to the voices and actions of others. My mother-in-law took the keys and ran the household while I stayed in bed. I lay with my face towards the wall, dry-eyed and wordless. Ingefried fed me gruel sweetened with honey and I swallowed because it was less effort than to refuse. I heard her and Thorgunn working together. I knew they were talking about me but had no interest in what they were saying. Then, one day, the fire was lit in the bathhouse. I was carried out, helped to wash and left in the steamy heat, alone. I lay on the smooth, warm wooden bench. My body felt clean, fresh and warm but this seemed only to intensify the agony in my mind. I thought of my murdered father, my mother who had denied me and my love who had left me. My tears were unfrozen and I cried myself to sleep.

I woke when I felt the cold draught from the door opening and closing. My head heavy with the heat and my vision blurred by the steam, I accepted the horn of

57

sweet mead and drank it down. Someone lay down next to me. In my confused state I thought it was Ragnar and I responded with passion to Hauk's embrace.

The night after Hauk had come to me in the sauna, I retired early and closed the curtains around the bed. I lay there listening to sounds of the household preparing for the night. The table was cleared. Bedding was spread on the benches and on the floor. Soon I could hear snoring from the karls and servants sleeping in the hall. Then the bed curtains parted and Hauk climbed in next to me. I turned my back to him and pretended to be asleep. His hand slid along my body under the covers. I went stiff.

'What now, Sigrid? You were frisky enough in the sauna yesterday. Does it take hot steam and mead to get you in the mood every time?' Hauk spoke softly but couldn't disguise the dissatisfaction in his voice. His hand gripped my shoulder and rolled me over onto my back. I kept my eyes shut so I didn't have to look at him. 'Now listen, your father is dead, your mother has been abducted and both your brothers have disappeared. You have no one but me.'

I still had no voice but, in any case, there was nothing to argue with in his conclusion. I nodded my head once to show I understood. His hand moved across my body. His fingers began stroking me. I tried to push him away and he got angry.

'What's the matter with you, woman? You liked it well enough yesterday. What's different? I know a man has had you before. Ingefried tells me you were raped. It is better if you help me believe that. Now treat me like a husband.'

* * *

58

Ingefried knew before I did. 'Are you unwell, Sigrid? You're pale and you keep leaving the hearth. I've several times had to save your stew from burning.'

'My stomach turns at the smell of cooking. I thought it would pass but it has persisted. Maybe you have a herb to help settle me.'

She smiled. 'And has your body given blood the usual way at each moon?' I hadn't thought to follow the changing shape of the moon so I didn't know. 'No herbs for you my child. In another turn of the moon, we'll be sure and then we can tell Hauk his first son is on his way.'

'I'm with child? But I ...'

'Too soon to say for sure but these are the usual signs.'

I went limp and had to sit down while Ingefried, beaming, went off on a long tirade about my mother's pregnancies, miscarriages and childbirths. I didn't listen. My thoughts were so crowded they seemed to be fighting inside my head. A baby. What was I to do? Ingefried brought me back when she stopped and put her face close to mine. Her demeanour changed, gone was the sparkle. Her eyes stared with the light blue of a cold winter's day and her lips trembled.

'When did you first know a man, Sigrid? Who, apart from Hauk, could be the father? I told him you'd been raped by one of Hakon's men but I know I told a lie. So how long ago did you lose your maidenhood? Can we make Hauk believe the child is his? Oh, Sigrid, bastard or not, my Gudrun's grandchild must not be put to death.'

6.

I was the cause of Hauk's death. I regret the way it happened. He wasn't a bad man, my father was right about that, and I brought him much humiliation and little comfort.

I was expecting Ragnar's child. It was a great happiness to me but also tinged with dread. Hauk would not be able to accept a bastard without losing the respect of all those who were already laughing about his reluctant bride. Ingefried was beset with worry.

'Don't tell Hauk just yet,' she said, 'if you wait you can make out the child is his. Then we can say it was early. Don't annoy Hauk. You must keep him thinking it is his child.'

I waited another turn of the moon then I spoke to Hauk. I went to meet him as he led his men back from the day's work. They had been clearing a new field and their weariness showed in their slow step. I greeted them, smiled at Hauk and, for the sake of my unborn child, I took his hand and led him to one side. I could hear the men snigger when they thought themselves out of earshot. This was part of my plan; it wasn't just Hauk who had to believe in my deception, they must all think I had turned into a dutiful wife.

'Hauk, husband, I'm carrying your child. If Freya wills, you shall have a son.' At first he looked at me without expression. Then the tired furrows on his brow lifted and he laughed out loud as he picked me up and swung me round and round until I had to plead with him to be careful lest he dropped me.

'Sigrid, I would never let you fall.' He held me then, tenderly, my head resting on his chest. He stroked my hair and kissed my brow and in a voice hoarse with feeling, he whispered of how he had loved me since he first saw me at the Thingmound many years before.

'Sigrid, my little wife, all will be well now, won't it?'

'Yes, Hauk.' I was glad he couldn't see my face.

Hauk stopped spending time with Lydia. I persuaded him to order her to do the same work as the other serfs. I smiled when I heard her shrill protest. It was a cheap victory and cost me dear later on. Hauk was attentive to me when, over the next few months, I struggled with my huge body. I kept pretending I was happy but sometimes my sorrow broke through. I blamed the pregnancy, I blamed grief for my family and for a time Hauk was persuaded. But when I asked that, if the baby were a boy, he should be named after my father, Hauk shook his head.

'Kveldulf was a good man but names carry meanings.' I knew what he meant; wolf of the evening – a shape-shifter. My meekness melted away.

'What are you saying about my father, Hauk?' He remained silent and would not meet my eyes. 'My father was a brave man, a warrior, a clever man. My … your son could do worse than be named after him.' He turned then and walked off. Later, his mother came to sit with me with her spinning.

'Don't goad Hauk about his lack of fighting prowess,' she said, 'he's my only child. I don't want

61

him to think he has to seek honour in battle. We need him here.'

I should have listened to her then. But I didn't. I never considered Hauk as a person. He was the man I had married to please my parents and to avoid being left an old maid. I had run away before the marriage had seen three moons and, since my return, I had been sick with grief. Now I needed him to be father to my child. I neither contemplated what kind of man he really was nor what I kind of man I was turning him into.

* * *

I was mindful of my duties as a wife during the day but I could not control my dreams, which became increasingly vivid and disturbing while the child was growing in me.

'Come sit with me a moment, wife,' Hauk said to me one morning when I brought him his breakfast. I joined him on the tree trunk he had felled, steadying my bulk by holding on to his shoulder.

'You speak in your sleep.' I had taken care, as always, to sit on his uninjured side but now I wished I could see the colour of his scar to judge his state of mind. 'You call out names.' The silence that followed sat heavy on my chest. Hauk took a deep breath. 'Names!' Now his voice was angry.

Bile of fear rose in my throat. I swallowed and whispered: 'What names?'

'Ragnar. Who is Ragnar?' There was violence in his question. I knew I must not swoon, I must not let on.

'Don't shout at me, Hauk. He's a boy I knew when I was a child. I saw his father killed. I don't even know if anyone has told him. I keep dreaming of the killings.' I was crying now.

Hauk seemed less sure of himself but he continued, 'So who's Thorfinn? And Olvir?'

'Olvir! But Hauk, you know who Olvir is. He's the lad who came with me from Becklund. Hauk, my dreams are full of what I witnessed. I can't help what I see then.'

'Sigrid, I'm plagued by doubts. Say the child is mine. Say you love me.'

'The child is yours.' That much I managed to lie but I could not bring myself to speak of love to him and I pretended to choke on my tears. He put his arm round me.

'Sigrid, little wife, all will be well. I promise you, we shall rebuild Becklund and then we shall have two of the best farms in Cumbria and great wealth to pass on to our children.'

* * *

My baby announced its arrival in the middle of the night three new moons after the midwinter sacrifice. I woke and at first I thought it was my nightmare continuing to squeeze my ribs. Then I realised and rose to summon Ingefried from her bed. She called a serf and ordered a fire in the bathhouse. I went outside. Frost glittered on the hard ground and on the branches of trees and shrubs.

'Walk around a bit,' said Ingefried and covered my shoulders with my fur-lined cloak. I threw it open, thankful to cool off. The icy air stung my chest and the pain abated. When it returned, it was worse than before and I groaned.

'Listen, Sigrid, this is just the beginning. Your waters haven't even broken yet. Don't whimper. Grit your teeth!'

Once the sauna was warm enough, Ingefried made

me lie down on the bench with my legs open. She tut-tutted and made me walk around again. The pains came and went. The sun rose. There were voices outside, Hauk and Thorgunn. Ingefried was talking to them.

'It's a bit early but I'm sure all will be well.'

'More than a bit early! Let me see her. I want an answer once and for all!'

'Calm yourself, son. You mustn't upset her now.'

'You most certainly will not see her. This is women's business. Go away. Your child will be brought to you in the usual manner. Thorgunn, please take him away. I'll send for you if we need you.'

My waters broke and gushed, warm and sticky, along my legs on to the floor. The pains came at regular intervals and wrenched my insides until I screamed. So the day passed into evening.

I knelt on the bench, shivering under another contraction. In the heat and steam Ingefried tried to make me breathe deeply and work with the baby. But I was full of dread and my cleft was tense and my breathing out of time. She left me with a serf-girl and when she returned she sent the girl away and made me drink a most foul concoction. Then I remember a great fog. Pain still sliced through my body, but it didn't seem to matter. I heard screams, which may have been mine. There were voices, the voices of my nightmares and the faces that came with them, my mother denouncing me, the sound of the sword on my father's neck, the thundering hooves of the horse carrying Ragnar away from me, the crackling of the flames destroying Becklund. Then I was back there, back in my father's hall. But the roof was caving in. I had to hold it up or it would collapse on top of me. I became a giant. My strength superhuman, I strained and pushed to keep those mighty beams from crushing me. I heard myself scream. My body was torn apart, my strength waned. I floated on a cloud with my head in my mother's lap.

I woke with a headache like thunder and a vile taste in my mouth. I was alone. The fire in the sauna had died out. I was covered by a linen sheet and a soft cured skin. The bench underneath me felt wet and cold. I lay on my side and there was sick on the floor. The smell made me heave and retch but I was empty. I closed my eyes. I had no memory.

Outside there was a great noise. People cheered and clapped their hands. The door to the sauna opened. I gulped the fresh air. Ingefried came to my side. She handed me a swaddled bundle.

'Your son,' she said. 'Hauk has sprinkled him with water and named him Kveldulf.'

So, despite his doubts, Hauk accepted my son. He didn't have to do that. He could have turned me out for the mere suspicion of bearing another man's child. But then he would have lost the rights to the land at Becklund. Nor did he reject the child as a result of rape. A legitimate son and heir was what he wanted, so that's what he claimed. He honoured me with a gift of a pleated gold finger-ring and let every household in the area know he had a son.

It did him no good. As soon as I looked into the eyes of my newborn son, I knew he was Ragnar's and I knew I had to find my love and bring his son to him.

* * *

Four new moons after Kveldulf's birth, Hauk left with some of his men to go trading. He'd been gone two days when I handed Thorgunn the keys and told her I intended to take my son to Becklund. I saddled the grey mare Moonbeam and, ignoring Thorgunn's protests, set off alone with my baby strapped to my back. I was not headed for Becklund. I would go to Ragnar's family at Buttermere to find out what had befallen him.

I took the route I had walked when I ran from Swanhill and my quarrel with Hauk over Lydia. I was able to ride the first part of the journey. The gentle rolling gait of the horse rocked Kveldulf to sleep. When the path became too steep, I had to dismount and lead the mare. This woke him and he cried. I was already tired and glad of a rest so I put a halter on the horse and sat down. I parted my pinafore and put the baby to my breast. He was a big feeder and I was filled with pride and love. In the silence, I became aware of voices and the sound of a horse's hooves. Carefully so as not to cause my baby distress, I stood up and looked round me. The sound seemed to come from the way I had just travelled. Looking down the path I saw a large grey horse with two people on it, a woman and a child. With a sigh, I sat down to await the arrival of Ingefried and Olvir.

'Sigrid, this is too much! I'm too old for this!' Ingefried clung to the horse I had taken from Thorfinn. Olvir was panting hard from the effort of leading the horse over the steep ground.

'Who asked you to come? I didn't intend to be away for long. There's no need.' I held the bridle while Olvir helped Ingefried off the horse.

'When you go off without talking to anyone, I know you're up to no good.'

'I told Thorgunn.' Ingefried's snort brought Olvir out in a giggle. I slapped him for his insolence but halfheartedly since I was fond of the boy.

'Where are you going really, Sigrid?'

I knew she had guessed, so I told her.

'To Buttermere. I need to find out where Ragnar is.'

Her eyes shot firebrands at me. She ordered Olvir to take our horses to water and when his back was turned she hissed, 'Yes, I thought as much! Ragnar Sweinson, the outlawed son of a traitor.' She slapped me across the face. 'When will you grow up? You're a wife and mother! You behave like a woman without shame, a disgrace to your family. What would your mother say? How would your father feel?' By now you'd need to be a furlong away not to hear. Kveldulf stopped feeding and began to cry. I saw Olvir's shoulders stiffen as he dragged the animals with him along the beck. I rubbed my stinging cheek.

'You can't do that! I'm your mistress.'

'You are a child I brought into this world. I nursed both you and your mother and that gives me the right. When you conduct yourself like a mistress, you'll find the respect you think yourself entitled to, will be given without grudge.' She took Kveldulf from me and shushed and rocked him until he stopped crying. We stood silently glaring at each other.

After a while, Ingefried said, 'In one thing you are right. Kveldulf should breathe the air at Becklund and there's no harm in him touching his grandfather's stone even if it isn't finished. But there will be no other visits for you, my girl.'

So the four of us set off for Becklund. On the steeper parts of Mosedale we had to lead the horses but we still made good time and arrived shortly after midday. The farm was much changed since my last visit. Bard, the

67

freeman Hauk had put in charge of the work, received us with ale and bread.

'Welcome, Sigrid Kveldulfsdaughter. You arrive alone, without your husband?' He gazed at me from under his bushy, grey eyebrows.

'Thank you. Yes, Bard, my husband is away trading and I felt a great longing to visit my old home and bring my son here.'

'It will be some time before Becklund resembles the home you knew.' He pointed towards the farmstead where work had started on the main buildings. The cookhouse was re-roofed and in use. I looked at the remains of my father's hall. The stone walls had been repaired and earth banked up on the outside. Large roof-timbers were stacked up to dry. When ready they would be put up in the shape of an upturned boat and covered with turf. Inside it would again be warm and smoky with the smells of cooking and … I began trembling and had to turn away.

Bard's rumbling voice was soft as he touched my elbow and turned me towards the lake.

'The rune-writer is at his task. It will be a fine stone as befits your father's memory. Would you like to see it?' He must have seen I was too overcome with my memories to answer, for he continued, 'I see your son is hearty and hale. May I call your people to meet him?' He sent for all the thralls and free men and women to come and pay their respect to Kveldulf. The men approved his sturdy little limbs and the women fussed over his round cheeks. And my baby waved and smiled and made happy, gurgling noises.

Bard led us round the farm. We saw the fields put to the plough and the young animals growing fat on the rich pasture. I carried my son through the meadow and the trees towards the lakeshore. There was the stone, a large slab of grey it would stand taller than a man. A rune-writer was chipping out an image of Odin on his eight-legged horse Sleipnir and with his two black ravens, Hugin and Munin by his shoulder. It was far from ready but it would look imposing. Set on higher ground, it would be visible from the water. I put Kveldulf's little hand against the stone and he clenched his fingers as if he were trying to grasp it.

'It is good of your husband to so honour your father and look after his people.' Ingefried's voice was insistent and in front of everyone I had to smile and nod agreement. Too soon we had to leave. With my whole being I wanted to stay there and help turn the farmstead back to what it was.

I whispered to Kveldulf. 'This is yours, all yours. One day we will come back here and be happy. You, me and your father.'

* * *

When I told my infant son stories of his grandfather's exploits as a warrior – stories I had to make up, since my father never spoke of them himself – Hauk would sit quietly, regarding me out of the corner of his one eye. Thorgunn tried to speak to me about him again.

'He's as strong and courageous as any man but his eye makes it hard for him in a fight because he can't see if anyone comes at him from the right. And, Sigrid, he has his pride. Many times I've had to persuade him to stay here while others went raiding. But he would perish in battle. I worry every day he will leave and come to harm.'

From time to time, I tried to settle down to my

marriage. Ingefried would remind me of Hauk's good nature, the stone for my father, his acceptance of my son, his care for the elderly serfs and freemen of Becklund. It was true that Hauk tried hard to win me over. But I had my son as a daily reminder of Ragnar. My love for him smothered any grain of love or even friendship I could have nurtured for Hauk.

The servants and thralls of Swanhill had never showed me the kind of respect I remember my mother receiving at Becklund. They obeyed me but with surly faces. I didn't let it worry me. I had other things on my mind and as long as they did as I ordered, I didn't much care about why. Whenever I beat a servant, Ingefried would try and advise me.

'A little kindness gets you further than the stick and harsh words.' But I didn't listen.

We had been married nearly two years when Hauk had a spell of bad luck. Sometimes he would return from a hunt with game for the spit but more often than not he came back empty-handed. His attention to me diminished. I didn't mind. I hardly noticed. I lived in a fantasy world where Ragnar would call for me and carry me away. Then the herring catch failed.

'It's her fault,' I overheard the thralls whisper. 'She's cursed by the gods.' I could feel their resentful eyes on my back as I moved round the farmstead. At first I ignored it but soon it made me feel uncomfortable. I began to listen in when they thought themselves alone and, from behind a woodpile, I heard two of the women discuss me in unflattering terms. Then one of them said, 'All was well before she came, when Lydia was his woman.'

'He goes to Lydia again, you know. I saw them.

Things could change around here.' A malicious giggle then she continued, 'And if they do, Mistress Sigrid had better watch her back. He looks after her now, but if he's intent on returning to the soft arms of Lydia ...' They moved out of my hearing. I leant on the rough woodpile for support. It had never occurred to me I had anything to fear from the serfs.

* * *

Then Hauk told us he was leaving. 'King Olav the Red is calling men to arms. I have a mind to join him.' The statement was so unexpected neither Mother Thorgunn nor I reacted to it at once. I heard Lydia cry out and whisper to herself where she sat at the end of the table among the other slave women. Then Thorgunn found her tongue.

'You would fight for the King of Dublin? What good will that do you? You have no cause in common.'

'I will join his fight against Æthelstan and his rule. It's time to make a stand and make sure we keep our own laws. Æthelstan is getting too powerful. We need a Norse king in Jorvik again.'

'The quarrels between kings have nothing to do with us, my son. You have a wife and child to provide for. You have me. I was looking forward to a peaceful old age. What will become of us here if you're killed in battle? Honour won't put bread on the table and, as for whose law we live by, I doubt it will make much difference to ordinary people.'

It was the longest speech I had heard from my mouse-like mother-in-law. But Hauk didn't pay any attention to her. His eye was fixed on me. I opened my mouth but the words would not come. All round the longhouse, the servants and thralls stared at me. Every breath could be heard over the crackling of the fire. The words I ought to say, *husband do not go*, hovered in the smoke-filled air. But I was mute.

When I didn't speak, Hauk returned to the piece of alder he was fashioning into a bowl. The knuckles stood out white on the bronzed fist and his shoulder heaved with the force he put into digging the gouge into the wood. His breathing followed the movements of his arm; short intake, holding his breath while the gouge bit then a long low grunt as the slice of alder curled away from the inside of the bowl.

Without looking up, he said, 'There's a large army gathering for a final battle against Æthelstan. Olaf Guthfrithson of Dublin and his hordes have joined Constantine the Scot. Danish princes and jarls from the islands have mustered.' He raised his head and looked me full in the face, 'Even the Manx Vikings are turning out.'

My hands began to shake and I put down my distaff, pretending to add more wool.

'Yes, they say the son of the traitor Swein Hjaltebrand is with them, trying to win favour with King Olaf.' He turned and spat on the floor. I flinched as if he'd aimed at me.

I should have told Hauk not to go. But I didn't. And then it was too late. My mind span a yarn of fear and guilt: fear of the hostile serfs if Hauk was killed; fear of Hauk killing Ragnar. Whatever happened would be my fault. I had no idea how but I knew it was my duty to stop it. So, when Hauk loaded his weapons on his horse, I handed the keys to the distraught Thorgunn. I held my son and breathed in the infant smell of milk and warm skin. I kissed his round cheeks, his downy head and his firm little fist.

'Mamammm,' he smiled and I felt like I was dying.

'I will be back.' I whispered. I meant to say so much more but tears I could not allow grew inside me and choked me to silence. I put him in Ingefried's arms. It tore my heart to shreds but where I was going was no place for a small child. Above anything else I wanted him safe. I found the sword Snakebite and the helmet my father had given me and the light shield Steinar and I had used as children. I took my cloak from its peg and went to join Hauk. He never looked at me.

'You'll need a horse. Take Moonbeam,' was all he said.

7.

Eight of our freemen came. We were also joined by Hauk's half-brother Kjeld, who farmed over by Croasdale, and he brought ten of his freemen. There were a number of trustworthy serfs, two of them women, who would look after the horses and set up camp. Olvir was among them, he was the youngest. He was seven years old.

We rode towards the sea where the sun sets. The men were in high spirits and talked of their coming exploits and of past glories. Only Hauk stayed silent. I rode on my own, apart from the others, full of confused thoughts about what I had done.

We reached the bay where Hauk and his brother Kjeld had knorrs and the men set to readying the boats. We set up camp on the edge of the sea. Hauk led me to shelter among the trees. He set down his pack and built a small fire.

'What brings you, Sigrid?' he asked. 'Have you come to make sure you become a widow?'

The damaged side of his face was in shadow but on the good side there were lines of sorrow which I knew were because of me. I felt a rush of shame and pity. He had done nothing to deserve what I had done to him.

'I seek no widowhood, Hauk. I mean to come with you.'

'I wanted things to be good between us, Sigrid. I

have tried my best.' He reached out. I thought then how much easier it would be if I could but like him, but it was remorse, not love, which made my hand meet his and my body lie down next to him. As he entered me I did as always, averted my face and closed my eyes. But this time Hauk wanted more.

He commanded in a harsh voice, 'Look at me, wife, look at me, look at me, look at me …' and each call was followed by a slap across my face. And I did as I was told and I looked at him and my short-lived compassion turned to hate.

When we sailed the next morning, I sat in the prow, breathing in the salty air. I let my headdress slip down and my hair float on the breeze. The cool wind felt good against my bruised face. I couldn't quite open my right eye. I put a careful finger to it and felt the tender swelling. My bottom lip had split open and I could taste the blood as I probed it with my tongue. Behind me, in the hold, the horses snorted and began to stir, unsettled by the rocking of the boat. I slid across to soothe them. I caught Hauk smiling as he looked at me. He was in a good mood. Earlier that morning, thinking he had tamed me, he had treated me with indulgent good humour as he ordered me about. For the time being this suited me and I assumed a quiet demeanour as I helped prepare the knorr for departure. But, in the furnace of my chest, my anger burned hot.

We sailed south, hugging the shoreline as far as the bay of shifting sands, where we set course across open water until we found land again and here our voyage took us past a sandy shores and the place called the Black Pool. I had once been there with my father when he traded in this area and I recognised the busy harbour with its rows of wooden piers. We crossed the estuary of the River Ribble and that was my last familiar landmark. From then on I was in unknown waters and a very long way from home.

The wind swung against us and the men had to use the oars. Our light knorr still made good speed. There were other ships heading the same way. Some were knorrs but most were long, sleek drakkens with so many oars I lost count as I stared at them across the waves. Towards evening we drew close to the shore in search of a beach. I sighted three vessels at anchor and called out to Hauk. I saw horses grazing close by and a glint of metal on board. This close to the place we had been called to muster we were unlikely to meet with enemies but we still made sure our weapons were within reach. None of us knew the colourful standard fluttering in the feeble breeze. It had four sides so did not belong to a Norwegian or Dane who favoured three-sided banners. I could make out red and gold and the outlines of two black ravens, facing each other with their wings spread open. As we drew close, Hauk took my place in the prow. A stocky warrior in rich armour stood with his back to the mast in the largest ship. He said something in a melodious accent, I did not recognise.

'From the islands in the North, I think,' said Hauk. I found the man hard to understand at first but, from Hauk's answer, I knew he must have asked who we were. Hauk spoke freely stating our intent to take part in the fight against king Æthelstan. As I grew used to the chieftain's way of speaking, I learnt he was a sworn man of the Earl of Orkney. This earl had called his men to support Olaf Guthfrithson, King of Dublin, and King Constantine the Scot in their struggle against King

Æthelstan of the Saxons and Mercians. He invited us to share the stag, roasting over hot embers and ale brought in large barrels.

The men spent the evening in merry companionship and they all had their fill of ale. I was happy to eat with the women and as darkness fell I retired to the knorr and slept on board alone. The men woke late and, having sworn everlasting friendship, decided to travel the rest of the way together. We passed the place where the River Mercey flows into the Irish Sea. Many hundred ships had converged on the south side of the estuary. We rowed along the coast until we found a sandy bay to pull in.

We moored in the vicinity of a small hamlet. There was rain in the air and Hauk decided to stay on the boat and rig up the sail for shelter. The horses were unloaded and led to grazing. Olvir and Ole the Toothless were to watch over them. They were joined by a group of children from the hamlet who offered to look after the horses against payment. I was helping build a fire to prepare the evening meal and gave some apples to the leader of the young gang.

'Three apples,' he exclaimed, 'is that all your horses are worth to you, Lady?'

I laughed at his cheek. He was about nine years old and reminded me of my brothers. I grew melancholy and doubled the pay. This earned me another slap from Hauk. This time I hit back. It took him by surprise and he fell over. This caused much merriment among the children and drew bawdy comments from our own company as well as our Orkney friends. Hauk's roar carried his fury above the laughter. He scrambled to his feet, drew his sword and came at me. I ran towards the knorr to find my sword but stumbled over the hem of my pinafore and fell. Hauk lunged at me. I saw him and rolled to the side. The sword hit the empty ground next to me. I scrambled to my feet and drew my knife. All I could see was Hauk's contorted face with the scar red and bulging as he walked towards me with lifted sword.

A spear blocked his way. It was wielded by a grey-bearded Orkney warrior in mail shirt and helmet.

'You don't tame wild things with blows, Northman, try kindness and a little of what they all like.' He laughed and gestured to his crotch. Hauk made to attack but thought better of it and scowled.

'She's my wife. I'll use her any way I want.'

'But she'll not be much use dead, will she?' The warrior grinned.

'No, and I don't mean to kill her. I shall mark her. She'll carry my mark on her pretty face and then we'll be equals.'

From then on I made sure to keep my weapons about me at all times. I took to wearing leggings and a man's tunic. I wouldn't stumble again. I also made sure not to turn my back to Hauk.

A village elder accepted payment and agreed to keep the boats safe for our return. One of his men offered to guide us towards Brunanburh, a fort by Vin Moor. This is where king Æthelstan had challenged King Constantine, Olaf of Dublin and their allies to a battle which would decide once and for all who would rule over the north of England.

On Vin Moor a large rectangle had been marked out with hazel rods. On one side was a river and on the other woodland. The ground was as even as it could be in this area of heather and tall grasses. This was to be the battlefield. At either end of the field the two armies had set up their camps. On our side this was a higgledy-piggledy mass of tents, all of different sizes and colours, clustered around the different standards of the many kings, princes, earls and chieftains gathered together to support King Olaf and King Constantine. The English side looked more orderly with straight lines of tents and standards. Their camp seemed to spread for many furlongs and a great many warriors could be seen moving around there.

Our friends reported to their liege the Earl of Orkney and were allocated a space for their tents and cooking fires. Hauk was reluctant to part from them but his brother Kjeld convinced him we must join the Dublin Vikings and serve under King Olaf. The king himself had settled in a town north of the moor where he awaited the arrival of King Æthelstan. While Hauk and his brother went in search of the king, I prepared our camp. The men unloaded the carved tent poles and put them so the dragon-heads looked to either side, keeping guard. At the back, two pieces of hazel served to support the crossbar, then the heavy cloth was draped over the frame and secured with wooden pegs and stones. Each of our tents held two or three men. Most of the tents around us were of this size but further along I could see larger ones and some woven in colourful patterns.

Olvir and Ole the Toothless were sent with the horses to find grazing. Others went to obtain provisions in nearby farms. Both sides had agreed not to plunder but I dare say much food and other goods changed hands without due payment all the same.

I built our fire. As usual the serf-women assisted me

with sullen faces. All around us women prepared food and men sat around talking, playing dice and tending their weapons.

'I don't like all this waiting around.' I overheard one warrior tell another over a shared horn of ale. 'Negotiations are a waste of time. And, I suspect, new reinforcements arrive for the English every day. They must have a mighty army by now. If we'd attacked straight away they wouldn't have time to rest and settle in.'

'We're growing stronger by the day ourselves.' His companion sounded a bit the worse for drink. 'Just look at our neighbour here, sword at her side and shield within reach. A couple of shieldmaidens like her and how can we lose?' They slapped their thighs and roared with laughter. I felt anger warming my cheeks.

'Mind you,' said his friend,' she's not been all that victorious, has she, Yngvar? Look at the black eye and split lip.'

I could no longer keep my temper. I was about to confront the insolent oafs, when the one called Yngvar spoke words that made me shiver.

'Ah, but you don't know what the other one looked like, do you, Thorfinn?'

The name shot through me like a red hot arrow. With not a thought as to the consequences I turned. A heavy jowl, a broken nose and a large red welt across the left side of his neck. I felt a rush of fear as I stared at the man I had left for dead. I dropped the log I was holding and turned away.

'Be still, calm yourself, good lady.' The man called Yngvar called out. 'We mean no harm. A little innocent banter, that's all.'

Behind me, Hauk had overheard. His scar stood out purple and his voice rang with fury as he challenged the two men.

'Don't, Hauk,' I said, 'it is not serious.'

But Hauk drew his sword. The two men had to respond and reached for their weapons. I grabbed Snakebite and stood, next to the husband I hated and pitied, facing two battle-scarred warriors. My heartbeat rang in my ears and my legs trembled. I could sense Hauk shaking but whether with fear or anger, I couldn't tell. A small crowd gathered around us and among much merriment someone remarked on the spectacle of a wife having to defend her man. That put a stop to any possibility of Hauk backing down. He took a step towards our adversaries. I followed but they retreated.

'We should not fight amongst ourselves. Let's save our strength for Æthelstan's fyrd.'

Although he was still pleading, Yngvar raised his two-handed battleaxe and started moving towards us. His companion shrugged his shoulders and followed. An appreciative murmur swept through the group of onlookers but stopped when a commanding voice from somewhere behind me shouted.

'Hold it!'

Hauk hesitated. Yngvar lifted his battleaxe to strike. I rushed forward and thrust Snakebite into Yngvar's unprotected belly but it was too late. With a roar Yngvar had let his axe fall on Hauk's skull. It split his head almost down to his shoulders. Hauk fell to his knees then his body slumped to one side. Half his skull was sliced off and hung still attached by the neck. Blood and grey matter welled out and slid down his shoulders on to the grass. His arms and legs twitched as if he was trying to crawl away. Yngvar staggered and stumbled over Hauk's body. I couldn't retract Snakebite so had to let go. As Yngvar fell Snakebite was trapped against the ground and the weight of his body pushed her blade further in until it emerged from between his shoulders. I leapt aside to avoid Thorfinn's axe and drew my dagger. But Thorfinn was no longer a threat. He was blocked by a man on a horse. My arm was gripped from behind making me drop my knife.

'I said "stop"!' The voice was chilling in its calm. The man who had spoken was mounted on a splendid black stallion. The gold trim on his fine woollen cloak and the way other men fell away before him told me he was a man of importance.

I realised I was alone among strangers and enemies. Hauk was dead, his brother had no interest in keeping me safe and a man I had tried to kill was waiting for revenge. I made my decision in an instant. I fell to my knees and grabbing Hauk's sword from where it had fallen held it up with the handle pointing to the man on the horse.

'Noble prince,' I said,' please accept me into your service. My name is Sigrid Kveldulfsdaughter. I am trained to fight and I wish …'

I was interrupted by a howl of derisive laughter from the crowd around us. But Olaf Guthfrithson, King of the Dublin Norse, touched the handle of my sword and the laughter stopped. I shivered and looked up at the man who was to lead me into my first battle. He spoke to the crowd.

'Have you forgotten the stories about how in the lands of The North, shieldmaidens fought side by side with the warriors of old? Have you forgotten the brave

82

deeds of Hervör Heidreksdaughter who carried the sword of her ancestors and led her men in battle or Princess Alfhild of Goathland who went raiding at the helm of her own ship? Sigrid Kveldulfsdaughter will be our shieldmaiden. She will fight alongside you men of the North. She will bring us luck and she will be part of our victory.'

The laughter turned to cheer but I met Thorfinn's eyes and was chilled.

* * *

King Æthelstan was still offering compensation to King Constantine, Olaf Guthfrithson and their allies, suggesting that, for a sum of money, they should drop their claim on Cumbria. Some wanted to accept but others were full of greed and reasoned that, if they turned it down, Æthelstan would increase the sums of money. This had happened before and each new offer took many days to deliberate. Æthelstan sent a messenger to Constantine, a day-long journey. The allies debated and, because there were so many of them, this could take several days. A messenger then took the reply to Æthelstan, and more time passed. Meanwhile the warriors waited and only much later did we learn that, while his enemies argued, Æthelstan used the time to bring more men to his army.

While this was going on, I had time to bury Hauk. His brother Kjeld blamed me for not making Hauk stay at home and himself for not being there to defend him. We spoke harsh words and after the last embers of the funeral pyre had died down we parted with much ill-feeling between us. Kjeld spoke with Thorfinn about compensation for the deaths of Yngvar and Hauk.

'We need no more killing between friends and

neighbours. There is a gathering at the Thingmound after harvest-time. Let's meet there and put each our cause to the Lawmen.'

Thorfinn agreed with this, and Kjeld, claiming he'd only come to help his brother, returned home with his own and Hauk's men. After they left, Thorfinn stayed in his tent for two whole days and nights. Then he came over to where I was now camped alone. He sat looking at me for a long time. His gaze made me uncomfortable and I made sure my weapons were to hand. Then he spoke in his rumbling voice.

'There have been two deaths here, woman. Your husband caused his own demise and he has been revenged. But Yngvar's passing was your doing. He was a good man and has family in Rannerdale. It will be better for them if you pay blood-money than if I kill you in revenge. This is what Kjeld and I agreed. But now I have thought this matter over. If you or I perish in battle …'

He fell silent but kept staring at me.

I felt my skin tingle and my muscles tighten. I knew that, should he ever recognise me and remember what had passed between us by Mosedale Beck, he would not be satisfied with blood-money; he'd want nothing less than my life.

That night I was kept awake by Thorfinn's drunken singing. He drank grave-ale for Yngvar, composing bad verse in his honour. He eventually grew silent except for the occasional hiccup and guttural murmur. I fell asleep but woke, thinking I heard a rustling sound outside my tent. I sat up, drew my dagger, waiting to see who my attacker was: Thorfinn, driven by drink to seek early revenge; or one of the warriors who ogled me as I moved round the camp. Fingers clawed at the tent cover. The front flap opened enough for me to see the outline of an arm. Without a word, I stabbed it. There was a cry, high-pitched and feeble. I rolled forward. An empty sleeve was pinned to the ground. I opened the tent flap. A small figure, halfway out of his too-large tunic, lay shaking with heavy sobs.

'Olvir, oh, Olvir! I didn't mean to hurt you.' I dragged him inside the tent and closed it. The dagger had cut his sleeve but only grazed the thin wrist.

'You're supposed to be on your way home. What's happened?' He curled up on my lap and I cradled him like a baby until he stopped shaking and his crying abated.

'I've come back to look after you, Sigrid. I didn't want you to be alone.'

* * *

I couldn't ask Thorfinn about Ragnar without giving away who I was. So, for two days, I roamed the part of the camp where the Manx Vikings had put up their tents. I spoke with the women and thralls and some had heard of Swein Hjaltebrand but none knew what had become of his son. Apart from Thorfinn, I saw nobody I recognised from Jarl Swein's household. Like a foolish kitten chasing butterflies, I had left my child, the most precious thing in my life, to pursue a mirage. I fell into a deep melancholy and the longing to hold my son in my arms became a like a constant ache in my breast. I decided I must find a way to escape Thorfinn's watchful eye and get back home. It meant breaking my oath to Olaf of Dublin but I figured he'd have more pressing concerns than my desertion.

No sooner had I made my decision than we were

called to battle. There was no way out. Shortly after daybreak, a group of warriors moved against Æthelstan's camp in a surprise attack. It failed. Æthelstan's watch spotted them and sounded the alarm. The enemy had the higher ground so, without the advantage of surprise, we had to retreat, line up for battle in the allotted field and wait for the horns to sound. By now the sun sat high in the sky and the heat turned my helmet to a crown of fire. Sweat ran down my brow. I blinked to clear my eyes of the stinging. Then I took my stance, my shield held in front to protect my vitals and my right arm wielding Snakebite. I was ready. Thorfinn stood next to me. He told me he wanted to make sure we both made it to the gathering at the Thingmound. It was a threat, not a promise of friendship. His eyes were shot with red, his jaw worked in a circular motion and he was beginning to foam at the corners of his mouth. Neither of us wore a mail shirt, he because the mushroom-brew made him feel invincible, me because it was too heavy.

The war-horns sounded on the English side. Ours answered; a long drawn out note followed by many short bursts. With a rush of bile to my throat I saw the long line of Æthelstan's fyrd move towards us. I bent forward and was sick on the ground.

'Just take it steady.' muttered a voice behind me. 'And let your hair loose. It will unsettle them and encourage us. They will think you are one of those demons they believe in and we will see our shieldmaiden all the better.'

I shook my hair free of pins and combs. Then I straightened up, determined to meet my fate with the same courage my father had met his.

The English weapons sparkled in the bright light. The men beat the rhythm of their steps on their shields and the sound was like rolls of thunder. Their battle-cries soared above the field and met ours in the air as if a contest of sound preceded the real fight. Someone broke our ranks and rushed forwards, followed by others until we all joined in a wild scramble across the field. The air above us filled with arrows, spears and throwing axes. Some found a target and men fell. Blood flowed from the first wounds. Our pace increased. I raised my shield and joined in the war-cry of the Cumbrian Norse: 'Odin, Odin'. All round me, men were running. I ran with them. Leaping and stumbling over the uneven land, slipping on the heather and the brushwood, we stormed with a loud cheer, headlong towards death.

The front men careered into each other with a mighty crash. I was not far behind. When I reached the enemy, I angled my shield upwards, remembering to make my short stature an advantage. I ducked a swinging sword. Snakebite found her way under the warrior's guard and stung his crotch. He screamed and crashed, writhing, to the ground. I had felled my first enemy in battle.

I used my shield to deflect an axe wielded by a huge red-haired berserker. The two-handed blow knocked my arm sideways across my body and the force of it swung me round. I knew he would aim for my unprotected back and leaped aside. His axe missing its target made the redhead stumble and bend sufficiently low for Snakebite to reach his throat. She drew blood but not enough and the warrior bellowed in fury as he straightened up and lifted his axe to finish me off. He expected me to pull back but I dived towards him, ducked under his axe and drove Snakebite into his belly. My sweet sword slid into his flesh and opened him up like a herring being gutted. He lowered his axe but I clung to him and the axe-head couldn't reach me without him having to change his grip. My shield-arm embraced his large, hairy torso and my shield was lodged behind his right arm. With my other hand, I tried to hold on to Snakebite, who wouldn't retract from his belly. I had to stay close or the berserker would smite me down with one blow. His blood soaked the front of my tunic and the warm reek of his intestines filled my nostrils. He let go of the axe with one hand and grasped my hair trying to pull me off. Then his knees folded and he fell, dragging me down with him and pinning me to the ground. We lay like two lovers in a deadly embrace. His breath turned to a shallow rattle. His body became slack and heavy. Over his shoulder, I saw Thorfinn finish an enemy by cutting off his head. I called him and he helped free me. He glanced at the body of the berserker and nodded at me.

'Odin is on your side today. You fight well.' We set off in pursuit of our enemy and, for that day, our quarrel was put aside.

My memory of my first battle is like a wool blanket with holes in it. The entirety is dark and confused but shards of clear recollection burst forth: the flared nostrils and gaping mouth of a charging berserker; the severed leg of a Scottish warrior next to his twitching body; the crushed skull of a Viking spilling grey and red matter on to the tangled heather; and later, having to step on the piles of bodies of dead and wounded warriors.

How many did I kill on that battlefield? Thorfinn

told me a full dozen but I don't know. As I grow old, I believe one should honour those warriors by remembering them but the battles are too many and too long ago. We stayed together, Thorfinn and I, on Vin Moor. He saved my life, and I his, many times over until we were separated towards the end of the day.

One by one the banners of Constantine, Olaf, Hilrinc, Anlaf, Inwood and other kings and earls I didn't know, were lowered. King Athelred's dragon banner remained, proud and erect and his men raised the victory-cry. We had lost the battle. The defeated armies withdrew although some continued to fight from sheer fury. I was overcome by a sense of sad weariness. There seemed no point in going on. My body hurt from many cuts and bruises and I had a limp from a sword cut to my right knee. It began to rain. I walked away and sought shelter among the shadows of the forest until night would hide me.

I was not the only one leaving the field. As I hid between a tree and a boulder, I saw men running, some alone others in groups. Some threw down their heavy shields to be able to run faster and one left a banner behind, a banner with two black ravens. So, the men from Orkney were leaving as well. I crouched lower in my hiding place and from there I witnessed much slaughter of the defeated. Their pursuers, drunk on victory and hatred, cut down the injured and listened to no pleas for mercy or offers of reward.

8.

The rain fell heavy and straight. I had lost my helmet and my hair hung wet and cold on my shoulders. I thought of my father. Had he too run away from a lost battle? Is it the action of a coward to flee when there is no longer any hope?

Thor rode his chariot across the sky. The volatile god vented his fury on the clouds and the sparks from Mjölnir lit the darkness in mighty strokes. I put down my shield, my sword and my knife. It would not do to challenge the hammer-wielding god by carrying weapons. A stand of hazel gave some shelter against the storm and I curled up on the wet ground. Had my actions on the battlefield angered the Æsir and brought him out in all his terrible glory? Had he come to punish me for running away?

But you can't hide from a god and I resolved not to be such a coward as to stay shivering in a bush. I crawled out and met the storm on trembling legs but with my head held high. And Thor was placated and rode away. The flashes when he threw his hammer and the crashes when it struck home receded into the distance and I was left alive but alone in the darkness on Vin Moor. Around me the sound of thunder was replaced with the moans of the dying and the screams of the lost. There was movement, shadowy figures, animals, humans and all things in between. I picked up my weapons again and, limping on my injured leg, started off in the direction I thought the camp would be.

During the battle it had been impossible not to trample the bodies of the dead, wounded and those who had just tripped and fallen. I hardly noticed in the end. I just concentrated on keeping upright and fighting for my life. Afterwards, in the dark, it was different. I stumbled, slipped and fell over inert bodies. My hand caught a soggy stomach wound and the stench made me retch. One body let out a moan, another rolled over, limbs moved. The death-rattles of men, who had a few hours ago been alive, mingled with cries of pain and pitiful pleas for help. It echoed in the mist like a choir of Helheim.

I kept walking. Lights moved around, torches used by people looking for spoils or searching for survivors. I kept clear of them, not trusting friend or foe in the dark. I saw two women tugging at the arm of a dead warrior and grunting with the effort of prising a heavy armlet over his stiffening elbow. That could have been me, I thought, lying naked, dead and cold being robbed of my weapons and jewellery and then left for the wolves and the crows. There were plenty like them, pulling off mail shirts and helmets, gathering up weapons to sell to the survivors. But there were others too. Men and women searched for husbands and other kin or for friends. They moved without stealth, calling the names of those they sought. And among those calls one sounded my name.

'Sigrid! Sigrid Kveldulfsdaughter! Siii-griiiid!!' The cry was interspersed with loud sobs. It was the voice of a child. Brave little Olvir, conquering his fear of the dark and the dead, had come searching for me. I called in reply and soon held the shivering, crying boy in my arms.

Olvir led me back towards the camp. 'I have packed the tent.' he said in a defiant voice. 'I don't think we should stay here any longer.' He pulled up snot through his nose. 'I heard all them kings and princes, and them are dead, and so are most of the warriors except the ones that ran away.'

I had no idea how to get home but I tried to sound confident.

'Yes we shall leave for home but I need to rest and wash my wounds.'

'Oh, Sigrid, you're wounded! So you fought like a proper warrior.' Olvir sounded full of awe and squeezed my hand. The darkness hid my grim smile.

Our tent and few other belongings were piled in a heap. Next to it sprawled Thorfinn. He was on his back and the ground trembled with his thunderous snores. I shook him but he didn't react. It was close to daybreak. Olvir fretted.

'Everyone's running away. I think we should too or they'll come and kill us. They do, you know. I saw them killing people who were running and wounded. Please, Sigrid, leave him and let's go.'

But Thorfinn would know how to get us back home. I tried again to rouse him.

'Sigrid, pleeease! We must go. It's almost light.'

I aimed one last kick at Thorfinn's back. It didn't even interrupt the rhythm of his snores. So, for the second time, I left him for dead, but this time I left his horse as well.

We tried to move in the shelter of the forest but Moonbeam stumbled on the deadwood and the lower branches got caught in the load on her back. Olvir was exhausted and I was limping. The wound on my knee had not been cleaned and dressed. It throbbed and sent arrows of pain through my whole leg. The few hunched figures I saw moving in the early dawn mist were no threat. So I decided we would ride and follow the track we had arrived on. If we watched out we would be able to run for cover, should anyone approach. Olvir climbed up in front of me on the horse and, at once, fell asleep. I steered Moonbeam through what remained of the camp.

It proved larger than I had realised. Evidence of our defeat showed everywhere: in the wrecked and abandoned tents flapping in occasional gusts of wind; in the reek from the wet but still smoking campfires; in the weapons, clothes and boots strewn on the trampled ground. There were reclining figures, dead or alive made no difference to us. We rode slowly. The mare's hooves seemed to echo through the silence. I kept searching, still hoping I would spot Ragnar. He wasn't there. I began to wonder whether he'd ever been part of King Olaf's army.

I had been so sure the gods would lead me to him. When I left little Kveldulf behind at Swanhill, it had been to go and find Ragnar, to stop Hauk killing him and to bring him back to Becklund. I had felt so sure he would get a pardon from King Harald. Why should the son be held responsible for his father's crime? But since then, I had seen the fierce hatred of kings and I had witnessed the slaughter of the defeated and I knew there was no mercy and there would be no pardon.

They came out of the mist in silent, swift ambush. Moonbeam reared and Olvir and I tumbled off. I cried out as my already battered body hit the ground. Olvir crawled across to me and sobbing threw his arms around me. I couldn't get up. I sat among a multitude of horses' legs, cradling Olvir, waiting for the end, hoping it would be swift.

Twelve warriors in mail shirts and helmets and one man dressed in a black, full length tunic with long sleeves and a hood over his head. He had no weapons and round his neck, instead of the golden neck-ring from a warlord, hung a large silver cross with the dead god Christ on it. I had heard of this kind of man, a monk. But I had been told they didn't fight. So what was this one doing here? Dazed, I looked up at him.

He stared back. Although my hair hung loose, I was still in man's clothing and my weapons were on my horse. It was obvious I had been part of the battle.

'But this is a woman!' His voice was little more than a whisper.

'Oh, I recognise her!' said one of the warriors. 'She fights as hard as any man and I saw her slay more than one of ours.' He dismounted and gripped his axe.

'No!' The monk shook his head so his hood fell down. The shaved patch in the middle of his head glistened. 'You can't kill a woman with a child in her arms.'

'Makes no difference, she has killed as much as the others.'

'No, I can't allow this. Put your axe away.'

'No survivors, the orders were quite clear.'

'I answer to King Æthelstan himself. On his authority I order you to leave the woman alone.'

'On your head be it, Master Scribe, but what shall we do with her then? She's not like the other women who fight when they have to and with what weapon they find. This one fights like a warrior. I've seen it.'

A third man got involved: 'Why don't we take her with us? A real, live shieldmaiden like in the minstrel's songs, the king should see this for himself.'

Again I was the object of amusement. This time I didn't mind. I was still alive.

King Æthelstan had set up court at Brunanburh. I rode there escorted by the monk and his party of warriors. They led a row of packhorses laden with the spoils from defeated warriors. Olvir sat in front of me on Moonbeam and one of the soldiers carried my weapons. The rest of our possessions were thrown away.

We rode through the gate in the wooden palisade and up to a house the size of a giant's hall. The King's little scribe gave orders and our horses were relieved of their burdens and led away. One of the warriors pushed me and was about to hit me with the hilt of his sword. The scribe held up a hand.

'No! I will not have the woman or the child mistreated. They are under my protection until the King decides otherwise.'

The booty was carried into the hall and we followed. Olvir clung to my hand and looked around with open mouth. In spite of my exhaustion I, too, was overcome by the splendour of the hall. Every wall was covered in rich hangings and there were oil lamps and candles suspended from the beams. The hearth held a lively fire and the roof was so tall the smoke all but disappeared, leaving the air in the hall clear. There were a great many people gathered, mostly men looking weary after the battle, many with blood-soaked bandages. I wondered whether anyone would let me take care of my injured leg. I tried to put my weight on the other foot but I was trembling with fatigue and found it hard to keep my balance. I stuck close to my protector, trying to keep out of the way of the stealthy pushes and blows from the warrior behind us. He had seen me limp and enjoyed kicking my bad leg.

An ox roasted over the fire. Everyone seemed to be eating. Women bustled back and forth with drinking horns and steaming platters piled high with meat. The smell of food made me realise I hadn't eaten for a day and a half. Olvir sniffed the aroma. He looked up at me and whined.

'Sigrid, I'm hungry.'

'Yes, I know. Me too.'

'Will they give us some food?'

'I don't know. Better be quiet. We mustn't annoy them.'

Olvir let go of my hand. Our guards were looking elsewhere as he slipped away. I watched him sidle up to a matron and smile. It worked, it always did. That boy would never go hungry. He returned to my side with a slice of meat, part of which he put in my hand. But whereas Olvir was able to avoid the guards' attention, I couldn't.

'That's not for you!' The meat was snatched from me and I watched it disappear between the heavy whiskers of my guard. My insides screamed with hunger but I was not allowed to forget there were those who wanted me dead.

Then the monk gave a sign and moved ahead. The guard took the opportunity to take my arm in a painful grip and push me forward. As we passed the hearth I could see the far end of the room. On a dais, behind a huge table, sat King Æthelstan. His chair had carvings of eagles' heads on the back and armrests. There was no mistaking the King. He wore a broad diadem set with lustrous jewels in many colours, his cloak was of finest wool trimmed with precious stones and gold threads. He was surrounded by men, some in fine clothes but some of them still carrying the mud and tears of yesterday's battle. Next to the King sat a young warrior. His face was pale and tired under a golden diadem almost as rich as the King's. This must be Edmund Ætheling, the King's younger brother. Fourteen years old and already battle-hardened.

Our scribe spoke to one of the lords seated by the King. The lord looked my way and I saw him smile in amusement. He turned and spoke to the king.

'Sire, look what Ansgar brought. A real, live shieldmaiden.' The King didn't hear him but the young prince looked at me and laughed.

'Ansgar, what a splendid jest!'

'It's not a jest, my Prince. I have come to find out what to do with her. She has a child with her too. It really is most … ah … most …'

The Prince roared with laughter and Ansgar fell silent. Then Prince Edmund leant forward.

'And what's a wench in armour doing at the King's court?' We now had the full attention of everyone and Æthelstan himself listened with a smile on his thin lips.

'With your permission, Sire.' A tall man had been whispering with one of my guards. 'This is no ordinary wench. She has slain many of your faithful warriors. Ulf the Proud, I saw it myself how she ran him through with her sword, and Halfdan the Pale.' He was interrupted by a lanky boy with a blood-soaked rag round his head, rising from his seat by the fire.

'Eidor the Beardless also, I witnessed it.' He swayed and sat down clutching his forehead.

Now others joined in, shouting names and calling for my blood. I wondered had I really killed that number of warriors? Only the little scribe objected but was shouted down. I fell to my knees. It had worked once. Maybe it would work again.

'Noble, merciful Lord, King Æthelstan. I have come due to events I could not control. I was forced to take up weapons. I know my old allegiance to be false. I know you, noble Lord, are the rightful ruler of all of England and I have come to pledge my trust and offer my sword in your service.'

Angry voices started up behind me but the King silenced them with a wave of his hand. He leant forward and looked me up and down.

'You speak well, woman, even if it's all nonsense. What is your name? And is it true you have slain so many of my warriors?'

'My name is Sigrid Kveldulfsdaughter.'

Someone hidden behind the gathering around the king drew a sharp breath. I continued to talk but slowly, not sure how much to tell.

'My father was accused of breaking his faith with King Harald and slain. But he wasn't a traitor. He wasn't!!' I couldn't stop myself, I shouted my grief and despair at the King.

I broke down and cried. Gradually I noticed that somewhere a lute had begun to play, soft and searching at first, then spreading warm notes of healing and comfort through the tense air. Silence spread through the hall. My tears abated and I looked up. The King lounged in his chair. The Prince leaned on the table resting his chin in his hand and his eyes looked at a dream somewhere beyond the rafters. The soothing melody weaved its way through the gathering and all around the hall men and women slowed down and became still and peaceful. Then the King spoke:

'Yes, Thorstein, I do believe we have found your sister.'

9.

My sister-in-law Freydis emerged from behind the dais. She held out her hands and helped me up from the floor. The pain in my knee made me wince. She put her arms around me, kissed my cheek and whispered, 'Don't worry, Sigrid. We'll look after you.' She led me towards the music and my heart sang.

Thorstein, dressed in a fine, embroidered tunic, sat with his lyre on his lap. His long, slender fingers stroked the music from the strings, just the way I remembered. He did not look at me. His eyes were open but had lost their colour. The skin around the eyes was red and scarred.

'What …' I began and looked at Freydis. Her smile reflected all the sadness she had suffered.

'Hakon blinded him.' she said.

I embraced the brother I had thought dead. His fingertips slid soft and searching over my face.

'Little sister. How I wish I could see you. Oh, Sigrid, what mischief has brought you here?' He hugged me and with his cheek against mine whispered, 'You will not be safe here. I can protect you but only for a time.'

The debating had started up again and I heard prince Edmund chuckle.

'Trial by combat. Let's make her fight for her life.'

Ansgar cut in: 'What blasphemy! A woman! And

anyway, there's been enough bloodshed. Send the poor, misguided creature home.'

'Oh, be still, all of you.' The King sounded tired. 'She isn't just anyone. She's Prince Hakon's niece and he may not want her killed in his absence.'

I let out a cry and Thorstein shushed me and rocked me back and forth.

Æthelstan continued,'And she has long ears! Bring her to me with her brother. And leave us alone, I wish to speak to them.'

Freydis led Thorstein to the King and I followed. As I was given a seat on the dais next to Æthelstan, there was a movement behind my shoulder and Olvir emerged, cheeks bulging with food. I pushed him down to sit on the floor, out of sight.

'I would address you as "princess" but I believe your mother reneged her title when she ran away with your grandfather's housekarl.' Æthelstan's voice was disdainful. My mind ran in circles trying to make sense of what I'd heard. Thorstein stretched out his hand and Freydis took it and placed it on mine.

'It's true,' he said, 'our mother is the daughter of King Harald of Norway, the one they call "Finehair".'

I kept shaking my head. I should have known. Did not Hakon call my father his brother-in-law before he killed him? Still, I could not accept it. My heart hammered against my ribs, my wound throbbed, sending ever more intense pains through my leg. I shivered, feeling sweat break out over my whole body. I was grateful when a commotion at the other end of the hall claimed Æthelstan's attention.

Freydis took charge. She obtained permission to take me away against the promise of returning me the next morning. I followed her stout, bustling figure into a small hut with a sunken floor. Olvir made himself useful banking up the fire over the embers and fetching water. Freydis removed my leggings. She tut-tutted when she saw my wound. She called Olvir.

'Go and collect as much cobweb as you can find. It must be clean, no flies no dust. Do you understand?' Olvir nodded and ran off.

Freydis cleaned out the cut with hot, salty water. I gritted my teeth but couldn't help letting out a groan. She put cobweb and crushed herbs on it and tore a strip off Thorstein's undershirt to tie them in place. While she tended me she told me how she and Thorstein had survived the attack on Becklund.

'I'm not ashamed, Sigrid,' she said. 'When the ships arrived and the men came ashore, I knew I must save Thorstein and his music. I ran in the house and fetched the lyre and I ran to warn Thorstein. But I must have passed him on the way. The field by the birches where he'd been working was abandoned. I heard the noise from the battle. Sigrid, you must understand this. There was no point me returning to the farm. What could I have done to help?'

'Calm yourself, my love.' Thorstein put an arm round her shoulder. 'So many times I have told you. You did the right thing. There can be no blame. Sigrid, say you understand this!'

'I do. I also didn't help. I hid under the grain store. I saw father killed.'

Freydis sighed. 'I waited until the fighting stopped. The Norwegians were feasting, thinking themselves safe with all of our people dead or tied up. I walked among the burning buildings. Your mother stood with prince

Hakon and Thorstein lay on the ground next to your father's body. They built a pyre and laid Kveldulf on it. Your mother performed the rites, slashing her arms and wailing. They were about to put Thorstein on the pyre as well when they realised he was not dead. He was brought to and ...' Freydis sobbed. 'Oh, Sigrid, there was nothing I could do. Hakon himself held the white-hot sword blade to his eyes ...'

'But I'm here, my love, and you are my eyes and my guardian angel.' Thorstein took up his lyre and played.

I slept and when I woke, Freydis was at my side. She knelt on the earth floor. In her hand was the same sort of cross with a man on it, I had seen around the neck of the scribe Ansgar.

'... and heal my beloved sister-in-law as you did my husband. In the name of ...' Her voice was a quiet mumble. Olvir sat on a low stool with his chin in his hand.

'Does that work?' he asked.

'God in his mercy healed Thorstein and he may do the same for Sigrid but it worries me she is still a heathen.'

'What's a "heathen"?'

'Someone who has not been baptised into the true faith,' Freydis said. When the boy looked no wiser, she added, 'Someone who is not a Christian. Have you heard of Christianity, Olvir, about the one true God and his son Jesus, who died for our sins?'

'What's "sins"?'

'Oh dear, I can see I have a lot to teach you.'

Olvir straightened up. 'I have heard about Christians. Some of the thralls were that. They'd sing and pray, just like you did then. It never happened though, what they prayed for.'

'How do you know?'

''Cause they prayed for freedom but they're all dead or they were taken by Hakon and I bet he was a lot worse than Kveldulf for a master.'

'The Lord moves in mysterious ways. Oh, Sigrid, you're awake! I have some broth for you.'

I sat on the edge of the bed, which stretched along most of the wall. On the bed opposite, Thorstein lay, cradling his lyre, his milky eyes staring into the ceiling.

'Is he asleep?' I whispered.

'Yes!' answered Thorstein and the mischievous smile of our childhood jokes spread across his lips. Olvir laughed and I joined in, feeling happy for the first time since I saw the burning ruins of Becklund. I sipped the hot brew and felt strength and hope return.

'The King will see you now.' The man was not one of the warriors I had arrived with. He allowed Thorstein, guided by Freydis, to come and I noticed Olvir sneaking in, hidden behind Freydis' voluminous dress.

'Ask him to take you to baptism.' Thorstein had time to say before we entered the hall.

The King sat as he had the evening before with his advisors and Prince I bent my knee to the King.

'Merciful King, Lord of all of England, I seek your forgiveness and your pardon. My past trespasses weigh heavy on my conscience and I crave the cleansing power of baptism under your protection.'

'Yes, baptised you shall be, but first I wish to find out a bit more about you.'

'I am Sigrid Kvel ...'

The King interrupted me with an impatient wave of

his gloved hand.

'Yes, yes, I know all that. When it comes to your family background I seem, if anything, better informed than yourself. What intrigues me is how you ended up fighting in this battle at a place so far from your home.'

His eyes glittered in the firelight. I trembled before this ambitious and ruthless monarch. It was said about him that he had a hand in his own father's death. He held most of the country and his armies were ever ready to quash rebellions. He had more than once ravaged the town of Jorvik and he meant to be the unrivalled ruler of the whole of Cumbria and Northumberland. Five kings and seven earls lay rotting on Vin Moor as proof of his power. His gaze seemed to penetrate my heart. He would not take kindly to lies and evasions. So I told him the whole story: Ragnar; the attack on Becklund; the deaths of Swein Hjaltebrand and my father; my marriage to Hauk and my baby.

'Then I followed my husband to stop him killing the father of my child. It was a foolish act, which I deeply regret.' I managed to finish before the tears choked me. I had lived with my lies and deceptions so long, they had burnt holes in my mind and I was relieved to let go of them.

The King stroked his stubbly chin, making a rasping sound. He had listened in silence, except at the mention of Ragnar and his father, when he leant to one of his nobles who whispered some information to him. Then he said to the scribe, 'Brother Ansgar, prepare for her baptism. And, for the love of God, get her into some women's clothing.'

Freydis got a dress in the Wessex fashion for me. I struggled with the narrow sleeves and the veil but the material felt soft against my bruised skin. I would have liked a bath as well but Freydis explained that the Saxons didn't bathe as frequently as we. I thought of the bathhouse at Becklund and how it was fired every week so we could all cleanse ourselves. I washed, as well as I could, in water brought in a bucket from the river.

'Better remove this.' Freydis took my golden pendant in the shape of Thor's hammer. I snatched it back.

'It's mine. Father gave it me.'

'It's a heathen symbol. You are coming to the true faith, Sigrid, you must let go of the old ways. You could have this re-fashioned into a small cross.'

'This is not the time to argue, Sigrid.' Thorstein's voice could be as soothing as his music.

'I could look after it for you.' Olvir stretched out a hand to which clung the evidence of his last meal. I turned down his offer and hid the pendant under my dress.

Back in the hall, Brother Ansgar brought a large cross, a big leather-bound book with gold clasps and a basin of water. I knelt and Freydis showed me how to put my hands together to pray. My father always said that oaths taken under threat didn't count and, as far as baptisms were concerned, the promises only lasted while you were in the service of that king. He claimed to have been christened twice, when serving two different chieftains, but he always stayed true to the old gods. I kept this in mind as I kissed the cross and the book. My head was sprinkled with water and Brother Ansgar said prayers over me in a language I didn't understand. It was over with quite quickly and I learned that Freydis would be my godmother and responsible

106

for teaching me how to be a good Christian woman.

* * *

I soon realised this would not be easy. The first stumbling block came when I was required to give up my weapons. I had thought I would get them back once I had sworn loyalty to Æthelstan but it turned out that 'good Christian women' don't carry weapons. I was much distressed to be deprived of Snakebite.

'What will happen to my sword?' I asked the soldier who took it from me.

'The King will find use for it. Although I don't see it being much good to a fully grown warrior. Nicely balanced though. Would do for a young boy to practise with.' He swung Snakebite in the air and smiled when he saw me raise my hands to grab for it.

'So you fought in the battle then, did you wench?'

I nodded, unable to take my eyes off Snakebite.

'You promised it to me, didn't you, Mother?' Olvir! The boy got everywhere. The warrior looked from Olvir to me and back again.

'How did you get in? This is the King's hall.'

'He's with me.' I put an arm round Olvir's shoulders.

'Is he your son? You seem very young ...' I didn't hesitate.

'Yes this is my son.'

But it made no difference and that's how I lost Snakebite but gained the foster-son who would stay with me and support me through many dangerous, difficult times.

Being a 'good Christian woman' was not going to suit me and besides I had a baby I ached to return to. My opportunity came when Ansgar sought me out to question me about my homeland.

'There are mountains with grazing for the sheep, forests full of game and rivers and lakes full of fish.' My voice became hoarse with homesickness.

'What about the people? Are there still heathens there?'

'Both Christians and others. We don't argue about it. There's enough to fear from Scottish raiders and pirates.'

'Scottish raiders … ah … I see …Scottish raiders.'

'There are some towns where we trade.' I tried to make it sound a bit less frightening for the little man. I realised that, if I could persuade him to go to my homeland, he would need a guide. 'And in Cockermouth, I believe, there is a small church.'

'So there is a Christian community there?'

'Oh yes, but they need support, Brother Ansgar. They are quite isolated.'

'And would you be able to lead me to them?'

'Oh yes, Brother Ansgar, I would.'

* * *

Two weeks later I was travelling home in the company of Brother Ansgar and two other monks. Æthelstan had already left for Jorvik and, I heard later, the poor town was, yet again, ravaged as punishment for supporting Olaf Guthfrithson. Part of the King's entourage was my brother the minstrel and his wife. I had tried to persuade Thorstein to return with me and claim Becklund. He laughed.

'I spent my childhood trying to get away from there. I'm not going back now.'

He dictated a letter, for Ansgar to write down, where he passed his right to Becklund to me and my children for all time. I would miss him but found comfort in the thought that he had realised his dream of being the minstrel at the court of a powerful lord. True, he could not see all the things he had fantasised about, but Freydis was at his side, describing and explaining. I believe he was happy. He said he was.

Moonbeam was restored to me and Olvir sat behind me, singing and chattering as we rode. Tied to my body, under my clothes, I wore Thorstein's letter to the Lawmen at the Allthing. Whatever awaited me at Swanhill, I would still have my home at Becklund.

Brother Ansgar paid a trader to take us as far as Cockermouth. Setting out we sailed past a great number of vessels. Many looked abandoned and some of these were drakkens of Norse construction with forty and fifty pairs of oars and fierce dragon-heads in the prow. I reflected that the chieftains who had arrived in these with their warriors were now, most likely, just piles of sun-bleached bones on the battlefield of Vin Moor.

Part Three:

Respect

10.

I had to bring Brother Ansgar to Swanhill. There was nowhere else for him and he was so afraid of the new land and the strange people in it. The other two monks stayed a while in Cockermouth before setting off in opposite directions to convert heathens.

'Look, there it is!' I shouted my delight and excitement when I finally spotted Swanhill. Trembling, impatient to hold my son in my arms again, I urged Moonbeam to a tired trot. Brother Ansgar called after me but I left him to find his own way. A black cat ran across the path and made my mare stumble. This was a bad omen but, in my relief that the journey was over, I ignored it and rode in through the gates, hooves clattering against the paved walkways. When I pulled up, Olvir slid off the horse and ran towards the hall shouting for Ingefried.

I remained mounted, looking at the people gathered in the yard. I was met with silence and sullen looks. Some even had their weapons handy. The thralls stared and whispered among themselves. That didn't worry me. I hadn't expected them to be pleased. The free men were a different matter. Some had seen Hauk killed and had brought the news home. I greeted them with respect one by one and they responded in kind but, in some cases, with suppressed hostility.

Bard, my father's old housekarl from Becklund, appeared. He took the reins from me and helped me dismount. We exchanged formal greetings but not even he had a welcoming smile for me. His grey eyebrows almost covered his eyes and his mouth was set in a firm line.

'Sigrid Kveldulfsdaughter, you have been absent a long time.' He looked at my dress. 'You return a Saxon woman?'

I answered in a loud voice to make sure they could all hear me. 'No, Bard, I'm no Saxon but I *am* a changed woman and much will change here too.' Then quietly I said just to him, 'Have you completed your work at Becklund? I thought you were staying there.' He shook his head.

'Kjeld has set me to run Swanhill and watch over his nephew, when he can't be here himself.' He added in a whisper, 'Take care.' Whether warning or threat, I could not tell.

I walked towards the hall. Olvir had left the door open and I saw movement inside. Lydia appeared. On her arm, his golden head resting on her shoulder, sat Kveldulf.

'My son!' I reached out to take him. I cried out in anguish when he turned from me and buried his face against Lydia's neck.

'Hand me my child, Lydia.' My voice was hoarse and tears dimmed my vision. She obeyed with a superior smirk. Kveldulf screamed and kicked and reached out to her, crying: 'Mummy, mummy'. His little feet hammered against my stomach and he wriggled in my arms. I clutched him to me regardless and kept saying: 'I'm your mummy. It's me.' He didn't

112

listen. He continued to kick and try to get away from me. Lydia looked on, a triumphant smile on her lips. The whole meaning of my life fell to pieces. My son, the sole reason for my survival, had been stolen from me. I screamed at Lydia's smirking face.

'You have put a spell on him, you offspring of trolls, you daughter of a snake, you …'

But she no longer paid attention to me. Her gaze had moved to something behind my shoulder. Her face transformed, her mouth softened and let in a rasping breath, her eyes opened, round and luminous before filling with tears. This stopped my curses and I turned to see Brother Ansgar clambering off his horse. He came up to us, limping after the long ride.

'Sigrid, such language! You should be grateful the lady has looked after your child.'

Lydia rushed past me, threw herself on the ground before Brother Ansgar. She embraced his knees. She kissed the muddy hem of his habit. She grasped his hand and covered it with her tears. Between her loud sobs she said again and again.

'Padre, mea culpa, mea culpa.'

He put his hand on her head and said something, which I couldn't hear above Kveldulf's screams, Lydia's sobbing and the rising wave of confused chatter from the assembled household.

Thorgunn appeared next to me. She put a piece of honeycomb into Kveldulf's screaming mouth and took him from me.

'You have been away for a long time.' she said. 'He has forgotten you. Come inside now.'

'Where are the keys? You're not carrying the keys.'

She patted my arm. 'I'm glad you're back, Sigrid.

We have much to talk about. Come now.'

I turned at the sound of a rider leaving the yard. 'Where is he going?'

'Kjeld's man. He'll be breaking the news of your return to my stepson Kjeld.'

I noticed then the keys to Swanhill attached to Lydia's belt. Things had indeed changed at Swanhill. Thorgunn took me by the hand and led me inside. I looked around.

'Where is Ingefried?'

'Come sit with me by the hearth, Sigrid. Shhh, Olvir.'

Olvir lay with his face to the wall on one of the benches. His whole body shook with deep, rasping sobs. I sat down by him and stroked his hair. Thorgunn sat next to me. Her face was pale. She rested her cheek on Kveldulf's head and sighed. When she spoke, I had to listen to things I did not want to hear.

'Sigrid, Ingefried took ill shortly after you left. She was a wise woman and a good friend to me. Life has been difficult since she entered the halls of Odin's fair wife.'

'Ill? But how? I don't understand. She's dead?' Thorgunn patted my arm. I heard the crackling fire, Olvir's sobs and distant voices from outside. Ingefried, my conscience and my guide, the one constant in my life, the one link with my past – gone. I let out a moan.

'Sigrid, there is no time to mourn. She left me a message for you. I think it is important you should hear it at once. You need to act to secure your future and that of your child.' The urgency in Thorgunn's voice cut through my grief. When she saw she had my attention she continued: 'She said you must gain the confidence and loyalty of your people – free men and women as well as servants and thralls. You must tell them there will be no more beatings and you must promise to treat them with fairness. That's the first thing. Then you must go to the next assembly of the Allthing and lay proper claim to Swanhill and Becklund in your son's name.'

'Why do I have to lay claim to what's Kveldulf's by right?'

'His rights have been challenged.'

'By whom? Who has dared? On what grounds?' My raised voice unsettled Kveldulf, who with a frightened look at me, wriggled down from Thorgunn's lap and toddled over to the door.

'Keluf out,' he said, 'to mummy.' His words were like knives tearing open my chest. A whine escaped from my lips and I bit my knuckles to stop it growing into the scream I could feel welling up inside me. Thorgunn took my hand.

'Be wary of Lydia. She is Kjeld's woman now and she has wielded the power here since he returned. She also has your son's heart and you need to win him back.'

I had not been so naïve as to think it would be easy to return to Swanhill. But I always thought, and this had sustained me, that my baby would be there waiting for me. Instead I found I had been ousted not only as mistress on the farm but also as Kveldulf's mother. I would need to gain the respect of my household – I always knew I'd have to do that – but I never thought I would be a stranger to my beloved son. My whole reason for striving seemed to disappear and exhaustion settled on me like an iron yoke. Thorgunn stroked my arm.

'You must be strong, Sigrid,' she whispered. 'We need you to be strong and see us through.'

Somehow, I found the courage to go and face the assembled household out in the yard. Brother Ansgar sat by the water trough speaking to Lydia and three other thralls. His face was burnt red by the sun but his smile was benign. He looked like a man who has found his vocation. He did not seem to notice the hostile glares from the other thralls and servants. Kveldulf sat on Lydia's lap. The rest of the household stood in small groups talking. As I opened the door, all fell silent and turned to stare at me. I beckoned to Brother Ansgar to come inside. He made the sign of the cross over the thralls before joining me.

I sat down in the high seat and invited Brother Ansgar to sit on my right. Thorgunn brought ale, bread and salt and I welcomed Ansgar to my home.

'What's ailing little Olvir,' he asked.

'There has been a death while we were g ...' My voice failed me. I had to stop and blink away my tears. Brother Ansgar looked at me, his eyes kind and sad.

'It has not been an easy homecoming for you, Sigrid. Put your trust in the Lord and all will be well.'

Thorgunn eyed him with suspicion as she put two bowls of curds in front of us. But Ansgar had no time for food.

'Sigrid, this must become a Christian house without delay. First free your Christian thralls. Then the rest of your household must be received in baptism.'

I thought this over. Even if I wanted them to be baptised the household would never obey me. And thralls were valuable. They worked the land and they could be sold when times were hard. I couldn't afford to

116

let them go. Besides they were not all Christian and to free some would cause dissatisfaction among the rest and among the servants. On the other hand, Brother Ansgar had influence over Lydia and I would need him on my side to persuade her to let me have my baby back. I decided to delay.

'These things cannot be rushed, Brother. There's much I need to see to. While I have been away, a thrall-woman has been in charge. I must regain my place as the mistress of this farm before I can change anything at all. Please come with me. I shall retrieve the keys to Swanhill then we shall be able to discuss this further.'

Lydia bridled, when I demanded the keys from her. 'Kjeld master now. He to me give keys. He …'

'Kjeld was master during my absence. I'm back now. Give me the keys, Lydia.' She looked to Brother Ansgar for support.

'Who is Kjeld?'

'My husband's half-brother. He has no lawful claim to the farm. It belongs to my son. He thought I was dead and so he took charge.'

'Kjeld master now.' Lydia insisted but Ansgar shook his head and under his watchful eye she handed me the keys. I ordered a feast to be prepared in celebration of my safe return and to welcome Brother Ansgar to Swanhill. I didn't feel like celebrating but there were things I had to put straight which couldn't be delayed.

I gave order for food and drink to be prepared and invited Ansgar to walk round the farm with me. As we set off towards the lake, Olvir caught up with us.

'I'll come with you, Mother,' he said and blew his nose in his fingers.

'I'm not sure you can call me "mother" now we're

back.' I ruffled his hair and put my arm round his shoulders to soften the rejection. 'Everyone here knows you're not my son.'

'I know you're not my real mother but I'm an orphan and now Ingefried is dead as well. A ... nd,' he put great emphasis on the word, 'you call Ansgar "brother" and he isn't.'

'Maybe,' Brother Ansgar used his most soothing voice, 'maybe foster-mother is a better name. Who is going to object to that?'

'You will have to call me that then, Olvir.' I took his clean hand and squeezed it.

'Brother,' I said as we watched Olvir throwing stones into the lake, 'I have not told you this before. I was not a good mistress when I lived here. I treated many of my people harshly and there are some who wish me dead. My life may not be safe.'

'Sigrid! But I thought ... I'm sure you said ...' Ansgar's voice betrayed his fear.

'I need to convince them that things will be different. I must do it in my own way. Your safety depends on this as much as mine does.' I gave him time to think this over. Poor Ansgar, he usually had a group of warriors to defend him should there be any danger. His breathing became shallow and he clutched his cross with shaking hands.

'I must ask you, Brother, not to contradict me or object to anything I say to the household tonight.' He nodded and I thought he had understood.

We returned to find preparations for the feast in progress. Women rushed back and forth carrying platters and bowls but without the usual chatter. Men brought firewood and set up the trestle-tables. Someone

118

had brought a barrel of ale. I sat in the high seat with Bard on my right and Ansgar on my left. I seated Lydia with Kveldulf on her lap next to Ansgar. She looked confused.

'I want you to hold Kveldulf and feed him.'

She looked at Ansgar. He nodded. She lowered her eyes and bowed her head.

'Yes, Mistress. Thank you.' She spoke in a quiet voice, without her customary sneer. Ansgar smiled. Perhaps he thought he had forged peace between us. But I knew Lydia was, more than ever, my enemy and Swanhill could not hold the two of us.

Everyone had their fill of meat and ale. The atmosphere improved but not as much as I had hoped. I waited till the household had finished eating before I stood up to address them.

'I return to you a different woman. Not only my clothing but my intent and my mind are changed. While I was away, I saw much misery and many things done which were wrong and it made me think about my own actions. I have understood that I didn't always treat you with fairness and I have decided to make up for that. There will be no more beatings without good reason. I give you my promise I will run this farm and look after you, feed you and keep you safe. Brother Ansgar brought me back home and he will stay here a while.'

A subdued murmur spread the length of the hall. Then Old Ake, who was deaf and spoke with a loud voice, without knowing, said to Swein Threefingers, who sat next to him on the bench.

'What's that monk doing here? Nothing good will come of having him here. And she's wearing a strange dress. Don't tell me she's gone and got herself

119

baptised.' Other voices joined in.

'They say Christians don't sacrifice to the Æsirs.'

'They don't.'

'There will be terrible revenge.'

The voices grew loud and created a great clamour. I tried to make myself heard but my voice was drowned out in the shouting.

'How will the harvest grow?'

'Will this Christus keep the trolls away?'

'A dead god, whoever heard …'

'With only the one god, how will everything get done?'

I spread my arms for silence but to no avail. Bard stood up. He looked at me. His face was grim and fear welled up inside me. Whose side was he on? I reached for my axe behind the seat. Bard shouted above the noise.

'Listen to me! You have to hear what Sigrid Kveldulfsdaughter has to say. Don't worry about baptism. I was baptised once. It doesn't make any difference, doesn't have to. It depends on whether you're serious or not.'

Bard's wife Brita stood up and shook her fist.

'But I don't want to, whether it means something or not.'

Others joined in.

'Let her try to make us.' The noise and shouting grew and grew.

I stood up. I raised my axe and let it fall on the table with a blow to make drinking-horns and soapstone bowls rattle. The crash made everyone draw back in startled silence. I shook like Loki when the snake's venom hits him. I thought of my mother and straightened my shoulders the way she used to. I tried to make my voice strong and commanding.

'This,' I pulled out my Thor's Hammer amulet and held it aloft for all to see. 'This is my pledge to you there will be no forced baptisms at Swanhill. I wear the likeness of Mjölner round my neck, like the rest of you. The gods of our ancestors shall be held in honour as before.'

'Sigrid, in God's name, woman!' Ansgar shot out of his seat next to me. I put a hand on his shoulder and pushed him back.

'Sit, Brother.' I whispered. I held up my small silver cross. 'Men and women of Swanhill look at this and compare it to Mjölner. The cross and Thor's hammer are not all that different.'

'Blasphemy, blasphemy,' Ansgar groaned. I kicked him to silence.

I waited a moment to let people consider my words. Some of the men and women began to nod and talk to each other. Bard leant over and spoke to reassure Ake the Old and Swein Threefingers. He may have been Kjeld's man but before then he was my father's man and he was on my side. My breath came easier and I was able to continue.

'Brother Ansgar will stay with us. You may want to listen to him or you may not. This will be your choice, but you must treat him well. He is my guest here.' Mentioning Ansgar's position as Æthelstan's scribe would not do him any favours in this company so I was grateful nobody asked how I had come to know him. I looked around the hall, allowing my eyes to rest on each man, woman and child in turn. There were more frowns than nods. I still had to go on. I could not avoid the issue that must be on everybody's mind.

'I have returned to make Swanhill prosperous and safe. I have given you my pledge to treat you well. As to the reason and manner of my husband's death, that is a matter for the Lawmen at the next Allthing and not for gossip. There may be some who seek to blacken my name to further their own interests. My husband died sword in hand. His was an honourable death and he has entered the halls of Odin. He has been avenged and I shall raise a stone to his memory. My son, Kveldulf Haukson is the true heir to Swanhill and, as his mother, I am in charge until he reaches maturity. Now I want you to accept my promise of better times at Swanhill.' Bard led a chorus of cheers which, after a look at his face, most of the household joined in with. I allowed my trembling knees to give way and sat down.

* * *

Next morning I rose before anyone else and went down to the lake-shore. There I shed my Saxon clothing and immersed myself in the cold, clear water. I swam out into the lake and, floating on my back, watched the sun rise above the fells. When the cold got too much, I returned to dry myself and put on my accustomed garments; the pleated under-dress and colourful woven pinafore of a Norse woman from Cumbria.

Later that morning a thrall came running into the yard. 'Sigrid Kveldulfsdaughter, men on horses. Some are in their mail shirts and helmets.'

I sent him to gather those working in the fields and told everyone to arm themselves but to stay out of sight in case the visit was a friendly one. As the group of riders approached, a call went out from one of the freemen.

'It looks like Kjeld. I recognise the horse with those black and white markings.'

I hastened to send for ale and stood in the middle of the yard, ready to receive Hauk's half-brother. He rode in, the hooves of his black and white stallion striking sparks from the cobbled walkways. He pulled up in front of me with his entourage until I was surrounded. I took a deep breath, planted my feet in warrior-stance and held out the drinking-horn.

'Well met, Kjeld Gunnarson. Will you dismount and share ale and bread with us?' He glared at me and threw the reins at Olvir who had, as always, turned up from nowhere.

'So, you survived then,' was his reply. I knew I must be careful not to provoke him so I just nodded and handed him the ale. He drank long and deep before passing it to the man next to him. Then he looked around, as if gauging the mood of the assembled men and women. Bard stepped forward to stand shoulder to shoulder with me. This earned him a furious look from Kjeld. Then his gaze came back to rest on me. He pointed to the hammer of Thor and the cross hanging next to each other among the trinkets on my neck-chain.

'What in Odin's name is that?' Next he spotted Brother Ansgar flapping along the path from the lake, followed by Lydia. His eyes narrowed to malevolent slits. 'I don't believe this. You clever vixen.' He spoke in a low voice almost to himself. Then he turned to Bard and spat on the ground. 'So, Bard, you have handed over to the woman who drove my brother to his death.'

'My master's wife, the mother of his son, has returned to resume her place on Swanhill.'

'So that's how you think it stands.' He looked from

Bard to me. We remained facing each other in hostile silence for some time. Then Kjeld spoke. 'I will meet you at the gathering of the Allthing this autumn. You have a lawsuit against you for the death of Yngvar Anlafson of Rannerdale. You also have no right to Swanhill.' I had no time to reply. He turned, mounted his horse and rode off. We watched them disappear through the coppice.

'You will need champions for when you go to the Allthing.' said Bard. 'I'll support you but you'll need many more.'

'You can count on me too, Foster-Mother.' said Olvir and puffed out his chest.

The thought of the lawsuit didn't worry me. I was prepared to pay blood-money to Yngvar's family. That was only proper. I knew I had no right to Swanhill, it would be inherited by Kveldulf and I would be in charge until he reached maturity. I should have paid more heed to Kjeld's threat. He held a deep hatred towards me and he was a most resourceful man.

11.

The gods were good to us that year and brought a fine harvest. I worked alongside everyone else in the fields and returned each night exhausted, to peaceful sleep. Kveldulf was getting used to me but Lydia was still the main figure in his life. He called her 'mummy'. He called me 'mummy' as well but only when prompted by Thorgunn. I made sure Lydia was busy in the fields and had Thorgunn care for Kveldulf. Brother Ansgar too was given a sickle and encouraged to help, but after he proved dangerous to himself and others, he was excused. Instead he was set to assist Thorgunn around the house and to watch over the smaller children. He seemed to enjoy this and they could be heard singing and talking together. But then the parents complained that he was trying to convert them and I had to instruct Thorgunn to make sure Ansgar didn't influence the children against their parents' wishes. She told me she did her best but every now and then we still heard the children sing his hymns. His faith in my ability to protect him was unshakeable, however much I tried to explain the insecurity of my own position.

'I have the Lord on my side and I must do his holy work,' he said when I tried to make him less strident in his missionary efforts. I allowed him to say mass for the Christians and, so as not to offend the others, I told him to use the bathhouse for this. He entreated me to join them, reminding me of my baptism. I was conscious of the need to keep him on my side in my dealings with Lydia, so I made excuses rather than refuse outright.

One morning I sat away from the rest when Thorgunn and Ansgar brought breakfast to the workers in the field. I beckoned to Thorgunn to join me. We watched as Kveldulf toddled across the stubble to topple over into Lydia's lap.

'I have meant to ask you, Thorgunn. You never told me how Ingefried died.' She clasped her hands and took a deep breath.

'I've been waiting to tell you, Sigrid, but I find it hard to speak of. My grief is mixed with a feeling of blame. I should have been able to heal her and keep her well for your return.'

'There can be no blame on you. I know you will have tried your best. What was the nature of her illness? I cannot remember her other than in good health. All through my childhood, she was always there, strong as an ox and tough as old leather.'

'But remember, she was old and after you left she began to feel it. She complained about fatigue. Then she seemed to just fade away. We made strengthening brews for her but nothing helped. She couldn't work in the end, she was so weak. And then Kjeld came back.' She fell silent.

'And?'

Thorgunn covered her face with her pinafore. 'Oh, Sigrid, you know I would have saved her if I could. She was my friend. Such a good friend. But there was nothing I could do.'

I pressed my fists to my chest as if it were possible

to calm my heartbeat.

'The cliff. He threw her off the cliff.' I forced the words through the ache in my throat.

'He was about to. We both knew. But Ingefried had her pride. She was not going to wait for Kjeld to send her to Frigga's hall. She went herself. I woke that morning and saw her getting dressed in her finest clothes. I followed ...'

'Stop! No more. I can't ... no.' I closed my eyes and fought to stay calm but my tears would out. Thorgunn, her hand stroking my back, waited but a brief moment before she continued to tell me what I did not want to hear.

'I followed her outside and persuaded her to ask the runes before she did anything that couldn't be changed. Together we cast the sacred marks on the ground and read them. But there was nothing good in their message, nothing. So then she knew Kjeld would throw her down the cliffs. There would be no grave-ale drunk for her, so she made her decision to take the leap. We walked to Angler's Crag and I stayed with her while she prepared herself. She gave me her message for you. Together we chanted the sacred words, I watched her leap and alone I chanted the lament to Frigga, entreating her to make Ingefried's journey swift and painless. She was very brave.' I nodded. Yes, she would have been.

I gained some comfort from knowing that Ingefried had made her own decision and that she had not been alone. But in the next few days, as I thought of the manner of her death, I found it increasingly hard to understand the nature of her illness. She was old but she was strong and she had promised to wait for me and to look after Kveldulf. Where had this wasting disease come from and how had it happened so quickly?

* * *

The time came, in the early autumn, when day and night are of equal length. There was an undercurrent of resentful anticipation among the men and women who did not listen to Brother Ansgar and that was the majority. To reassure them, I made the usual preparations for the harvest celebrations. The women made corn dollies and wreaths of such plants that bore berries. Baskets of apples and mushrooms were lined up next to loaves of bread baked from this year's wheat and barrels of ale brewed from this year's barley. One evening I took the two silver offer-bowls from the large chest and polished them with fine sand and soured milk until the relief of Odin and his ravens sparkled in the firelight.

On the appointed day those of our freemen who had farms of their own joined the rest of the household. They all brought their own offerings and I led the procession of freemen, servants and thralls to the copse of oak trees, where ancestors and gods received homage at the prescribed times of the year. As we left the house, singing and in high spirits, I saw Ansgar, Lydia and the rest of the small flock of Christians gather in the yard. They said their prayers in voices loud enough to present a challenge. Some of my people shouted at them to be quiet and Old Ake shook his fist. They took no notice. The little monk was getting far too confident. I decided to speak to him again about the limits to my authority in the household, and the challenge to my very right to run the farm. I sang louder and increased the pace of the procession to get away from the offensive noise.

Among the trees the remnants of the midsummer

sacrifice were still in evidence; wreaths of dead flowers and leaves; the bare bones and tattered fleece of the first lamb; empty baskets, some in their original places, some torn and scattered by the wind, or dragged round by animals. I held one bowl of ale and one of milk aloft and, walking round the copse, daubed the rocks and the base of the trees. The food was set down in the centre and I intoned the song of praise to Frey and Freya. We sang to thank them for the harvest and ask them to keep our women, animals and soil fertile. We sang the song of farewell to the god Baldur, as he began his journey to the underworld and we implored him to return and bring another spring and summer with him. We opened a barrel and drank of the ale and ate of the food we had brought.

When we arrived back at the farm, Brother Ansgar had erected a wooden cross in the yard. He and his followers stood clustered around it, singing their plaintive songs. This was too much for my people and their ale-fuelled anger broke free. Swords and axes are not carried to offerings but, amidst shouts of fury, knives were drawn. Some of the men began to move towards the group by the cross. I shouted at them to stop and tried to run in front to place myself between them and the Christians. Bard's firm hand round my arm held me back.

'No, Sigrid, there's nothing you can do. They're angry and they're drunk.'

The little group dispersed. Four thralls and Lydia's three young children ran, leaving only two figures by the cross. Lydia stood with her arms spread out shielding the trembling Brother Ansgar, who had fallen to his knees.

'Keep away!' she screamed. 'Keep away. Ansgar holy man.' The angry mob surged forward, shouting and waving knives. I managed to tear my arm from Bard's grip and ran past them to stand in front of Lydia.

'There will be no killing among my people!'

They didn't hear me but kept advancing. I held up the two offer-bowls I had just used in the sacrifice. The mob hesitated but they still had their weapons at the ready. They gathered in a half-circle in front of me.

'Listen to me. There must be no taking of life on this sacred day. You have come from the place where we have sacrificed to the life-givers. There must be no bloodshed.'

There were some angry mutterings but after a while one of the freemen lowered his knife and said, 'We have shared your sacrifice, Sigrid Kveldulfsdaughter, but some of us are not sure of you. You still wear that thing next to Thor's hammer.' He pointed to the cross Freydis had given me. I unthreaded it from my neck-chain.

'You are right. I should not wear this.' I held it up and folded the top bit so it had only three arms. 'Look the cross turns into Thor's hammer. Do not doubt me. Have I not led you in the ancient rites? Have we not shared the offerings with our gods?'

'So why do you keep these offspring of trolls? Why do you allow them their vile practice?'

'Brother Ansgar saved my life. I cannot …'

I was interrupted by a snort of incredulity. Swein Threefingers had a weak head for ale and now he slurred, 'You're telling us that wretch in skirts saved you?'

Bard shook him by the shoulder. 'That's enough!'

The next to give voice to her resentment was Brita.

'And anyway, what about the rest? Their worship will bring down the anger of the Æsirs; crops will fail, animals will be barren.'

Bard glared at her but she ignored him. I turned to her.

'The others are my thralls. They work for me. They work alongside you. They have just helped bring in the best harvest for many years. You said so yourselves.' A murmur of uncertainty worked its way through the crowd.

But Brita had not finished. 'And her,' she pointed at Lydia. 'We don't understand why you haven't got rid of her. She took your place and now, look at what she's getting away with. There's been no punishment, nothing. I have known you since you were a child, Sigrid Kveldulfsdaughter, and I've never seen you let anyone get the better of you before.'

Her words stung. The time had come. I must show I was strong. I must be the undisputed mistress. I turned to Lydia and, in a low voice so only she could hear, I whispered with all my pent-up venom, 'How did Ingefried die, Lydia? Do you know the punishment for a thrall who kills?'

She drew a rasping breath. Her face turned as white as a dead man's skull. In one slow movement, she fell to the ground in front of me. She kissed the hem of my dress and cried in a voice full of fear and remorse, 'Forgiveness! Please, forgiveness!'

In the silence which followed, even the wind seemed to hold its breath. Then a confused murmur grew to excited chatter which Bard broke by cheering. They all joined in as one. Nobody knew what had passed between me and Lydia but they could all see her power was broken. Trembling with relief, I took my bitter-sweet victory. My suspicions had been proved true. Lydia had a hand in Ingefried's death. I turned and led the way inside. Out of the corner of my eye I saw Bard pick up Lydia and bring her and Ansgar. A couple of lads pointed to the cross and Bard nodded. The pieces were later used for firewood.

'Tonight is not the time for judgement. Tomorrow I shall hold court.' I explained to the household. They accepted and, amongst much whispering and talking, prepared their beds. I gave orders for Ansgar to be tied to one of the benches and for Lydia to be tied up and left in the bathhouse. When all was quiet, I slipped out and went down to her. She sat shivering on the stone shelf but when she realised it was me, she got up and knelt on the floor in front of me.

'Forgiveness.'

'The truth!' I stood above her fighting the impulse to run her through with my dagger. She fell silent.

'The truth!' I kicked her. She fell and wriggled away from me. 'Speak, you vermin!'

'I no kill! No, no.'

'What did you give her?' She moaned and writhed on the floor. I bent over her. 'I'll kill you here and now if you don't tell me.'

She could hear I meant it and started to cry.

'Hauk good to me. Then you come. For me bad. You take Hauk from me. I want hurt you, I make your baby mine.' She snivelled and wiped her nose on her sleeve. 'I never hurt your baby.'

'What about Ingefried?' I said and shook her.

'Ingefried stop me taking Kveldulf. I give herb to make tired, then I take baby. She too, too tired. But,' her voice rose to a shriek: 'I no kill, never, never. She go, she just go. One day not here.' I dragged her outside and in the faint light from the moon I tried to see in her face if she was lying.

'What did you say to Kjeld?' She squirmed. Her eyes slid away to avoid mine.

'No say to Kjeld.' I drew my dagger and pointed it to her neck. She whimpered: 'No, please, no. I tell. I say to Kjeld, she tired. I say, she old. I no say kill ...' Her voice died away.

'You told him she was too old to work. That's what you told him wasn't it?' She lowered her head.

'Forgive,' she whispered. 'I do bad. But I no want her to die.'

* * *

I was to preside over my first court. I had realised that, to satisfy the freemen, I would have to punish Ansgar as well as Lydia. The other Christians were regarded as poor, misguided creatures and it would be sufficient to mete out hard labour, less food and a beating.

I sent Thorgunn and Olvir with the younger children to look for mushrooms in the woods. They took Lydia's three children as well. Some argued that the oldest, a girl of six, should stand trial but I ruled that any child under eight was not responsible and had been made by their parents to take part. The household arranged themselves on the benches along the walls. Some looked feverish in anticipation of the punishment, they hoped would be given. There was always the possibility of settling old scores and rejoice in the misfortune of enemies. Many, myself included, saw the opportunity for revenge as well as justice.

The accused were brought one by one to stand in

front of me. I sat, alone, behind the table. I dealt out mild punishments to the thralls as I had decided beforehand and nobody argued against it. I was relieved. I saw no advantage in making more enemies by being too harsh to them.

Then Brother Ansgar was brought in front of me. Pale and puffy-eyed he clutched his cross to his thin chest.

'Brother Ansgar, you are accused of bringing the farm into danger by your open denial of the Æsirs, the very gods who ensure our safety and prosperity. You have broken my trust. You were given safe conduct and a place to follow your religion. But that was not enough for you. You staged a ceremony to challenge our harvest sacrifice and to insult our gods. I kept you safe and you defied my authority. I recognise my blood-debt to you. I will spare your life but you are banished from Swanhill.' Here several voices offered dissent.

'He must die or the gods will take their revenge on all of us.'

The monk began to shake and whisper his prayers.

'No,' I said, 'a life for a life. He saved mine. I cannot take his.'

'But,' said Ake the Old, who had been listening with his hand cupped round his ear, 'that cancels out the debt then, doesn't it?'

I had to admit it did and I felt a great fear for the little monk. I knew, I must get him away from Swanhill and find him a place of safety.

Lydia looked around her as she was dragged in. If she was searching for a friendly face, she was disappointed. I had not realised how much the others had resented it, when Kjeld took the keys from

Thorgunn and handed them to her. She was just a thrall and she was put in charge of the household, above the free women, above Thorgunn. He must have done it because he knew she was very capable. Even I had to admit she was. But he had done her no favour.

I repeated the same accusation Brother Ansgar had been charged with. Lydia listened. She seemed to have recovered from last night and stood with her back straight and her head held high. But her hands trembled as she clutched her string of beads with the cross. She must have spent the night rehearsing what to say.

'I Galician princess. I Kjeld's woman. You must leave me alone.' The hall filled with derisive laughter and jeers. I raised my hand for silence and was gratified when the household heeded my gesture.

'You are a thrall belonging to Swanhill, nothing more. I deal with you as I please.' Murmurs of approval spread along the benches. Lydia stepped forward, bent towards me and said in a low, ingratiating voice, 'I give back your baby.' She didn't speak quietly enough. The women sitting closest heard her and passed it on in an angry whisper, which grew to renewed clamour as others joined in. Brita raised her hand.

'I wish to add to the accusation.' I looked at her. 'She also has taken advantage of her position to do less work and to let her children do less and have better food.' Several others nodded and mumbled their support. I had no way of knowing whether this was true or not but it would make no difference. I went on to my real grievance. 'Lydia, I also accuse you of causing Ingefried's death. You gave her herbs that made her tired. You then told Kjeld she was too old to work. She knew that he would have her toppled over the edge of

Angler's Crag.' I had to swallow hard to keep the tears away. I clasped my shaking hands in front of me on the table. When I continued my voice sounded frail and small in the silent hall. 'She didn't wait. She leapt to her death. You brought about the death of the woman who was a mother to me.'

It was like the whole assembled household had held their breath and then let go all at the same time. The furious shouting drowned out Lydia's plea for mercy. My spirit soared on the wave of human voices. I was glad I had not taken Ansgar's advice to free the Christian thralls. It meant I could pass judgement on Lydia without reference to the Lawmen. My voice sang with power and determination as I spoke her sentence.

Lydia was taken out and dragged down to the lake. Her hands were tied behind her back and she was put into one of the small boats. Her last journey was watched by all the people she had lived and worked with at Swanhill. Some had been her friends but that was all in the past. The manner of Ingefried's death had turned all against her and there were no words of comfort or pleas for mercy on her behalf. She cried the names of her children, Maria, Jesus and Anna. She said the words of her prayers in her own language. Bard took the oars and rowed with steady strokes out into the middle of the lake, where it is at its deepest. Lydia sat slumped between two grim-faced men. She was shaking her head and looking to the sky.

'¡Cristo Jesús ,' she shouted, 'los niños, los niños! ¡Jesucristo, salvame!' The rest of the household stood on the shore watching, their excited voices mingling with the everyday farmyard sounds. Ansgar stood close behind me, mumbling his prayers. Across the lake

Lydia's cries floated towards us. 'Maariaaa, Jesús, Aannaaa.' Then her feet were tied, she was lifted over the side and thrown into the water. She surfaced once before she disappeared and the lake was silent.

Bard returned and came straight up to me. He bent his knee and offered the hilt of his sword. I touched it and thanked him for his service. One by one the others followed. Servants and thralls bent their knees in subjugation. I was mistress of Swanhill. At that moment, Kjeld's scheming to deprive me of my right seemed no threat at all.

12.

It was getting close to the time when the Lawmen would ascend the Thingmound and sit in judgement over wrongdoing and local disputes. Bard approached me one day after the work in the fields was through.

'Sigrid Kveldulfsdaughter, you are young and inexperienced in the matters of lawsuits, you will not mind if I offer my advice.'

'But it should be a simple matter. Kveldulf inherits Swanhill from his father. I inherit Becklund from mine. What can go wrong?'

'I hear from his freemen that Kjeld is busy gathering supporters for his claim to Swanhill. As the brother, he may be able to argue his right to at least a stake in the farm. It would be as well for you to have some freemen of good standing, or chieftains would be even better, to champion your cause. Your blood-debt to the family of Yngvar Anlafson of Rannerdale can be used against you and you should try to clear it in advance of the Allthing.'

I heeded Bard's advice and sent gifts of animals, cloth, fleeces and jewellery to those of my neighbours I thought could be persuaded to support my claim to Swanhill and Becklund. I sent a message to Yngvar Anlafson's family that I was prepared to pay blood-money and they accepted my offer. To raise money for all this, Bard took some animals to be sold in

Cockermouth. I was grateful for the help from my father's old housekarl and rewarded him with an arm-ring made of twisted strands of silver.

Two local chieftains, Bjalke Sigtryggson and Helgi Thorkilson sent word that they had fought alongside my father and would champion my cause without fail. Others accepted my gifts but gave no firm undertaking. Only one returned my offerings. I tried to figure out how many supporters Kjeld would have but I didn't know the area well enough to be able even to guess.

'He is a great leader,' said Bard. 'He will be able to call on many to support him.'

'But my cause is just.' I felt like stamping my foot but Bard shook his head.

'That, Sigrid, will be up to the Lawmen to decide.'

I sacrificed a heifer to Odin and daubed the rocks and trees in the sacred copse with its blood. I carved the runes for justice on tablets of wood and hung them from the branches of the mighty oak tree in the middle of the copse. Then I felt I had done what I could and now I must trust to the wisdom of the Lawmen.

I rode with my freemen, their wives and children, my servants and thralls to the gathering by the Thingmound. Bard appointed some trusted servants to stay behind and defend the farm but even without them we numbered almost thirty. We set up our tents and prepared a fire-pit. The children were given leave to join in the games and competitions. They disappeared for hours, only to reappear when there was food. Kveldulf had grown fond of Olvir and insisted on following him around. They came back exhausted at the end of each day and Kveldulf fell asleep in my arms while Olvir told me about who had won the wrestling, who had tried to cheat at archery and who had claimed the price for the football game.

'Do you not take part yourself, Olvir?' I said, thinking he was missing out because he felt he had to look after Kveldulf. He looked away and said in a small voice, 'It's a bit rough, Sigrid. There's an awful lot of shouting and people fight and get hurt.' Then he turned back and looked straight at me. 'But I'll have a go if you want me to. I don't want you to feel ashamed of me.' I laughed and reassured him I knew no braver man than him and the games were not important.

'I'm quite fast. Maybe I could go in a race. Would you come and watch?'

The next day I was there as Olvir lined up with the other boys. I had some difficulty keeping Kveldulf out of the way. He didn't understand why he couldn't go with Olvir. The race went along a prepared track. Most of the brushwood and bracken had been cleared, leaving a grassy surface, uneven and slippery but still better than the ground of a battlefield. The boys were shouting and laughing, taunting each other and pushing for a good position. Olvir stood to one side looking worried. He was one of the smaller participants and I hoped he wouldn't take defeat too seriously.

The starter sounded his horn. One over-eager boy in the front row slipped and fell, pulling three others down with him. The others tried to swerve to avoid them but another couple stumbled over the pile of kicking bodies and crashed to the ground. Those who managed to avoid the melee were slowed down and this gave Olvir, who was far out on the edge of the field, the opportunity to take the lead. I could see he was running too fast and would tire but I was pleased he was there. Then I was distracted for a moment. The boys who had fallen did not bother to run. They turned on the unlucky lad, who had tripped them up and a fight broke out. A crowd gathered and I moved away to avoid them. I was brought back to the race when Kveldulf called out, 'Olvir! Look, Olvir tired.' My foster-son was now at the back of the group of runners. The track went up a slight hill and he didn't have the strength to keep up the pace he'd set. The track turned and levelled out. Olvir, managed to run along the inside of the bend and caught up with the pack but he was well behind the leaders. Coming back down the slope, two boys let their legs run away with them and tumbled down the hill. Olvir managed to run round one and leap over the other. He stayed on his feet and finished in the middle of the pack. Kveldulf squealed with excitement and I set him down so we could both go up to our little hero and congratulate him. Like most of the boys, he lay on the grass fighting for breath. When he was able to speak, he said: 'Next year I'll win.'

I couldn't spend much time watching the games. Each day I sat at the base of the Thingmound and watched the Lawmen take their seats on the rock. The oldest of them was nearing the end of his life. His white beard was like a thin, wispy cloud around his furrowed face. The other, Mord Lambason of Keskadale, was still a vigorous man, capable of work and fighting. He had known my father and I had hopes he would support my claim. As the Lawmen recited the laws, I listened with more intent than ever before and I was reassured there was nothing to stop Kveldulf inheriting Swanhill, nor to me taking over Becklund.

There was much visiting of old friends among the

families at the Allthing. Thorgunn and Brita went round with the other freemen's wives. I took Bard and some others with me and went in search of champions in the coming lawsuit. We sought out Bjalke Sigtryggson and Helgi Thorkilson and both stood by their promise of support. They came with me to help persuade others that my cause was just. Now and again I caught sight of Kjeld and his followers. There did seem to be a great many of them.

I had come prepared with generous amounts of food and drink and now I invited a number of respected chieftains and farmers to share it with me. We put up a large tent made from four sails and supported by sturdy timbers. I had ordered a replica of my father's shield to be made and this I hung above the entrance to my tent. Tied to my waist under my clothes I wore the letter from Thorstein.

Thorgunn and Brita served up a great feast. Lawman Mord Lambason of Keskadale agreed to be my guest and I seated him on my right. He spoke of my father and praised his courage but not his wisdom.

'We all wish for friends like your father,' he said. 'But to support a blood-brother when your king has denounced him is to bring disaster on yourself and your family. Kveldulf knew that. He was gallant but foolish.'

I could never see the manner of my father's death as anything other than a cruel injustice but I couldn't afford to offend Mord so I kept this to myself. I showed him the letter from Thorstein and he agreed it was legally binding. We parted with friendly words.

My claims were to be judged the next day. I spent the night outside my tent trying to read my fate in the glowing embers in our fire-pit. I counted the number of firm champions I had and the number of possible supporters. I closed my eyes to picture Kjeld and his entourage. Did he have more than me? Would it matter? I watched the sun rise over the silent field of tents and fires. Kveldulf cried out in his sleep and I went and picked him up. My precious son, I must not fail him.

There were several lawsuits to be heard that day and it was afternoon before it was my turn. Kjeld rose to speak.

'Sigrid Kveldulfsdaughter has no claim to Swanhill for her son. The boy is a bastard. He is not the child of my brother Hauk Gunnarson of Swanhill.'

Mord and the other two Lawmen looked at me. I stood as struck by a thunderbolt from Thor's own hammer.

I found my voice and shouted, 'That is a slanderous lie. Hauk sprinkled his son's head with water. He named him Kveldulf for my father.'

'Did anyone witness Hauk accepting the child as his?' asked Mord.

'Yes, I did.' Swein Threefingers stepped up.

'This is not a witness, he's a thrall.' Kjeld smirked. I looked around at my freemen. None of them had been present.

'Hauk sent word to our neighbours. I appeal to you, who remember, to say so.'

Bjalke Sigtryggson and Helgi Thorkelson led a group of my supporters to say they remembered the tidings that Hauk of Swanhill had a son. But Kjeld had more supporters and they all mentioned that Kveldulf, although said to be born early, had been a large, healthy baby and they all thought I had deceived my husband.

'Hauk told me he suspected Sigrid of having

cuckolded him.' Kjeld shouted.

'That's a lie!' I was shaking and sweat formed on my brow.

'Not only that but she caused his death.' Kjeld described how Hauk died before the battle of Brunanburh. This turned many against me and I lost some of my supporters although not Beorn and Helgi nor their men.

'A man doesn't need the permission of his wife to go to battle.' said Beorn. And if he challenged Yngvar, that was his decision too. You can't blame Sigrid for it.'

'She drove him away with her constant taunts and tales of her father. He felt belittled in his own home.' Kjeld had turned red in the face and looked ready to attack me. He was told to calm down.

'Does the boy look like Hauk and his family?' The old Lawman asked. 'Bring the child here.' Kveldulf was sent for and arrived, riding on Bard's broad shoulders. He smiled and laughed and with his curly fair hair and green eyes, it was clear to all that he did not look like Hauk.

'He's too young,' I tried. 'It's too early to say what he'll look like.' The Lawmen deliberated but the mood had turned against me. I stood in front of the mound, looking up at them, feeling very alone. Then they passed judgement.

'Kjeld Gunnarson, we judge you the legal heir to your brother's farm at Swanhill.'

Kjeld and his supporters cheered.

I screamed, 'You're naming my son a bastard! It's wrong! You do me wrong!'

Mord shook his head.

'It is the law, Sigrid Kveldulfsdaughter. Do not

144

question our judgement, your next claim depends on it.'

His reproof helped me gather my wits. Bard stood next to me. He whispered, 'You still have Becklund.'

Yes, he was right. Kjeld could not take that away from me. Still shaking, I stated my claim and produced the letter from Thorstein. This was accepted and I began to breathe again.

'But were there not two sons born to Kveldulf Arnvidson?' asked the older Lawman. 'Your other brother is your elder and has first claim. Do you have anything from him? Do you know whether he is still alive?'

I shook my head, unable to speak.

'Does anyone here know?' Mord looked around. Nobody said anything.

'My brother Steinar Kveldulfson's marriage was without issue. As his nearest living relative I have the right to look after Becklund until he returns or is proved dead.' My voice was so hoarse, they couldn't hear me. I had to repeat my words. The two Lawmen nodded amongst themselves and I took heart. I would have a home for me and Kveldulf.

Then Kjeld stepped forward and spoke.

'All this is no use. The farm was forfeited by Kveldulf Arnvidson, when he turned traitor to King Harald and was outlawed. An outlaw cannot own land. There is nothing to inherit.'

'No! No!' I heard my own desperate scream rise above the shouts of Kjeld's supporters. 'My father was not a traitor. Never!'

But it was to no avail. The Lawmen ruled that my father had broken his oath to King Harald. I appealed to the assembly that King Harald was not the law in

Northumbria but the gathered chieftains were mindful that their own authority depended on the allegiance sworn by their followers according to Norse law. They held that any man who failed in the allegiance to his lord was outside that law and had no right to land.

* * *

I was now homeless, bereft of supporters and friends. I was no better than the servants I used to beat.

Flushed with triumph and leering through his whiskers, Kjeld asked permission to bring up the matter of compensation for the death of Yngvar Anlafson of Rannerdale. I could make no claim for Hauk. I had revenged his death by killing Yngvar. His family were prepared to accept the blood-money I had offered. But money from Swanhill was no longer mine to use. With no home nor means to earn a living, I would not be able to pay the debt. I put my predicament to the Lawmen. I was given one turn of the full moon to pay.

There was not a glimmer of sympathy in Mord's face as he said, 'The law states that, unless you pay within the stated time, the family will have the right to claim a life for a life.'

Kjeld, flushed with triumph, laughed. Then he said, with a hateful sneer and a look at my son, 'Not just any life. Like for like – a *male* life.'

Part Four:

Ring Giver

13.

When I lost my lawsuits at the Allthing, I had some offers to join the households of well-to-do chieftains. The way their eyes slid over my body made it all too clear what my position would be, a servant-woman at the disposal of her master. I turned them all down.

I returned to Swanhill only to collect my few belongings. I embraced the tearful Thorgunn and bade farewell to the faithful Bard and the other freemen and thralls. Then I put Kveldulf in front of me on the stallion I had taken from Thorfinn at Mosedale Beck. Olvir rode my little mare, Moonbeam and followed me. Brother Ansgar, had, with the help of the Christian thralls, been hiding out in one of the shielings. When we turned out of the farmstead he rode up on his brown gelding and, without a word, joined us.

I headed for Buttermere. Where else could I go? We took the route past Mosedale Beck. I had not been there since the time I looked for Thorfinn's corpse and a shiver ran down my spine as we passed the place. We stopped to rest and water the horses. Ansgar sat down next to me.

'The girl said you had to leave and I'd not be safe any more.'

'Yes, I sent her to tell you. I used you, Brother Ansgar, to get away from Æthelstan and I will try my best to keep you safe until you can return to him.'

'No, no, as I keep telling you, Sigrid, the Lord, in his wisdom, will use me for his own purpose. If it is his will that I be a martyr here, then I shall go with pride and ...'

I put my hand on his sleeve.

'Yes, Ansgar, but does your God want you to throw away your life by provoking people to anger. Angry people don't listen. Stop insulting the Æsirs and you'll have a much easier time. Also, you should understand that many more would listen to you if you didn't insist they abandon their own gods.'

'But, Sigrid child, have you not heard me? I keep telling you, there is only one God. You have to deny all your heathen idols and false gods. I must bring that message to the people here. You were the means by which the Lord brought me here. He surely must have a purpose for you too in his service.'

I had to admire his persistence, at the same time as I despaired of his failure to learn from his mistakes. But it was my actions which had brought him to dangers he didn't even seem to recognise. I had a duty to keep him safe until he could return to court.

The low lying stretch of land between Crummockwater and Buttermere was part under water, which slowed our progress. Our approach attracted the attention of the farm dogs, who started up a tired-sounding chorus of barking and howling. People assembled by the gate to the enclosed yard. Even from a distance, I could see that the gate hung loose and the wall had crumbled in several places. As I came closer it became clear that the farm had suffered great damage which had not been repaired. Part of the roof on the hall was burnt, the blackened rafters stood outlined against the sky. A bedraggled-looking group of people received me. A tall man limped in front and bade us welcome. His name was Beorn and he remembered me from the visit to Becklund.

'It seems a long time ago, Sigrid Kveldulfsdaughter. Things have not fared well with us.'

Ragnar's mother, Aisgerd, received me at the entrance to the hall. I held up Kveldulf and she never expressed any doubt that he was her grandson.

'He looks like Ragnar when he was that age,' she said. 'I don't know where he is, Sigrid. I have not seen him since he fled from Hakon.' Her voice was sad but her eyes shone when she looked at Kveldulf. He had spotted a litter of piglets and toddled off towards them, arms outstretched.

'Svine, svine, little svine,' he called.

We were invited in and served with curds and coarse bread. I explained our situation and asked if Aisgerd would give us shelter. Her lips trembled when she heard of the threat to Kveldulf's life.

'Of course, you must stay here. What little I own is yours to help pay your debt but I doubt it will be enough. We live a simple life. I have but few servants and thralls to do the work. Nobody visits the family of a traitor. My daughters live with me, unmarried, cursed by their father's actions. Three full moons ago we were attacked by cattle-raiders and lost much of our stock. They killed one of my servants and the best of my dogs. It was the second raid since we settled here. I don't feel safe but have nowhere else to go.' She began moaning and rocking in her seat. 'How my life is blighted by the actions of that husband of mine. Swein caused so much suffering, so much.'

I sat, at a loss for what to say, waiting for her to calm

down. Brother Ansgar leant across and took her hand.

'You must put your trust in our Lord Jesus and he will lead you to salvation.'

I tried to kick him but he moved his foot out of reach. Aisgerd pulled her hand free and got up.

'My people will be back, wanting their evening meal.'

'We shall help. Brother Ansgar will fetch water, if you tell him where from.' He answered my glare with one of his sublime smiles.

We settled in to life on the farm at Buttermere. Despite their losses, they kept ten cows and numerous sheep up on the fell. But with only five men – four of them old, the fifth a boy – very little land had been ploughed. Aisgerd's daughters, Thora and Gyda were with four of the thralls up on the fell, tending the cattle. I saw them only occasionally when one of them came down from the hills with the butter and cheese they had made and to collect provisions for another week. It was strange to be in a place so empty of children. One of the servant women had a girl of about eight and a lad of ten but that was all. The household made Olvir welcome and everyone fussed over Kveldulf.

Aisgerd seemed to have spent more time bemoaning her ill fortune than trying to improve it. With the two girls and the strongest workers away in the summer shieling, I found the household looked to me for guidance. The house must be repaired but first we needed food for the winter. I set the men to plough the neglected fields. They shook their heads when I led Thorfinn's stallion and my mare out and shackled them to the plough. It was against our ways to use good

151

horses for ploughing, they muttered. But when I showed them that by alternating the horses with the oxen, they were able to get twice as much done, their objections stopped. After all, who was left on the farm to ride a great stallion?

Olvir and the other children collected firewood and the old women foraged for mushrooms, leeks, apples and other wild food to store for the winter. I made Ansgar help me repair dry-stone walls and prepare the meadows for the return of the animals from their summer grazing. I found he was not as useless with tools as he had seemed during the harvest at Swanhill. When I asked him about this, he smiled.

'I have thought about what you said and I have come to realise that, around here, people need practical help as well as salvation. Jesus Christ told of the good farmer who prepares the ground so his seeds grow well and give a good harvest. If the scribe has to turn farmer in order to prepare the minds of the people so he can sow the word of our Lord, then so be it.' I noticed then his hands, blistered and grazed, with dirt under broken nails.

* * *

The blood-money I owed Yngvar's family was due to be paid and I rode to Rannerdale to speak with them. I brought what was left of my dowry; two drinking-horns inlaid with silver, the tapestry, my brooches, neck-rings, armlets and finger-rings, some fine linen and furs. Aisgerd gave me fifteen silver coins and a bowl made of gold and silver with pictures of Odin and his ravens. She offered her jewellery too, but it would have left us all destitute.

'I shall come with you though, Sigrid. I am on

friendly terms with Yngvar's family. He was one of Swein's housekarls before we came here. I may be able to persuade the widow and her son to take some of the payment in animals.'

It was a short ride to Rannerdale but on the rough ground our progress was slow. We dismounted to ford Grassgarth Beck. As I helped Aisgerd back on her mare, I heard the sound of hooves behind us. I led our horses out of sight behind the trees. Dragonclaw, the sword I had obtained as replacement for Snakebite, slid silent and ready out of her scabbard. I crept up to the track. The rider stopped and looked round. I stepped out of my hiding place and challenged him.

'Brother Ansgar!'

He looked embarrassed. 'Sigrid, I felt you should have a man with you on this errand. Olvir wanted to come too but Kveldulf cried when he tried to leave and we decided ...'

'You decided! Since when were you and Olvir in a position to say whether you go or stay? Who's taking food to the people in the shieling?'

Ansgar drew a deep breath and straightened his shoulders.

'It's all been seen to. The boy Bjarne and his sister will do it.' There seemed little point in sending him back so Ansgar joined us for the journey.

Yngvar's farm in Rannerdale was as modest as ours in Buttermere but there was more life and movement. A pack of barking dogs followed by a gaggle of children ran to meet us.

'Aisgerd, Aisgerd! Have you brought Gyda? Will she tell us stories?' They stopped short when they saw me and Ansgar. 'Who have you brought? Who's that funny man in a dress?'

The older boys took the bridles and led our horses into the yard. A comely woman, with auburn curls escaping from her neat headdress, greeted us and bade us go inside. A small child sat on her hip, regarding us with wide-open, blue eyes. Aisgerd introduced the woman as Yngvar's widow, Hrodney. She asked us inside and sent a girl to fetch bread and ale. Before the girl returned, a young man stormed through the door and confronted us.

'My father's cowardly murderer! I demand retribution.' I stood up and faced him.

'I killed your father in a fair fight after he killed my husband. There was no cowardice and no murder, just one killing to avenge another. I regret it happening but it was the destiny the Norns had woven for us.'

Hrodney put her hand on her son's shoulder.

'Anlaf, son, we have agreed to accept weregeld.'

He shook her off and with an angry gait went and sat in the high seat. Anlaf was, at fifteen, head of the household and Hrodney deferred to him. The young man, full of his new-found authority, was greedy and unyielding.

'We will take your goods as part-payment but it is not enough. For us to give up the blood-debt, we want you to serve as our thrall for a full year.'

I resisted the urge to slap his leering face. Work as a thrall-woman and be used for his pleasure. His mother reddened and looked at me then at him then at the floor.

'What I'm offering is a fair sum for a free man.' But Anlaf shook his head.

'Not *any* free man, a landowner.'

His mother said to him in an entreating voice,

'Perhaps we should wait for Thorfinn to return from the fell and ask his advice.'

'Thorfinn!' Aisgerd and I said at the same time. The man I had twice left for dead, thinking I would not meet him again. So he'd escaped Æthelstan's soldiers and now he was here. I thought the Æsirs had turned against me and prepared me a cruel fate. Aisgerd, ignorant of my previous run-ins with Thorfinn, slapped the flat of her hand on the table.

'Thorfinn is with you? Why? Since when? He is one of my husband's housekarls. His duty is with me.'

The odious boy looked at her with his insolent grin: 'Traitors have no claim on anyone's loyalty. Dead traitors even less so.'

Aisgerd looked like he'd slapped her. She lowered her head and I saw a tear following a furrow in her sunken cheek. Hrodney took her hand and kissed it.

'Forgive my son his lack of respect,' she said. 'He is young and the loss of his father still weighs on his mind.

The thought of Thorfinn arriving to find his stolen horse tethered by the trough in the yard and find me in the house, made sweat break out on my brow. I tried to hurry a decision.

'I can contribute animals to make the sum fit for a landowner.'

Anlaf shook his head. 'We have plenty of animals. We need workers. We're clearing more land. A strong, healthy thrall is what we need.'

His eyes were fixed on me and I pulled my shawl tighter across my chest. Brother Ansgar had been quiet throughout but now he spoke.

'I shall offer myself in Sigrid's place. If you need help to clear the land, a man is more use than a woman with a small child.'

Hrodney, with a relieved smile, agreed at once. Anlaf frowned but had no argument. And so it was settled.

* * *

We had paid the blood-money but we still had to survive the winter. The cows were brought back from the fells and with them came Thora, Gyda, two female servants, a male servant and a male thrall. I set the men to repair the roof, the women to proof the walls and the children to collect fresh reeds to cover the earth floor. The cows had given good milk during the summer and our stores were full of cheese and butter. But the harvest had been poor. With six good workers gone with the cattle for the summer, there had not been enough hands to gather it all in. Autumn brought rain and cold winds. Despite our efforts, the ploughing had to be abandoned before all fields were done. It was too wet. As grass and weeds invaded, we tried to put some cattle to graze on the stubble but their feet rotted in the mud and we had to bring them in.

We had to decide how many animals we could feed until spring. Two heifers, a bull-calf and two sows were selected for sale or barter against salt, a new ploughshare and other items we could not produce ourselves. Anlaf visited to discuss a time when a trading party from the three farms along Buttermere and Crummockwater could set off together for the market in Keswick. The arrival of the young man caused a stir in the household. Aisgerd received him with a polite but cool greeting. I heard the two sisters chatting and laughing with him and realised how little company of their own age they had. I took Olvir and Kveldulf picking mushrooms to keep out of the way of Anlaf's ogling.

Ten days later the animals were driven off. Thora and three of the men went. They would join the party from Rannerdale and one from a farm further along Crummockwater. Gyda was upset not to be allowed to go and maintained a sullen silence until her sister returned four days later.

Aisgerd seemed relieved to hand over the decision-making to me. When her daughters returned from the shieling she continued to treat me like a daughter-in-law and honoured me by asking my advice in everything. Her two daughters were more reserved. I became aware of a distance between them and Aisgerd. They spoke with her only when necessary and mostly about practical matters. At the same time, they were very close to each other and spent most of their time together. The sound of their talking and singing surrounded them like an invisible shield. They showed more warmth towards the old servants than towards their mother.

Thora and Gyda made no comment about me and Kveldulf coming to live on the farm. And yet, they would have heard rumours. They must have had questions. They showed me neither friendship nor hostility but spoke as little to me as to their mother. I found myself much in Aisgerd's company. She had been very lonely since the flight from Manx and Jarl Swein's death and she seemed pleased to have someone to confide in. We sat side by side in the late autumn sunshine carding the last of the summer's wool.

'You see, Sigrid,' she said, 'I haven't been able to make myself raise a stone or hold a funeral for Swein.

Many think ill of me for this. They say that, whatever he did wrong, he paid for it and he was a Jarl and entitled to a decent sending off. I think that's why all the housekarls, well, except for Thorfinn, have abandoned me. They just stopped calling in, one by one they drifted off. They can't all be dead, can they now?'

'Why didn't you honour him? My father got a stone and, I was told, a funeral.'

Aisgerd snorted. 'That's different. Your father put his blood-brother above his king. It was foolish but brave. He remained an honourable man to the end. Swein had no honour. He robbed from friend and foe alike without any thought to the consequences. I have to say …' She threw down her carding combs and her voice shrank to an angry whisper. 'You should know, and your father Kveldulf should have known, that Swein would never have done for anyone what your father did for him. Your father's death was a waste of a good man. I should have warned him. It's on my conscience.' She hid her face in her hands and began rocking back and forth. I put a hand on her shoulder.

'Calm yourself, Aisgerd! You are not to blame.' I thought of the arguments I had overheard between my parents. 'My father had plenty of warnings. Yours would have made no difference.'

Aisgerd was, at first, reluctant to speak of Ragnar, but the story came out bit by bit. Not that she had much to tell. Ragnar had stayed a couple of days with her but when they got news about the events at Becklund he had realised he would not be safe. He had not told her where he was going. It was better for her not to know.

'Two summers have gone since I saw him and not a word. But, Sigrid, he's alive. I would know if anything had happened to him. You do believe me don't you?'

I nodded. Yes, I thought, I would know too if anything had befallen my son.

'You see,' she said, 'you never feel for your man what you feel for your children. Your love for your children overrides all other.'

I wasn't so sure. I thought of the way I had left my child. How I had been in the grip of a fever. That hadn't changed. The memory of Ragnar's embrace made my body tingle and my breath quicken. Despite my disappointment not to find him at Brunanburh, there wasn't a day when I didn't imagine him entering the farmyard to take me in his arms, and there wasn't a night when I didn't dream of him making love to me. I knew I would never leave my child again but I also knew that I would go searching for Ragnar at the slightest hope of finding him.

14.

So we formed a bond, the mother and the lover, both waiting for Ragnar. And in the background, sufficient to each other, keeping themselves apart, were the two sisters. A tension developed between us which grew into the winter. I thought they felt displaced in their mother's affection and tried to involve them in our conversations. They were polite but cold. They ignored Olvir and only Kveldulf could sometimes raise a smile from them.

'I think it's got to do with men,' said Olvir.

'What has?' We were catching our breath from sawing up a tree, blown over in the latest storm.

'Those two. Thora and Gyda. The way they are. I seen them looking at that boy from Rannerdale when he came over.'

I knew I should have slapped him for gossiping about the girls but I was intrigued. Olvir never needed encouragement to share his observations with the rest of the world so he continued, 'Stands to reason. They should be married by now. They're as old as you are. But they must be desperate to even look at that ...'

'That's enough, Olvir. You owe them respect.'

I picked up my end of the saw and Olvir went to his side of the tree. It took a long time to saw through the whole trunk. When the last cob rolled away, ready to be chopped into logs, the sun was low in the sky. We would have to return tomorrow with one of the oxen to drag the wood back to the farm. On the way home, it became clear that Olvir had more to say.

'I think it's because they haven't got any dowries.'

'Yes, that's possible.'

'And I think they blame us.'

'What!' I stopped, my mouth wide open. Olvir turned and looked at me with raised eyebrows.

'Think about it,' he said, 'where did the last of the money go?'

'Olvir, who have you been talking to? Have you been listening to people without them knowing?' When I thought about it, I had to admit that, however he came on his information, Olvir was probably right. The coins and the bowl, used to pay Yngvar's weregeld, may have been set aside for a dowry. I decided I had to ask Aisgerd about this.

She was adamant. 'No they were not for dowries. The reason being that no suitable men would consider marriage to the daughters of a traitor and I will not consent to having one of my husband's housekarls for a son-in-law, nor a poor farmer's son from Rannerdale.' I chose not to remind her that my father had been a housekarl, albeit to a king.

'But what will happen to them if ...?' This was the first time I had contemplated the possibility of Ragnar not returning and the words would not be forced through the tightness in my throat.

'If Ragnar doesn't return, you mean. Well, then I'm afraid you'll have to come clean about who Kveldulf's father is, so he can have the farm.'

I thought this over. It would make little difference to me. Since the Lawmen's ruling, nobody thought Hauk was Kveldulf's father anyway. My reputation didn't matter. I was not interested in finding another husband.

'I would be glad to do that but, even supposing people believed me, does Ragnar have a claim on the farm? He's an outlaw. I lost Becklund because my father was branded an outlaw. How safe are you yourself here?'

'Safe enough as long as Ragnar keeps away and nobody else claims the land. That's the sad truth of it. Oh, Sigrid, do you see now why I hate that man so much? Funeral and a stone, after all the misery he's caused.' She did not mention the matter again but I often saw her lost in thought and the lines on her face grew deeper.

* * *

The winter was hard on us that year. We decided to keep eight of the cows. Olvir and the other two children worked hard collecting fodder. Kveldulf tagged along, preferring their company to adults. He now called me Mummy and he had stopped asking after Lydia.

With careful housekeeping, the food should last. We had slaughtered all the pigs bar two sows and the boar. Salted and smoked hams hung from the ceilings next to strings of sausages. Other meats were packed in salt in large barrels. Trout and pike had been plentiful and were dried, salted or smoked. The only things we would find difficult to stretch through the winter were wheat and barley. Our crop had been meagre and Thora had not managed to buy more than fifteen bushels at Keswick. The bark from oak trees would have to be dried, ground up and mixed in with the grain for bread making.

At midwinter, on the longest night, we held a good

162

sacrifice. Aisgerd did me the honour of asking me to perform the ritual killing of the hog we were to offer to the Æsirs in return for their protection and to ensure the safe return of the sun. The animal was hoisted, kicking and squealing, by its hind legs to a branch of the sacred oak. I plunged the sacrificial dagger into its throat, letting the blood drain into a silver offer-bowl. We brought it back to the farm and daubed the lintels above the doors and the four corners of the hall, the dairy and the byre. The Yule log was carried in and Beorn showed Bjarne and Olvir how to start it burning from the small piece saved from last year.

'Then you have to watch it and keep feeding it into the fire so it doesn't go out. It must last the full thirteen days and we must have a small piece to save for next year to start the new log.' Bjarne and Olvir nodded and Beorn smiled at me: 'It's good to have some youngsters to pass the knowledge to.'

I watched the log burn and thought of the Yuletide at Swanhill. I had been big with Kveldulf, trying to make Hauk believe it was his child I expected, while I dreamt about being reunited with Ragnar. I had been bad-tempered and unfair in my treatment of servants and thralls and their resentment of me had been heavy in the air. I had cared nothing for the farm or its people, only myself. I was not proud of how I had behaved then. If only there had been time to divorce Hauk. If only Becklund hadn't been destroyed. If only my family … but there was no point in opening up old wounds.

Beorn and Bjarne brought out their flutes and Olvir used an upturned bucket for a drum. I blinked away my tears and joined in the song about summer and the happiness it would bring. Then we put up the trestle-tables and shared with servants and thralls what the earth had provided. Perishable food, like offal and sausages were plenty and we all had our fill. The ale was weak due to the shortage of barley but it was strong enough to loosen tongues usually held to silence.

'They had a good harvest at Rannerdale,' said Gyda, glaring at her mother with red-rimmed eyes.

'Anlaf's lack of charity and greed got them an extra pair of hands. That monk should have been here.' Aisgerd tapped her finger on the table. 'Things could have been very different.' She looked up as if suddenly struck by a thought. 'And Thorfinn! He should be here! Your precious friends have robbed us of his help as well.'

I could see from Thora's face that she'd rather Gyda had kept quiet. It was never a good idea to provide Aisgerd with an excuse to unleash her pent up bitterness. But Gyda had not finished.

'It's hardly their fault that she,' she nodded in my direction, 'had to pay blood-money.' Everyone heard her. A thick silence settled over the household. It made the air difficult to breathe. My heartbeat quickened. I felt my cheeks blush as Gyda went on: 'Three extra mouths to feed. My dowry gone …'

'Shush, Gyda!' Thora put her hand over Gyda's mouth. Gyda tore it away and shouted, 'Her and her brats. It's all her fault.' She slumped over the table, resting her head on her arms. Aisgerd, red-faced, her hands in tight fists, looked at Thora.

'You may take your sister outside. She can sleep in the byre tonight. Make her comfortable then come back here.' Thora obeyed without a word.

* * *

The next morning Gyda was gone. We searched but the muddy ground yielded no clue to where she was headed. Some of the men took the boats and searched the shores. Women and children spread out across meadows and woodland. I lent Beorn the Lame Thorfinn's stallion and he rode up on the fell to see if she'd gone to hide in the shieling. It was late afternoon before the calling and searching stopped and we returned to the farm. Aisgerd took to her bed and lay facing the wall, refusing food and drink. That's when I realised Olvir hadn't come back. I went to the stables. Moonbeam was gone. I got on Ansgar's gelding and followed the deep imprints of the horse's hooves on the track towards Rannerdale. I met Olvir by the ford. He looked more than usually pleased with himself.

'I had to leave her at Rannerdale. Well, she wasn't ever going to come with me, was she? But she's safe at least. Mind you, I'm not sure how happy they were to see her.'

I knew he kept chattering to stop me telling him off and he kept Moonbeam at a distance to be out of my reach.

'You should have told me where you were going. I've been worried.'

'Yes, but I knew you'd understand and I didn't want you to come with me because of that horrible boy.'

'What boy?'

'The one who wanted you for his thrall-woman – Anlaf. And in case Thorfinn was there. He'd never recognise me. I'm very good at not being noticed.' He sounded very confident and, as he relaxed and came closer, I grabbed hold of his ear and shook him.

'Don't ever do that again! You think you can get away with anything, don't you? But one of these days your luck will run out and ...' I let go of his ear and put my arm round his shoulder. 'I don't know what I'd do if anything happened to you.' He rubbed his cheek on my arm. Then he looked up at me with his gap-toothed grin.

Gyda returned the next day. She was brought back by Thorfinn, perched in front of him on his horse. She slid down when they came to a halt and stood in the middle of the yard, looking at a loss. Thora came running from the byre and led her inside. Thorfinn remained standing, looking round. There was nowhere for me to hide. I took a deep breath and stepped up to him.

'Welcome, Thorfinn. We are grateful to you for returning Gyda to us.'

He nodded. 'I heard you survived. Good, you deserved to. You fought well. And you paid the blood-money. Kjeld did well by Yngvar's family.'

'It was not Kjeld's doing. I would have made fair compensation. But I lost my husband and I have had no compensation. Thanks to Kjeld's vile slander I also lost my home.'

He looked at me and I noticed he'd changed. His eyes were no longer bloodshot, his hair was combed and he had trimmed his beard. He turned towards the house and said over his shoulder, 'All settled by the Lawmen. Nothing to be done about it now.'

He left me standing in a fog of angry confusion. I was brought back by a nudge and an urgent whisper,

'Sigrid, you need to go in and find out what he's here for.' Olvir took my hand and led me towards the house.

'Marry!' Aisgerd was red in the face and short of breath. 'Marry!' I slid on to the bench and looked for Gyda. She sat slumped at the back of the hall, as far away from her mother as she could get. Thora knelt in front of her with her arms encircling the heaving shoulders. Thorfinn sat by Aisgerd with a sheepish smile on his heavy face.

'Yes, Aisgerd Rolfsdaughter, I shall marry Hrodney Rainesdaughter, Yngvar Anlafson's widow.'

'I know who she is!' Aisgerd sat back, her lips so dark they looked blue. I got up to fetch her some ale, wishing there was strong mead at hand.

'Calm yourself, Aisgerd,' I whispered.

'So I … eh … I … um …' Thorfinn scratched his beard. I thought I knew what was coming.

'Yes, Thorfinn, what else?' Aisgerd sounded resigned. She must have known too.

'Well, I thought it best … what with all that's …' Thorfinn drew a deep breath and straightened his shoulders. He spoke fast, like he'd been taught what to say. 'When your husband died, I was released of my oath to him. I just wanted to tell you I will not be a housekarl to your son. I shall settle down and be a farmer and your neighbour.' He could have added he would be her equal. I was grateful he didn't, this was hard enough for Aisgerd as it was. She closed her eyes and leant on the table.

'So, the last one of my husband's housekarls shall abandon me to my hardship. Have you forgotten when you came crawling here, covered in blood, an arrow sticking out of your neck, with no memory of what had befallen you? Have you forgotten who cared for you, tended your wounds and fed you with her own hand until you were strong again?'

They were too involved in their talk to notice how I choked on my drink of ale and kept coughing to clear it. So that's how Thorfinn had survived our encounter by Mosedale Beck, wounded, not dead and no magic –only Aisgerd's healing touch. Through my tortured efforts to breathe, I heard Thorfinn.

'Aisgerd Rolfsdaughter, I have not forgotten the debt I owe for your care. I will not see you and your family go short.'

'You said you would find my son.'

'I went looking for him. I didn't find him but I have news.'

My heart seemed to stop and then it beat so fast my whole body shook. I closed my eyes. I wanted to hear but I dreaded what he might have to say. Thorfinn looked down at his hands.

'He was not with King Olaf's army which ... ahem ... was just as well since ... erm ... we were badly beaten. I spoke to a man who heard that Ragnar was on his way to Neustria to offer his services to William Longsword. I ... ah ... I wish I could bring you better news than this.'

I stifled a sigh. The news was good enough for me. Ragnar was alive.

Thorfinn left. Aisgerd returned to her bed and stayed there. She would not speak to Gyda. The poor girl probably didn't mind. She was pale and her eyes stayed red and swollen for several days. She did her work as before but there was no singing and no stories to fill the long evenings. Before he left, Thorfinn asked me whether there was anything we needed to survive the winter. I told him we were short of grain. He did not tell me how he got away after the battle of Brunanburh and I had not the courage to ask. I began to think he lived a charmed life, as berserkers are said to do.

15.

The weeks after Thorfinn's visit were cold and windy. Then came the blizzards. The snow stung our eyes and settled on our clothes. On one side of the yard it gathered into a drift three feet high. We had to dig our way through it to get to the dairy. Whenever there was a lull in the storms we fetched in water and firewood. The beck froze and we had to smash through the ice to fill our buckets. But we kept warm around the hearth and we did not go hungry – that would come later when the stores ran low and before nature would supply us with new crops.

The storm blew itself out and the sun made the world glisten brilliant white. It made me think of Norway, where, all year round, snow lay on the tallest mountains where the giants live. My mother never spoke of her life in Norway; what I knew was from Ingefried's stories. I wondered where my mother was and whether she too looked out at a sparkling snowfield somewhere.

Beorn the Lame took Olvir and the other children ice-fishing and they brought back fresh perch. Kveldulf learnt to make snowballs and during a happy afternoon he and I built a snowman with twigs for nose and arms and a crown of holly. Aisgerd was not well. The smallest task, the shortest walk, made her struggle for breath and she spent most of the time sitting in the high seat. I took over the running of the farm. I didn't mind. I was glad to help but I worried about Thora and Gyda. I tried to ask their advice but Thora would look down and say that I must do as I saw fit. Gyda shrugged her shoulders and didn't answer at all.

Shortly before the Spring sacrifice, the time when day and night are of equal length, Thorfinn paid us another visit. He brought three bushels each of wheat and barley. Aisgerd was much encouraged by his arrival and presented him with a whole cheese in return for the grain. Thorfinn was reluctant to accept it.

'I told you, I don't forget a debt. I won't let you go short, Aisgerd Rolfsdaughter.'

Aisgerd sat up at table and seemed almost like her old self, enquiring about his new life as a married man.

Thorfinn turned red in the face and stuttered. 'We are well, over at Rannerdale, and ... eh ... well you see.' He smiled somewhere between embarrassment and pride and he looked not handsome but a lot less ugly when he continued, 'Hrodney is carrying my child. Sometime this summer I shall be a father.'

I looked at him. There was little left in his appearance to remind me of the ferocious berserker I had fought alongside at Brunanburh or the ruffian who tried to molest and capture me by Mosedale Beck. It wasn't just the neat hair and beard. He seemed calm, almost subdued. I couldn't help wondering how long it would last. I joined Aisgerd in congratulating him and wishing Hrodney an easy birth.

It turned out to be more than Hrodney's influence that had changed Thorfinn.

'I have been baptised,' he said. 'The blessed Brother Ansgar has led me and Hrodney to become Christians, all our servants and thralls also. It is quite wondrous

171

how my life has changed since Hrodney took me in.'

'And your stepson, Anlaf, is he well too?' Thora spoke from where she sat with her arm round her sister. I could see Thorfinn struggling for the right words and I realised what had befallen poor Gyda when she turned up at Rannerdale after her row with Aisgerd.

'Anlaf Yngvarson is well. He ... ah, that is to say, we ...'

Aisgerd interrupted him. 'There was never an understanding between us regarding those two. Don't feel disconcerted. My daughter brought shame on herself and her family by running away and throwing ...'

Gyda stood up and screamed.

'I did no such thing! We had spoken ...'

Her voice broke and she ran crying from the hall. Thora followed her but before she left she turned to Aisgerd and her look was full of hatred. Thorfinn put his elbows on the table and leant his head in his hands. Aisgerd stretched across and patted him on the shoulder. I waved to the thralls and servants to move to the other end of the hall and got up to follow them. Aisgerd held me back.

'Stay with us, Sigrid. You are as much my daughter as either of those two. Now tell me, Thorfinn, what shall we do about this? I don't want any bad feelings between our families. I have done much thinking and I have come to accept I am no longer the wife of a chieftain and I cannot continue to behave as if I were. Marriage to your stepson would get one daughter off my hands and we might be able to negotiate a settlement. But has the boy changed his mind now? Tell me honestly, without shame.'

'The boy is not minded to marry. He wants adventure. He wants away from the farm. He torments me with his constant nagging about raids and fighting. Always out in the yard practising with sword and axe. Did well at the Allthing in the wrestling. He's a strong lad.'

'What does his mother say about this? You have no plans to go a-viking, have you?' Thorfinn looked shifty.

'Ahh, ahem … old habits, Aisgerd Rolfsdaughter, we had some good times even when we weren't in luck. You know what I mean, Sigrid, don't you? Brunanburh, now wasn't that swordplay worthy of Thor himself? I've composed a verse or two about it, just to remind myself.' His eyes lost their focus and a dreamy expression spread across his features.

'Behold brave warriors of Brunanburh
That brown and barren field, where …'

Aisgerd interrupted him with a disdainful snort. 'You men! It's time to give up the "old ways", Thorfinn. And anyway, who will be looking after your wife and child if you take off again?'

'Oh, I have no plans,' he widened his eyes in an innocent stare, 'but I think maybe Hrodney would like me to go along and keep an eye on Anlaf. Well, that's if he were to go, that is.'

An idea, not yet a plan, was beginning to form in my mind.

'Where would you go, Thorfinn?' He looked at me, startled. 'If you were to go at all, that is'

'Oh, I don't know. They say there's fortune to be won in Neustria and Normandy. But I don't have a ship, I'm not a chieftain. I just dream of fortunes abroad.'

'That's enough of that. And you a Christian too.'

173

Aisgerd put an end to Thorfinn's dreaming but I knew there was a seed there, ready to be nurtured.

* * *

Aisgerd decided to approach Hrodney about Anlaf and Gyda.

'This is not easy for me, Sigrid, but I have to accept my situation. Two maids on the farm is not good. I would like you to ride there and speak with them. I'm not up to the journey.'

She was right. She found walking difficult and spent most of her time indoors. I set off with such gifts as we could afford: a soft tanned skin; some ribbons woven by Gyda to show off her skills. I saddled Moonbeam. The stallion could have done with the exercise but I didn't want to risk Thorfinn recognising his old horse and perhaps regaining his memory. I don't remember asking him but Olvir came with me for part of the way and I was glad of the company. He had grown over the winter and his leggings and the sleeves of his tunic were too short.

'We have to get you some new clothes. How old are you, Olvir? Do you know?'

'I've just turned eight. Before the spring sacrifice.'

'You seem very sure?'

'Ingefried told me. She told all of us and said we had to remember.'

'Who was your mother?' It had never occurred to me to ask him before. He'd just been Olvir who was always there.

'Unn, she died when I was born. Ingefried looked after me.'

He was a thrall-woman's child. There wasn't much point in asking who his father was. It could be any of

174

the men at Becklund. I wasn't sure I wanted to know but it stayed in my mind as I sent him back and continued on my own.

* * *

At Rannerdale I was met by the usual gaggle of children and dogs. Hrodney welcomed me and sent one of her children to find Thorfinn. She brought curds and bread. The bread was good with less bark in it than we had at Buttermere. We made small talk about the weather, the farm and the expected baby. Anlaf and Thorfinn joined us. I brought out the gifts and apologised for their meagreness. They praised the intricacy of Gyda's weaving and the softness of the deerskin. By now, we all knew the purpose of my visit.

Anlaf was awkward and had to be prompted to offer praise. He treated me with great respect. But the way he looked at me, when he thought himself unobserved, the way he blushed if our eyes met, made me feel as uncomfortable as his previous insolence. I wondered what had caused the change in him.

Hrodney and Thorfinn were as enthusiastic as Anlaf was reluctant. I would return to Buttermere with the message that Thorfinn and Anlaf would visit soon. Before I left, I enquired about Brother Ansgar. He was at Keswick market, a trusted servant rather than a thrall.

'But he knows nothing about farming!'

'No,' said Hrodney, 'but he knows about money and bartering. Many of the Saxons like to deal with him because of the religion. They trust him and there's less trouble. We trust him too.' I could but marvel at how the little monk had prospered. I was sorry to miss him and left my greetings for him.

Thorfinn accompanied us part of the way home, as

175

was polite, but in reality he wanted to talk.

'We suffered a bad defeat at Brunanburh.'

'Yes, it was hard.' I was still on my guard with Thorfinn. I wasn't sure how deep the change in him had gone. It is a big step from violent berserker to peaceful farmer. And the worry that he'd regain his memory nagged at me. But he seemed relaxed and friendly as with an old comrade which, in a sense, I was.

'None of our fault, though. We fought well.'

I could no longer keep my curiosity under control. I had to ask: 'How did you get away? Last time I saw you, you slept like a dead man. I couldn't rouse you.'

He grinned and his eyes shone with the pleasure of the memory: 'Well, ah ... you see, I borrowed some clothes and a helmet from a Mercian who didn't need them any more and pretended I'd fought for Æthelstan all along. How did *you* manage?'

I told him as much as I thought he needed to know. I made sure he understood my kinship with King Harald Finehair.

'And, I think, maybe Hakon took my mother back to Norway.'

'So she may still be alive. A real lady, your mother, she treated us well.' A thought made furrows on his brow. 'But there was this wench ...' he looked at me. 'It wasn't you was it? Cut my hand?'

'You should have been more careful where you put it, Thorfinn.'

I made a joke but every muscle in my body was prepared for flight. He stared at me under lowered brow. His knuckles showed white on his clenched hands. I held my breath. Had I pushed my luck too far? Suddenly, he threw back his head and his laughter rumbled like a rockfall.

'I should have known,' he snorted and steadied his horse, which had been startled by the sudden noise. 'I should have known. A real shieldmaiden – already a warrior queen in the making.' He pulled up his horse and turned so we were face to face.

'Sigrid Kveldulfsdaughter, we have done much fighting together and minded each other's lives like good comrades.' He looked me straight in the eye and offered his right hand. We clasped each other's wrists in a warrior greeting and his voice was warm when he declared: 'There is no bad blood between us.'

I agreed but wondered how he would feel if he ever recalled how I almost killed him by Mosedale Beck.

* * *

It was another full moon before Thorfinn and Anlaf arrived at Buttermere Farm. They were accompanied by Brother Ansgar. I was pleased to see him again and noted how strong and healthy he looked.

'Working the land, Sigrid. It is good for me to breathe God's fresh air instead of standing in the scriptorium copying documents all day, important as that work may be. I always knew the Lord had a purpose for me here.'

I was amazed at his conviction and wondered to myself if he realised that two of his converts were dreaming of raids and battle-glory. After greetings had been exchanged and the guests settled inside, a sulky Anlaf was prompted to hand a carved scutcher to Gyda.

'Funny kind of a love-token,' Olvir whispered to me.

'It's because of her skills in weaving ribbons. The scutcher will help her prepare the flax.'

'He still doesn't seem very keen, does he?'

'I suppose he's a bit shy.'

'Not shy of looking at you, though. See, there he goes again.'

'Stop it, Olvir. This is nothing to do with us. Let's go.' I picked up Kveldulf but was called back by Aisgerd, who wanted me to be part of the bartering. I made it clear to Olvir he would not be needed and he scuttled off with Bjarne to take the field workers their midday meal.

A traitor's daughter or not, Gyda was of an old, high-ranking Manx family and a desirable addition to the household at Rannerdale. Their demands for dowry were modest. She had her jewellery and she'd get linens and fleeces. The rest could be raised by selling some animals.

'Perhaps the horse I arrived on,' suggested Ansgar. 'I would be willing to take it to market and get a good price for it.'

We accepted and I knew this was my opportunity to finally get rid of Thorfinn's stallion. It would fetch a better price and maybe make Gyda more favourably inclined towards me but, more importantly, it would rid me of the last link with that day by Mosedale Beck.

'Then there's the question of the bride-geld.' Thorfinn looked pleased with himself. 'We can offer you a thrall-girl to take over Gyda's work on the farm. She is with child so we're giving you two thralls.' The way Anlaf glared at Thorfinn made it clear who the father was, but that was no concern of ours. 'Brother Ansgar's time as a thrall with us comes to an end this autumn but we are willing to release him early so he can help you with the spring ploughing.' Everyone agreed these were very good terms and Thorfinn had done well by Aisgerd.

We drank good mead to seal the agreement and Thorfinn grew talkative. After reminiscing about Brunanburh, I steered the conversation on to Becklund and I told of how I had lost my claim to my family home. Thorfinn shook his head in sympathy.

'Did you know my father had been branded an outlaw?'

'No and it seems harsh.'

'Sometimes I feel that, if I could only talk to my grandfather, he would change the verdict.' He looked surprised.

'Have you not heard? Harald is dead and Eirik is king. Your other uncle, Hakon, the one who … ahem … slew your father, well, he's left England and gone to Norway to challenge his brother for the crown. Now that will be a battle. They are both great warriors, those two.'

'I didn't know. Who do you think will win?'

'Hard to say. But they will both be looking for swords to support their claim.'

At this point Aisgerd put a stop to his deliberations.

'None of that concerns us here. Sigrid has this farm to look after. She doesn't need another one.'

I could see no advantage in upsetting her and so we listened to her memories of her life in Ireland before she was given in marriage to Jarl Swein and taken to the Isle of Man. Her comments about her dead husband were, as always, bitter and I saw Thorfinn growing uneasy. After a polite interval, he and Anlaf took their leave. I went with them as far as the gate to wish them a safe ride home. They mounted their horses but before they rode off Thorfinn turned to me and said: 'If you decide to go, send for me.'

* * *

Ansgar stayed with us and two weeks before midsummer he and I led the bridal party from Buttermere to Rannerdale. Aisgerd was not well enough to undertake the journey so Gyda was accompanied by Thora and two of the servants. We were greeted by the assembled household at Rannerdale and the family from Low Kid Farm. Horns of sweet, strong mead were handed round. I thought back on my own bride-ale and how I had humiliated my father.

This time it was not the bride but the groom, who was reluctant. Gyda, her hair bleached and braided, in her best clothes and jewellery was all smiles. She was introduced to those present as Anlaf's bride and the future mistress of Rannerdale farm. Then Thora and Hrodney took her inside the house. After a short while they came out and told Anlaf that his bride was ready. He had drunk more than his share of the mead and now, supported by his friend Ulf of Low Kid Farm, he staggered towards the house. In the middle of the yard they stopped and turned. They walked on unsteady legs past the house and disappeared behind the corner in the direction of the privy. This caused many jokes which were interrupted by a group of children running into the yard and Olvir's frightened scream.

'Smoke! There's a fire! It looks like Buttermere.'

16.

We left only enough people to defend Rannerdale Farm, the rest joined me in fetching our horses from the meadow and getting helmets, shields and weapons ready. Thorfinn and two others rode up Rannerdale to Whiteless Pike thinking to cut off the escape of any raiders that way. Anlaf and Ulf came at a stumbling trot from behind the house. They dunked their befuddled heads in the water trough. Dripping and fumbling to get their weapons and armour ready, they joined me by the horses. I threw off my pinafore and tucked the hem of my dress into my belt. Straddling my mare I led them on the more direct path through Great Wood. My face burned and I spurred Moonbeam in front of the others. The house we had repaired, the animals we had reared and kept alive during the winter and, worst of all, Aisgerd with only Beorn the Lame and a handful of women and thralls to defend her.

The wind blew into my face and soon I could smell the smoke. It was acrid. They had set fire to the fresh hay as well as to the buildings. The bellowing of frightened animals mingled with the terrified screams of women and excited, high-pitched yells of the raiders. I urged my mare on. One of our dogs lay on the track with its throat cut. I steered my mare around it and drew Dragonclaw.

There were five of them but they all looked strong

and were armed with spears and clubs. I rode in through the broken gate and headed for a red-bearded villain. He heard me and turned. I looked into his staring eyes. His mouth opened. Then Dragonclaw slit his throat. The mare neighed as she was splattered with the warm, dark blood. One of the raiders saw me and threw his spear before he ran. His aim was poor and it only grazed my arm. It was a scratch, no more, but enough to provoke the battle-fury and the strange detachment it brings.

Moonbeam bridled but I forced her on. Out of the corner of my eye I saw Anlaf and Ulf, their swords flashing in the sun as they chased one raider and a herd of cattle towards the lake. The remaining three raiders climbed the fence to the meadow and headed for the slope towards Whiteless Breast. I followed. My mare jumped the fence with ease. One of the marauders stopped and raised his spear. He had no fear and his aim was good. I had no choice but to turn my horse. She took the spear in her neck. She reared and her neigh rose to a wild scream. As she crashed on to the grass, my leg was trapped under her quivering body. My enemy gave a triumphant shout. His eyes glowed fierce under a tangle of black hair. He made no hurry but started towards me with a confident stride. I brought Dragonclaw down on the mare's flank. She jolted trying to get up. I managed to snatch my leg from under her. In my frenzy, I felt no pain, only a violent hatred of the marauder who had attacked my home and my people.

I got to my feet. Dragonclaw felt hot in my hand, eager for combat. I took my knife in my other hand and went to meet the Scot. I saw him hesitate. Without his spear he had to rely on a dagger and his club but he was taller than me and had a wider reach. He growled and began an attacking run down the hill. He raised his club, ready to strike. I waited until he was almost upon me before I ducked, sidestepped and with a swift turn let Dragonclaw slash his arm. She found the wrist and his dagger fell to the ground. He roared and swung round to face me. We crouched and began circling each other. I now had two weapons to his one but he could use both arms for more force and better control of each strike. One blow of that club would crush my head. He lunged at me a few times and I leapt aside. The club is a forceful weapon but it is slow. I tried to use my speed and agility to advantage and twisted and turned to come at him from different angles. He was alert and ready to parry attacks from any direction but his breathing was laboured and each time I jumped to one side he was a little slower to respond. I began to feel confident and that is never wise because the gods like to punish such pride. I sidestepped, stumbled and fell on my back. My scream echoed alien and distant. With a satisfied grunt my enemy lifted his club. I rolled down the slope and got back on my feet. His club hit the ground with a dead thump.

Then he began to retreat up the hill. Encouraged by his laboured breath, I followed. Step by cautious step, striking out at each other, we worked our way up the grassy slope. I tried to get within reach to let Dragonclaw stab at him but he was on his guard, with the club a constant threat. I tried to overtake him to force him back down towards the farm where there was help. I tried to trick him. I looked over his shoulder with a smile as if there were reinforcements on their way. But he ignored it. His clever eyes stayed fixed on my face as he tried to read my next move.

Instead, it was I who was distracted. The hem of my dress began working loose from the belt and with the hand that held my dagger I tried to pull it tight again. The Scot saw his opportunity and brought his club down on me. I slipped, lunged sideways, tried to roll out of the way. This time it didn't work. My raised left arm took the full force of the blow. I heard the bone crack and a searing pain burnt its way up towards my shoulder. The air left my lungs in a piercing scream. I cried a desperate plea to Thor for help. Through a mist of pain I heard my enemy's triumphant bellow and saw his torso upright and both arms raised to swing the club. The great warrior-god heard me and sent a wave of strength to my sword hand. I twisted round and thrust Dragonclaw into the villain's exposed belly and up under his ribs. He staggered backwards and fell like a tree. In a last effort I crawled away and from a distance of a few feet I watched his eyes lose their lustre and red froth well out through his mouth.

I sat hunched supporting my injured arm. The battle-fury left me and I could hear the sounds around me: cattle lowing; men and women calling; dogs barking; and, somewhere above me, men shouting. I could make out the foreign ring of the marauders' voices. They were coming towards me. I looked around for a hiding place but there was nowhere on the bare hillside. Whimpering with exhaustion, I got to my feet. I had to let go of my broken, battered arm. As it hung unsupported at my side the pain throbbed and stabbed, and my vision blurred with tears. I rubbed my eyes with my sleeve. Then I gripped Dragonclaw and, using my foot to brace against the dead Scot's body, pulled her free. Chanting the warriors' battle-call, 'Odin, Odin', I turned to face the enemy, prepared to die with honour.

Two men came running down the hill pursued by two others on horseback. I recognised Thorfinn and his neighbour. The Scots headed towards me. If they got to me before my friends got to them, I would enter Valhalla that day. They had lost their spears but held their clubs in front as they ran. I raised Dragonclaw. Thorfinn had spotted my plight and urged his horse on but I could see he would not catch up in time to save me.

Then a shout from behind me. 'Sigrid! Get down!'

I crouched and first one, then another spear flew past me. The first landed in the chest of one of the marauders the other missed but made the remaining raider veer away from his path and away from me. Ulf and Anlaf steered their horses up the hill in pursuit.

'We'll get him!' Their calls, shrill and excited, mixed with the groans of the injured man. Thorfinn finished him with his axe.

Then he helped me back to the farm. My pain was no more severe than the anguish I felt for those I had come to think of as my family and household. I looked around for them while Thorfinn fashioned a splint for my arm. Ansgar came limping up to me.

'Sigrid, you came just in time. We have the nithings on the run!' I hardly recognised the peaceful little monk. His face was streaked with soot and sweat and above his left eye a mighty lump had formed. In a state of high excitement, he waved a sturdy staff. 'I shall take the boy Bjarne with me and we shall find the cattle and bring them back, every single one, I promise.'

'But, Ansgar! Brother, you are hurt.'

'A scratch, Sigrid, no more.'

He left with Bjarne, who was dirty and in torn clothing but otherwise looked unhurt. Beorn the Lame sat leaning against the fence. He looked dazed and had a bloodstained rag round his head. One of the thralls lay dead, his skull split open and his white hair stained with blood and matter. For the rest, I called them all by name and took stock of their injuries. Bjarne's mother and another thrall-woman had been raped and were in the lake to wash out the vile seed. The rest were frightened and angry but had only grazes and minor wounds. One person was missing.

'Aisgerd, where is Aisgerd?' Someone muttered she must still be in the house. I went inside to look for her. She sat slumped in the high seat. Around her were broken chests, torn clothing and scattered treasure. Her face under the stained and crumpled headdress was as grey as sorrow itself. I believed her dead and let out a wail. But she opened her eyes and when she saw me she tried to straighten up.

'Sigrid,' she said in a low, weak voice, 'daughter. You must take over now.'

The hangings on the bed were torn but the timber was sound and I collected what blankets and fleeces I could find. Thorfinn carried Aisgerd over to the bed but before she lay down she said: 'Sigrid, you shall sit in the high seat.'

'I will until you feel strong again.'

She nodded and closed her eyes.

* * *

We had interrupted the plunder and destruction and, while I fought on the hillside, the people on the farm had managed to pull the burning thatch down from the dairy roof. It still smouldered on the muddy ground,

186

spreading dark choking smoke. The byre had burnt to the ground but the roof of the main house was covered in turf and the timbers were undamaged. I noted all that would need repairing, thinking to myself we had done it before, we could do it again. I began to plan what to do first: there would be injuries to see to; the cattle would need rounding up and bringing back.

I called the household together and took my place in the high seat. We tended wounds and were refreshed with food and drink. The Scots were after cattle and silver. They had caused much damage but many things were found scattered around the house and yard. I told everyone our wounds would heal and the farm could be repaired. I promised a proper burial for the thrall who had been killed. The fire in the hearth was rekindled and, as the evening closed in, a sense of tired relief spread through the room. My own peace of mind may have been assisted by the valerian in the drink I was given against the pain in my arm.

Ansgar and Bjarne returned and drove eight cows into the meadow. I nodded in appreciation as Thorfinn told me the news and made sure they had food and had their wounds seen to. At least I think I did. Then Anlaf and Ulf arrived with another seven heads of cattle. My head swam with the valerian but I was still in the high seat as I saw them enter in a swirling fog. Two youngsters, one short and stocky with a head of chestnut curls the other tall and lanky, his hair so red it seemed on fire. Their faces flushed, their eyes bright they seemed to float towards me all smiles and swagger. The household shuffled and moved back to let them through. They stopped in front of me, bowed their heads and knelt. Between them they held a bundle made from a tartan rug, tied up with a thong. They undid it and the contents of their makeshift sack spilled out on the floor. Five severed heads came to rest in front of my feet, hair clotted with fresh blood, eyes dull and mouths open as in a last plea for mercy. The room around me began to sway. I gripped the sides of my seat and the pain from my broken arm jolted me back. I tried to focus on Anlaf and Ulf. They were still on their knees, offering me their swords. Only half conscious, I heard Ulf speak for both of them, swearing allegiance to 'the noble granddaughter of the great King Harald, the brave warrior-maiden of Brunanburh' and pledging their services on my forthcoming expedition to Norway. I was at a loss. What should I do? How could I reject them after they had saved my life? But how could I accept their homage with no property from which to make gifts? And how did they know about my dream to go to Norway? The great god Odin took my right hand and guided it. I watched it move, no longer under my control and felt it grip first the hilt of Ulf's sword then that of Anlaf's. With beaming faces they got to their feet.

'We shall serve you well, Sigrid Kveldulfsdaughter, as Odin is our witness.'

I think Thorfinn and Beorn took the heads of the Scots. These would be displayed along the track taken by the robbers, to make it clear to anyone else minded to attack the farm that we were no longer an easy target for their raids. I was helped to bed and drifted off into confused sleep where tartan-clad raiders paid me homage while Anlaf and Ulf sailed a dragon-ship up Buttermere calling me to come and lead them into battle.

The next morning Thorfinn and his companions saddled their horses for the return ride to their farms. Before they left I took Thorfinn to one side. He confirmed that Anlaf and Ulf were now my sworn men. So I had not dreamt it.

'Those two seem to know many things about me, Thorfinn.' He fiddled with his beard and didn't meet my eye.

'Oh, now ... well ... I suppose it's possible they ... um, overheard me composing, you know, some verses about the battle of Brunanburh. I may even have mentioned you when ...'

'When ale loosened your tongue perhaps, Thorfinn.' I shook his hand. 'Friend, I shall not forget the service you rendered me yesterday and neither will Aisgerd.'

I promised Anlaf and Ulf that, when I was ready to make my journey to Norway, I would send for them and the messenger would bring them rings to seal our bond.

I went alone down to the lake shore. I sat for a long time watching the ripples on the water, considering that I was now a ring-giver, a chieftain. I recalled my father's words about the responsibilities this carried.

'The men who you can call upon to fight for you have a right to expect gifts and land in return.' I looked at the ravaged remnants of Buttermere farm. I wondered where I would get the riches to enable me to bestow gifts on my karls.

17.

The time after the raid was hard. Hardest of all was to raise the spirits of the household. The raid was the third in the four years since their arrival at Buttermere and many thought it pointless to rebuild only to wait for the next group of marauders. Beorn the Lame was plagued by headaches since the blow he had received during the fighting. Aisgerd spent her time either in bed or sitting by the hearth, with her hands idle in her lap, staring into the fire. Thora and some of the strongest workers took the animals up on the summer pasture. The rest of us struggled to get the fields ready for sowing, cut down enough trees for the repairs and cope with the general work on the farm.

But, with some help from our neighbours at Rannerdale and Low Kid Crag, we managed. By the time day and night were equal in the autumn, we had the animals safely under cover in a new byre and the gods had rewarded us with a good harvest. Later, when Brother Ansgar held his lonely celebration of Martin mass, we had repaired the broken fences and the house was, once again, warm and comfortable.

Brother Ansgar was less fervent in preaching Christianity to the household at Buttermere than he'd been at Swanhill. I thought he had finally understood that people resent being told their beliefs are wrong. It turned out his reticence had another reason.

'Sigrid,' he said one morning when we took our rest after chopping up logs for the fire, 'I have sinned grievously against the Lord's Commandments. I have no confessor to give me absolution and I fear dying in this sinful state.'

I failed to recognise a single bad act of Ansgar's in all the time I had known him. It could perhaps be something he had thought or wished; apparently that counted as well as acts in his religion. The Commandments, I knew, had things about not wanting what belonged to others. But Ansgar had never shown any interest in neither women nor possessions. I sat in confused silence.

When he got no response, he continued. 'If you would but return to the true faith, you could hear my confession despite being a lay-person. In extreme circumstances, I'm sure the Lord would allow it.'

I thought, was this a trap? No, Ansgar was clever but incapable of deception.

'Brother, you know I was converted under duress. I am not a Christian in my heart. I would like to help you but, if it's true that your God can see into people's minds, then he will know.'

He sighed, a long, trembling breath which made me realise how he suffered.

'Oh, Sigrid, I cannot carry this any longer. I must unburden myself. When those poor wretches attacked the farm last spring, I tried to talk to them but they have a different tongue, which I do not know. I showed them my cross. I waved it in front of them and that's when it happened. Dear Lord, I feel such remorse!'

'Ansgar, what happened?'

He hid his face in his hands and I could only just

make out his words.

'One of the raiders tried to take my cross. He grabbed it and wouldn't let go. I should have turned the other cheek. I should have let him take it. But …'

'But what did you do, Brother? Did you kill him?' I found it hard not to smile at his distress.

'No, but I hit him with my staff and I felt anger, such anger, Sigrid. They spared no one, the buildings were on fire, old people were struck down along with the young. Two of them violated our women, right there on the ground. I was carried by my sinful anger to use my staff as a weapon and I beat them off and I continued to strike around me.'

'But, Ansgar, I'm sure your God allows you to save women and to defend those weaker than you from attack.'

'Yes, he does. But he does not condone what I felt.'

I remembered then Ansgar's flushed, excited face as he set off to gather the animals after the raid. The prim little scribe from Æthelstan's court was, indeed, a long way from home.

'What *did* you feel, Brother?'

He didn't answer at once. He sat with his head in his hands. Then he spoke in a hoarse whisper. 'Sigrid, I felt triumph, I felt joy, more than I've ever felt before. I wanted to go on smiting the marauders even after they ran. What if I'd killed one of them, Sigrid? I forgot they are God's creatures. I wanted them dead. I have broken my vows. I am unworthy of serving the Lord. Bjarne tells me I growled like the Fenris wolf. How can anyone listen to me preaching the love of our Lord after that?'

'No, no, you're wrong about that at least! Remember Swanhill? Have you not noticed how they all treat you differently here? They like you because you work with them and fight for them. What you felt was the battle-fury. We believe the god Thor sends it to us to give us courage. Maybe your god does the same.'

He thought about this for a long time. His hands, once white and soft with ink-stains on the fingers, now brown and calloused like the rest of us, played with his precious silver cross. Then he sat up straight.

'Of course kings and warriors pray to Our Lord and the Saints for victory and make gifts to churches and monasteries. But I cannot believe …'

'Why not, Ansgar? The battle-fury helps with the pain as well and you took a blow on the head, did you not?' I saw the furrows of worry leaving his brow.

'So you think maybe the Lord has a purpose for me after all and I have not fallen from His grace.'

I was pleased to see him smile again but I sighed at the thought of the renewed vigour of his missionary zeal which I sensed would follow.

* * *

A few days after Midwinter, a half-score of sheep escaped from the enclosure. I rode with a couple of the dogs up on the fell to look for them. Olvir and Kveldulf wanted to come and, since it was a bright day, I agreed. Kveldulf rode in front of Olvir on the gelding. He had grown very confident and I heard him chattering to Olvir. He had decided he needed his own dog. This was Thorfinn's doing. He had promised the lad a puppy from his next litter and Kveldulf was too young to understand that the puppy was not yet born. He made daily enquiries about whether Thorfinn would come that day with his dog. Olvir tried to explain but wasn't getting far. I just enjoyed listening to them while watching the fells for signs of sheep.

We found them but the day was fading and I decided to drive them to the shieling and leave them in the enclosure there overnight. We sat resting before our return ride when the peace was broken by the old hound. He snapped out of his sleep and stood up. He sniffed the breeze and a growl rose from the back of his throat. Swift joined in.

'Olvir, take Kveldulf and the dogs inside the hut! Try to keep them quiet.' I climbed up on the wall and scanned the horizon. Something moved over on High Snockrigg. I strained my eyes to see a rider appearing over the crest of the hill. I leapt down and got my spear and Dragonclaw. The boys ran inside and I kept a look out from behind the wall. Long before I could see clearly, I knew it was him.

I walked towards him, whispering his name. 'Ragnar, Ragnar ...'

When he came within earshot I heard him calling me. I threw my weapons on the ground and ran to him.

Nothing in my dreams, nothing in my memories were as sweet as that reunion. Ragnar threw himself off his horse and picked me up as if I had no weight at all. He swung me round and round until the sky became the ground and we fell on the frozen ground, dizzy and drunk on excitement. I lay on my back laughing and crying.

He leant over me and said, in a voice filled with wonder, 'Sigrid, my mother tells me I have a son. Is it really true?'

I nodded and, with his face against my neck, he whispered my name over and over. I kissed his hair and we held each other hard and close.

Then a shriek from near by. 'Siiigriiid!! Let her go, you nithing!'

We sat up to see Olvir come storming down the slope swinging Dragonclaw with both hands.

Ragnar sprang to his feet and drew his sword. He stepped back and looked down at his small assailant.

'What in Odin's name is this?'

I sat up and laughed.

'Olvir, calm yourself! It's Ragnar, Kveldulf's father, my …' I hesitated. Ragnar looked at me.

'Husband?' he said. Olvir straightened up and bristled. 'I'm Olvir. I am Sigrid's foster-son and I look after her.'

Ragnar's mouth twitched as he put down his sword and offered his hand. Olvir, with a sideways glance at me, put down Dragonclaw and let his hand disappear into Ragnar's.

I led the way back to the shieling. Olvir walked next to Ragnar.

'She fought in the battle of Brunanburh, you know.' His voice was bursting with proprietary pride.

I went inside, picked up Kveldulf and let the dogs loose. I waited for their excited whining and tail-wagging to stop. Then, with a silent prayer to Freya that Ragnar would accept the child as his, I set Kveldulf down.

'Ragnar this is your son.'

When he saw the stranger, Kveldulf turned and buried his face in my tunic. Ragnar frowned. A cold shiver made its way down my spine. With trembling hands I picked up Kveldulf and tried to make him look at Ragnar but he hid his face in my shoulder.

'Kveldulf it's your father. Look at your father.' It

was no good. The child picked up my anxiety and began whimpering. I pleaded with Ragnar. 'He's shy. He doesn't know who you are. He's too young to understand.'

Ragnar looked at Kveldulf, a wrinkle formed between his eyebrows.

'I may need some time to get used to this. I don't know anything about children.'

'Nothing to it,' said Olvir in his most superior voice. 'Kveldulf is a very easy child to look after.'

'Olvir, go and fetch Ragnar's horse.' I had to get the boy out of the way, in case there was a limit to Ragnar's patience.

'Aisgerd says he looks like you.' I pleaded.

Ragnar's gaze shifted from our son to me. His features softened into a smile.

'Sigrid, I believe the boy is mine. Don't fret. But right now I just want to be alone with you.'

His eyes were still as green as the sea over sand. I relaxed and felt my breathing quicken as my body responded to his look. I swung Kveldulf round to sit on my hip and lifted my face to Ragnar's. I lost track of time and place as we kissed but was brought back by an angry little voice.

'Here's the horse. He hadn't got far.'

We put Olvir and Kveldulf on the gelding and I rode with them until they were close enough to the farm to continue alone. When I returned to the shieling it was getting dark and Ragnar had lit a fire. He spread his cloak and pulled me down to lie with him on the ground.

Like once before, we stayed all night, and through the broken roof the stars and the moon witnessed our bodies' pleasure in each other. From time to time we slept but we talked little. There was too much to say and many things were difficult to speak of. A fine drizzle fell towards morning, the sun hid behind clouds and soon the rain increased. The gods were telling us it was time to go home. I became aware of my muddy man's breeches and coarse woollen tunic. My hair was matted and tousled. Ever since my arrival at Buttermere I had neglected my womanly looks and now I felt embarrassed in front of my lover.

'I would have dressed better …' I mumbled. Ragnar laughed and hugged me.

'You weren't exactly a picture last time I saw you either.'

As he picked up his cloak I noticed the rich fur-lining and now I also saw the fine wool and braiding of his tunic.

'You have done well while you were away?'

'William Longsword was grateful.'

Most men like nothing better than to describe the honours they gain in battle but Ragnar seemed evasive. I wondered why. I soon found out.

* * *

Olvir had been looking out for us and, when we dismounted, he came running into the yard. He ignored Ragnar and called to me.

'Sigrid, he's brought women. He's no better than that Hauk.' I swung round to face Ragnar. He glared at Olvir then he turned to me with an apologetic look on his face.

'They're thralls, Sigrid. They were given to me by William Longsword.'

I turned and ran to the house. Inside, the people were

getting ready for the day. Huddled in a corner were five newcomers, three men and two women. One of the women was tall and strong-looking. Her hands showed the evidence of hard work and her face spoke of sorrows. She was no threat to me. Then I noticed the other one. She was young. Her skin was white against her rich dark hair. She wore a green embroidered gown, trimmed with gold ribbon and fur. Round her waist sat a belt made of finest leather with a large silver buckle, and around her neck hung a thick gold chain with many beads and trinkets. My chest tightened as I saw a baby at her breast.

I bared my teeth in fury. A woman to challenge me for Ragnar's love. A baby to challenge the rights of my son. I put my hand on Dragonclaw and she slid out of her bed ready and eager. I would spill the blood of the abomination right there in the hall. Ragnar came up behind me and took my arm in a firm grip.

'Sigrid, they are thralls.'

I wanted to vent my fury on his treacherous face with my fists but he pinned my arms to my sides and held me tight.

'Sigrid, you are my woman,' he whispered. 'You are my wife.'

My eyes filled with angry tears. He really thought that would make it well, did he? He turned me to face him, held me close and continued to whisper softly in my ear. My rage sat like a lump in my throat and I couldn't speak. I squeezed the handle of Dragonclaw and held my body stiff and unresponsive. Then a blade of clear thought cut through my fury. If I couldn't kill them, I would get rid of the woman and her hateful brat another way. A high-born, female slave would fetch a good price. Held firmly in the vice of Ragnar's arms I thought some more. Money would buy a passage to Norway. Maybe Odin had sent the wretch my way to help me towards my goal. I made my decision, relaxed my head onto Ragnar's chest and took a deep breath before looking up at him.

'So they can be sold then, Ragnar, can't they?'

He hesitated. I thought he blanched and held my breath. He looked at the woman with the baby. I felt his heart beat through his jerkin. He looked at Kveldulf where he sat on Aisgerd's lap, then at me.

At last he spoke. 'It shall be as you wish.'

The woman cried and wailed in a foreign tongue when she was put on to a horse and led away. Brother Ansgar made his usual complaint about the evils of buying and selling people. He would not take part in the trade but in the end he agreed to go with Thora and Beorn to Cockermouth. They got a good price and returned safe. Ragnar showed no regrets. He presented me with the money the way a husband would compensate a wife for his transgressions.

We kept the other thrall-woman. She was needed on the farm. She seemed resigned with her lot and did the work she was given to do. Of the men who came with Ragnar, two were thralls. They too were welcome additions to the farm. We would be able to clear new fields and build a larger byre.

The third man was a young Frankish warrior who had attached himself to Ragnar, half friend, half servant. His name was Lothar and his presence caused Thora to bleach her hair and wear her best clothes. She blushed each time his soft, brown eyes looked in her direction and she smiled as I had never seen her smile since I arrived at Buttermere.

Ragnar had brought gold and silver coins from Neustria. He presented me, his mother and Thora with jewellery. Gifts were set aside for Gyda but it was not deemed safe to announce Ragnar's arrival even to his own kin at Rannerdale. So the feast we held to welcome him home was enjoyed only by the household at Buttermere. But what a feast it was. We filled our stomachs with fresh game, smoked ham, cheese and the dried fruits and nuts from our stores. Ansgar brought provisions from Cockermouth – wheat was in short supply, but he had bought some barley and we brewed strong ale. We no longer had to be careful with our supplies; we had money to buy what we needed. We just had to make sure people didn't start asking where this new-found wealth came from. Ansgar had brought back some wine and I tasted this drink for the first time. I found it not to my liking but Ragnar had got used to it while fighting in Neustria. That evening he led me to the sleeping alcove and from then on we lived as master and wife of Buttermere farm.

* * *

I knew each day might be our last together unless I could persuade Ragnar to join me on an expedition to Norway. But he had other ideas.

'To your uncle, King Hakon, I'm an outlaw – in that land even more than here. I don't have the protection of being of his blood. But I can get land in Neustria or Normandy. Why don't we go there?'

'Because this is my country. This is where I want to live. I want a pardon for you, I want to clear my father's name and I want Kveldulf to have Becklund. And what will happen to Aisgerd and Thora without you? I don't

200

want you to be on the run for the rest of your life and only see you for a few days when you think it's safe.'

'I'm not on the run when I'm in Neustria. It's a fair country. The soil is rich and the air warm.'

'And there is constant fighting, so I still wouldn't see much of you.'

'Who told you that?'

'Lothar told Olvir and he told me. It's true though, isn't it?'

'Olvir. He interferes too much for my liking. Who is the little rascal?'

'He came with me from Becklund. I have taken him as my foster-son. Kveldulf is very fond of him.'

'I've noticed. He's also very possessive of Kveldulf; I hardly get to see my own son.'

'No! I'm sure …' I thought a bit. Maybe Ragnar was right.

I joined Olvir when he went to fetch water from the beck. 'I'm very happy to have Ragnar back, Olvir.'

'Uhu.'

'Is that all you have to say?'

'Well, what else is there? Ragnar is back, you don't need me any more. Do you?' His voice quavered and a drop of snot was forming on the tip of his nose. 'Beorn thinks maybe you'll send me …' He stopped in a hoarse whisper.

'Send you where?'

I sat down on a rock and pulled him to me. He sobbed against my shoulder and it took a while before he could answer.

'To market.'

'What? Olvir! I'd never do that. How could you believe it?'

'You wouldn't?'

'No never. You're my foster-son. I thought we decided that a long time ago. You shouldn't listen to Beorn.'

Olvir stopped sobbing but his little body was still tense.

'I hate him.' he hissed.

'Look, Olvir, Beorn is not unkind, he just likes to tease. This time he has gone too far. I'll …'

'No, not silly old Beorn … him, your Ragnar.'

'Why do you hate him?'

'You won't want me around and I'll be all alone.'

'Olvir, I'll always need you to look after me and Kveldulf.'

'He doesn't like me to be with Kveldulf.'

'He's Kveldulf's father. It would make me very happy if you helped Ragnar and Kveldulf to get to know each other. I'd like Ragnar to find out what a good lad you are as well.'

He wiped his nose on his sleeve and looked at me from under his unkempt fringe. A reluctant little smile spread across his face.

18.

With Ragnar back, I became aware of my appearance. I stopped wearing men's leggings and tunic and got out my women's wear. I joined Thora in making soap to bleach our hair and we helped each other fashioning it into plaited coils under our headdresses. While we indulged in these female pursuits Thora spoke of her life.

'I was jilted. The Irish chieftain, who was betrothed to me, turned me down when my father was outlawed. I have hated this place so much but there seems no escape. Mother would not allow any of the housekarls to woo me – not that I liked any of them much, but they were all leaving for other places and I would have gone with any of them just to get away.' She stopped combing my wet hair and we changed places. 'Sigrid, I'm sorry Gyda and I weren't welcoming to you when you arrived. I'm sure Gyda feels the same. I know she's grateful to you for arranging her marriage. Mother would never have agreed if you hadn't persuaded her.'

I wasn't sure I had done much to help poor Gyda but I decided I might as well take the credit.

* * *

We had some weeks of harmony. Ragnar took charge of the work on the farm. I spent more time indoors, cooking and weaving. I still had no great skill in either of these. I had always preferred the work outdoors. But it felt different when it was for my man and my family and, for the first time in my life, I made an effort to keep the snags out of my weft, to make sure the bread wasn't burnt and the servants took the salted fish from the oldest barrel first. In the evenings we listened to tales of Ragnar's and Lothar's adventures. It would have been so easy to leave things like that. We didn't receive many visitors at Buttermere, the house of an outlaw is shunned by most, but whenever there were signs of anyone approaching Ragnar and Lothar went into hiding with all their armour at hand. I was always aware of the need to watch out, taking care it would not become known that Ragnar had returned. I shared the sleeping-alcove with him as if we were married but how could we be? You cannot celebrate bride-ale with a man who is not supposed to be there. Then there was our child. Ragnar would not be able to show up at the Allthing to acknowledge Kveldulf as his son. My child would remain a bastard for as long as his father had a price on his head.

With more workers on the farm, Ragnar and I had more time to be together. He would come in the house and, amongst much laughter and comments from the household, carry me outside to the waiting horses. I treasured those outings, not just because of the lovemaking but because we had time to talk. Little by little, I tried to convince Ragnar the journey to Norway was worth the risk.

'Hakon and his men have never seen you. You could travel in disguise.'

'Sigrid, not that again. I am a Manx warrior. I do not sneak about dressed up as anything else.'

'You're sneaking about now, hiding all the time.'

'That's different. Come here and stop talking nonsense.' He pulled me close and I was soon lost in his kisses.

One evening, when we all sat by the fire, I persuaded Aisgerd to tell us the story of when the god Thor dressed in women's clothing to enter the giants' land and regain his hammer. We all laughed as Thor swung Mjölner and split the head of Thrym, the foolish giant who thought he would marry Freya but found Thor's angry face under the bridal veil. I felt Ragnar's eyes on me all through the storytelling. He knew why I had wanted that story. He didn't laugh with the rest of us.

'He had to get it back really, didn't he,' said Olvir, ''Cause he needed it to fight the giants or they'd get the better of him.'

'Yes,' I said. 'And he'd have to run and hide every time they came to Asgard.'

Ragnar was quiet the rest of the evening and later when we retired to our bed, he sighed.

'I know what you're going to say, Sigrid. If the Æsirs can go about in disguise then so can I. But …'

'I'm not asking you to put on a dress, Ragnar. Just use another name. And think how good it will be when you can take your place among the other Norse, a free man on your own land.' He nodded and sighed. I pressed on: 'Your son no longer a bastard. Although for that you'd have to marry me, of course.'

'Steady on now, that's taking things a bit too far.' He laughed and ducked under the covers to avoid my fist. I smiled. I knew then I would have my way.

* * *

In spring the sun returned to us and brought fresh growth. I took the golden neck-ring I had removed from

Ragnar's thrall-woman to Beorn the Lame. He had some skills with blacksmithing and from the twists of gold he fashioned four simple arm-rings. One, a small one, I gave to Olvir. The other three I sent with Olvir and Ansgar to Rannerdale with a message to be ready to join me after the spring ploughing was finished. I decided not to tell them about Ragnar until we were all ready to set off. I also decided not to tell anyone, I was now certain, another child was on the way. I was pleased, of course, but the news would give Ragnar another argument against our journey.

* * *

One day in early summer Thorfinn, Anlaf and Ulf came riding in full armour to Buttermere. I was sent for from the meadow where a cow was having difficulty calving. I left Beorn in charge and went to get cleaned up. The farmyard echoed with the happy greetings of men who had not met for years. As I approached, the men from Rannerdale turned from Ragnar and knelt in front of me. Ragnar watched, puzzled at first, then he was outraged.

'Since when do men of Manx pledge their swords to women? Thorfinn, you were my father's man. You owe allegiance to me.' Thorfinn stood to face Ragnar.

'Your father is dead, Ragnar. I am released from my oath. Sigrid Kveldulfsdaughter is no ordinary woman. She's the granddaughter of King Harald Finehair. I fought alongside her at Brunanburh. She is a great warrior and I have given her my promise of support. This is how it stands.'

Ragnar went pale and left us. All eyes were on me. I couldn't run after him. I was a ring-giver not a servant girl. But it was hard to watch him stride towards the horse-meadow when all I wanted was to call him and plead with him.

Aisgerd appeared in the doorway and bade our guests to enter. Ale was served and servants rushed to prepare a meal. I left Thorfinn exchanging news with Aisgerd and went to look for Ragnar. He had saddled his horse and Lothar had brought him his armour but they seemed to be arguing. Thora stood with her hand on the stirrup.

'At least say goodbye to your mother and your son,' I heard her say. I looked round for Kveldulf.

'Where is Kveldulf Ragnarson?' I said. They all looked at me. Olvir, coming from behind the hall carrying an armful of firewood, shook his head.

'I thought he was with Aisgerd.' he said. He dropped the logs where he stood and ran towards the copse.

'The brook,' screamed Thora and ran off. I gathered my skirts and headed for the lake. Behind me I heard the household calling out, their voices growing fainter as they spread out beyond the safety of the yard.

I didn't stop to remove my shoes but plunged into the water. The cold made me gasp and I slipped on the smooth pebbles. I waded between the rocks where Kveldulf liked to play. I could still hear the others, worry making their voices shrill and some on the edge of tears. Beorn got the small boat and, with Bjarne's mother in the stern peering into the depths, he rowed along the shore. I looked under the long grass on the edge of the lake. I scratched my arms plunging them in among branches overhanging the water. The sunlight played cruel tricks against the waves. Time and again I thought I saw the pale face of my son under the surface. I cried and raged and pleaded with the gods. I promised a golden sacrifice if they returned my son to me. I knew

I'd gone further than Kveldulf would have managed but I couldn't stop. I was wet through, my dress was torn and I shivered from cold. But I was oblivious to everything except that I had lost my child.

Then I heard Ragnar call. 'Sigrid, Sigrid I have found him.' No words ever sounded so sweet. I clambered out of the water and saw Ragnar carrying our son in his arms. Behind him scurried Olvir and Bjarne.

'He was in the dairy,' said Ragnar. 'He'd followed the damned dog.'

Kveldulf was laughing and chattering. He clasped a squirming puppy to his chest.

'Look, Mummy! Tofinn bring Keluf puppy. Bad puppy run away.' he said, 'Keluf catched puppy.'

Faint and trembling I put my arms round my man, my son and his little dog. I sobbed with relief. Ragnar told the boys to run back to the farm and tell everyone we had found Kveldulf. Then he set Kveldulf down and held me till I stopped shaking. We sat down on the grass and watched our son play. I put my hand on Ragnar's.

'Don't leave us.'

He looked at me.

'Am I no longer the master in my own home, Sigrid?'

'Ragnar you are the master of Buttermere farm but Thorfinn and the lads are free men. Thorfinn has a farm of his own. He is no longer a housekarl. He is his own master.'

'That's not what it looked like.'

'It was their choice. Thorfinn promised support for me to seek pardons for you and my father. The lads just want adventure. Thorfinn made some verse, you know how he does when he's in his cups, and they think I'm a

208

warrior-queen.'

'So you did fight in that battle?'

'I didn't intend to. I went there to look for you.'

'Me! Why?'

'Hauk was going to find you and kill you. I followed him and then ... oh, Ragnar, there's so much we haven't talked about. What has happened has not been of my doing. I have been through danger, I lost my home. I have tried to keep your son safe and be a help to your mother. Don't abandon us now.'

He didn't answer. He went to fetch Kveldulf and the puppy who had been chasing round and were straying too far. When he returned, he looked grim but held out his hands and helped me stand up. Then he put his son to ride on his shoulders and we walked back to the farm together. As we drew close he stopped, let Kveldulf take his puppy and walk ahead. A little smile pulled at the corners of his mouth.

'I suppose this is my punishment for bedding a shieldmaiden. Do you remember, Sigrid, at Becklund?'

I nodded.

'I remember. You were better than me,' I almost added 'then' but stopped myself in time.

He smiled a proper smile and kissed me. Then he looked at me, his head tilted to one side.

'Just tell me one thing now. These four years I thought Thorfinn dead by your hand. How come he's here, alive? Have you compensated him for the time you brought him so close to Valhalla?'

I took a deep breath. I had forgotten Ragnar knew.

'He made it back to Buttermere, I don't know how, neither does he. Aisgerd healed him but he has no memory of what happened.'

'Are you going to tell him? What will happen if he remembers? He seems affable enough now and he clearly thinks highly of you but he has a fearsome temper. He was known for it.' Ragnar walked next to me. He didn't see me shudder.

* * *

In the evening we held a great feast and both ale and talk flowed freely. Ragnar was subdued. I think he was at once proud and resentful of my position. I took care to defer to him but I could not change what had been done and promised. Thorfinn got drunk and sentimental and spoke of the glorious days of raids and feasting. The young men hung on his every word and Aisgerd's efforts to extract information about Gyda got scant interest. Thorfinn spoke of my exploits in the battle of Brunanburh. Ansgar tut-tutted and shook his head.

'All in the past,' he kept muttering. 'All different now. Why rake it up?'

Lothar struggled to understand. His command of the Norse language was still hesitant. Olvir, who had appointed himself Lothar's guide, helped explain to him. He had learnt enough Frankish to be able to translate and to add a few embellishments of his own. When the story turned to how I had slain the redheaded berserker, Lothar could not hide his amazement.

'The Mistress Sigrid did that? A lady ...' he laughed and shook his head. Ragnar, grim-faced, got up and left the hall. I followed him outside.

He went down to the lake and stood in the light of the half-moon. He picked up pebbles and threw them into the water, one by one, as if there was something below the surface he tried to kill. When I joined him, he growled like a wolf. 'You're showing me up. I'm a

210

Manx warrior. Our women don't try to be like men and behave like, like …'

'So, on Manx, who defends the farm if it is attacked when the men are away?'

'Why, the men who have been left behind.' The way he shrugged his shoulders made anger swell my chest.

'Like who in this case? Who did you and your father leave to defend your family here in Buttermere?' He edged away from me but I had gone too far to stop now. I grabbed his arm. 'When the farm here was raided, who was around to defend it? Three raids! People killed, women raped, cattle stolen. Your mother and sisters could have done with their own swords and spears then.'

He swung away from the lake and faced me. In the pale light his eyes were dark hollows.

'Raids! Why was I not told about this?'

'Three years you were away, Ragnar! There's been too much to tell. Nobody wanted to spoil a happy homecoming with sad news.' I could have added that, when the warrior returns, his people listen to his tales, they don't complain to him about their own past misfortunes.

He sighed and rubbed his temples with his fists.

'I'm lost, Sigrid. I don't know the life here. When I'm fighting, I know what I'm about. I'm my own man, answerable only to the king who has hired me and only for as long as it suits me.'

'Yes, I know. It's a simple life but it cannot go on for ever. Sometime you have to grow up and …'

His laughter sounded angry, like a sneer.

'Grow up, is it! So Sigrid, warrior-queen, you think going to Norway will set everything right. You set off with an old berserker and a couple of youngsters. What do you hope to achieve with that gallant force? Norway is not a safe place. There are many who would challenge your uncle for the throne. Or is there more you have forgotten to tell me about? Is there a splendid drakken waiting for you somewhere, with a crew of seasoned warriors?'

'Don't mock me, Ragnar Sweinson! I'm not waging war. I'm not going raiding. I think I've seen what that leads to.'

'You say too much, Sigrid Kveldulfsdaughter!'

By now we were facing each other, shouting and waving our arms, too absorbed in our quarrel to notice we had an audience. Aisgerd, leaning on Olvir, walked towards us with unsteady step. Ragnar saw her first and fell silent. He looked shaken. Aisgerd's breathing sounded like air forced through a blacksmith's bellows. In the moonlight she seemed an apparition from Helheim.

'My happiness has been great these last few months since you returned home, Ragnar. I am not asking that you should stay here. It is not the way of men. But remember that, as long as you are an outlaw, your son remains a bastard and can have no inheritance. I shall die soon. I would go to Frigga's fair halls with a light heart if I knew the life of my grandson was safe.'

'Don't speak of death, Mother,' said Ragnar, and I thought I heard tears in his voice. He walked off along the shore. I knew there was no need to run after him because just then the moon broke free of the clouds and painted a straight, wide path of silver on the lake. Odin showed his approval of my plans and he would make Ragnar see it too.

I returned with Aisgerd and Olvir to the house. Our people looked worried and Thorfinn got up. I waved to him to sit. The air in the hall was heavy with unspoken questions and nobody seemed able to find anything to talk about. Aisgerd sat pale and silent with Thora and Olvir stroking her arms and patting her hands. In the end the gloomy atmosphere got too much for me and, against my better judgement, I asked Thorfinn for a *drapa*. He thought a while and muttered to himself then he rose and declared:

> 'Sigrid fair and fearless maiden
> with her faithful followers abide
> by Aisgerd's audacious son.
> In blessed bountiful Buttermere
> brave and resolute Ragnar
> Cumbria's proud son ...'

Nobody had noticed Ragnar coming back. Now he interrupted Thorfinn.

'Please stop before the gods call down a curse and punish us all for your awful poetry.'

I thanked Odin. Ragnar looked himself again, tall, handsome, his green eyes teasing and laughing, my hero as I had dreamt him and known him since a girl. His mother opened her eyes and smiled, household and guests all relaxed and laughed. Ragnar went up to Aisgerd and knelt in front of her.

'A son can carry out his mother's request without shame. If it is your wish that I go with Sigrid to Norway then so I shall.'

A tear made its way down Aisgerd's withered cheek. She spoke with effort.

'For my grandchildren, even if I never see you again.'

'You shall see me a free man and you shall see my children grow to be brave warriors and fair maidens.'

Ragnar reached out for me. I took his hand and he pulled me out of my seat.

'Sigrid Kveldulfsdaughter, shieldmaiden and ring-giver, I will not be your karl but I will be your man and your husband.' He pulled the widest, most beautiful ring off his arm and offered it to me.

'You want me to be *your* karl?' My reply set the hall alight with merriment. Ragnar laughed with the rest. Had he really tried to trick me?

'No Sigrid Kveldulfsdaughter, I want you for my wife. We shall both owe allegiance to each other. You are who you are and I shall match you and surpass you and you shall be proud of me and proud to be my wife. Thor, the god of fine adventures, has spoken to me and shown me the way my destiny lies.'

* * *

We prepared to leave Buttermere. Ragnar buried most of his hoard below the post next to the high seat. He showed Aisgerd and Lothar and told them to be careful how they used it. We took coins and such items as were easy to carry and use for payment and barter. Ragnar insisted on wearing his mail shirt, helmet and two swords.

'You cannot hide being a warrior,' he said and so it was left. The only disguise he agreed to was to grow his coarse, red beard and to plait his long hair to make him look like a Neustrian. He would go under the name of Robert d'Ivetot, after a Viking settlement in Neustria. Thorfinn too wore full armour and Anlaf had his father's mail coat and helmet. Ulf had a good leather tunic and a helmet his father had captured from an Irish warrior. It was old but had been polished with such vigour it shone like fire in the sun. I strapped on Dragonclaw and put my helmet in a sack behind me on my horse. My shield had to be left behind as it would not go with my status as a widow, travelling with her two sons, Kveldulf and Olvir, in the company of a small bodyguard and a monk. There was some debate about whether Ansgar should be included in the party but he argued that Hakon was known to be a good Christian and would look with favour on a party with more than one devout soul in it. He accompanied this opinion with a glance at Thorfinn, who made haste to agree with him.

Lothar asked to stay behind to keep the farm safe. Thora's blushes indicated that it wasn't just the farm he was intending to care for. Bjarne argued long and well to be allowed to accompany his friend Olvir, but when I explained that Lothar would need another man on the farm, he relented and agreed to stay.

Ragnar was right, it was not an army I led but a small group of adventurers. We had not the means to equip our own ship but in Jorvik there would be plenty of traders sailing for Norway.

19.

Jorvik, capital of Northumbria, was, since the battle of Brunanburh, in the hands of Æthelstan who had appointed as his representative my uncle Eirik Haraldson, also known as Bloodaxe because of the way he killed, so they say, most of the men of his own blood. Eirik Haraldson had been king of Norway for only one year. Then my other uncle, Hakon returned to oust him. Eirik turned the prow of his sea-dragon towards Scotland and England where King Æthelstan entrusted to him the peace of Northumbria. We had this information from a trader we met in Aldeburgh.

'King Æthelstan has both a victorious army and the support of the saints. God grant he brings us peace and prosperity.' He crossed himself. Ansgar smiled, Ragnar looked glum.

'What's Jorvik like under Eirik?' I asked.

'Peaceful. King Eirik is accepted by Danes and Norse alike and the Saxons are content he is Æthelred's man. Besides he has a fearsome reputation as a warrior and they say his housekarls are berserkers to a man. I can't see anyone mad enough to challenge him.'

The news about my uncle unsettled me. All the way from Aldeburgh to Jorvik I kept trying to work out how it would affect our journey. Should I make myself known to Eirik and his shape-shifter witch of a wife or would it be better to avoid them? They would not be able to help but if they felt slighted they could make things difficult.

We camped just outside the town walls. Jorvik was many times the size of Keswick or any of the places we'd passed through on our journey. Smoke from numberless buildings floated in the air as if the town lived under its own permanent cloud. There were vessels of all kinds moored along the river. In the town itself there were knorrs, riverboats and ferry boats. Further out beyond Jorvik we could see the tall masts of long ships, many of them with banners fluttering in the breeze. Ragnar and Thorfinn went to ask around and find out who was likely to have space on board for passengers. They and the two boys would offer themselves as crew so it was just me, my children and Ansgar, who would take up valuable space. They argued it would be quicker to get passage with a dragon-ship since a knorr would follow the coast and keep stopping to trade. To find a trustworthy ship's master would take some judgement. There were plenty of stories about hapless passengers who, after paying for their voyage, were sold into slavery by ruthless chieftains and traders. Ragnar and Thorfinn were hoping someone from Norway might think it advantageous to carry King Hakon's niece.

We were a somewhat unusual group of travellers. Women and their children came from Norway to join husbands in England but they rarely travelled in the other direction.

'The King will get to hear about us,' said Thorfinn, 'and if he doesn't the Queen will. Nothing escapes her. He may have his spies but she is a seer.'

'But why should they be interested in my business?'

I was looking for an excuse not to meet this malevolent woman.

'They probably aren't.' Ragnar shook his head. 'But they'll want you to show the respect they think themselves entitled to. Don't offend Queen Gunnhild. She's not one to have for an enemy.'

So I decided to present myself to the King and Queen. Brother Ansgar, who knew Jorvik and the way to the King's Court, accompanied me. I was glad to have him along. I had no reason to think King Eirik and Queen Gunnhild would wish me harm but there was so much I didn't know about my mother's family. I had already seen my father killed by one of them.

We went towards the city and joined a throng of noisy people bringing food, animals and other goods to sell. The open gates were as wide as six ordinary doors at home. They hung between towers so tall they seemed to touch the clouds. The walls on either side were not as impressive – earth mounds with palisades which bore the marks of much damage and careless repairs. I was jostled between oxen and sheep and I stumbled over geese. I was pushed from all sides by men and women carrying bundles and baskets, all eager to enter the city and barter their wares. By the gate, men in Norse armour demanded tax from anyone bringing goods or cattle into or out of the town. The levy was for the King, they said. I had to pay for the modest gifts I had brought for that same king. This grieved me but I thought it better not to argue.

I was relieved to leave the crush at the gates behind. The crowd spread out and I could breathe again. Inside the walls we walked between rows of fields and trees but soon the wide street was lined with houses standing so close together they almost touched. Narrow passages led between them and I spied cows, pigs and hens behind the houses and in deep cellars underneath them. We got to the river and crossed on a bridge as wide as the street and high enough for knorrs and other small vessels to pass underneath. It stood on sturdy timbers but I still thought that, surely, it would collapse under the weight of so many people and animals.

There were more buildings on the other side and Ansgar slowed our progress by his annoying habit of not being able to pass a single church without entering and saying prayers for the saints. I was impatient and apprehensive in equal measure and would stand shifting from one foot to the other, waiting for him to finish.

After three such detours, he said, 'It wouldn't hurt you to join me in a prayer or two, Sigrid. I fear the saints will punish you for your desertion.'

After another two stops we came to the inner set of ancient walls. These were in even worse repair than the outer ones but the gatehouse we stood in front of was the most imposing and frightening structure I had ever encountered. It was built of stone. How any mortal man had been able to pile the large blocks so high I could not fathom. There must have been magic at work here. I leant back to see the top of the tower outlined against the fast-moving clouds. It began to lean over me. It would crash down on my head. I tried to step back and out of its way but lost my balance. I would have fallen over had Brother Ansgar not grabbed hold of me.

'Steady, Sigrid, don't look up. You'll only get dizzy.'

I stood there feeling very small and frightened. Inside this malevolent tower were Queen Gunnhild and

King Eirik. I must not offend anyone who could threaten the future of my son and they most certainly could. I had made the decision to come here, I couldn't turn away now. I thought of my mother and straightened my shoulders.

Ansgar didn't seem in awe but struck the mighty oak door with his staff. Two guards in gleaming mail coats and helmets appeared above the balustrade. They looked down at us. Ansgar addressed them.

'Tell King Eirik that his niece, Sigrid Kveldulfsdaughter, is here to pay her respects.'

The giant warriors looked at each other then at me. Ansgar repeated his request. I tried to look confident. They withdrew. I heard them talk then they looked down at me again. One of them shrugged his shoulders and left.

We were kept waiting long enough for me to think we would not be admitted and I began to feel quite relieved. Then a broad-shouldered figure appeared above the balustrade and a clean-shaven face peered down at us.

'Who are you? I don't know of any niece to the King.'

'My name is Sigrid Kveldulfsdaughter, my mother …'

That's how far I got before Ansgar interrupted me.

'Father Wulfstan! Your Grace, I should say. Don't you recognise me? Ansgar, clerk at King Æthelstan's court.'

The man peered at Ansgar who removed his hood.

'Well, I say. Praise be to St Oswald. Dear Ansgar, I had quite given up hope of seeing you again. I beg your indulgence. I'll be with you shortly.' He disappeared and we were left to wait again.

'This is evidence of the power of prayer, Sigrid. Archbishop Wulfstan is the best person possible for us to meet here. He was …'

Then all at once there was a great banging and clonking as crossbars were withdrawn and the door swung open. Archbishop Wulfstan of Jorvik, dressed in a splendid full-length tunic trimmed with fur and elaborate embroideries looked to me like a prince or chieftain. Only the magnificent bejewelled crucifix on a thick gold chain around his neck revealed him as a man of the church. He waved at us to come in. Ansgar knelt and kissed his hand. I thought it better to do the same. With one hand I made sure my Thor's hammer amulet was hidden under my pinafore with the other I managed to bend my silver cross back into shape. I wished I'd thought of it before and displayed it in a more prominent place among the pendants on my neck-chain.

We were led through the echoing tunnel of the gatehouse into a cobbled yard. Here we faced a hall even greater than the one Æthelstan had inhabited when I was his prisoner after the battle of Brunanburh. But we were not going there. We headed for the entrance to the tower itself. We followed the Archbishop up some steep stone-steps to a door half-way up the wall. I didn't like being so far off the ground. Climbing a rock or a tree is one thing, this was quite another and I felt dizzy and clung to the wall.

Archbishop Wulfstan opened and ushered us inside. Then he made his excuses and disappeared down the stairs again. The stone walls loomed over me cold and forbidding. Scant daylight was afforded by a slit in the outer wall. Two warriors stood leaning on their spears.

One of them opened a door and Ansgar gave me an encouraging little push and told me to go through. I blinked to get used to the dim light after the bright sunshine outside. In the middle of the floor a fire sparkled on a small hearth. It was the only familiar object. Everything else made me feel I was in one of the caves of the mountain-king.

A voice from out of the smoky gloom. 'So you say you are Gudrun's daughter.'

A tall figure stood with his back to one of the slits in the wall. He did not sound friendly and again I thought I shouldn't have come. I strained my eyes but he stood in the light and all I could see was his broad frame towering over me. I stepped forward, dropped to my knees and held out my hands to him. He had the courtesy to take them in his and raise me which made me feel a bit better. He pulled me over to the opening in the wall and made me face the light.

'My sister's face, yes especially around the mouth. But those eyes … ah, well, not that it matters.'

He let go of me and went to sit down in a high-backed chair by the fire. I remained standing, unsure of what I was expected to do. I could now see my uncle more clearly. I had expected him to look like his brother but even allowing for him being older by many years he carried little resemblance. Brown hair in thin wisps under a fine embroidered cap, a thin, mean mouth and a long nose. He waved at me to come and sit on a stool next to him.

'So, niece, what is it you want from me?'

He eyed me with a speculative glint and made me remember my manners. I turned to Brother Ansgar who was ready with the gifts I had selected.

'I have not come with requests but to pay my respects. I am a widow of small means and my gifts are modest.' I handed over a small, embroidered wall hanging and a yard of ribbon woven in silk. It was all Thora's and Gyda's work, mine not being fit for gifts to anyone. But my uncle wasn't to know that and he received them with a gracious nod and praised the skills I didn't have.

'But what brings ...'

He didn't get to finish his question. There was movement outside the door. It opened and a lady stepped in with an impatient swish of her fine velvet gown. It had to be Gunnhild, the Queen, the witch, the shape-shifter. I made haste to rise and curtsy. She did not return my greeting but came close and, like her husband before her, she pulled me over to the opening in the wall. Her eyes glittered, dark against her milky-white skin.

'Yes, mmm, yes, I suppose it's possible. Gudrun looked a bit like that when she was young. The same stubborn set of the mouth, yes.'

I tried to control my anger at her arrogance but could feel my cheeks burn. She noticed and laughed. Then she let me go and went to sit by my uncle.

'Gifts,' he said and pointed to where they lay discarded on a chest.

'Yes,' Gunnhild didn't look at them. 'Well, what does she want?'

King Eirik shrugged his shoulders.

'We haven't quite got to that yet.'

He leant back in his chair, stretched out his legs and it seemed he was handing over to his wife.

'I have no errand but to pay my respects. I am

recently widowed and headed for Norway to look for my mother. I am told she was taken there and I wish to join her.'

'Alone?'

'Yes, apart from a small retinue of travelling companions.'

'Who are these companions?'

'Neighbours.' I offered no further information. Gunnhild became impatient.

'But do tell me about these neighbours.'

'Oh, just a couple of young men looking for adventure.' I felt sweat moisten my brow and my mouth dry up.

'Adventure? I assume you mean they look to join some chieftain or other. Well, how fortunate. My husband is looking for a crew. They would not get such a good opportunity in Norway, I'm sure.'

'They are bound by their promise to accompany me to Norway, after that I don't know their plans.'

'Why risk the journey? You don't even seem sure whether Gudrun is alive. We can offer you the safety of our home. There are plenty of noblemen who would be happy to offer marriage to the niece of the King of Northumbria.'

'I'm not looking for a husband. I have vowed to find my mother. I … I … had a dream, where she called for me.'

She was making sport with me, like a cat playing with the mouse before closing in for the kill. I tried to control my trembling hands, while cursing my decision to call on these two. Gunnhild leant forward in her chair.

'So you will have your son with you, then. I'm

surprised you didn't bring him to receive our blessing.'

'I have not brought my son. I left him in the care of his grandmother.'

'Ah, ha, ha. Now would that be the mother of your deceased husband or the mother of the man who sired the child?'

Oh, how she enjoyed letting me know the depth of her knowledge. King Æthelstan had listened well when I told him what had befallen me since my father's death and he had passed it on to this evil woman. I decided there was nothing to be gained by allowing her to continue to mock me and I stood up.

'I have called on you because, when I heard my uncle and his wife were here, I thought it my duty. I am grateful that you have received my modest gifts. With your permission, I will now return to my camp.'

'Oh, but I don't think we have had the pleasure of your company for long enough, not nearly long enough, dear niece.'

She waved a bejewelled hand to one of her maids and ordered wine. As the maid left, I saw Ansgar sidle out in her wake.

'Eirik, dear husband, don't you think we should invite these companions of Sigrid's to join us?'

'Aunt, Uncle, your graciousness is appreciated but a visit here is too exalted for the simple farm-boys I have with me. They are in my service only until I find my mother.' I remained standing.

Gunnhild gave me one of her chilling smiles. She looked at me with the eyes of the falcon she was said to turn herself into at will; small, dark, ruthless eyes. I tried to look away from them but couldn't. They bored into my skull. I felt the tug of her mind as she searched for my secrets. I trembled with the effort of keeping my thoughts hidden. We were locked in silent struggle until my uncle cleared his throat. Gunnhild shrugged, the corners of her mouth twitched.

'I must insist you stay in the safety of our court. I cannot allow you to go. Your farm-boys shall find adventure with the King's fleet. And, my dear niece, we shall send for your son and let him prosper under our protection.'

Her words made me shiver as if a cold wind had swept through the room. I must get Kveldulf to safety. She knew I had brought him. She would have him to foster. She would poison his mind. I would lose him for ever.

I stuttered. 'Your kindness is overwhelming but, as I explained, I must go.' I moved towards the door. I lifted the bar. The door swung open and I stepped outside. Two spears, wielded by tall warriors, crossed in front of me.

'Come back inside and close the door. You're letting the heat out. It's a chilly day.'

I went back and faced her. 'Am I a prisoner?'

'Ungrateful! Stubborn and ungrateful, just like her mother.' With that the Queen stood, waved at her husband to follow her and left. The door closed with a doom-laden bang. I heard a bolt sliding into place and I was alone.

I tried to look out of the thin slits in the walls. On one side I saw the courtyard, where warriors in armour filed into the giant hall. On the other side I saw the town stretch in front for many furlongs. I began to shiver. I saw no way out. The wind-eye in the thatched roof was too high for me to reach and even if I could get up there,

226

how would I get down from this cloud-scraper? I sat in the low chair Gunnhild had used. I paced back and forth. I thought of Kveldulf. Were they looking for him? Would they find him? What possible use could he be to them? I might be useful as a peace-weaver, a tool to bind a family to them by marriage, but my son – what did they mean to do with him?

I was a long time there in the cave-like little room, working up a furious fear for the future. Then I heard movement outside. Voices, indistinct men's voices. The bolt was drawn back and the door opened. A hooded figure slipped in and closed the door behind him. Brother Ansgar began to untie the rope he used as a belt.

'We must swap clothing, Sigrid.'

'We can't do that! What will happen? They might kill you!'

'No, Wulfstan will look after me. He's the Archbishop. He has power over Eirik. This is the only way. You go. I stay. Hurry! The King and Queen are in a meeting. You must be out of here by the time it's finished. Will you hurry, Sigrid!'

I had never heard Brother Ansgar raise his voice before and the effect was ridiculous. I sniggered but did as he said. Ansgar slipped behind the high back of Eirik's chair to remove his habit and handed it over with a thin, pale arm. I removed my pinafore and my pleated linen dress, picked up the habit and slipped it over my head. The coarse wool scratched my bare skin and I thought Ansgar had the better part of this deal. I pulled the cowl over my head and made to go, but then I hesitated.

'I can't leave you here, Brother.'

'You must. Don't worry, I'm Æthelstan's clerk.

227

Wulfstan won't let anything happen to me. Now listen carefully.' He explained how to get back to the camp and admonished me not to remain in Jorvik overnight. He made the sign of the cross. I tried the door. It opened and I slipped out.

The guards were leaning against the wall and took no notice of me. As I passed, they secured the door again and Ansgar was locked in. I trod carefully down the hated steps and drew a deep breath as I reached the ground. The soldiers opened the gates without looking at me. A monk's habit was an excellent disguise in this town and in the gathering dusk I soon jostled with the crowd leaving the town before the gates closed for the night. I got as far as the bridge over the rive Ouse before I was accosted.

'Father, please, Father.' A ragged man in Saxon clothing threw himself in front of me and grabbed my sleeve. Nobody took much notice but I figured they soon would if the man discovered that this father was a woman. I made a fist as the man fumbled for my hand and began kissing it.

'Please, Father, I have a sick child at home. The brothers at All Saints ask too much money and I am a poor man. The gates of St Mary's are closed for the night. My only son …'

He looked up at me and I withdrew my head inside the hood. I made the sign of the cross over him. If I spoke at all I would have to say prayers and I didn't know any. I put a finger of my free hand in front of my face, hoping the man would understand me to have taken a vow of silence. Then I walked away from him. He got up, grabbed my sleeve and tried to pull me along with him. This got the attention of the guards at the end of the bridge and they started to move towards us. The man, oblivious to their presence, continued to whine and beg. The guards increased their pace. One of them shouted something and the other drew his sword. I could fool the gibbering wretch at my feet but I would not be able to fool the guards. I turned my back to them, nodded at the man and allowed him to lead me away from the bridge towards the town I was escaping from.

The man's home was in a small side street. It was in poor repair, the thatch hung like a wet, shaggy mane over the eaves and the upright timbers were rotting at the base. He led me inside and in the faint light of a small fire I saw one child curled up on a pile of straw and two others sit huddled together next to him. All three were dirty and dressed in rags. The sick boy was asleep. Or so I thought at first. A slight tremble of one eyelid gave him away.

'My wife died and now my only son is struck down. Please, Father, heal him.'

I made the sign of the cross over the boy and wondered what else to do. I knelt beside him and put my hands together and pretended to pray. From inside the depths of the hood I got a view of the room. Rough plank floor, one stool, a few pots and pails, baskets and leather pouches hanging from pegs on the walls. It spoke of poverty and neglect. I turned my attention on the boy. He was dirty and unkempt but his round cheeks had a healthy blush under the grime.

'It's the fever, isn't it, Father?' The poor man wrung his hands. I flapped my sleeve in the direction of a bucket and a small bowl. The man stared and did nothing. Trying to keep my hands concealed, I rose and got some water. I took Ansgar's silver cross and dipped it in the water a few times, each time nodding and rocking as if I was chanting a wordless spell. Then I made the sign of the cross over the boy and threw the bowl of water on his face. The little rascal leaped up with an outraged scream. He stared at me with pale eyes, coughing and spluttering to get his breath back.

'A miracle!' His father threw his arms in the air before collapsing in a heap at my feet. He kissed the muddy hem of Ansgar's habit: 'Thank you, Father, thank you, thank you!' He rose and hugged the boy. 'My son,' he sobbed rocking from side to side, 'my son cured by a miracle.' Over his shoulder the boy fixed me with a malevolent stare. I made for the door but the man called out and again grabbed hold of my sleeve. He held up a small coin. I shook my head.

'But, Father, I must know your name so I can tell of the miracle you performed.' Having no other way of communicating with him I again shook my head and pushed him aside. He cried out and to soften my roughness I made another sign of the cross. I stumbled out of the door and walked as swiftly as the slippery walkway allowed. This was to no avail. The grateful father pursued me down the path shouting for all to hear about the miracle of his son's recovery. I increased my pace until I was running. Once back on the main road I dipped behind a cart and slipped into the shadows between two houses. I waited for him to pass first one way then the other.

It was getting dark by the time I crossed the bridge and approached the gates. They were about to be barred and one side was already closed. There were few travellers left and they were impatient and pushed and shoved to get through. I tried to walk as if I was in a

230

hurry but not so fast it would look suspicious. I had to join the crowd at the gate as it was pulled to. It was hard to see from inside my hood but I couldn't afford to risk anyone catching a glimpse of my face. I was pushed by a burly farmer squeezing past. One of the guards shouted at him and he stopped to apologise. I shrank further into the hood and waved an empty sleeve to show he was forgiven. Otherwise the guards took little notice of me except two of them bowed their heads in respect as I passed. My spine tingled with the anticipation of being called back. I was a couple of spear-throws beyond the gate when I heard the distant noise of horns, hounds and shouting. The alarm had been raised. Ansgar had been found. I invoked the protection of Odin for him, hitched up his habit and ran.

20.

I arrived at the camp to find everything packed and my companions waiting.

'Ansgar, but where is …?' Ragnar's voice cracked, betraying his anguish and I smiled and removed the hood. 'Odin's beard, it's you! Sigrid, at last! I gave a blood-sacrifice to Thor to keep you safe. We hear too much about this king and his wife.' Ragnar held me close for a brief moment. 'No time to talk now. We must hurry or the tide will be gone and the ship will sail without us.'

The ship *Cloudrider* was beached, on its own, behind a bend in the river. In the pale light of the setting summer sun I saw the fearsome carved head of a dragon with fire in his eyes and sharp teeth in his open mouth. This ship was as large as any I had seen in the estuary before the battle of Brunanburh. While our baggage was loaded, and Kveldulf and Olvir settled on board, I slipped behind a clump of reeds and swapped Ansgar's coarse, black habit for a spare dress of my own. So it was as a respectable widow I greeted the chieftain, Gunnar Sigfusson. He stood taller than most men, broad-shouldered with the dark, brooding face of one capable of great violence. His ship's master looked younger but bore the marks of someone who had seen many battles. They both treated me with respect.

'Better not mention Brunanburh,' whispered

Thorfinn. 'They both fought there but on the other side. Not that I'm frightened but we are greatly outnumbered. They weren't keen on the children but I mentioned your royal connections and Gunnar Sigfusson decided we might be useful to him. It seems he intends to stop in Norway for a while.'

I was allocated space for myself, Olvir and Kveldulf in the middle of the ship among all the chests, barrels and leather sacks holding treasure, goods to trade and supplies for the voyage. Our horses had to be left behind due to the heavy cargo. A man came with us from the town and paid a good price when confronted with so many swords. Ragnar, Thorfinn, Anlaf and Ulf were to join the crew for the journey and each had an oar to power until we were under sail.

Gunnar seemed in a hurry to leave Jorvik. He decided we would take advantage of the light evening and start our voyage straight away. This brought remonstrations from others, since a couple of men still hadn't returned from the town. Gunnar looked around and conferred with his ship's master. The sky was clear, the wind favourable, Niord, god of the sea and Thor who ruled the wind and waves, were sending us an omen that it was a good time set off. The helmsman called directions to the oarsmen. Some of the men began humming and others joined in a tune that followed the rhythm of the oars.

We followed the River Ouse to where it joins the Humber. Then we moved with the evening tide out towards the open sea. Gunnar stood in the prow looking out for waves breaking on shallows and rocks. I leant against a bale of hides and cradled Kveldulf in my arms. Olvir snuggled up to me and fell asleep. I lifted my face to the sky and allowed tears of relief to run down my cheeks. In the dim light from the moon, only one man noticed. Ragnar smiled and winked at me. He looked relaxed and happy pulling at his oar. I wiped my tears. I worried about Brother Ansgar. He was so trusting. I knew that Archbishop Wulfstan was more than able to protect him against Eirik but I had glimpsed the evil in Gunnhild and feared for my friend.

The crew took it in turns to row through the night with Gunnar setting the course by the stars. When the sun crept above the horizon, Kveldulf was the first to wake. He looked around him and squealed with delight.

'Mummy, look! Big boat.'

This woke the warriors nearest to us and one of them sat up and muttered about women and children on warships. I was grateful we were placed so my four companions were two on each side of me. For the first time I began to think of them as my bodyguard. Then I looked down the rows of oarsmen in front of me and behind me. There must be at least thirty pairs of oars. Even with their mail shirts and helmets stowed away in their sea-chests the men looked fearsome, each carrying the scars and wild demeanours of seasoned warriors. What could my four do against them all?

I looked at the broad back of Gunnar Sigfusson, who stood in the prow in the same position I had seen him last night. He said something to one of the oarsmen, who got up and took his place. Gunnar turned round and I got a proper look at him. He was built to instil fear, dark and solid, with a broken nose and eyebrows shadowing his raven's eyes. He made his way along the crowded hull towards me and with a trembling hand I felt for my knife. He knelt next to me, stretched out a large, hairy finger and tickled Kveldulf's chin.

'Well, here we have the seed of a true Viking. So you like riding my plank-horse, little man.' He looked at me and one of his eyebrows sat high in his forehead as he smiled. 'You may need to tether him to the mast. We have made enough sacrifice to Niord in the past. We don't want to give him our future as well.' Then he left me and went to the stern, where he lifted his tunic and pissed in a great arch over the side of the ship.

The rest of the crew followed his example, as did Olvir. Ragnar held Kveldulf so he could do the same. I began to wonder how to manage my own needs. In the small knorr with my father at the helm, I would stick my rump over the side in the stern and hold on to the rudder. One look at the helmsman put me right off that idea. I appealed to Ragnar who confirmed this was the best way unless I wanted to use a bucket.

'Just remember to empty it out on the leeward side,' he said and laughed.

I found one of the pails and spread my cloak around me for a little privacy.

Olvir didn't like the sea. While we followed the coast northwards, keeping just in sight of the shore, he kept asking why we couldn't sail closer to land. The dolphins and porpoises leaping and playing in the ship's wake held his attention only temporarily. He grew ever more anxious as the last of the land sunk below the horizon, the gulls abandoned us and the water became free of seaweed. He sat with his back to the mast where he knew he was out of the way and his face took on a pale greenish hue. The puppy, Striker, also didn't like the sea and lay like a dishevelled rag on Olvir's lap.

They looked a thoroughly miserable pair. To distract Olvir, Ragnar gave him some wood and suggested he should carve himself a set of hnefatafl figures.

'But how you'll manage once the wind picks up and we're on the open sea, I don't know,' he said with a shake of his head, 'we haven't even started off yet.' There was a shade of 'I-told-you-so' in Ragnar's voice which was not lost on Olvir and he set his mouth in a determined line, put Striker down and began whittling.

Kveldulf loved the ship and we had to lengthen his tether to allow him to get to the side, where he stood on Ragnar's sea-chest and laughed as the salty foam sprayed his face. Gunnar Sigfusson was greatly amused by him and the rest of the crew began to talk about him as a token of good luck. They passed him from hand to hand along the ship so he could stand in the stern patting the neck of the dragon and encourage it to fly across the waves. Then they passed him all the way back and he took his turn by the tiller, his little hand resting on the helmsman's huge paw.

During the first three days the weather was sunny with just enough wind to fill our sail and give us comfortable speed. The oars were stacked in the middle of the ship and the covers lowered over of the oar-holes. Ragnar and the rest of my 'bodyguard' engaged in swapping stories of their adventures with the crew. The child in my womb was growing and becoming more active and I was happy to rest. I spent my time dozing and talking to Olvir who gradually became used to the movement of the ship and began to resemble his old self. He had finished the figure of the king for his hnefatafl and we borrowed a board and the rest of the pieces from Gunnar and spent many hours playing.

Olvir had a good understanding of the strategy of the game and captured my king time and again. This was noticed and soon there were others who challenged Olvir to a game. He was very successful and in the end Ragnar explained that to win all the time might earn him enemies as well as friends.

* * *

On the fourth day of our journey, clouds formed on the side where the sun sets and the wind increased. The waves grew white foam on top and *Cloudrider* rolled and dived among the watery troughs and peaks. This time it was not only Olvir who felt bad. Anlaf and Ulf both spent time hanging over the side throwing up and so did a good dozen of the crew, some of them veterans of many voyages.

'They'll get their sea legs in a day or two,' said Thorfinn and patted his stepson on the back.

Soon rain began to soak through our clothes. The helmsman beckoned to me to bring the children to shelter in the low space below his steering platform. We wriggled in and lay there looking out on the rows of oarsmen. Kveldulf kept up a cheerful chatter about all he saw. We sheltered there for a long while and night settled over our heads. The wind kept increasing. The rigging wailed and whined and the sail bulged full to breaking point. The helmsman struggled to keep us riding into the waves.

'Too much strain,' he called, 'reduce the sail by half.' Before anyone could act, there was a sharp crack. He swore and shouted, 'The rudder's gone! Reef the sail! Oars out!'

Bereft of the rudder, *Cloudrider* swung broadside to the mountainous waves. I screamed and clutched my children to me as the ship listed, ready to topple over and spill us all into the foaming sea. Frantic activity broke out among the crew. A dozen oarsmen tried to keep the ship facing the wind. They had little success and she rolled violently with each wave. Others lowered the yard and tried to gather the rain-heavy sail.

Kveldulf, too young to sense danger and ever inquisitive, asked, 'Mummy, what are they doing?'

I swallowed bile and tried to sound confident. 'They lower the yard to make the sail smaller so we won't go too fast. And look at Gunnar! He's mending the rudder. No, Kveldulf, you can't go and look. You'd be in the way. Stay here and hold on to Striker.'

Gunnar leaned dangerously over the side of the ship, half in, half out, trying to replace the broken leather thong which held the rudder in place. Two of the crew held on to his belt to stop him falling overboard as wave after wave crashed over his head threatening to drown him. Some of the men began a chant to Odin, Thor and Niord and soon they all joined in. Kveldulf hummed along trying to make out the words. Olvir retched and cried. I held them both, feeling sick to death and wishing for the end to be swift.

But the end did not come. Gunnar straightened up and bellowed for the yard to be raised and we hoisted a much reduced sail. Our speed was just enough to enable the helmsman to steer into the waves again and the violent rolling was replaced with the lunging, dipping and diving again. We crashed into each wave with a noise like thunder, the cold, glittering water broke over the prow and gushed down over the crew. Then the ship slid down into the trough heading for the bottom of the ocean before it was brought up by the next wave rising,

rising until the wild salt-foam broke over the prow again. Those not incapacitated by seasickness and fear worked hard bailing out but for every bucketful they emptied over the side, ten were returned by the merciless sea. The night seemed without end and I thought *Cloudrider* would take us to the end of all time.

But she didn't and the next morning the sea calmed. The sail was increased but the rain turned more persistent and there was not sufficient wind to fill the wet, heavy expanse of vadmal. So the soaked, exhausted crew were ordered to put out the oars and soon they struck up the rhythmic humming, which helped them settle into their rowing.

'Look, Mummy, birds! Big, big birds!' Kveldulf's chubby little finger pointed to the sky. The men closest to us heard his shout and passed it on.

'Yes, there they are!' called the helmsman, 'The little warrior has eyes like Odin's ravens. I think we'll invite him along when we next go a-viking.'

This first indication of land was followed by others: seaweed; a dark line on the horizon; and, as we drew nearer, smoke. The crew began to speculate about where this land might be.

'Can you see yet if it's flat sand or tall rocks?' they kept asking, while debating whether it would be better to hit land in Denmark before going on to Norway.

'It could even be Friesland,' said one of the older men, 'depends on how strong that westerly was.'

All this talk unsettled me. What would I do in Denmark or this land called Friesland? I was not so naïve as not to understand that some of the crew would have liked to stop and look for somewhere to raid and then what would happen to me and my children? I was

relieved when tall rocks clad in green forest became
visible. We were headed for Norway. But what sort of
reception would I get there?

Part Five:

Quest for Justice

21.

It was four years since I had woken from my swoon and heard my mother deny me. 'The wife of one of our neighbours' she called me, before she sent me away with neither blessing nor kind word. Her face had been pale and her eyes dead. My father's severed head rested, blood-smeared, in the dust not two ells away from us. Were my mother's last words to me a rejection or, as Ingefried had maintained, a way to save me? Would she take my side, argue my case to King Hakon after I had borne the child of the man she had warned me against? What would I say to her? Was she even there or had she been married off to some chieftain far away? What would I say to the King? Who would help me plead? I missed Ansgar and began to include his god in my prayers and sacrifices.

Gunnar stayed near Kaupangen where he had a land claim to pursue. He invited us to stay with him but I was impatient to put my case to King Hakon. I was told the King would be at Nidaros, guest of the powerful Jarl Sigurd of Lade. Fifteen of the crew offered to accompany us there. Some wanted to go to other parts of Norway before winter set in, a few spoke of making the journey back to Iceland or joining other chieftains on raids.

We purchased horses and prepared for the journey. I

donned breeches to be better able to ride across the rough terrain. The mountains were taller than in Cumbria and a dusting of snow made the peaks of Dovrefjell sparkle in the sunlight. Along with the horses, some of the crew also procured women; young girls who would cook, prepare the camp and share their beds. I was happy to hand over all domestic tasks to them and spent my time playing with Kveldulf or discussing our plans with my companions. The new child was now so large in me that Ragnar noticed and wondered how, on the meagre rations on board, I had managed to gain so much weight. There was no longer any reason to keep the news from him.

'Sigrid, be damned, woman! You put yourself and my child in danger on this foolish journey. Have you no sense!'

I let him rage. He calmed down, as I knew he would, and then he was proud and excited.

'This time I shall be there to sprinkle the baby's head with water and declare it mine. I swear to you, Sigrid.' He stroked my emerging bulge.

To begin with we had tried to keep up the pretence that Ragnar was just the leader of my bodyguard but by the time we approached the Trondheimsfiord it must have been obvious he was much more than that. Our shipmates accepted this without comment. Ragnar's years fighting in Neustria and his strong rowing during our voyage had already earned him respect and this seemed to deepen as they recognised his status as my special man. More surprising but also more pleasing was the respect they showed me. I found out later that both Thorfinn and Olvir had told them I fought at Brunanburh and each had outdone the other in exaggerating my accomplishments as a warrior-maiden. They had also made sure the information would be passed on by swearing everyone to secrecy.

Dovrefjell was an enchanted place. I sensed giants and gods watching us from the top of the mountains. We rode in sunshine most of the way. There was cold, sweet-tasting water in the white-foaming streams and the gnarled, low-growing birch trees gave good firewood. Frey, god of plenty, sent elk and deer and guided our arrows to them. It would have been splendid sport had I not seen bad omens everywhere: a crow, shiny and black, diving from the clear sky to snatch a piece of meat from Kveldulf's hand; a host of hostile clouds bringing a sudden thunderstorm; an injured fox limping across our path, leaving a trail of blood.

* * *

We came to a spot near Nidaros which bore the marks of a holy place. A row of carved stones led to a tall wooden building with elaborately decorated beams holding up a roof of chipped bark. Inside stood a huge likeness of Odin with his two ravens one on each shoulder. He stood halfway up to the roof-beams. His large head, crowned with a splendid helmet and with the one empty eye socket, looked down on an offer-stone inscribed with holy runes and stained with the blood of many sacrifices. We stopped there. The air seemed full of spirits. I breathed in the mixture of dread and hope which fills a holy place. The remnants of the recent midsummer-blot were still there. A horse's head sat high on a pole by the entrance to the temple, several fleeces from first-born lambs flapped torn and frayed from the trees. I was surprised. Hakon had spent many years at Æthelstan's court and was known to be a

244

devout Christian. Yet here, in the splendour of the stone carvings and the temple building, was the evidence that rich powerful chieftains, perhaps even Jarl Sigurd himself, followed the Old Religion. I talked it over with Ragnar.

'I don't suppose it makes any difference, though. I will still have to be a Christian if I am to gain favour with Hakon.'

He shrugged his shoulders. 'I don't see the problem. While I fought for William Longsword I had to be a Christian too. You get used to it.'

'But their god is different, isn't he? It's not just about worship. That's not enough. Ansgar says you have to denounce your own gods as well. I can't do that. Odin saved my life at Brunanburh and Thor sent me strength to kill the raider at Buttermere. Frey has brought us good harvests and made our animals fertile and Frigga brought you back to me so we can be a family. What revenge will they take if I turn from them now?'

'You don't have to turn from them, just pretend to. We all do that, I've done it – so did your father and mine, several times.'

'How will they know? What if I'm made to denounce the Æsirs? What will they think? And I need their help, now more than ever. In fact ...' I looked around me. Ragnar followed my gaze and nodded.

'Yes, I've thought so too. What better place to ask for it.'

So we decided to hold a sacrifice there in the ancient, holy glade. I would be able to explain to the Æsirs why I was about to deny them and pray for their support. Thorfinn and Anlaf agreed it was a good idea and wanted to play their part. I didn't raise the question of their conversion to Christianity. I had always thought it a bit fragile.

I chose a good horse, a grey stallion. This was not a time to short-change the gods. Ragnar, Thorfinn and three of the crew led it into the temple. It took all their strength, for horses know what the stone is about. They don't go quietly to their death but fight and struggle. I stepped up and raised my axe. The horse reared. The men hung on to the bridle and kept it from moving out of my reach. I intoned the prayer to Odin. When the stallion's front legs came down I summoned all my strength and let the axe fall. The stallion's last terrified scream carried our prayers to Odin's ears. The great scull split and he fell, kicking, to the floor. The men tied him up and hoisted the great animal on to the offer-stone. I slit the throat and let the blood drain into the silver offer-bowl I had brought from Buttermere. The men joined their voices to mine and together we made a mighty chorus as we chanted the old words and called to our gods. Together Ragnar and I daubed the inscribed rocks and the base of Odin's likeness with the blood.

I took out my pouch and opened it to scatter the holy runes. The carved wooden discs fell to the ground and I bent down to read them. The signs were not clear. They spoke of friends but also foes, of gain but also loss. And, however I looked at them, I read danger. I stuck my knife into the belly of the horse and slit it open to allow the entrails to spill out. The sickly smell of blood, guts and undigested grass filled my nostrils. I plunged my hands into the carcass and ripped out the liver.

I lifted it to the statue and intoned, 'Odin, master of the runes, fount of all wisdom, hear me, give your servant a sign.' Blood gushed down my arms from the warm liver. I stared at the image with such intensity it made my eyes water but I could see no sign.

Then Olvir called from outside. 'Sigrid, come out and look!' I went out and there, among the carrion-birds that assembled above the glade, was a sleek, black raven. Odin was listening. It was time for me to find the King.

* * *

I had done all I could and I tried to sound and feel confident as I was challenged at the entrance to Jarl Sigurd's splendid farmstead at Lade.

'I am Sigrid Kveldulfsdaughter; my mother is Gudrun Haraldsdaughter, King Hakon's sister.'

It worked. I was shown in and my companions left their weapons in the wapenhouse and followed me. The hall at Lade was as large as the one I was taken to by Ansgar after the battle of Brunanburh. It had the same rich wall hangings and a dais at one end with a carved chair similar to the one Æthelstan had used. I felt this was the hall of a king not a mere jarl.

We were given seats at the end of the hall and offered sour curds and bread. The King and the Jarl were not expected for a few days and I reined in my impatience and prepared to wait. I tried to devote myself to the stream of questions from Kveldulf but my mind was in a muddle and my body so tense it shook with each heartbeat. I touched my Thor's hammer amulet under my dress for reassurance.

Five of the crew from *Cloudrider* were staying to offer their services to King Hakon or Jarl Sigurd. The rest made their farewells and drifted off to follow their own destinies. Some asked to stay and serve me but I thanked them for the service they had already given and Ragnar paid them in silver. They all left little gifts for Kveldulf, a carved horse, a silver clasp for his cloak, a little knife with mother of pearl on the handle, a pendant made of amber. They shook Olvir's hand praising his skill at the hnefatafl and, when they had all left, he had a full set of pieces for the game.

I was left with my so-called bodyguard: two warriors; two untested young men; two children. We sat together and the tension unsettled Kveldulf who began to whine. I picked him up and sat him to bounce on my knee.

'Trot, trot, you're riding to meet your grandmother.' His face lit up and he looked around.

'Aisgerd here? Kelluf get honey.'

'No, not Aisgerd. This grandmother is called Gudrun. Can you say that? Grandmother Gudrun, say it.'

He pouted and shook his head.

'That'll go down well with your mother,' Ragnar muttered. 'If she's here, that is.'

He was ill at ease without his two swords and kept glancing in the direction of the wapenhouse. I was about to make an angry reply when a tall man approached me. He wore a long tunic of coarse black wool and his only adornment was a silver cross inlaid with red and green stones. His attire reminded me of Ansgar's habit but this was no monk. He had the bearing of a warrior. He made a small bow to me.

'Your mother is ready to receive you now, Sigrid Kveldulfsdaughter.'

My body went limp and Ragnar had to help me to my feet while Olvir took Kveldulf from my lap.

'She'll meet you alone,' the messenger looked at my companions.

'I shall bring only my children,' I said. As I heard how feeble my voice sounded, I grew angry and straightened my back, determined to face my mother with my head held high.

*   *   *

'Sigrid!' My mother came towards me with her hands outstretched. She smiled and kissed me on both cheeks before embracing me. 'Sigrid, my child! Oh, my daughter. I thought I'd never see you again.' She held me at arm's length and looked at me. Her eyes were as clear blue as I remembered but her hair was white and thin, and her face bore lines of sorrow and suffering. 'You have grown into a beautiful young woman, Sigrid. Come, sit here by me and tell me ...' She was interrupted by the tall man clearing his throat.

'Yes, Toki?' She looked over my shoulder to where Olvir and Kveldulf stood and fell silent. I freed myself from her embrace and led Kveldulf to her.

'This is your grandson. I named him Kveldulf.'

She drew a sharp breath and I had the satisfaction of seeing her eyes fill with tears before she knelt down to greet my son.

He looked behind him at Olvir and asked, 'Is it Grandmother Gudrun? Will she give Keluf apple?'

Olvir avoided my eyes and scraped his foot against the floor.

'You'll have to ask her,' he said.

My mother took no notice of this exchange. She was looking closely at Kveldulf.

'So, he has his grandfather's name,' she said and stroked his cheek. 'Let's hope he has more sense.' But then she smiled again and held out her hand for me to help her stand.

Later, when Kveldulf had got his apple and entertained his new grandmother with some barely intelligible tales about his journey, Olvir put him to bed on one of the benches and sang quietly to him until they both slept. My mother's monk-like servant Toki got orders to find sleeping quarters for my entourage. There were no further practical details to sort out. We sat alone by the hearth, my mother and I. Her bearing was as straight and proud as ever but she looked very thin. When she was not smiling, her cheeks looked hollow and pale. I had not anticipated this. In my mind she had remained as always, tall and imposing, her body as strong as her mind. For a moment my own troubles seemed less urgent than to tell my mother that Thorstein and Freydis were alive. Her face lit up. She grasped the silver cross she wore around her neck and kissed it.

'Thank you, Lord, for returning my daughter and keeping my son alive. Thank you, thank you. Oh, Sigrid, when I sent you away from Becklund I thought I'd never see you again.'

'Why did you ...?' A tightness in my throat blocked the rest of my question and I bit my lip to stop the tears. She leant out of her chair and embraced me.

'I thought you'd understand. If Hakon had known you were my daughter, he'd have taken you as well. I wanted you to be safe with Hauk.'

I relaxed with her arms around me and allowed my tears to loosen the knot of anxiety in my chest. But even in my happiness, I knew this harmony between us could not last. In an attempt to keep hold of it and postpone the moment when I had to explain about Kveldulf, I asked her about her life at Nidaros.

She lived with her own servants in a small house on the farm belonging to the Jarl of Lade. Hakon had used her as a peace-weaver and married her off to a chieftain whose support he needed.

'My husband was a Jarl. Hakon seems to think he was the man my father intended for me. I didn't even remember him. He was killed while out hunting very soon after we were married. I had a child, which was still-born, a little girl.'

Her eyes filled with tears and I put my arms around her, too full of emotion to be able to utter a word of consolation. My poor mother. She kissed me.

'I am so grateful the good Lord has returned you to me, Sigrid.'

We sat silent, hand in hand. Then she shook her head and looked at me.

'It's a long, dangerous journey you have made. You must have a reason. I know Hauk is dead. Is your new husband with you?'

'You know! How?'

'Hakon receives news from Æthelstan.' She laughed without mirth. 'I hope the tales of your exploits at Brunanburh were exaggerated. But I've heard nothing else. I assume you have re-married.' She looked at my pregnant body. I drew a deep breath and prepared to shatter the peace between us.

As calmly as I could, I told her about Hauk's death, about the battle of Brunanburh, about Ingefried's death and how I had avenged her. When she showed no sign of wanting to interrupt, I went on to speak of how I had lost my lawsuit and become destitute. I described how Aisgerd had taken me in and looked after me and

251

Kveldulf. That's when she asked the question I dreaded.

'Who then is the father of the child I can see you carry?'

I straightened up and pushed my shoulders back. 'Ragnar Sweinson. Ragnar is the father of both Kveldulf and the child I'm expecting.' I ignored her cry and continued: 'I love him like I believe you once loved my father and …'

Her hand flew up to slap my face but I was quick and caught it halfway. I put it back on her lap.

'Don't pretend to me, Mother. I'm old enough to understand now. Yours was not a marriage approved by your family. You gave up everything to be with your man. How can you condemn me for doing the same?'

Her face went red as a hot fever, then pale as bleached parchment. I needed all my strength not to cower in front of her furious eyes.

'Don't dare to liken that boy to my husband! Your father was brave and honourable, too honourable sometimes. That Ragnar Sweinson is of bad blood. There's no honour in his lineage; it is rotten through and through.'

Her words hit me like blows from an iron fist. She drew her breath and sat quietly for a moment. Then she turned to me and, with a slow, gentle movement, put her hand on the cheek she had thought to slap.

'Daughter, don't you understand? I want what's best for you and a reckless pursuit of brief happiness is not it.' Her face darkened. 'I can never forget how Ragnar's father was the cause of my husband's death. Don't ask me to plead his case with Hakon. I shall do what I can for my grandchild but never for the son of Swein Hjaltebrand.'

I spent the next day with my mother. We played with Kveldulf, she embroidered and I picked up a spindle and distaff. We worked, ate and talked but all the time our disagreement sat between us like a ghost at a wedding feast. We both avoided any reference to Ragnar. Instead I told her about the rebuilding of Becklund, of the stone to my father, of how Thorstein and Freydis had escaped. I showed her Thorstein's letter. She read it and confirmed that the writing meant he left Becklund to me.

'But Steinar is my elder and has first right to the farm. Mother, you have told me nothing about my brother Steinar.'

She sat stiff in her seat.

'He hid during the fighting. Can you believe it? He hid while his father was killed and his brother maimed. My shame in front of my enemies was boundless.'

'I hid too.'

'It was too late by the time you arrived and you had no weapons. There's no blame attached to you.'

I felt sad for the feeble-minded, lumbering lump of a man Steinar had become. He was my elder by several years but he was my playmate and I had taught him to use sword and axe even if he never did manage the shield. I was fond of him.

'Where is he now? Is he still alive?'

She turned to supervise her serving women who were busy by the hearth. I thought she would not answer but then, with her back still to me, she said, 'I don't know.'

* * *

I had not seen Ragnar or any of the others for more than a day. Olvir, true to his habit, kept slipping in and out of the house and turned up at my elbow every now and again with news. These were as I would expect: Ragnar sulked; Thorfinn drank and talked; Anlaf and Ulf had joined other young men in weapons practice and games. I could only hope none of them would be goaded by bored housekarls into loose talk or fights.

'Who is that child?' my mother asked after one of Olvir's visits to our side.

'He was born at Becklund. His mother was one of the thralls.'

'People here think he is your son.' She studied her embroidery.

'What?'

'I know he can't be. You're too young. But you two look very alike, that's why.' She threaded a fresh length of silk through the eye of her needle. Then she put her embroidery down. 'Was his mother called Unn?'

'Yes, how did you know?'

'Unn was Steinar's woman. I think she felt sorry for him and, of course, he *was* the son of the master, despite everything. It would account for the family likeness.'

I had not been aware of Steinar having a special woman but by then he was busy working the land and I was still chasing round avoiding work and pursuing the pleasures of childhood. So Olvir was my nephew, my brother's son. We shared the same blood.

I was struck by a thought. The thrall Ketil had replaced Steinar as my companion and scapegoat. He had suffered many a thrashing on my behalf and would laugh it off as we embarked on our next adventure.

'Ketil, do you remember him? He died fighting.' I said. 'I saw his body and the man he slayed. Was he …'

My mother shook her head and smiled.

'No, he wasn't related to you by blood, although it is not always easy to tell on a farm, who has fathered which child.'

I spoke to her then of Lydia, Hauk's special woman and the mother of his three children. I should have known better than to expect sympathy.

'You have only yourself to blame, Sigrid. If you had been a good wife to Hauk, he would never have looked at another woman again. He had his heart set on you from when you were about ten, constantly pestering Kveldulf for you. This woman – what was her name again, Lydia – was only someone to keep him satisfied while waiting for you.'

So there it was again, only myself to blame, no Steinar or Ketil to pay for my misdeeds, only me.

22.

My uncle, Hakon Haraldson, king of Norway, 'Hakon the Good' some called him, arrived and agreed to see me. I put on new clothes provided by my mother, an undershirt of silk softer than anything I had ever worn before, a pleated over-dress of finest linen and a pinafore of purple wool with wide embroidered panels at the hem. I sneaked my Thor's hammer amulet out of sight under my shirt. But in full view among other jewellery on my neck-chain I hung my silver cross, restored to its original shape by the simple action of bending the top arm back into place. Mother helped me wash and braid my hair.

'Such a shame to have to cover it up,' she said and stroked my heavy tresses before fastening my headdress.

'What kind of man is King Hakon?'

'He is already showing the strength of a true king. Jarl Sigurd has given him much support and sound advice but he has his own mind. He has already made many laws and he has sworn to make the country Christian. I left Norway before he was born so I don't know him as a man, as my half-brother. We don't speak much. Too many things lay unresolved between us.'

'Has he offered weregeld?'

'No, nor has he said he's sorry for my loss. While he's generous and makes sure I lack for nothing, he avoids my gaze and is awkward in my company. He keeps me here to …' She shot me an appraising look. 'Well, never mind that. But one thing you should understand. It was humiliating for my father when I ran away with Kveldulf. My father would have named Kveldulf among his enemies but, believe me, if he'd wanted him killed he would have brought about his death very soon after we eloped. He didn't because it was not important enough. I was one of many daughters. Sheltering Swein was different. To King Harald, my father, that was an act of treason. There is no weregeld due for the killing of a traitor.' I gritted my teeth and nodded. I knew about that, I just didn't want to hear it.

The lack of family resemblance between Hakon and Eirik extended further than their physical appearance. Eirik had sat lounging in his chair, much like a viper sunning itself on a warm rock but ready for a swift strike. Hakon paced up and down the hall, leaping on and off the dais, the image of a wolf stalking his prey. He was handsome. His blond, almost white hair shone in the torchlight and his tall, broad-shouldered frame danced shadows on the wall-hangings. I realised he was about the same age as me. As we drew close he stopped and bowed to my mother.

'Sister, I trust this day finds you well.'

'Yes, thank you for asking. Thanks to your generosity, I lack for nothing. I have brought my daughter, your niece, Sigrid Kveldulfsdaughter to pay her respects.'

At the mention of my father's name, I thought I discerned a tightening of Hakon's chin. He didn't look at me.

'Niece.' His voice was gruff, devoid of warmth or welcome.

I bent my knee, waiting for him to offer his hand. He didn't. I looked up into his face. His eyebrows met above his nose and his mouth was an angry, thin line. Then, as his eyes met mine, there was a transformation from annoyance to surprise, then to a look I knew only too well, the look of a man who has seen a woman he wants. He held out both hands and helped me rise. I felt my cheeks burn in angry confusion. It was true I had come to meet him as a supplicant but as a woman of worth, my own mistress. With that look, Hakon reduced me to mere chattel, a thing he desired and would have as of right because he was the King.

I had intended to carry myself with dignity but also with humility. Maybe, if I had been able to do that, things would have worked out better. But my pride got in the way. Unable to control my temper, I snatched my hands back and met Hakon's admiring gaze with a scowl. I heard my mother draw her breath. She took my hand and put it back in Hakon's.

'Think, girl!' she hissed.

But the damage was done and Hakon's smile vanished. He dropped my hand and turned to my mother.

'You may attend our table tonight with your daughter. We shall discuss her future then.' With that he turned his back to us.

As I walked towards the door, I saw Ragnar at the back of the hall. He was struggling to free himself from Thorfinn and Anlaf, who held on to an arm each. His pale, furious face told me he had witnessed my encounter with the King. He broke loose, grabbed me by the arm and dragged me outside.

'What did he say to you?'

'Nothing, Ragnar. Becalm yourself.'

'How did he insult you? I shall avenge your honour, be he king or no.'

'Hush, Ragnar!'

A couple of Hakon's housekarls had followed us outside and were moving in our direction. Their hands were on the hilts of their swords. Ulf and Anlaf arrived with Ragnar's weapons as well as their own. Ragnar snatched his swords and axe from them.

'I saw the way he looked at you!'

Then my mother caught up with us. She slapped Ragnar across the face.

'Be quiet, fool! You'll ruin us all.'

She turned and spoke to the housekarls. They hesitated. They looked Ragnar over and stayed where they were. Ragnar stood silent, stunned, rubbing his cheek. Thorfinn bent his knee to my mother and pulled Ragnar down with him.

'Gudrun Haraldsdaughter …' said Thorfinn.

Mother had already turned and walked towards her house. We followed the straight-backed, composed figure in silence. One of the housekarls made some comment I couldn't hear and the other one laughed. I looked back to see them following us with their eyes.

'I can't help any of you, if you will not help yourselves. Sigrid, to my brother you are the daughter of a traitor. I persuaded him to meet you nevertheless. You could have smiled sweetly at him and possibly he would have listened. Be still, Ragnar Sweinson!' Ragnar hung his head and Mother continued: 'Instead you insult him. I doubt he'll see you again, unless he thinks of a use for you, which is quite possible.'

I knew only too well what she meant by 'use'. Like her, I would be a peace-weaver, a gift to bind one of his allies closer to him by marriage. I felt like a foolish child.

'Ragnar Sweinson, if you're going to challenge every man, regardless of rank, who looks at my daughter you will bring certain disaster to us all. Why did you come?'

'I came to protect my wife and son.'

I felt a warm glow inside me at this and could not stop myself looking at him. Mother snorted and shook her head.

'In your temper you have drawn the eyes of Hakon's karls. You could have got killed there. You're challenging a king. You are no protection but a danger to Sigrid and Kveldulf. You must leave. You should go now, tonight. You have nothing to gain by staying. You are an outlaw and I doubt very much Hakon will have any use for you alive.'

She paused and leant back in her chair. Ragnar got up and for a second time bent his knee in front of her.

'I also came because our marriage, although real to us, needs your approval. I can pay a generous bride-geld.'

Mother shook her head.

'Oh, I don't doubt it. I know how men like you get their riches. You may have gold, Ragnar Sweinson, but without land you're nothing.'

'Will you plead my cause with the King?'

'No.' She stood, indicating that there was nothing more to discuss.

Ragnar got up. He made to say something but my

260

mother cut him short.

'Go!'

Ragnar's hands shook as he lifted mine to his lips and the look he gave me pierced my heart. I made to follow him but Mother held me back. I wrenched myself free.

'But, Mother, you cannot let Ragnar be punished for what his father did!' I rushed after him. At the door my way was barred by Toki. He inclined his head.

'Forgive me, Sigrid Kveldulfsdaughter.'

He took my arm and walked me back to my seat. Thorfinn stood with his hand on his sword and a miserable look on his face. My mother had her hand on his arm.

'You must understand this, both of you. Ragnar was present at the raid on one my father's islands. In Hakon's eyes, he is guilty of treason the same way his father was. I assume you were there too, Thorfinn. But you were a follower and I understand you are now Sigrid's sworn man. You and the two boys should be safe enough. But you have to persuade Ragnar to go tonight. He is a danger to Sigrid and to Kveldulf. Do you understand? They will find out who he is. It is impossible to hide these things here. Whether you go or stay, Thorfinn, I leave to you but Ragnar must go.'

Thorfinn nodded and turned to leave.

'But where can he go?' I asked.

She laughed.

'A brave sword will always find a home and he is brave, your man, I'll give him that.'

I tried to leave but again she held me back. 'It's better you're not seen with him.' I noticed Toki had resumed his place by the door.

261

'Go with him.' I called to Thorfinn. He nodded and then the door closed behind him.

* * *

I attended Hakon's hall as ordered. Encased in a fog of misery, I was introduced to Jarl Sigurd but have no recollection of what we talked about. I sat between my mother and another female relative of Hakon's. She told me her name but I don't remember it. She talked and asked me questions. I heard her voice as from far away and, unable to answer, heard Mother speak on my behalf. The food put in front of me remained untouched. I looked in vain for Ulf and Anlaf. I wished Thorfinn would bring me a message but he, too, was nowhere to be seen. The King ignored me. All my hopes were dashed and all through my own impetuous action.

It was a relief when Mother said it was time to return to her house. We made our way between the trestle-tables and at the lower end of the hall Ulf and Anlaf rose to greet us. They looked like they had just arrived. Drizzle still coated their clothing in fine droplets. I told them to finish their meal before joining me. Back at the house the serving women had fed Kveldulf and were trying to get him to go to bed.

'Keluf want Olvir.' He looked at me with accusing eyes and trembling lower lip.

'I thought he was with you, here.'

The servants shook their heads. He had left with me and Mother.

'So he may still be in the hall.' Mother turned to Toki. 'Please see if you can find him there.'

'No, I'll go.' I rose but my mother pulled me back. She held my arm until Toki had left.

'You need to understand that Toki is not just my

servant, he is my jailor too.' I thought at first I had misheard her. She cleared her throat. 'Sigrid, you may find that Hakon holds it against you that not only did your father break his oath to his king but your brother Steinar has run off to join his enemies.'

'Steinar!'

'Yes, the coward has turned hero. Word has it he has sworn to avenge your father's death. I am watched at all times, in case he seeks me out. We are all under suspicion. Hakon believes we're all capable of seeking revenge.'

'And are you?' I whispered.

She didn't answer. She looked around at her household. Then her eyes held mine for a few breathless moments.

'How would that help?'

* * *

Olvir was not in the hall. No one remembered seeing him there that evening. I railed at Toki until he allowed me out, in the company of a couple of servants, to look for him. As I stepped out into the fine drizzle, Ulf and Anlaf joined me. They had been barred from entering the house but had taken up position by the door in case I needed them. They had last seen Olvir playing hnefatafl with a visiting Northumbrian trader, but it had been much earlier in the afternoon. I knew something must have happened. Olvir would never leave Kveldulf like that. We searched in ever wider circles, lighting our way with torches and calling his name.

'He likes to wander down to the harbour and chat to people. Maybe we should look there,' said Anlaf.

'But this late?'

'I hope nothing …'

Anlaf didn't need to finish. I was distraught and prepared to search the whole of Norway and beyond. As I turned towards the harbour, my mother's serving woman stopped me.

'You are overtired, Sigrid Kveldulfsdaughter. Think of your unborn child. Come back and rest. Your karls can go faster without you.'

Anlaf and Ulf soon returned, carrying a bedraggled Olvir. He was wet through, pale and hollow-eyed and his clothes and face bore streaks of vomit. He couldn't speak just kept closing his eyes and making retching noises.

'We found him at the start of the track to the harbour,' said Ulf. 'I don't understand how we missed him before. I'm sure we must have passed him. Looks like he was suddenly overcome by sickness. Strange. No one else is sick. Not that I know of, anyway. Here you are, little mite.' He put Olvir down on a bed and ruffled his hair. 'Maybe he had too much to eat. He has a way of getting the women to feed him better than the rest of us.'

I bent down next to him and, while stroking Olvir's cheek, I whispered to Ulf.

'Be careful, watch out, be my eyes and ears.'

Olvir opened his eyes and muttered: 'No, that's me. That's what I am.'

I shushed him. Then, in a loud voice, I thanked Ulf and Anlaf and told them to get some rest.

Olvir threw up several times in the night. I sat with him, holding his hand while he slept and supporting his head when he spewed. The next morning one of the serving women brought her mother who was a wise woman. Old Kirsten hobbled through the door, bent and

264

gnarled like an old oak. She brought her granddaughter, also called Kirsten, a girl of eleven who lived with her.

'So where is the sick child?' Old Kirsten blinked as her peppercorn eyes swept the room. Toki, probably annoyed at not being consulted, tried to shoo her away.

'We don't need witchcraft here. I shall ask the priest to attend the boy. He needs prayers, not heathen hocus-pocus.'

'This is not a question of religion, Toki,' said my mother. 'We shall ask the priest to pray, of course we shall, but Kirsten knows more than anyone how to use herbs to cure illness. We need her help as well as the Lord's mercy to get Olvir well.'

The old crone showed her empty gums in a smirk and was led to Olvir's bed. She bent over him, studied his pale features and stroked his damp brow.

'Show me what he has brought up.' I looked around. 'I don't think …'

'Yes, I saved it. Here.' Old Kirsten's daughter brought a vile-smelling pail from outside. Old Kirsten sniffed it, felt it and put some on the tip of her tongue.

'Hmm, I see,' she muttered. 'So that's how it is.' She made her granddaughter smell and taste the vomit as well and whispered to her. The girl's eyes became round and her mouth opened. Then Old Kirsten turned to us. 'Ladies, I need to talk to you.'

Mother and I sat her down away from the servants. She looked at us for several moments before she spoke.

'The child has been poisoned. Pink toadstool. It's treacherous. Small amounts will make the warrior brave but too much can send you to the next world. The boy will live. Give him a draft made of dried chamomile to calm his stomach. He will sleep for a long time now.

When he recovers, he needs building up. Nourishing food, of course, strong broth from marrow-bones mixed with egg and milk. Give him the dried leaves of wood avens and nettle pounded with warm water, add chamomile too. Can you get those things? If you don't have them, send my daughter to fetch some from me.'

I nodded and looked at my mother. She seemed as stunned as I was. Echoing my thoughts, Old Kirsten continued, 'The question of who may wish to poison a young child is for you to consider. I may be able to help you but not with herbs. It takes other powers and ceremonies, you may not agree with.' She pointed at the crosses on our neck-chains.

23.

'Where were you?' I held a spoonful of steaming broth to Olvir's mouth. He took a sip and swallowed.

'Don't remember.' He leant back and closed his eyes. Three days had passed and he was still weak but on the mend. Poisoned. I fought back my tears. Who would want to harm Olvir?

'Did anyone give you anything to eat?'

'Don't know.' He thought a while. 'One of the traders gave me a drink.'

'Which trader?'

'Don't know. Maybe the one I beat at hnefatafl. Oh yes, I remember it now. He gave me a drink and then he wanted me to come on board but I ran away. I didn't like him.'

A trader trying to poison Olvir in revenge for defeat at a board game? No. To be able to abduct him and sell him? A boy his age would fetch a good price. But there were better ways to make him drowsy than pink toadstool. And why risk abducting a child from the harbour with so many people around? Still, I had to accept it for now.

'You must take care. I need you, and Kveldulf does.'

His eyes still closed, he nodded. As I rose to leave him, I heard him heave a trembling sigh.

'Olvir, what is the matter?' He turned his face to the wall.

'Nothing.'

* * *

The knorrs had left the previous day and my mother and I discussed with Toki how best to proceed with our suspicion against the trader.

'But I don't understand it,' he said. 'These are well-regarded men, regular visitors to Nidaros. Why would they risk their reputation by killing a child? What in the name ...' He looked behind him. 'I wish you wouldn't sneak up like that, Olvir!'

'I'm sorry. I heard you talk. I'm not sure now. Maybe it didn't happen. Maybe I dreamt.'

I could see Toki's patience was about to run out, and intervened.

'Are you feeling strong enough to come and sit outside, Olvir?'

He nodded. Drizzle had given way to the pale sun of early autumn. I found a seat by the main cookhouse.

'You have never lied to me, have you Olvir? You are one person I can always trust to tell me the truth.' I heard him sniffle. 'I do wish I knew what really happened to you. It wouldn't be a very good idea to get all the King's men looking for a murderer if ...'

'Oh, Sigrid, please, I didn't mean ...'

I put my arm round him. 'Tell me what happened.'

'I can't.'

'Olvir, someone gave you a poisoned drink. You could have died. You must tell me who it was.'

'It wasn't anyone.'

'Don't tell any more lies. I know you were given toadstool. Tell me who.'

'I did it myself.'

I felt like life itself drained from my body. My arm

dropped from Olvir's shoulder. I closed my eyes, struggling with the thought that my foster-son, my faithful companion, had tried to kill himself.

'Why, Olvir? Why?'

'I can't tell you. Please, Sigrid, don't be angry.'

Angry, I thought, yes maybe that's what I should be. But instead tears blurred my vision and the cold hand of misery squeezed my belly.

'Why did you want to kill yourself?'

'I didn't. I took too much by mistake. I didn't mean to. I didn't.'

'Are you trying to tell me, you don't know how dangerous toadstool is?'

'No, yes, no, I do know, but …' He took my hand and held it against his cheek. It was wet. I wiped his tears and then my own.

'Where did you find it?' He sat silent with lowered head. 'Look at me, Olvir. Where did you find it?' He didn't move. I grabbed his head and turned him to face me. I had never had to do anything like this before. Olvir had never lied or been disobedient. 'Tell me! Tell me immediately! Don't lie to me!'

'I took some from Thorfinn. Please, don't tell him, please!'

'You took some. You stole!'

'Only a little in case I needed it.'

'What do you mean, need it? Why should you need the mushroom at all?'

'Please, Sigrid, I've said I'm sorry. I don't feel well. Promise you won't tell Thorfinn or Ragnar. Don't tell anyone. I don't want anyone to know.'

'Why did you need the mushroom, Olvir? Answer me.' The delay told me another lie was on the way.

269

'I didn't really need it. I just wanted to know what it felt like. I'm sorry. I must have taken too much or something.'

I leant back against the wall. Olvir was nine years old, bright and inquisitive. Maybe he was telling the truth. Maybe he had just been experimenting. But then …

'Why did you lie about the trader?'

He half-turned and gave me a sideways glance. Calculating. This was not the Olvir I knew. What was going on with the child?

'I said it 'cause he's a nasty man. He cheats.'

'Who did he cheat? How do you know?'

'He cheats at hnefatafl. I caught him. I saw and when I told on him, he tried to hit me.'

This sounded plausible enough but I was still uneasy. We sat in silence for a while but I couldn't regain the usual feeling of comfort and trust between us.

When we returned inside, Toki's voice stabbed like an icicle. 'The boy has uttered slanderous lies against a respected trader. How do you intend to punish him?' I shook my head.

'He has confessed and apologised. I know he's very ashamed.'

'He needs a beating.'

'I don't beat my children. I was never beaten nor were my brothers, nor will my children be.'

'It is the Christian duty of a parent to chastise their errant children until they learn obedience. And that duty extends to servants and thralls. The lad must be taught a lesson. He's far too confident and familiar for a thrall.'

'He's my foster-son. He may be born of a thrall-woman but …' I had never given Olvir his freedom. I

270

could have done it at the Allthing but I was too full of my own concerns then. So he was a thrall.

'Toki is right.'

My mother took charge. I had to accept that, in her house, she held the right to pass judgement. He was the son of her thrall-woman so Olvir belonged to her not me. As Toki led him outside, Olvir looked away from me. My brave, faithful, little champion, I had failed to protect him and he deserved better.

* * *

Autumn closed in; a sad, lonely time when nature itself seemed to grieve with me. I tried to keep busy but the occupations open to me were limited to the weaving and embroidering I had always found tedious. With too much time on my hands I fell into a deep melancholy. Accompanied by a serving woman and one of Toki's underlings I took long walks in the surroundings of Nidaros. The child growing inside me was used as an excuse to make it clear to me that I was not free to wander too far and my horse was kept in the royal stables. My thoughts were heavy with self-reproach. I was separated from my love, my children would be bastards for all time and there seemed little hope of returning to Cumbria. I wondered where Ragnar and Thorfinn were, and I wondered what had befallen Brother Ansgar who had so selflessly and pointlessly put himself in danger for my sake. I bitterly regretted my ill-temper with Hakon which had put us all in this hopeless situation.

My mother was concerned about my low spirits and arranged for me to learn to read. She had for some time taken instruction from Toki and from the priest at Nidaros. The lessons were heavy with Christian

271

preaching but I decided that to be able to read would be useful and anyway there was no point in upsetting her. Olvir joined us and learnt the Latin letters much faster than me. I was not entirely happy about the way he took an interest in the religious content but at least I knew where he was during our lessons.

It was during one of our lessons that I understood that my mother had a very definite aim to her learning.

'I wish to assist my brother Hakon in his efforts to bring the salvation of Christ to the heathens in this country. We have talked about establishing a holy community.'

'What do you mean by that?' I asked but before she could answer, Olvir was there, eager to show off.

'It's what Brother Ansgar belonged to. They all live together and pray and … um … and …'

'It would be a community of men and women who wish to devote their lives to the service of Our Lord. I shall take holy orders as soon as it can be arranged and Hakon has agreed to gift a house and some land. From there the word of God will travel across the land.' I looked at her eager face and felt I looked at a stranger.

I was too tired and dejected to exercise full control over my children. It didn't matter with Kveldulf. He was very happy at Nidaros. There were small horses from Shetland for him to ride. Anlaf made him a small bow and taught him to shoot. Ulf helped him train Striker, no longer a puppy, to fetch and obey commands. He began to speak like the Norwegians, in a chirpy, sing-song accent. He played with the other children and many adults praised him for his fearless nature. My mother spoilt him worse than anyone, claiming this was her right. Even Toki seemed to

272

approve of the lad. Hakon sometimes requested his attendance and this filled me with dread. Hakon had spent his childhood at Æthelstan's court as a token of the friendship between the two kings. Might Hakon have similar plans to keep my son at his own court?

Meanwhile I saw less and less of Olvir. My mother made arrangements to grant him his freedom and to have his status as my foster-son formally recognised. But she complained that he spent too much time at the hnefatafl board and had begun to play for money. He seemed to win more often than lose but this could make him enemies as well as friends and he was too young to exercise judgement in the matter. It was clear he ought to spend more time with other children.

'The only thing he excels at is running,' Toki's voice indicated this was not among the most important skills for a Viking. 'He goes for long runs alone and he shows great endurance and speed but he must learn to use weapons as well or he'll spend his life running away from battles.' I spoke to Olvir about this and he promised to pay more attention to fighting skills.

'But remember, Sigrid,' he said, 'I promised to win a race at the Allthing.'

'I worry about you. Where do you go when you run out alone?'

'Oh, all over the place.' He shrugged his shoulders and sauntered off.

* * *

Rain, darkened skies and a cold wind from the north made me spend more time indoors. I grew heavy but not even the approaching birth of my child could brighten my thoughts. Only in the evenings when we sat, warm and snug, around the fire and my mother told us stories, did I feel at peace. When I closed my eyes I could almost imagine myself a child again, safe and happy back at Becklund.

A great storm brought heavy snow. It lasted for three days and, to avoid getting lost in the blizzard, the servants tied ropes between the houses, barns and byres. When the wind abated, we opened the door and cold, fresh air pushed its way in to replace the smoke-laden fumes. Outside, everything was hushed and all contours in the landscape rounded and soft under the thick blanket of snow. Land, trees and buildings sparkled in the sunshine, blinding our indoor eyes. Then children and dogs began chasing round and the air filled with happy voices. Skis and sledges were dug out from the stores. Olvir and Kveldulf got skis and made determined efforts to keep up with the other children, who had developed their skill over many years and laughed at the beginners.

Then the Valkyries rode across the evening sky spreading fear, making people wonder what disaster was about to strike and who had brought it about. It is better to stay indoors, out of the way of their wrath but I was spellbound and couldn't move. As the winged horses raced across the sky, there were brilliant reflections from the armour of the riders and there followed in their wake shimmering waves of green and golden lights. They filled the darkness above me. It was beautiful and dreadful. I trembled with awe. Then one of the servants came up behind me and touched my arm. I turned round to ask what he wanted. Behind him I saw the impossible. Far away behind the trees, where the sun had set many hours before, a pale red glimmer coloured the horizon. Yesterday's sun was returning. Tomorrow's sun was rising from the wrong place. The harbinger of Ragnarok, the final battle between Gods and giants, the chaos when the snake of Midgard shall whip the sea into a giant wave, when the Fenris wolf will break its fetters and with fire burning in its eyes swallow the world.

I felt a stab to my stomach, fell to my knees and let out a groan of despair.

'No sound, Sigrid Kveldulfsdaughter. It will bring down the fury of the Valkyries.'

'The sun! Ragnarok!' I raised my arm but he caught it.

'Don't point. The light guides the Valkyries. It must not be mocked or disturbed. It is not the final battle, not yet.' He led me towards the house.

'My children!'

'Safe. They were brought inside so no light could descend and sever their heads from their bodies.'

I shivered. Another stabbing pain tore through me. My second child asked to be born. I wondered what fate befell a child born under the light from the armour worn by Odin's own shieldmaidens.

As with my first birth, I struggled and suffered great pain. The sauna was fired up and Old Kirsten was sent for. She arrived with her granddaughter Kirsten and bemoaned the lack of fresh shepherd's purse to deter evil spirits. She threw a handful of pine cones on the fire. They filled the air with a soothing scent of resin. In a brief moment between the birth-cramps I heard her ask my mother, 'What have you given her so far?'

'Silverweed and motherwort, small doses only. We keep very few strong herbs here.'

Old Kirsten nodded and asked her granddaughter, 'So what would you do now?'

'I would mix a small amount of rue with the white deadnettle,' the girl answered promptly and Old Kirsten nodded again.

'The Valkyries,' I panted. 'What will happen?'

Old Kirsten looked at me and pursed her lips.

'Hmm. Let's add some henbane. She may start raving but it will pass.' She came over to me and looked between my legs. She pressed her dry, claw-like hands over my belly. 'Ah, a breech birth. This is not good. I shall try to turn the baby but let's get something to still you first.' She waved Young Kirsten over.

'Watch carefully. Put your hand here.' They treated me like a slab of meat. Why did nobody listen to me?

I cried out, 'The Valkyries, are they still riding the sky? What will happen?'

The young girl put a hand on my forehead. 'They are gone. It is almost midday. Try to be still. The Norns will weave the destiny of your child whether you worry about it or not.'

The draught they gave me was as bitter as gall. I choked and coughed but was forced to drink. Then the walls began to sway and ripple. From the fire rose a cloud with red, glowing eyes, flared fiery nostrils and silver horns. Its hot breath filled me with the strength of a giant and together we roared the battle-cry of the Norse: 'Odin, Odin.' With my bare hands I fought a three-headed demon. He forced himself inside me and filled my belly with flames. They grew and grew, and I screamed and I heaved and I pushed until it tore me apart and I sank into a whirlpool of blackness.

When I woke, I thought for a moment I was back at Swanhill, that time had reversed and I had just given birth to Kveldulf. The headache, the nausea, the cloying smell of blood, birth fluids and sick were the same. I tried to sit and winced. My cleft was on fire. I felt I would never be able to move again. I moaned and called out for Ragnar. Someone rose from the bench opposite. I strained to see.

'Sigrid,' my mother put an arm round my shoulders to support me, 'you have another son, a healthy, strong boy. Drink this. No, don't worry it is only shepherd's purse to help staunch the blood. I have a poultice as well to put between your legs. It will sting at first but we must stop the bleeding.'

She washed the sweat from my body and dressed me in a fine shift. Toki arrived and carried me to the house. I could not hold back my tears when the red, wrinkly little face of my baby emerged from the swaddling. I loved him more than my life but to the world he was just another bastard.

Kveldulf was led up to my bed to see his baby brother. He was not impressed.

'He's too little. You said Keluf have brother to play with.'

'He'll grow. He'll be a baby at first, then he'll grow and you can play. Come and have a closer look.'

He crawled on to the bed and snuggled up. He giggled.

'He is suckling you just like the lambs! I did too, didn't I? But I don't any more.'

I felt a little less sad. 'Where is Olvir?'

Nobody knew. One of the women left to look for him but returned alone.

'I don't understand,' she said, 'he was here when Old Kirsten brought the baby. I remember him having a good look when the baby was bathed. I had to squeeze past him to be able to see anything myself.'

'I'm sure he'll be back,' said my mother, 'rest now. I'll wake you when he comes.'

* * *

When I woke, the hall was quiet save for the peaceful snores of the household. My baby rooted and I put him to my breast. Another greedy feeder, another brave little warrior. I was drifting off to sleep again, when there was a firm knock on the door. The servant closest got up and asked who disturbed the house so late.

There was an answer and the servant called out, 'It's just Olvir. Where have you been, child? We were out looking for you. You'll be in trouble again.' He pulled the bolts aside to let Olvir in.

When the others heard him they turned, muttered and prepared to go back to sleep. When the door swung open it was not Olvir who entered. Four tall, looming figures in bulging cloaks pushed their way inside. Their faces below the rims of their helmets were hidden under pieces of cloth. One made his way over to Toki and held a knife to his throat. Another threw a shawl over my mother's shoulders and pinned her arms to her body. The other two stood back to back, their swords drawn, in the middle of the hall.

'Stay where you are. Nobody will harm you. Despite our weapons, we have come in peace.'

'Ragnar!' I choked on a wave of tears and stretched out my arms. He removed his helmet and his disguise and embraced me.

'I told you I would be here to claim this son as mine,' he said and kissed my tear-stained face. 'Where is the new little warrior?'

I handed him the baby. He took it out of its

278

swaddling and placed it carefully in his helmet. He held it up for all to see.

'I am Ragnar Sweinson and this is my son.' His voice broke and he cleared his throat. 'My second son. And with you all as my witnesses I give him the name …'

'Harald,' I cried out, 'please may we call him Harald!'

He looked at me, mouth and eyes open wide. Then he smiled and said, 'If it pleases you, my brave shieldmaiden, he shall be named Harald Ragnarson. Now drink my friends, drink to the future of my new son!'

A small figure, insufficiently disguised to hide the fact that it was Olvir, had waited by the door. Now he stepped forward with a pitcher of mead. He took it round for all to share in the birth-ale. Only Toki refused. My mother sighed but drank. Then Ragnar returned the baby to me and kissed me.

'Odin, Thor and Frey guard you and our children till I return.'

We clung to each other. He kissed the sleeping Kveldulf. Then they were gone.

24.

Kings have enemies and it seemed Hakon, too, had his fair share. Eirik and Gunnhild had champions who were ever on the alert, looking for an opportunity to prove their loyalty. Then there were the Danes. Between Hakon and King Harald Gormson of Denmark, old rivalries festered, both concerning land and family as Queen Gunnhild was Harald Gormson's half-sister. Within Norway itself, there were chieftains who felt slighted and usurped and who could not be trusted. At Nidaros we were ever vigilant but Ragnar's appearance showed how vulnerable we were to surprise.

When they left and the door slammed shut, the hall filled with voices, my mother calling down the curse of all the saints on Ragnar, Toki swearing and shouting at the servants, excited chatter from the women. Toki rushed to the door. It was barred from outside. He ordered the men to help him use a trestle for a battering ram but was stopped by my mother.

'They will have horses waiting. It's dark. By the time you're through they will be long gone.'

Only Ragnar had revealed his face and spoken but the other three must have been Thorfinn, Anlaf and Ulf and helping them, bringing them news, bringing them to me – Olvir. So that's what his long, lonely runs had been about. This is what he needed mushroom-courage for. What would happen to him now? We had all seen him. He had answered the servant at the door. Toki knew he had led Ragnar to us. Would he ever be able to return? Ulf and Anlaf had not spoken and not been recognised, they were safe. Ragnar and Thorfinn were able to find shelter and survive on what the land gave. But Olvir was just a child. Where could *he* find shelter?

I was questioned repeatedly by Toki about Ragnar but in the end he had to accept that I didn't know where he was. I did my best to persuade him that Ragnar was no threat to the King or the Jarl but for several days I saw groups of housekarls set off to search for him and his mysterious companions. Ulf and Anlaf had been barred from my mother's house from the start and were not known by anyone there except my mother. She must have realised who the companions were and I was grateful she kept her knowledge to herself. One day while I rested and the household were busy with their various occupations, Old Kirsten's daughter brought me my midday meal.

'Olvir is with my mother,' she whispered, even though nobody was within earshot. 'He can stay there as long as he needs to. I'll bring them news and he'll carry it to your man. Oh, Sigrid Kveldulfsdaughter, how brave he is, your man, and how he must love you. All the women are talking about it.'

* * *

The midwinter celebrations at Lade were lavish but I was prevented from participating as the Jarl met with other chieftains in the temple to sacrifice to the Æsirs in the grand, old style and I had to keep up the pretence of being a Christian. I heard rumours that the King had problems persuading local chieftains to support him because he refused to eat of the sacrificial meat and when he drank of the mead he made the sign of the cross over the horn. The Jarl had tried to persuade him to compromise and, after much debating, he had agreed to eat a small piece of horse-liver. I would have gladly eaten his share and given my own horse to Odin as well if it would help keep Ragnar safe.

The Jarl and the King were away for several days and I had more freedom to move around. I walked down to Nidaros hoping to catch sight of Olvir. But he was never there and I didn't want to draw attention to Old Kirsten by visiting her hovel. Nobody did. If she was wanted she was sent for.

Nidaros was a busy port and trading post clustered around the mouth of the river Nid. It provided a good, deep harbour lined with wooden walkways and with piers sticking out from it, like piglets suckling a sow, to provide landing stages for the ships. The traders and craftsmen had houses and gardens all along the harbour and I enjoyed walking there, listening to them bartering and gossiping. I asked Toki why Jarl Sigurd had his farm on the Lade peninsula instead of at Nidaros.

'Oh,' he said, 'Nidaros is the domain of the King. That was established by Harald Finehair, your grandfather, when he conquered the land and Jarl Sigurd's father agreed. The low-lying area behind the trading post is used for the assembly of the Allthing and that is sacred ground not to be claimed by any man for himself.'

'But Lade has no proper harbour, just the beach.'

'Ah, but you see, the Lade peninsula has good farmland and grazing, enough for the Jarl to bestow land on his many faithful followers. And then there are many other beaches dotted around the peninsula where they

282

have ships so in times of unrest they can be sent for, to support the Jarl both on land and sea. Lade is not a bad place at all for a Jarl's court.'

Kveldulf accepted that his father had gone away. He knew from the other children that fathers did so from time to time. He took longer to get used to not having Olvir around. During the day he was happy and busy but at night he complained and shed bitter tears. I missed Olvir too. I was comforted to think he would be safe with Old Kirsten and her granddaughter. Those who asked were told he was her apprentice. I gathered he used skis to move across the snow-covered ground and, throughout the winter, he met up with Ragnar and Thorfinn at different hiding places to exchange news. Old Kirsten's daughter brought little presents from Ragnar to Kveldulf, carved animals – so many he had enough for a whole farmyard. I couldn't tell Kveldulf the presents were from his father, he was still too young to keep a secret. Ragnar would know that and I felt he sent the keepsakes as messages for me to let me know we were in his thoughts.

My longing for Ragnar was like a constant ache and the worry for him gnawed at my insides. I was watched and followed everywhere. I had no one to confide in except my two faithful karls, Ulf and Anlaf. As I recovered from the birth I joined them in weapons practice and it eased my mind to have to concentrate on the physical exertion of swordplay and the vigorous throwing of the spear. When I was overcome by sadness I walked through the pine forest behind Lade, up on to the ridge. I sat on a rock with Harald in my arms staring out to sea. In clear weather I could see, past the outer peninsula, the vastness of the ocean. There beyond the horizon were England, Cumbria and Becklund. I wondered whether I would ever be able to return there.

Sometimes I envied Ragnar and Thorfinn their life out in the mountains, free from the worries and cares of daily life on the farm. I longed to join them, to break out of my restricted world in my mother's house and breathe the clear, cold air of freedom. But I had my children to love and protect, and I could go nowhere.

* * *

Soon after Kveldulf turned four we enjoyed a warm beautiful spring. The animals had been moved to grazing on the slopes above the settlement, waiting for the weather to warm up sufficiently for them to make the migration to the high mountain meadows. Six full moons had come and gone since Harald's birth and he was greedy for solid food to help his teething. He could sit up and was trying to crawl. Kveldulf was disdainful but the rest of the household were enchanted. I thought every now and then of how the Valkyries rode across the sky before he was born and I wondered if it meant he would meet with a bad end. Two weeks after his birth, a fire broke out in one of the warehouses in Nidaros and I tried to be reassured that this was the event foretold by the lights. All through the spring, whenever something bad happened, I felt it took away the threat to my baby and his future. I saw the lights again that winter, several times but never so clear, never so brilliant and threatening as the night before Harald was born.

I decided it was almost summer and cleaned my fur-lined cloak in cow's urine to keep it for next winter. As I draped it over a bush to air, I became aware of a commotion from the direction of the harbour. I saw servants hurry into the house. Kveldulf rode up on Morning Star.

'Mummy, there are some ships. I think they are emn ... eme ... enemy. Anlaf says I have to hide!'

Fear for my children gripped me like an eagle's claw. My mother came out shouting for Toki. My heartbeat quickened as I watched frantic activity break out all round me. My mother's household seemed to have rehearsed this. They emerged from the house with food, bedding and the chest of valuables. Toki brought horses and within a short time the women and children of the household were ready to move – all except me. My fear had transposed into determination and, while Toki had his back to me, I kissed my children and entrusted them into the care of my mother. She tried to argue but not for long and I thought there was a measure of pride in her voice as she said, 'You are your father's daughter. I can't do anything about that now. God go with you.'

There was no time to get upset and think about whether I was doing the right thing. Like the mother-wolf, I followed my instincts to fight whoever was threatening my young. I changed into tunic and leggings, unwrapped my helmet and strapped Dragonclaw to my side. I collected the spear, bow and arrows I had stashed away in the rafters. Ulf and Anlaf arrived in full armour. Anlaf brought the light, lime-wood shield I had used for sword practice. I saw riders set off to muster the Jarl's supporters from around the Lade peninsula. The King and Jarl Sigurd were on the move, surrounded by their housekarls and with their banners fluttering in the breeze. I cannot deny that, as we set off towards the harbour, I felt a surge of excitement.

I counted nine sails. The wind was in their favour. White foam sparkled where the keels cut into the waves. The sails were taut and full and in the prows open-mouthed dragons snarled. We followed the King's banner down towards the piers and the trading settlement of Nidaros. The Jarl and his hird were on the beach further around the bay. Two of his warships were pulled up there and warriors were already struggling to drag them off the sand and into the shallow water.

King Hakon's ships were in the fiord. There were three of them and these were launched to meet the attack. Seven old knorrs were tied together to form a barrier across the mouth of the river and protect the piers and storehouses of the town itself. But there were further piers outside of this barrier and that's where we headed for. The King's housekarls stood ready to form a shieldwall around him. I could see some of them popping the dried mushrooms in their mouths chewing and spitting. One or two were beginning to foam about the lips. Despite Hakon's strict Christian rule over his household, I heard as many invocations of Odin and Thor as of Christ, and I reached inside my tunic and pulled out my own Thor's hammer amulet. This was no time to put doubt in the minds of the Æsirs. I needed their protection and had to show that I kept their faith.

Men and some of the women from the trading settlement positioned themselves among the houses lining the harbour. Some were armed with bows and arrows others with clubs, sickles, hay-forks, anything that could be used as a weapon. I remembered the advice of the old warrior at Brunanburh and let my hair hang loose over my shoulders. It drew attention to me and all round I heard broken whispers.

'Sigrid … Sigrid   Kveldulfsdaughter … king's niece … Brunanburh … shieldmaiden …' Olvir's and Thorfinn's stories were coming back to haunt me. For the sake of my love and our sons I must live up to those stories. I mouthed a silent appeal to Thor and Odin for courage.

The ships came close enough for us to see some of the banners at the top of their masts. They sailed under colours I thought I had seen at Brunanburh but not recognised.

Around me, people strained their eyes while speculating and cursing.

'Is that Harald's banner? Can you see if it's that piss-head Harald Gormson! I have unfinished business with him.' A grey-bearded man in full armour tested his bowstring.

'No, I wager this is Eirik's doing,' answered a warrior and rammed his helmet down on his wild mass of red hair.

'The witch Gunnhild, more likely,' said another scratching his half-shaved chin.

'Ha, the Danish fart-bags don't need her, they're quite stupid enough to think this up for themselves,' a youngster drawled. His trembling hands gave the lie to his casual tone.

I said nothing but thought the banners looked more like those of the warriors from the Orkney and Shetland Isles. I made sure Dragonclaw slid easy in her fleece-lined sheath, planted my spear in the ground next to me and lined up my arrows.

The first of the King's ships steered straight for the largest of the attacking dragonships. The oarsmen pulled hard and we heard their chants across the water: 'Odin, Odin.' They crashed into the enemy ship and the air filled with the noise of splintering timbers, wild warrior shouts and the terrifying screams from the first wounded. The second of the Nidaros ships placed itself broadside to try and block the approaching enemy. If one of the others had got to her earlier they could have stopped several of the attackers but these were under sail and could not manoeuvre round them very quickly. Three dragons sailed past them and made for the harbour, another two were forced to fight and the remaining three headed for the Jarl's forces on the beach below Lade.

A score of small rowing boats set off from Nidaros. On board, archers crouched behind a row of shields. Braziers were lit and rags soaked in tar were wrapped round arrows, set alight and fired. The sail of the front ship caught fire, the sheep-fat, used to make it waterproof, helped the flames spread and rise to the top of the mast. The remaining two ships had lowered their sails and put the oars out. Chanting our battle-cry and banging our swords against our shields we awaited the onslaught. Ulf and Anlaf stood on either side of me. Ulf, as the elder, stood to my left. I saw him trembling and beads of sweat made their way down his tense face. Anlaf, on my right hand, turned and threw up on the ground behind him.

'Take it steady,' I said, remembering how I was sick before the battle of Brunanburh. The dragons drew closer. I picked up my bow and selected the first arrow.

Despite warnings to save their arrows until they could pick their targets on board, Ulf, Anlaf and many others began shooting before they were within range.

288

Their arrows dropped harmless, wasted, into the water. The first ship reduced the number of oars. Oarsmen turned archers and the air sang to the tune of twanging bowstrings and the swishing of arrows flying in all directions. We had the advantage of firm ground but even so their arrows began to hit home. An old man next to Anlaf fell with blood gushing from a neck-wound. A woman came out from the shelter of the houses and tried to staunch the blood with a rag. I moved across and picked up his arrows.

'What's his name?' I asked the woman.

'Olaf.'

'Tell him Sigrid Kveldulfsdaughter will send his arrows to seek his revenge.'

The first ship closed in on the piers. Warriors lined the sides, waving their axes and swords, shouting and chanting, banging their weapons against their shields. Then the noise changed as spears and throwing axes were hurled. I waited behind my shield till I was sure of my aim and a warrior in a silver-crested helmet fell with my spear through his chest. They took heavy losses because the water was too deep for them to wade ashore and it took time to manoeuvre the ship up to the pier. In the crush some fell or were pushed overboard and, weighted down by their heavy armour, sank without any other trace than a few bubbles bursting on the surface of the water. One young warrior, eager and impatient tried to leap too soon. He slipped and fell. His battle-cry was silenced when his chest was crushed between the ship and the pier. His shipmates landed on the sturdy planks and formed a shieldwall. Dead and injured were trampled or kicked aside. The line of men behind their shields moved towards the shore. The defenders waited, ready to fight them before they could set foot on land.

The first enemy warriors were strong, battle-scarred berserkers with foaming mouths and staring eyes. They hewed around them with heavy, two-handed axes in great, wide strokes. The planks of the pier were slippery, painted with blood and the water beneath turned red. They seemed invincible and cut a path through the ranks of our warriors. The rest of the crew followed and fought their way step by blood-soaked step onto the shore. I saw that what had looked like an impossible task was about to succeed, simply because the defenders got in the way of each other. I stepped back. Ulf and Anlaf followed me with questioning expressions. I led them back from the road and towards the row of houses. I picked up as many axes, spears and arrows as I could carry and motioned to them to do the same.

We climbed on to the turf-covered roof of one of the houses. We threw the short-handled, solid axes and they did their duty, splitting helmets and skulls, breaking arms and slashing through leather jerkins to draw blood. When we ran out of axes we sent death through spears and arrows. In this manner, we picked off many of the rearguard of the attacking hoard. They had no way of retaliating, their spears and axes thrown already and now returning to them.

The other two ships drew up to piers further along the harbour. We slid back down from the roof and ran to join the men meeting the fresh crews. Again they were led by groups of ferocious berserkers and our losses were great. My shield took a blow from an axe so hard the blade stuck to the wood. When the warrior drew back I was pulled along. Anlaf lunged at him and gave a

290

wild shout as his sword slashed through the warrior's wrist severing his hand, still clutching the axe. He finished by skewering the man through the stomach, like a herring being threaded onto a stick for drying. He removed the axe from my shield and was fumbling to secure it in his belt when I pushed him aside to parry a sword-cut from a stocky, bearded Viking. Dragonclaw sang out in triumph and the man dropped to his knees.

'Watch out, Anlaf. We're not finished yet. Leave the plunder till later.'

The King's hird had formed a shieldwall between the piers and the mouth of the river and now the horn sounded for the rest of us to join them. We retreated step by step, seeking what shelter we could behind the row of storehouses and workshops. I thought bitterly that again I was on the losing side in a battle. I looked at my uncle, safe surrounded by his housekarls. His helmet was inlaid with gold and sparkled in the sunlight. The same helmet he had worn the day he ordered the killing of my father. There came over me a blind hatred so strong that all I wanted was to spill Hakon's blood in revenge. I moved out from the shelter of the buildings screaming my fury and, with Dragonclaw slicing anything and anyone in my way, I moved towards the King.

25.

What would have happened if I had got to the
shieldwall? Did I really think I would be able to get
through the double line of the strongest warriors in the
realm and kill the King? I was brought back to reality
when Ulf cried out in pain and went down first on his
knees then sideways on to the ground. I shouted at
Anlaf to shield Ulf. Then I faced his enemy. He was a
youngster like Ulf himself. In my state of single-minded
bloodlust I cut his throat before he had time to lift his
sword. Then everything changed. The first line of the
shieldwall broke off and advanced through our
diminished ranks towards the invaders. As they passed
us I had time to look at Ulf. A sword had cut through his
leather jerkin. I couldn't see how deep the wound was
but we dragged him out of the way and left him sitting
propped up against a wall.

The housekarls had set to work and the invaders
were on the run, with nowhere to run to. Their ships in
the harbour had been set on fire by the returning rowing
boats. Out on the fiord, Hakon's ships had sent two
enemy dragons running and were returning to make sure
there were no survivors from the ship they had rammed.
The one with its sail on fire had managed to avoid them
and rowed back out to sea. The attackers knew that
Hakon would give no quarter. They tried to run to the
Lade beach where all three of their ships had managed

to land and their comrades were a great deal more successful. Some escaped by slipping in among the houses or dropping into the water and hiding under the piers. A few got to their allies on the beach. Most were sent on their way to Odin's great gathering at Valhalla.

Jarl Sigurd and his hird were having a difficult time. They were mighty warriors but three crews were more than enough to match them in number and the confusion when they had tried to launch the Jarl's ships had led to many falling prey to enemy swords and axes. We could hear the roar of their warrior chant: 'Odin, Odin'. It was clear they needed support quickly. The rest of Hakon's housekarls came up behind me. They were moving apace and I stepped aside to let them pass. As they drew level Hakon turned towards me. Our eyes met. I remembered then the choice I had made to forego vengeance and seek a pardon for my father. I bowed my head in greeting and supplication. Then I nodded to Anlaf and together we followed the king.

The Jarl's men gave a huge roar when they saw reinforcements were on the way. Some of the attackers lost heart and tried to get back on their ships. One dragonship was put to oars but was intercepted by the King's returning fleet. The attack had failed and while many of the berserkers fought to the end, others chose to run. The ones who ran towards the hill behind Lade met with the men from the farms on that side and although many died, some were spared and became thralls to the farmers who had lost men in the attack. Only a few got away – but the ones who did caused such sorrow to me I still hurt at the memory.

* * *

Anlaf had taken a spear in his thigh and was helped to

return to the farm. He was elated and would not stop blabbering about his exploits. He had done well. Thorfinn would be proud. I left him before the excitement gave way to pain. I didn't think he would want me to see him then.

The battle-fury leaked out of me as I walked back towards Nidaros. I was glad I hadn't reached the King. It would have meant death to me, not him. Revenge, maybe it would come one day but the Norns, who weave the stories of all our futures, had decided that now was not the time. I became aware of the ache in the shoulder of my shield-arm. My head also hurt. I vaguely remembered a blow to my forehead. I decided to wait before removing my helmet. Surviving attackers would have dropped their painted shields and it would be difficult to tell enemy from friend. The sun sat low in the sky but it would stay light for some time yet. The track to Nidaros was full of men and women. Some were returning home, some looking for their missing husbands and sons, many were looting.

I found Ulf where we had left him. His hands clutched his sword, his eyes were closed. I thought he was asleep and spoke softly to him. He didn't wake up. I saw the blood-soaked grass around him and with a stab at my chest I realised I must tell his mother of his death. He fought well. He died with his sword in his hand. This night a Valkyrie would come on a winged horse and bring him across the rainbow bridge to Valhalla. His father would accept that and be proud but how could I tell his mother?

I shouted at a couple of women who were about to come to blows over a thick, gold neck-chain from a dead warrior.

'There's more than enough loot here for both of you,' I said. They stopped and looked at me with hostile expressions. 'I need help to carry the dead warrior to the farm at Lade. I will pay.'

'There will be many funeral pyres here tomorrow,' said one of them. 'There's no need to move him.'

'He was my karl, he saved my life and I owe him a proper funeral ale.'

They looked at each other and spoke together. Then one of them came forward and looked closely at me.

'Not many women fighting in the battle,' she said, 'not in full armour. You are the shieldmaiden from Cumbria aren't you? We heard about you. Word has it you fight like an eagle defending its nest.'

The other woman nodded. 'We are grateful you helped defend our town. You must be tired. Would you break bread with us? Would you take a drink?'

I realised my tongue was sticking to the roof of my mouth. I couldn't eat the proffered bread but drank greedily of the ale. All round us the injured moaned and cried for help and mercy while women wailed their laments for the fallen. When I had drunk, one of the women brought a horse and they helped me lash Ulf's lifeless body across its back. It was a heavy walk back to Lade and I was plagued by thoughts about how mothers bear their sons, as I had done, only to lose them in battle. Then I felt foolish when I recognised that my mother could equally have lost her daughter. She had known that and sent me off with her blessing. Ulf's mother would have done the same. Her grief would be heavy but she would be comforted to know her son died a hero.

I led the horse past the dead, the injured, the looters

and the searchers. There can be no time more sorrowful than the aftermath of a battle. Later we would celebrate with a great feast but now the weariness of pain and loss lay like a thick cloud over victors and vanquished alike.

* * *

At Lade, King Hakon and Jarl Sigurd were seated in the yard receiving reports of how the fighting had gone, who was dead, who was injured and who was still alive. Servants and thralls had begun preparing a feast. Women, children and old people returned from their hiding places. There was much talk of the three ships that had escaped. One of them had a badly burnt sail and would need to find anchorage so the crew could repair it. At least one had flown the banner of an Orkney chieftain. Many worried that they would join together and mount another attack. One of the King's ships' masters would raise a fresh crew and mount a search the next morning.

The Jarl's reeve saw me arrive and spoke to the King. He gestured to me to approach. I left Ulf's body in the care of the servants. Hakon looked at me. It was a very different look from the one that so angered me when we first met almost a year ago.

'Greetings, niece, I am glad to find you alive. I have seen with my own eyes that the tales of your courage were not exaggerated. Had you been a man, I would have offered you a place at my table to fill one of the gaps left by my fallen housekarls. Tomorrow we shall speak of how I can reward you. Until then,' he rose and handed me an armlet of heavy, twisted gold. I didn't hesitate. I accepted the arm-ring and put it on. I was now tied to King Hakon, I owed him allegiance but that worked both ways. Becklund would be the weregeld he owed for my father's life and a pardon the admission of the wrong he did. I felt at peace with the choice I had made.

I looked in vain for my family but was told their hideaway was in the rugged terrain up in the hills above Lade and they would not have had the news of our victory yet. I found Anlaf and held him while he sobbed his grief for his friend. He helped me lay the body on a bier. We collected wood and lit a mighty fire under it. We drank funeral ale and took it in turns to praise the gallant young warrior, who would now be on his way to Valhalla.

'We shall meet him there, shall we not, Sigrid?' Anlaf was pale and red-eyed but calm now.

'Yes, you fought well, both of you, and we shall all drink together in Odin's great hall.'

We sat there all night until the last embers turned to ash and Ulf was gone.

* * *

I took Anlaf to my mother's house for her servants to look after. There was still no word from her or Toki although the rest of her household had returned one by one. Too tired to get changed, I lay down on my mother's bed and fell into deep, dreamless sleep. I was woken by one of the women.

'Sigrid Kveldulfsdaughter, Jarl Sigurd sends word asking for your mother. What shall I say? The sun is sinking in the sky and there's no sign of her or the children.'

I sat up and, heedless of my dirty, bloodstained clothing, got up to speak to the Jarl's messenger. He led me to the hall where King Hakon and the Jarl sat in conference. Neither commented on my appearance. It did not differ from that of most of their retinue. The Jarl looked pale and tired. The King was like me, dirty and dishevelled. He nodded to me.

'My sister and the Jarl's wife have not returned. I believe your children are with them, are they not?' I nodded, too overcome to say anything. 'We sent some men to search for them. They returned with the news that the hideaway in the forest is empty. It showed signs of a struggle. This was left behind.'

I couldn't hold back a cry of anguish. In the King's hand nestled one of Kveldulf's little wooden animals.

The following day groups of men rode out in different directions to search for those missing. I asked to join them but the King refused. I spent my time pacing the perimeter of the farm until he summoned me.

'Niece, it saps the courage of others to see you give in to your worry. The sauna stands ready. Your mother's household is at your service. People need to see you in command here as well as on the battlefield. Go and dress as behoves a royal niece.'

I noticed then he had changed into a splendid robe of red velvet with gold braid and on his combed blond hair sat the royal diadem. I was pleased to be addressed as 'niece' but embarrassed to have let myself down and apologised to him. He should not have to remind me of the necessity to act with dignity. My mother had shown me that all through my childhood. I knew I must follow her example. Her servants looked relieved when I ordered fresh clothes and asked one of the women to comb my hair.

Towards the evening I was summoned to join Hakon and Jarl Sigurd in the great hall. A lookout had brought the news that a small number of people were approaching on foot. They were some of the Jarl's household who had taken refuge in the hideout. My mother and my children were not among them. Also missing were Toki and Jarl Sigurd's young wife. They had been taken hostage by a group of about fifteen warriors and we were told to expect a messenger from them the next day. I tried to think what my mother would have done in this situation. In my memory she had always remained calm which had reassured the household. I tried to do the same. I supervised the preparation of our evening meal and sat in my mother's seat while we ate. The only thing I didn't do was to lead them in Christian prayer. I no longer felt it necessary to keep up the pretence.

The messenger from the hostage-takers was spotted by one of the guards. The King sent for me. I was brought into the Jarl's private room. He and the King were seated at a table and a stool was brought for me. A rising tide of voices from the hall announced the arrival of the messenger. The heavy drapery separating the Jarl's room from the main hall was pulled aside. Toki entered supported by one of the housekarls. He limped badly, his tunic was bloodstained and his cloak torn. When he struggled to kneel in front of the King, he was offered a seat. He shook his head and instead knelt with downcast eyes.

'My Lords, I have failed you. Your families are at the mercy of the chieftain formerly known as Jarl Olaf and his brother Helgi. I have been sent to tell you their demands.'

The Jarl went up to him and helped him to his feet.

'Your wounds speak for you. There is no shame in your defeat.'

'Who are they?' asked the King. 'The ships carried the banners of some minor chieftains from the Orkneys. Are they with the treacherous marauder holding the hostages?'

'No, none that I know – some of their men perhaps.'

I had fought to stay quiet but now the question uppermost in my mind broke out.

'My children, my mother, are they hurt?'

Toki shook his head.

'No, they are unharmed. All the hostages are unharmed,' he added with a look at the Jarl, who nodded.

The King glanced at me and I sat back and managed to remain silent for the rest of the talk. The chieftains wanted parley. The Jarl would speak to them but King Hakon was furious with the one called Olaf. He had once sworn allegiance to Hakon but, after an armed rebellion, had fled the country.

'We must find them and kill them. I don't parley with traitors.'

I had heard him say those words once before. He said it to my father before he beheaded him. I closed my eyes, gritted my teeth and reminded myself how I had decided to restore my father's honour.

'Impossible,' said the Jarl. 'They know the country too well. They will have gone into the mountains, they will keep on the move and they will have lookouts. It's better they all leave. If they escape into the Upplands they can cause mischief among the chieftains there. If they join up with the crews that escaped after the battle, we can expect another attack. Better they go to the other side of the sea. And we must think of the safety of the hostages. I want my wife back.'

They argued some more but the Jarl was determined and, when he offered to pay the ransom himself, the King gave in. Toki went to take the reply to the hostage-takers and horses to enable them to travel to the meeting place. I decided I had to find a way to accompany the King to the parley.

26.

The parley took place the next day. I waited on my horse by the gates. Hakon looked displeased but couldn't, in front of everyone, send me away after all the praise yesterday.

'Remember, niece, you are a witness not party to these talks.' I nodded and followed him and Jarl Sigurd as they rode out onto the plains before Lade.

Rain hung like curtains from the sky and I got soaked while we sat on our horses waiting for the hostage-takers. At the appointed time, three horsemen emerged out of the mists. They stopped while still out of range of bows and arrows. King Hakon and Jarl Sigurd rode to meet them. I followed but took care to stay behind the two lords. The Jarl opened the talks.

'So you've had enough of fighting warriors, Olaf. You're scared of men and prefer to fight women and children. Will that bring you the praise and reputation you crave? The world will laugh when they hear that the cowardly piece of dog-shit called Olaf Biornson runs from the battle to fight with old women and babes in arms?'

I tensed in my saddle and almost cried out. How could he say such things? At such an insult, surely the chieftain would either draw a concealed weapon and attack the Jarl or ride away and send us the severed heads of his hostages. But he gave a loud, braying laugh and stayed sitting on his horse, rain dripping from his wet clothes.

Then Hakon spoke. 'Olaf Biornson, oath-breaker and traitor, trying to buy your miserable life with the lives of women and children. Return your captives or be cursed by the Lord God and his son Jesus Christ for all eternity'

The chieftain bent forward and spat on the ground.

'That's what I think of your god, Hakon Haraldson, usurper and traitor to the Old Religion. And as for the toothless old mongrel at your side, tell him I shall enjoy his woman tonight. She is already looking forward to the feel of a real man.'

The Jarl retaliated with a sneer. 'We shall catch up with you and your mangy crew long before that and, by the time we're finished with you, my dogs will be feasting on your entrails and your heads will be set on spikes for the crows to peck.'

It was the other chieftain's turn.

'You two old women couldn't catch a crippled crone. We're armed and ready. We'll make you eat your own turds!'

The trading of insults and threats seemed to go on and on. I felt impatient at this time-wasting but despite being drenched by the persistent rain, neither side showed any sign of urgency.

Finally something changed.

'Your wife is worth something to you then, Sigurd?' The comment was so casual in the middle of the abuse, I almost missed it. The Jarl ignored it. Olaf continued,

'She's worth a lot to me. My manhood stirs when I think about her soft body.'

Jarl Sigurd had to clear his throat and Hakon took

over with a stream of threats. The hostage-takers turned their horses round and began to slowly ride away. I couldn't hold back a cry. This earned me a sharp look from Hakon. Olaf and his companion turned back.

'For a free passage and three chests of gold, I might decide to return her to you.' Hakon replied with derisive laughter. This marked the beginning of the real negotiations.

Several times one party or the other turned their horses and threatened to ride away. Then at last, the ransom was decided. The hostage-takers would get free passage, a knorr to take them across the sea and a quantity of gold. The gold was the main stumbling block. Hakon had none to spare for traitors but the Jarl was both able and willing to pay as Olaf Biornson must have known. He settled for a chest full of gold, one third coins and the rest ornaments and jewellery. They decided to meet the next day on the beach below Lade. The knorr would be there but no other vessels, the gold would be handed over, the chieftain and his men would leave and the hostages would be free. When that had been made clear, the men dismounted and for the first time, got within reach of each other. They spat in the palms of their hands and shook on the deal.

'How do you know they won't kill the hostages or take them away?' I asked the Jarl as we rode back to the farm.

'Oh no, I have known Olaf Biornson since we were both young. He is a man of honour. He won't break his word.'

* * *

The rain continued through the day and into the night. I performed my duties as head of household and tried not

304

to think of my mother and children, wet and frightened, and all the things that could go wrong with the release of the hostages. We were finishing the evening meal when there was a knock on the door. A serving woman went to open.

'Olvir!! Oh, my dear little boy. Where have you been all this time? We've been so worried about you.' She fussed and exclaimed while bringing a soaked and exhausted Olvir up to the fire. I leaped out of my seat and embraced the wet, dishevelled little figure. He was out of breath and shaking with cold. I refused to let him talk until he had been dried off and given hot gruel to eat. He insisted he must talk to the King.

'Olvir, you'll never be admitted to the King. Even I am not allowed to just go and talk to him any time I want.'

'But his life is in danger. I must see him and tell him.' He looked flushed. I wondered if he had a fever.

'Tell me first and we'll decide what to do.'

'When they hand over the gold tomorrow, some of the men will run over and kill the King.'

'How do you know that?'

'I heard them.'

'Who? Odin's beard, Olvir! What have you been up to?'

'I saw the people run from the attack and I followed them. Kveldulf and the baby were there. I wanted to help. But then I saw Toki so I didn't go to them I just followed at a distance. Then the men came and took your mother and Kveldulf and the baby and some others and I stayed hidden and followed them too and today when the chieftain came back he told them all they would get lots of gold for the hostages and then I saw some of the men nodding to each other and they went away like if they were going for a piss and I heard them talk and they hate the King and they want to kill him and they're going to.'

I thought for a moment. Olvir did have a knack of creeping up on people and listening in. But he was very young and didn't always understand what he heard.

'Who were the men?'

'I don't know. How am I supposed to know that? Sigrid, you must believe me! If I don't tell the King, he'll die and it'll be your fault.' He cried and a deep cough rattled in his thin chest. I put another shawl around him and together we went to seek the King.

We were stopped at the entrance to the hall. I explained to the burly housekarls and, after a delay, we were admitted. The King and the Jarl sat together close to the fire. They didn't believe us. Jarl Sigurd had heard from Toki about Olvir's lies about the trader and now he was outraged by Olvir's slander of yet another man of high standing.

'But it isn't the chieftain himself. He doesn't even know.' Olvir trembled in his frustration at not being believed. The Jarl looked furious.

'Olaf's men will all be under oath to him. There is no threat. The hostages will be freed.'

I wondered how much of the Jarl's conviction was made up of his desperate wish to see his wife again. I turned to the King.

'Forgive me, uncle. I would feel easier in my mind if you would at least have your housekarls around you.'

'No!' interrupted Jarl Sigurd. 'It would be the end of the exchange. We must show that we trust Olaf and personally I have no reason to take the word of this urchin over his.' With that we were dismissed.

Olvir cried so hard I had to give him some mead before he was in a fit state to listen to me.

'We need Ragnar to help us with this. You must tell me where he is.'

He shook his head. 'They've gone west, the other side of Nid. It's another five days before I meet them again. I don't know where they are.'

It was up to me. There was no one else. I must not despair. I thought for a while. Maybe there was a way to thwart the assassins' plot.

'I must act on my own and rely on Odin and Thor to help me.'

'And me!' Olvir, pale and exhausted but always at my side.

'Yes, be alert and ready to get Kveldulf and Harald to safety if anything happens.' There was nothing else he or anyone could do. I was alone in this.

* * *

The next morning Hakon ordered the beach to be cleared of people and a small knorr was pulled as close to the shore as it would go. A chest was carried down and left in the sand under the guard of Jarl Sigurd's most trusted housekarls. It was not long after midday when the horn sounded for the arrival of the hostages and their abductors. The people of Lade were kept well away by King Hakon's housekarls and stood in silent rows watching the event. The hostages had been on horseback but were now helped to dismount. Double lines of Olaf's warriors walked, swords drawn, on each side of Toki, the two women and my two children. The Jarl's wife was in front with one of the abductors holding a knife to her throat. Behind her my mother carried Harald and Kveldulf walked between her and Toki holding on to their hands. Having seen that they were unhurt I looked away before any emotion could cloud my judgement. I had to keep calm and concentrate on the task ahead. I concentrated on the hostage-takers and tried to read their intent on their faces.

The hostage-takers lined up on the beach, close to the water's edge, fidgeting and adjusting their weapons. The hostages stood in front of them and the chieftain Olaf Biornson and his brother in front of them. The Lade housekarls stayed out of range. The silence was broken only by the screams of the gulls and the waves breaking on the sand. I felt sweat trickling down my back and my stomach was in a hard knot as I went to stand next to the Jarl and Hakon. They took no notice of me. They stepped forward, cloaks thrown back to show they were unarmed, and faced the two leaders of the hostage-takers. I went with them, stiff with anticipation. Hakon looked at me then. His eyebrows met over the bridge of his nose and his chin tightened but he didn't send me away. Olaf Biornson opened the lid of the chest and I saw the glow of gold as he lifted pieces aside to be able to see the coins at the bottom. The splendid jewellery, drinking horns, bowls and coins caused a murmur of anticipation among the hostage-takers. I fixed my gaze at the men and tried to figure out who would make a move on the King. I managed not to look at my children but I could not shut out the sound of Kveldulf's voice as he called out.

'Look, there's Mummy! Mummy, Mummy!'

I heard my mother shush him. The eager little voice tugged at me and I had an overwhelming urge to rush over to him and cover his dear little face with kisses.

My hands shook, my eyes watered and my vision began to blur. I shook my head and blinked away my tears. The chieftain and his brother lifted the chest and staggered with it down to the water. They loaded it onto a small rowing boat and took it out to the knorr. Their men followed wading through the shallow water towards the boat. When the two men with the chest passed them, the hostages began to walk towards us. In this general movement three men turned from the water and rushed for the King.

One came from the left. Toki saw him, stepped in front of him and threw his arms around him. He took the man's knife in his chest and they fell together. Hakon's men were with them in an instant.

The other two came from the right. I ran in front of Hakon and drew the short sword I had concealed under my pinafore. The two assailants were distracted and called out warnings to each other. The one in front pointed his dagger at me but my sword pierced his belly and he fell writhing to the ground. The other changed direction and ran away from us with great lumbering strides. I pulled out the other weapon I had managed to secret under my clothes, a small, sharp throwing axe. I raised it and took aim.

'Don't kill him! Sigrid, don't kill him!'

It was my mother. Her cry startled me and my aim failed. Instead of landing, sharp edge first, between his shoulder-blades the axe glanced off the side of his head. He staggered and lost pace. Two housekarls caught up with him and cut him down. They dumped his twitching body at the King's feet.

The rest of the hostage-takers had the oars out and were escaping. The air filled with noise, screams and curses. Olaf Biornson stood in the stern of the knorr cupping his hands round his mouth to make himself heard.

'None of my doing!' he shouted. 'Not my men!'

* * *

All that was no longer of any concern to me. Shaking with relief, I ran to embrace my children. I took Harald from my mother's arms and knelt next to Kveldulf, holding both my sons close. I kissed their soft, round cheeks and told them again and again how much I'd missed them. Through Kveldulf's excited chatter, Harald's crying and my own sobs I heard my mother quietly keening. It took some moments before I realised and got up to look at her. She stood with her eyes fixed on the dead assassin. Her voice was barely audible as she intoned the lamentation for the dead.

'Mother?'

But she was unable to speak. Olvir arrived and took Harald and Kveldulf from my arms. I rose and grabbed my mother by her shoulders. I didn't want to but I had to know. I heard my own voice, shrill and trembling.

'Mother, who is that man? The man who tried to kill Hakon. Who is he?'

She looked at me with dead eyes and whispered, 'Be quiet … your brother.'

I turned to run across to where Steinar was breathing his last. My mother threw her arms around me from behind and held me close.

'Don't move,' she hissed into my ear. 'Think of your children! Whatever you do, stay away from him.'

That brought me to my senses. I clung to her. I buried my face in her shoulder and the material of her dress muffled my agonised scream.

'I killed him!'

'You didn't know. It's not your doing.'

'Yes it is. It is. I killed my brother.'

'The housekarls killed him.'

'Oh, Steinar!'

'Shh, Sigrid, be quiet, be quiet! The king must not know who he was. He must not find out. The children, think of the children.' I knew she was right and I clenched my teeth to stifle my crying. 'Sigrid, we shall grieve later.'

We held each other in a trembling embrace. My mother kept repeating, 'The children, the children ...' and it helped to steady us, so, when Hakon came towards us, we were able to greet him. He seemed to think our tears were those of joy and relief at our reunion. I never knew how much he noticed or understood. Maybe he knew it was Steinar but he never let on and so we never had to answer for my brother's attempt on his life.

Toki died from his wound and was given a hero's funeral. My brother Steinar's head was cut off and displayed on a stake next to those of the other two would-be assassins. Their bodies were thrown to the dogs.

Part Six:

Vengeance of the Gods

27.

A ship was launched to follow and capture the other hostage-takers. It took too long to get going and the men returned and confessed they had lost sight of the knorr. The King was in bad humour with the Jarl, who kept to his belief that the assassins had acted without the knowledge of Olaf Biornson. The Jarl seemed not to care about anything else than the joy of having his wife safe with him again. He laid on a great feast to celebrate the victory over the attackers, the return of the hostages and the foiling of the conspiracy to kill the King. All I wanted was to be with my children, to grieve for my brother and try to come to terms with what had happened to him and the part I had played in that. But my mother and I were both required to attend the feast. With death in our hearts we dressed in our best clothes, coiled our hair and straightened our shoulders.

We greeted King Hakon and Jarl Sigurd where they sat at the head table on the dais. The Jarl's wife sat by his side and next to her sat one of the Jarl's younger brothers. Next to the King were two empty seats and when we rose from our curtseys he beckoned us forward and placed us there with me next to him in the place of honour. The hall was silent and I felt all eyes on me. My hands shook and my legs were so weak I had to be helped up on to the dais. Hakon spoke in a loud voice for all to hear.

'Niece, you have earned my trust and my gratitude these last few days. I shall have to think of a suitable reward for you.'

It felt like the chair and the dais disappeared from under me and I floated on thin air. Becklund and a pardon for Ragnar – they were there for the asking. But now the moment was here, I couldn't find the words. My lips wouldn't move, my tongue stuck to the roof of my mouth. I tried to swallow and find my voice. Hakon's eyes were on me. I had to speak.

'I … ahh, I …'

My mother tugged at my dress.

'It's honour enough to be here,' she hissed.

I'm sure Hakon heard but he didn't move a muscle in his handsome face. I saw the cold strength of the man and the ruthlessness of the King in those features.

'Sire, it is honour enough to be here and to be allowed to serve you.'

He bowed his head in recognition.

'We shall consider and return to the question later. Now tell me, niece,' he sat back as a wench served me with meat and wine, 'about the battle of Brunanburh.'

* * *

Back in my mother's house we argued about what I should request from Hakon.

'Ask for Becklund but no more,' said my mother. 'Don't overreach yourself or you'll end up with nothing. Don't even think about a pardon for your father so soon after Steinar tried to avenge him. And as for the son of that Jarl Swein …'

'I saved his life! He owes me more than a farm.'

'Hakon is King and will decide for himself how to reward you. He may prefer to give you land here in

Norway. It would keep the land in the family and still show him as generous and fair.'

'Land, here in Norway! But I …'

'There are worse places, Sigrid. You and the children will be very far away from me if you return to Cumbria. I may never see you again.'

'But Becklund, Mother, Becklund! How can you bear to be away from there?'

'You forget I grew up here. My last memory of Becklund still haunts me.'

'But you'd come back there with me, wouldn't you?'

'My darling girl,' she laughed and shook her head. 'There's only room for one mistress at Becklund. Here I have my own household and, if the Good Lord so wishes, I shall have a community of believers to look after too. And besides, it really wouldn't suit me to live at Becklund with you in charge. Don't look at me like that. I know you did very well here in my absence and you have run your own household too. I don't doubt your ability but I am no Aisgerd, there's no use pretending I would sit quietly while you ruled.'

What she said made sense but it meant I had found her, only to be separated from her again. And yet I felt such a longing for Becklund. I had spent my whole carefree, happy childhood there and I wanted that for my children. Norway was beautiful but it was not my home.

'I shall ask for Becklund and a pardon for Ragnar.'

'No, leave the pardon. When dealing with kings and chieftains it is better to ask for too little than too much. Make it easy for Hakon. Land is easy; it doesn't involve honour.'

* * *

315

When night fell and all went quiet I could no longer keep the thought of Steinar away. When I closed my eyes I saw his head on the stake, his eyes being pecked at by carrion birds and his mouth open in an agonised howl. Afraid of sleep I got up and wrapped a shawl around my shoulders. The fire had been banked up for the night but I stirred it to life and got some warmth. Resting my feet on the hearth I sat with my elbows on my knees and looked into the glowing embers searching for some answers to the senseless death of my brother. What could I have done differently?

A movement in the dark hall made me look up. My mother sat down beside me and put her arm round my shoulder. She knew my thoughts.

'It was not you who killed him. They would have caught him sooner or later and they would have given him a slow, painful death. Remember, it was his choice. The Lord knows I tried to talk him out of it but in the end I couldn't stop him and he did what he thought he had to do.'

'He stayed true. He followed the path of honour.'

'Oh, honour – where did it get him – and your father for that matter? No, you did the right thing and your children will thank you.'

'Down in the harbour, when there was fighting, I turned on Hakon. I was going to …'

My mother put her hand over my mouth.

'Sigrid! Shhh, don't say it. In the end you served your king. You saved his life. That's all that matters.'

'But I betrayed my father.'

'No, you found a different way to serve his memory. Hakon will never pay weregeld. A king does not admit to a wrong killing. He must always be seen to be right.

316

But if he gives you Becklund it would be the same as both pardon and weregeld without Hakon having to say it. That's justice enough and you have to be content. People will understand. They will know you restored your father's honour.'

'And Steinar?'

'There was nothing you could have done to change his fate.'

I nodded, thinking I had understood her.

'No, we can't change the destiny the Norns have woven for us.'

'Oh, Sigrid, that's wrong. It's not what I meant. The Bible teaches that the Good Lord gave us all a free will. We make our own decisions. Steinar chose his destiny. I grieve but I have to accept and so do you. I pray for his soul. I ask Christ, the merciful, to take pity on the poor, misguided man who was my son. I shall pay the priest to hold masses and say prayers to speed Steinar's soul through purgatory. He had the mind of a child and Jesus said to let the children come unto him. Thanks to you, he does not have blood on his hands and I'm sure the Lord will know that and take it into account.'

My mother's belief didn't help me. Steinar had remained true to the Old Religion and he fulfilled his duty. Later, I thought about him arriving in Odin's great hall. Nobody had considered him a warrior before. My father would, at last, be proud of what his son had tried to achieve. That was some comfort to me but didn't absolve me from my part in my brother's death. I didn't sleep that night. My mother said her prayers over and over. I envied her certainty and her belief in forgiveness. I was far from convinced that my gods would be so merciful and I knew I had a debt to pay.

* * *

The next day there was a steady stream of people entering the court. Farmers and local chieftains came to show their loyalty to Hakon, to account for loot and thralls they had taken and to listen to the stories of the battle, already exaggerated and glorified. I was surprised to hear that I had single-handedly fought off ten berserkers before they even had time to step off the ship. Would this have been when I stood with Ulf and Anlaf on the roof throwing axes and spears at them? Or was it when I followed in the wake of Hakon's hird chasing the attackers towards the beach? I learned much about the forging of poems and songs that day and I never looked at a hero in quite the same way again.

Anlaf revelled in the attention he got as my karl. With Toki dead and not yet replaced Anlaf was accepted into my mother's household. The women fussed and fawned over him and he made the most of his injured leg. Odin only knows what lies he told about his courage and mine. Olvir, too, had stories and information about the battle and he wasn't even there when it happened.

An unwelcome effect of all this praise was the attention paid to me by some local chieftains. Did they see me as a warrior queen ready for bedding or a strong woman who could run their farms or simply as Hakon's niece and a way into the royal household? I began to worry. A king's memory can be as long or as short as it suits him. How long would Hakon's gratitude last? How long before I was a part of his political games?

The talk was not all about victory and glory. Three ships had escaped, albeit one with its sail in flames. Fishermen reported seeing two warships on the open sea heading west. But the damaged dragon-ship had vanished with its crew. And then there was Olaf Biornson. Was he gathering a fresh crew, waiting to attack from a different direction? Was he heading north towards allies in the Upplands? Every day the Jarl's and the King's ships set off to guard the entrance to the fiord and at night warriors in full armour stood guard over the ships in the harbour and on the beaches all round the Lade peninsula.

Four days after the hostages return we were still celebrating and chieftains and jarls were still arriving to share in the feasting and pledge their loyalty. In the constant coming and going, I wondered how the housekarls were able to tell friend from foe but someone in the King's household always knew who everyone was. I was tired of attention and took as many opportunities as I could to spend time with my children. We paddled in the Ladebeck and chased butterflies in the meadows. We borrowed a small rowing boat and went fishing in the fiord. I took care not to go close to, or even look towards, the small island where my brother's head sat with those of the other traitors on a line of stakes, displayed for all approaching ships to see. It was hard enough to hear the shrieks of the gulls and know what they were fighting over. When gripped by dark moods I held on to the thought that my children were safe and that returning to Cumbria was no longer an impossible dream. Anything else I pushed aside like a difficult task to be dealt with later.

* * *

It was during one of our little fishing-expeditions that Kveldulf called out from his seat in the prow.

'Who's that? There! It looks like Father and Tofin.

And more men.' I followed the direction of his finger and then I saw as well; four men on foot followed by two on horseback. It looked like Ragnar and Thorfinn. It had to be them. Fear emptied my lungs of air. My heart leaped to my throat. They would be killed! I must get to the guards before they got to Ragnar. Anlaf and I took an oar each and brought us to the beach in a few strong strokes. I left the children with Anlaf and ran sobbing with fear. I saw the housekarls set out with bared swords. I tried to call out to them but I was too far away. As the housekarls closed in, Ragnar and Thorfinn dismounted, removed their helmets and sheathed their swords. The housekarls surrounded them, swords and axes glinted in the sun. I screamed but, like in a nightmare, no one heard. The housekarls kicked the four men on foot and they fell clumsily to their knees. I could no longer see Ragnar and Thorfinn.

People came running from all directions. King Hakon and Jarl Sigurd stood by the entrance to the hall. I arrived, stumbling and out of breath and was jostled by men and women eager to find out what was happening. I pushed my way forward until I could see. They were there, unharmed but closely guarded. But why were they giving themselves up?

Ragnar and Thorfinn removed two bundles from their horses. They were led between two columns of housekarls who had to beat their way through the excited crowd. They stopped at a respectful distance from the waiting King and Jarl. Still flanked by the housekarls, Ragnar and Thorfinn knelt and gave their names in confident, proud voices. Neither King nor Jarl showed any emotion or gave any response. Ragnar and Thorfinn put down their sacks and emptied the contents on the ground. Golden drinking horns, neck-rings and bejewelled belts mingled with coins in the dust. A murmur of excitement and appreciation spread through the assembled crowd. Then the captives were relieved of their blood-soaked burdens. When these were untied, six heads, bloody, hideous and gaping, stared up at the King.

The crowd cheered. The King stayed silent. The noise died down and everybody looked at him. I couldn't see how he had a choice. Even knowing who Ragnar and Thorfinn were, even knowing how they had mocked his housekarls by sneaking into my mother's house to see the newborn Harald, he must accept their homage because in front of him, with his hands tied on his back, knelt Olaf Biornson and next to him rested the severed head of his brother Helgi. But still Hakon stayed silent. I held my breath. The yard was so still I heard the cooing from the dovecote behind the byre and the humming from the hives in the meadow. Jarl Sigurd whispered to Hakon. He gestured at the housekarls and Ragnar and Thorfinn got their swords back. Ragnar held up Bearkiller and Thorfinn Iceflame. With stony face and reluctant hand, Hakon touched the proffered swords, accepting their homage.

That evening I sat again with Hakon and Jarl Sigurd at their table on the dais. Ragnar and Thorfinn had places close to the top of one of the trestle-tables running the length of the hall and I was able to look and smile at my love and our friend. I don't imagine he'd been invited but Olvir sat between Ragnar and Thorfinn, and the servants didn't shoo him away. Jarl Sigurd asked to hear how just two of them had overpowered the whole of Olaf Biornson's crew. Thorfinn gave his

321

account with one of the appalling *drapas* he was wont to compose. There was no stopping him. He stood on the bench to declare. Ragnar looked at Olvir and they shook their heads and laughed. Drinking horn in hand, Thorfinn spoke:

* * *

'Hiding from the hand of Hakon
Warriors willing to prove their worth
Waiting to win the favour
Of high-born Hakon the Good

Ship stranded with smoking sail
Looking for loot from Lade
Vile Vikings pouring their venom
On faithful followers of Finehair's son.'

* * *

Ragnar pulled a face and tugged at Thorfinn's breeches until he toppled backwards off the bench.

'Friend,' he said, 'I think the Jarl just wants to know what happened.'

Everyone in the hall, king, jarl, guests and household laughed. I suggested that maybe Thorfinn could take his time to compose his *drapa* while Ragnar told of their adventure.

'We were hid ... ah ... hunting in a spot two day's riding away to the west.' Ragnar's embarrassed grin gave him away but the King let it pass. 'We spotted a fleet heading for the Trondheimsfiord, so we set off to see what help we could render. Other dragons came from the harbour and we saw some fierce fighting. Two of the ships turned. They were under sail and heading

322

west at speed. The others sailed on towards Nidaros. The next day we came across another ship. It was beached in a small inlet and the sail was spread out in the sand. The crew were trying to repair it where it was damaged by fire. We stayed hidden waiting for an opportunity to attack. Men went in small groups hunting for game and collecting fresh water. We sent those to Odin's hall. The others grew suspicious when their comrades failed to return and stayed by the ship. They had lookouts during the night but one or two of them fell asleep and didn't wake up again.'

Ragnar paused to drink from the horn he shared with Thorfinn and the hall filled with noisy approval. He wiped his unkempt whiskers and continued, 'A couple of days passed then a small knorr joined them. At first they all seemed pleased to see each other but it soon went sour. We couldn't hear what the disagreement was about but weapons were drawn. Then the sail from the knorr was hoisted on the dragon and the crew made ready to leave. None of the men from the knorr joined the dragon. When the ship was out of sight they dragged a large chest from the knorr, emptied the treasure it contained into sacks and began walking inland. We followed. At nightfall they set up camp. By morning there were only four left. You know better than I who they are and what they have done.'

It all sounded a bit too easy for me but the King, the Jarl and all others in the hall seemed happy. Ragnar smiled enjoying the praise heaped on him. I wondered what the King would do. There was a clear expectation for him to honour and reward Ragnar and Thorfinn.

'You are an outlaw,' he said and the hall fell into horrified silence. I half rose to get to Ragnar's side. My

323

mother pulled me back. Hakon waited a moment before he resumed. 'You were made so by my father after a treacherous act committed by your father against him. Your actions here have been brave and have put me in your debt. You shall no longer live outside the law and under threat to your life but there is no place for you in my service. It would be better if you left Norway.'

Ragnar blanched when Hakon first spoke but, as he grasped that he was pardoned, he smiled and rose from his seat.

'I am grateful to stand again a free man. I am sorry you have no use for my service but it is your land and I must do as you bid me.' He drew a deep breath as if he was gathering pace for a run up before jumping a hurdle. 'Lord, I have a request.'

I saw his knuckles white against the tanned skin on his fists. My mother sat next to me, tense and alert. The King radiated displeasure. He was on the spot. It would be difficult to refuse the new hero. The hall was silent as a grave and even the smoke from the hearth seemed to hang still in the air, waiting to hear the King's reply before dispersing. I clasped my hands to stop them shaking. What would he ask? How dared he risk the displeasure of the King? I couldn't look at Hakon but I heard him, gruff and curt.

'Speak it.'

Ragnar bent his knee. He spoke clearly but his voice trembled with emotion.

'I have no use of riches or even land. All I want is the woman sitting next to you for my wife.'

'The audacity!' my mother said under her breath but I thought I heard a note of admiration in her voice.

The rest of the people in the hall cheered and

clapped, especially the women and I'm sure I saw several of the maids dry their eyes on their aprons. The King looked at me. Over his shoulder I saw the Jarl's wife nod and smile.

'Please, Uncle,' I managed to whisper. Hakon nodded. He looked relieved.

'Then so be it. I shall tell the priest to celebrate mass for you and to hear your vows.'

* * *

A Christian wedding was not what I'd had in mind but the King made it quite clear it was that or nothing. Ragnar rode off with Thorfinn to unearth the silver he had buried for safe keeping and my mother and uncle each accepted their share of the bride-geld. My mother gave most of her share back to me for my dowry.

'I don't need it,' she said, 'and I want to know you'll have the means to look after yourself and the children.'

'But you have accepted the bride-geld, haven't you? Please say you accept Ragnar as my husband.'

She did not answer and she had no smile for me when she helped me put on my best clothes and dress my hair with meadow-flowers for the marriage ceremony. Then she spotted my Thor's hammer amulet.

'You cannot enter the house of God wearing that!'

'It won't show. I'll wear it under my dress.'

'No. Just this once, please do as I say. I'm not asking you to throw it away.' I submitted and she removed it from round my neck. She turned it over in her hands. 'Where did you get it from?'

'Father.'

Her eyes filled with tears and her hands shook. I took the amulet from her.

'We should be friends on this day, Mother.' She

nodded.

'Let me put it somewhere safe for you.'

'No.' I went to the door and called Olvir. 'I want you to look after this for me until after the ceremony. You'd better wear it under your tunic. I'll get a ribbon.'

'No need. It can hang next to mine.'

'What? Do you have a hammer amulet of your own?'

He nodded and pulled a small amulet worked in silver from under his shirt.

'I was going to show it to you but so many things have happened. Ragnar gave it to me.' He blushed and grinned. 'He said I'm his son and never mind the "foster".'

'Ragnar said that?'

'Yes, when I told him about Harald. He was so pleased, you see.'

He looked so proud and happy I had to hug him.

* * *

I rode a white horse with leaves and flowers on its bridle. In front walked two pipers playing a joyful tune. Around me walked my children, my mother and all the women of Lade. Even the Jarl's wife did me the honour of accompanying my bridal train. They all sang as we came down the slope to Nidaros. A simple wooden building served as a church until Hakon's plans for something grander could be put into being. Hakon met us by the gate. We entered and my eyes watered against the smoke from the incense. The strong smell, after the fresh air outside, made me feel nauseous and I hoped against hope that the ceremony would be brief. Hakon led me between rows of guests up to the large table where Ragnar and the priest waited, their faces set in scowls of mutual dislike. Hakon placed my hand in Ragnar's and stepped aside. We stood hand in hand and looked at each other.

Ragnar winked and said in a low voice, 'So here we are at last, my little shieldmaiden. I see they took your weapons off you, as well. Odin knows how we are supposed to defend ourselves against this ferocious priest.' I bit my lip to stem my laughter. The priest cleared his throat and glared at us but all through the ceremony we kept looking at each other and giggling behind our hands. The priest said prayers for us and we exchanged vows. That is to say, Ragnar had to take an oath for himself whereas Hakon spoke for me. I've always maintained that means I'm not bound by some of the more extravagant promises he made on my behalf.

Then the priest and his two helpers sang some of their tuneless, morose chants which seem to last for ever. Behind us the guests were made to kneel and get up several times. I could hear some of them grumbling under their breath. Then, at last, the drawn-out mass was over.

Ragnar heaved a sigh of relief and, under the guise of a kiss, whispered to me. 'By Frigga's hair when we get back home we shall celebrate such a bride-ale as people will remember for generations to come.' Then he gathered me in his arms and carried me through the throng of well-wishers out through the door towards the meadow where our horses stood ready saddled.

'But the feast!' I cried. 'We can't just leave!'

I struggled to get down and the housekarls, led by Thorfinn, called out bawdy remarks involving rutting stags and reluctant does. Ragnar laughed and swung me over his shoulder, every inch the warrior claiming his prize. And who was I to object? He was, after all, my hero and always had been.

28.

In accordance with Hakon's wish, we prepared to return to Northumbria. I pointed out to Hakon we had no place of our own to return to.

'Your parents' farm, wherever it was, what about that?'

I choked on a wave of anger. He looked genuinely puzzled, as if he had never been there, never burnt it, never killed my father. I am proud of the way I managed to control my emotions and, without going into detail about his part in it all, I explained how I had lost Becklund.

'It is a fair place, Uncle. There's a beck with sweet water, a lake with pike, trout and other fish, the grazing is good and deer roam the woods. Nothing would make me happier than to see my children grow up there.'

He looked over to where Olvir and Kveldulf threw sticks for Striker to fetch. Then he looked at Harald sitting on my hip. He stretched out a finger to tickle the baby's cheek. Please don't cry now, I thought. Harald was of an age when he disliked strangers but, thank Odin, he smiled and blew bubbles at Hakon.

'You shall have your farm. You have earned it.' He nodded and turned to walk away and I was left wondering if I had heard him right. Was that all there was to it? But how would I persuade the Lawmen at the next Allthing that Hakon had promised me Becklund?

They would hardly take my word for it. Should I call after him? He'd perhaps be annoyed. Ask to see him later, alone and put my request to him.

Then, as if he felt my anxious thoughts, he said carelessly, over his shoulder, as if it were of no great consequence. 'I'll get my scribe to prepare a writ with a pardon for you father so you can inherit the land he possessed.' Behind his retreating back I sank to my knees and hugged Harald till he squealed. This was more than I had dared hope for. My father's name cleared, by me. I had done it! The whole purpose of my journey to Norway, the dangers, the worry, all of it justified with that one sentence: a pardon for my father.

* * *

Before Olvir had gone to hide with Old Kirsten, my mother and I had been talking about telling him who his father was. She still wanted to tell him but I hesitated. The Norns had woven him a cruel fate. He had revealed the plans to kill the King. He had betrayed his father and caused his death. Not knowing who it was he betrayed did not change that.

I knew Mother made her confession to the priest regularly and I was not surprised when she brought up the issue.

'Is Olvir baptised?'

'No.' I suppressed the 'nor shall he be' that tried to follow.

'It would help him accept his situation if he had the comfort of a priest and the forgiveness of Our Lord. You do wrong to deny him absolution. What if he should die with this on his conscience?'

'There's nothing on his conscience. He didn't know who Steinar was and he didn't know it was Steinar. You

330

haven't told him, have you?'

She shook her head. 'But he has a right to know.'

'No, he's too young to be burdened with such guilt, Mother. Please let's wait till he's older.'

'He should be told so he can pay his penance. He will be able to confess to the priest here and be absolved.' Her answer seemed glib to me and provoked a fury I couldn't control.

My voice was heavy with scorn as I replied, 'Oh yes, I forgot, that's how you Christians do it. You perform a bad act, confess, give some silver to the priest, say a few of your prayers and then you're clean and can start all over again.'

'Sigrid, the blasphemy! No this is too much! Your heathen slander. I thought you had turned to the true faith but as soon as that Ragnar returns you revert to your false gods.'

'Leave Ragnar out of it! I make my own decisions. I wore the cross to impress Hakon not because I had joined your faith.'

'Sigrid! That is weak and manipulative and deceitful and …'

I heard no more. I threw down my weaving batten and left the house. We didn't speak for two whole days after our argument. It grieved me. I loved my mother. I had come to admire her strength and value her advice. But she had persisted in her dislike for my husband. Nothing he did was good enough. Kveldulf loved him and revelled in his attention. Harald gurgled with pleasure when Ragnar picked him up. Olvir roared with laughter at his jokes and blushed with pride when Ragnar praised his efforts with the sword. But to my mother he was the son of Swein Hjaltebrand, the man

331

who had brought death and disgrace to our family at Becklund.

* * *

It was some weeks later that, among the ships and knorrs that came and went in the harbour, one arrived from Jorvik. It was laden with goods for sale and gifts for the King. It also brought seven passengers. Six were missionaries to help Hakon spread Christianity in Norway. The seventh came to call on me one day at my mother's house. I didn't know him at first. I only had a brief glimpse of his shaven head and heavy jowls when he opened the gates to the King's tower in Jorvik to me and Ansgar. When I recognised Archbishop Wulfstan of Jorvik, my confusion was complete.

'Your Grace!' If uncertain, my father used to say, bend your knee. It gives you time to gather your thoughts. So, to my mother's delight, that was what I did. But I didn't kiss the proffered ring. He still made the sign of the cross over me.

'Brother Ansgar was most insistent I should see you and bring his greetings in person. It seems you two have a habit of getting each other out of tight situations.' He smiled a tired smile that never reached his eyes. He turned to my mother who kissed his ring with an enthusiasm that more than made up for my refusal.

'It is an honour to receive you, Your Grace.' She invited the Archbishop to sit in the high seat and we perched on stools next to him. The servants were sent to fetch wine and raid our stores for such luxuries we reserved for our most important occasions: almonds; dried fruit; and bread sweetened with honey. The Archbishop emptied his goblet in one go and relaxed in his seat. Olvir and Kveldulf stood at a respectful distance, round-eyed and silent, until the Archbishop waved them to him.

'Ansgar is my friend too,' said Olvir.

'And mine,' nodded Kveldulf. 'He used to sing songs with no tune and let me ride on his shoulders.'

The Archbishop tilted his head back and his booming laughter filled the house.

'Yes, I gather he got up to all sorts of things and, I agree, his voice is terrible.' Mother placed a hand on each neck and pushed the boys onto their knees. Wulfstan made the sign of the cross and blessed them. Then he gave them a handful of sweets and waved them away. Kveldulf ran outside to boast to his friends about the important visitor with gold braid on his fur-lined cloak. Olvir crouched next to my seat and I let him stay.

We enquired about the voyage and about events in England. Æthelstan had died and been succeeded by Edmund, the young prince who had goaded me when I was a prisoner after the Battle of Brunanburh. The arrival of a young inexperienced king had stirred the Northumbrians to send my uncle Eirik Bloodaxe away and again turn to a Norse King of Dublin for leadership. I was worried about this.

'Will it mean more fighting? Will Cumbria be affected?' The Archbishop shrugged.

'The fighting will go on until the English accept that we have our own laws. The Norse will never subject willingly to English rule.' My mother was not interested in the defence of the Danelaw, as the Archbishop called it.

'My brother King Hakon will be sad to learn that his foster-father has gone to join the angels.'

'Yes, it's never easy to bring such news. But I have

333

also brought missionaries to help convert the heathens of this country. Your brother speaks highly of you, Gudrun Haraldsdaughter. I understand your desire is to establish a religious community here at Nidaros.'

'I feel my calling is to serve God in any way He sees fit.'

'Your brother has offered to set you up in a suitable house and I shall personally instruct you and bless this undertaking before I leave.'

I couldn't help feeling pleased for my mother when I saw her face light up and her eyes fill with tears.

* * *

Archbishop Wulfstan did not intend to stay long. He planned to return in only eight days' time. Ragnar and I decided to travel with him. I assumed we would use the knorr Wulfstan had arrived on but Hakon had other plans. He equipped a dragon-ship for the Archbishop's journey. He put Ragnar in charge of it and entrusted him with Wulfstan's safety until he reached Jorvik. The ship was to be Ragnar's reward. It was generous. Hakon made sure nobody could say he'd been less than grateful to Ragnar for capturing his enemies.

It was a beautiful vessel: forty oars; a sail in green and brown stripes. The sleek clinker-built hull spoke of swift travel and the shallow draught would carry us up rivers and close to shore.

'What shall I name her?'

'It's yours, Ragnar. You must decide.'

'I thought *Storm-Wolf* and I'll put a wolf's head in the prow.'

'Why a wolf?'

'A thanks to the Norwegian wolves that spared us last winter when we camped out.' So it was agreed and

Ragnar carved a splendid wolf's head with pointed ears, sharp teeth and a tongue of fire.

That night I dreamt about Becklund, a dream so vivid I could smell the sweet air blowing down from the fells, feel the soft, rich grass under my feet and see the sunlight play on the rippling waves of Loweswater. I walked along the shore up to the small knoll where the stone for my father was clearly visible from anywhere on the lake. In the ribbon encircling the face of the tall granite-slab, the runes read:

"Gudrun Haraldsdaughter raised this stone for her husband Kveldulf Arnvidson of Becklund, brave sword, faithful friend, honourable man."

I held up King Hakon's writ to the stone as if my father were there, as if he could hear me when I read out the pardon that meant he was an outlaw no more, and I was his rightful heir and owner of Becklund. I turned from the lake-shore to the farm. My father's hall lay in smouldering ruins as it did the day King Hakon and his men burnt and plundered it. But, beyond the blackened rafters and tumbledown walls, a new building rose before my eyes. I stood back and admired the solid stone foundations and the heavy wooden door. A woman as tall as a tree with broad shoulders and strong arms came walking across the meadow. Her long yellow hair blew around her face and she wore many arm-rings. She held a sword in one hand and a weaving batten in the other. She went up to the hall and entered. I tried to follow but she closed the door and shut me out. I woke up with the dream vivid in my mind. Why had my father's fylgia turned away from me?

* * *

There was little to pack but we had horses to sell and

provisions to buy. Kveldulf became inconsolable when told that his pony must be left behind. Ragnar promised him another one when we got home but the boy cried for days. Hakon gave us ten thralls to help man the oars, the Archbishop paid his fare in silver and we had no difficulty recruiting men among the bored warriors and adventurous youths of Nidaros. It was obvious that they expected Ragnar to go raiding, once he had delivered the Archbishop to Jorvik. Some days it felt to me like the place teemed with impatient and excited men waiting for the wind to change so they could start their adventure. It was not what I had in mind but I couldn't ignore Ragnar's delight in his ship and I knew I would not be able to hold him back forever.

I don't know what made my mother change her view of Ragnar. Maybe the time she spent with the Archbishop, preparing for her religious community, softened her and brought a more forgiving turn to her thoughts.

'Sigrid,' she said one day, as we worked together at our looms, 'I have been thinking that perhaps, if Ragnar were another man's son I might have liked him. He loves you truly, I can see that. He is good with the children and kind to my servants. Maybe I shall be able to approve your marriage with my heart when I have got used to thinking of him as a man in his own right.'

It was a grudging admission but it would have to do. I would not get anything better at that time. I hugged her feeling a little tearful at the thought of our impending separation.

'Mother, I shall try to live so you can feel proud of me.'

She smiled.

'You will live your life as your conscience tells you. I am proud of you. I may not agree with everything you do but I *am* proud of you. Never doubt it, my daughter.' She was silent for a while. Then she put down her batten. 'There's one more thing. I want to say goodbye to Olvir as my grandson the same as Kveldulf and Harald.'

'Is it not enough that he is my foster-son?'

'No, it's not the same.'

'If I let you tell him, will you promise not to involve the priest?' She hesitated but I stood firm. 'I don't want the priest talking to Olvir when he's upset.'

She nodded. I noticed her hands were shaking.

'I shall do it now. Send him to me. Then wait outside.'

* * *

Olvir came out of the door like an arrow off a bowstring. I was ready for him and caught him. He struggled and we tottered and stumbled around on the uneven ground but I held on to him.

'Let me go! Let me go!'

'No never. You are my son and I'll never let you go.'

'Foster-son, foster-son, fost ...'

'Forget that. You have earned your place with me as mine and Ragnar's son. Do you hear? You're mine and Ragnar's.'

'No, I killed my father. I killed ...'

His voice rose to a scream, broke to a sob and stopped. I held him tight and, step by step, I led him over to the bench next to the house. I sat him on my lap. He didn't resist. His eyes closed, he wailed against my shoulder, a most desolate sound.

We sat there for a long while. People passed us,

looked and walked on when I shook my head. There was nothing anyone could do to help my poor Olvir. Ragnar returned from hunting. He sat down and put his arm around both of us.

'What ails my eldest son?'

'I'm nobody's son.'

Ragnar looked at me. 'I thought you weren't going to tell him.'

'His grandmother insisted.'

His eyebrows met over the bridge of his nose and his eyes turned black. He sat with his head bowed for a moment then he said, through gritted teeth, 'I suppose it is her right.' He got up and took Olvir out of my numb arms. 'We shall seek healing at Odin's temple. Come.'

* * *

It was just the three of us. I left a message for Mother with Anlaf. Then we rode across the fields and meadows into the pine forest and along the track we had followed when we first arrived at Lade. Ragnar held Olvir in front of him on his large stallion, Raven. I followed on Thorfinn's horse and led a small mare by her bridle. It was almost two full moons since the summer solstice. The evening closed in and here among the trees it was getting dark.

'Had we better stop for the night?' I asked, but Ragnar shook his head.

'For this to work we must be there for sunrise. Don't worry about the horses. They know this path. We came here often when we were hiding out.'

Even the light of a crescent moon would have helped but it was overcast and not until we arrived at the clearing did it become light enough to see. Ragnar left me holding Olvir and set to building a fire in a small circle of rocks already black from earlier camps.

'We stayed here several times,' he said. 'Sit here. You can lean against this stone. How's my son? Is he asleep?'

Olvir lay slack-limbed on my lap. His eyes were open and stared with an empty pain no child should have to bear. I didn't dare let go of him. I sat with my back against one of the carved stones lining the path to the temple. Ragnar lay down next to us. He stayed silent but throughout the night he kept the fire going. I began to speak of my brother to Olvir and maybe I was speaking to myself as well. Since Steinar's head had been set on a stake on traitors' island, I had shut away all thought and all feeling about him. But here, in the holy grove with the flames of the fire dancing shadows around me, I felt the presence of my brother.

I spoke of our childhood at Becklund, our games and our quarrels. I spoke of the day our father was killed and we both failed to avenge him. I spoke of his son Olvir, his courage and steadfastness, how he had stayed with me at Brunanburh, stood by me when I was without friends and helped me save the King's life. I talked and cried and the night passed.

'Steinar, I know you are feasting with our father and his warriors in Valhalla. I know the ancient law says you took the honourable path. I chose to live and make a future for our children, your son and mine. Maybe I was wrong. Oh, my brother, if I had known it was you! I mourn you and I crave your forgiveness.'

A gust of wind made the treetops sing and the first ray from the sun fell on my face. It felt like a soothing caress. Olvir opened his eyes. He sat up and looked at the trees above him. He raised his arms towards the

339

swaying branches.

'Can you hear him, Sigrid? Listen, he whispers with the wind. He's forgiven us.'

* * *

Olvir fell asleep. We made him comfortable and sat down a short distance away.

'It's not the end of it though, is it, Ragnar?'

He was silent for a long while before he put his arm around me and answered.

'Your brother was not a vengeful man. He chose his path and you chose yours. He will have forgiven you – Olvir heard it and I think he was right.'

'Yes, I don't believe Steinar wants retribution. But the gods? It's their commandments I have violated.'

'I honestly don't know, Sigrid.' The thoughts and worries I had tried to ignore must be acknowledged. I could keep it to myself no longer.

'Can we sail the North Sea in this state?'

'I brought three horses.'

'Yes, I realise. But can we do it on our own? A horse? They're not like sheep and cattle. They know what the stone is for. They fight and struggle.'

'Raven.'

'Ragnar, you can't sacrifice Raven! Your own horse!'

'For this, I shall. Come, there's no point in delaying this.' He got up and helped me to my feet. Then he fetched Raven. The beautiful creature followed him with complete trust into the temple and up to the offer-stone. I collected the embers from our fire and in front of Odin's likeness I burnt wild sage and juniper. I breathed in the powerful aroma and intoned the sacred chant to attract the attention of the mighty. Raven trembled. Ragnar spoke quietly to him and stroked his muzzle. They stood together Ragnar and the faithful horse that had carried him safely away and shared his time as a fugitive. Ragnar made the horse bend its front legs, like he was kneeling in front of the altar. Then with a movement so swift I never saw the beginning of it, Ragnar lifted his axe. One blow of the mill-sharpened blade severed Raven's head from his body. It fell sideways. The legs thrashed and kicked. Blood spurted from the neck. I used my apron to soak it up and daub the mighty pillars and carved likenesses. Ragnar stood with lowered head next to Raven's body. His trews were soaked in blood and his lips moved silently.

It was time to open the animal and read the intestines. I put more herbs on the fire and stood in the smoke swaying and chanting until I felt my mind opening up. It was more powerful than I had ever experienced before. I tried to say the sacred words but my tongue swelled in my mouth and I struggled to move my lips. Odin's single eye fixed on me and grew and grew until it was all I could see. I was alone in a mist with the staring, all-seeing eye. I fumbled for my knife. It seemed to tremble and wriggle in my hand. I called on Odin to aid my sight. I put the point between Raven's front legs and pressed until it pierced the hide. Then I slit the stomach open. Entrails spilled out on the stone floor like a clutch of writhing snakes. The sickly smell of undigested grass and dung filled my nostrils. I reached inside the carcass for the liver. I held it up to the image of the god. It felt heavy. Blood drained from it down my arms. Then I saw that it was a vile thing I offered to the god. It was swollen and pitted and dark green in colour. It gave off a foul stench. My whole

341

body was seized with trembling. I wanted to shout to the god and beseech him not to reject my offering. But my voice made strange sounds, words without meaning. The god bore down on me. He picked me up and carried me high, through the roof and into a thick cloud.

* * *

'Sigrid! Sigrid! Wake up.' Ragnar's voice. Why was he calling me? I wanted to sleep. Now he shook me as well. Why couldn't he let me sleep? I opened my eyes. I was lying on the ground with the cloudless sky above me and the clean grass under my body. I turned away and was sick on the ground. Olvir, his eyes large and frightened handed me a leather flask with water. I rinsed my mouth. Then I swallowed a mouthful and, realising how thirsty I was, I emptied the whole skin. Ragnar sent Olvir to collect more water before he turned to me.

'What happened to you in there? Was it the smoke? It was heavy, I felt quite dizzy myself.'

'The liver was spoilt, Ragnar. You sacrificed Raven in vain. The gods will not forgive me.'

'No, no, I saw the liver. There was nothing wrong with it. You had a bad turn from the smoke. The gods accepted the gift.' I shook my head but he had got up and entered the temple. When he returned he carried the roasted liver on a stick.

'Here, look at it. There's nothing wrong with it. We shall share it to honour the gods.' He handed a piece each to Olvir and me. I looked at it. It seemed perfectly healthy. Ragnar and Olvir bit off mouthfuls and chewed. I cut off a small piece and put it in my mouth. I had no time to chew or swallow. I was immediately sick. Ragnar blamed it on the potent herbs I had breathed in and would hear no other. I tried to join in his and

342

Olvir's joyous relief. But, while I was comforted to know that Odin had accepted a sacrifice from Ragnar and looked on him with favour, I couldn't rid myself of the memory of what I had seen. I knew the gods demanded another sacrifice from me and would exact it when it suited them.

29.

'Oars out,' called Ragnar and the rowers on the harbour-side pushed *Storm-Wolf* away from the pier and out into the Nidaros harbour. The crew cheered and the crowd who had come to see us off joined in. I looked around for Kveldulf. He stood in the stern, next to Ragnar, legs planted firmly apart, thumbs hooked into his belt, every inch of his four-year-old frame showing him for the warrior he was destined to be.

Storm-Wolf moved out of the harbour leaving the piers and the walkway with the houses and workshops behind. In the distance the mountains loomed half-veiled in the drizzle. I waved to my mother until she was but a small figure among the others. Then I went to sit with Archbishop Wulfstan. He nodded and made room for me next to him by the mast. I sat on a chest, a last gift to me from my uncle Hakon. He had made a big show of filling it with precious gifts: a silk gown; golden candlesticks; silver coins; and a large silver cross with the god Jesus hanging on it. I determined to sell that last item at the first opportunity.

Next to me, Olvir was still waving. He too received precious gifts from both the Jarl and the King – at least we thought the box of silver coins, the suit of clothes and the fur-lined cloak must be from those two. I reassured Olvir that, as the gifts were anonymous, there was no need to thank anyone.

'But why don't they say?'

'So you won't have a reason to say, I told you so, about the nithings who planned to kill the king.'

'And they should apologise. They weren't very nice to me then.' It offended the child's sense of fairness and I had to explain that kings and jarls never apologise, as their positions mean they must never be seen to be in the wrong.

'Everybody's wrong sometime,' he muttered.

I sent him to join Kveldulf and Ragnar in the prow.

'Make sure Kveldulf is safe and not in the way,' I said but the real reason was to distract him. I caught Ragnar's eye over the heads of the crew. He saw Olvir clambering towards him and nodded. I kept my eyes on the Lade-peninsula to my right in order to avoid looking at the island we had to pass on our way out of the fiord. All I wanted was to leave it behind. Thorfinn steered a course as far out from it as possible. I mustn't dwell on what the island held. I looked at the men in front of me, pulling at their oars, some with smiles, some with frowns and some with dreamy expressions. They began humming to the rhythm Thorfinn set and the ship gained pace.

I could look away. I could shut my eyes. But the sky filled with the tortuous screams of savage, scavenging birds and that sound would not be shut out. They shrieked like demons of death and laughed like callous creatures from Helheim.

'No, don't look that way!' I heard Ragnar shout. I saw him covering Olvir's eyes. Olvir screamed and struggled. Ragnar pressed the boy's face to his shoulder, rocking him slowly from side to side. He talked quietly to Olvir as he held him.

'What ails the lad?' asked the Archbishop. 'I must say his father is very patient with him.' The disapproval in his voice riled me. I blinked away my tears, cleared my throat and answered.

'Olvir is not Ragnar's son, nor mine. His father's head is among the ones you can see on the island over there, stuck on a spear on Traitors' Row. He was my brother, he ...' I tried to say more but my chest contracted, air could not reach my lungs and my voice died. I covered my face to stifle my sobs then I gave in and cried into my pinafore.

'Ah yes, of course,' I heard the Archbishop say to himself.

The crew stopped singing and silence spread across the ship. I wiped my face, straightened my apron and looked at the men in front of me. They all had one hand off the oar to touch their amulets. Some clutched Thor's hammers, some the cross of the Christ – others had both of these and other tokens as well. We had passed the island and they were all now facing it. They may have tried to avert their eyes but the screams of the birds, as they fought over the ragged remains of the traitors' heads, forced their gaze in that direction. We all searched the sky and saw gulls, shiny white or granite grey and the fast flapping skuas. But of the brilliant, black ravens, Odin's messengers, there was no sign to say that the Lord of Law and Wisdom had accepted the King's judgement on my brother.

'Put your backs into it, you vermin off a dog's scabby pelt!' Thorfinn's booming voice made the men grip their oars with both hands. They had lost their rhythm and some of the oars on the starboard side clashed. Thorfinn roared and in a couple of strokes the smooth movement of men pulling their oars in unison was restored. There was no need to move so fast out of the fiord but nobody seemed to mind. It is a sobering thought that, at some time or other, we had all been somebody's enemy and could, if the gods had so willed it, have ended up with our heads on the end of a stake, our eyes and tongues pecked by carrion-birds. All were relieved to leave the sight of Traitors' Island behind.

As the fiord widened and the sea lay endless before us, the rain stopped and a pale sun showed through the wispy clouds. Ragnar ordered the sail to be raised. The spar was lifted off its crutches and the men began the heavy work of pulling it and the sail to the top of the mast. The sail, unwieldy and wet from the earlier drizzle, sprayed those underneath it with a cold shower. The men laughed and swore and pulled harder at the sealskin ropes. The sail hung like a tired sack. Then it gave a small flap, as if testing the wind. Then the green and brown stripes filled out and we were on our way. The oars were pulled on board and stored in the middle of the ship. Men made themselves comfortable, sprawling on the crossbars wrapped in their cloaks with their caps pulled over their eyes to sleep off the drink from last night's feasting. Others brought out hnefatafl boards or dice and looked for opponents willing to accept a challenge.

'Noooo!' I started at the sound of Kveldulf's furious scream. He was trying to wriggle out of the harness Ragnar had fitted him with and tied to the nearest crossbar. 'I'm too big for that! Far, please! Olvir doesn't have one.' Ragnar laughed and tested his son's tether, straightened his tunic and ruffled his hair. He spoke to Olvir who nodded and turned to watch the sea in front.

Ragnar, with frequent stops to exchange a few words with the men, made his way down the ship towards me. He was still grinning and his green eyes held mine.

'I'm afraid Kveldulf has your temper, Sigrid. Like you he will not listen to reason or ... arggh!' He tried to leap aside to avoid my kick. 'And if that doesn't prove my point ...'

'Ragnar!' I felt my face go hot and cast an embarrassed glance at the Archbishop, who rocked with laughter. Ragnar knelt beside me and took my hands.

'We're going home, Sigrid. Our troubles are over. We can start again and all thanks to you and your stubbornness.'

'My what!' But Ragnar's smile, as always, made me smile too. The heavy fetters of sorrow and worry lifted from my body. 'Yes we are, aren't we? At last we are going home, home to Becklund. Oh, Ragnar, hurry *Storm-Wolf*, tell her I cannot wait to see my Cumbria again.' I leant back against the mast, closed my eyes and gulped in the salty air with its promise of a new life. Ragnar squeezed my hands and looked at the Archbishop.

'You will have heard of my wife's brave deeds at Lade, Your Grace.'

'Yes indeed and of yours, Ragnar Nithingsbane.'

'Nithingsbane? Is that what they call me?' I opened my eyes to see Ragnar's cheeks flushed with pride and I had to stop myself hugging him, he looked so much like Kveldulf then.

'Yes, and with reason. You captured the escaped nithings who attacked Lade.'

'And is there a name for my wife as well or have the people of Nidaros forgotten what she did in their hour of need?'

'I believe Sigrid Kveldulfsdaughter is commonly referred to as the Cumbrian Shieldmaiden.' The Archbishop's disapproving little sniff reminded me that a Good Christian Woman does not engage in swordplay. 'You are blessed with two strong healthy sons.'

'Three,' Ragnar corrected. 'My youngest is asleep below the steering-platform.'

'But I thought ...'

'I told His Grace about Olvir's parentage.'

'Sigrid, I may not have sired Olvir but you know he is equal in my affection to Kveldulf and Harald. Your Grace, let me explain. Olvir became my true son one black, moon-free winter night when he dared the wolf packs and the pale fetch of the forest to find me and bring me the tidings of Harald's birth. I tell you, that boy can match any man on this ship in courage – no, he can better us all, for he had neither sword nor shield, only his speed and devotion to Sigrid.'

The Archbishop nodded approval.

'So quite the little warrior then.'

'No, he'll never be a warrior. He was born a thrall and so had no weapons practice until this year. I have worked hard with him and he tries had but it's too late, he lacks killer instinct. There's something else about him, though. He knows letters. He learnt by listening when Sigrid was taught at Lade. And he'll take the last piece of silver from the whole crew here by beating them at hnefatafl. Yes,' he shot me a glance and laughed, 'I have warned him not to do that.'

'Hnefatafl?' The Archbishop's generous eyebrows shot up into the fur trim of his hat. 'You don't say. Well, I shall have to challenge him. It will help pass the time. Can we call him?' A message was relayed from mouth to mouth and reached Olvir who turned from his lookout post to make his way to us. His face was red and swollen from crying. He looked unsteady and nervous moving on the ship which rolled slightly. Most of the men knew him and many put out a steadying hand to help him along.

'I hear you are fond of the noble game, young Olvir.' The Archbishop was already busy setting out the pieces and Olvir's smile widened. Ragnar and I left them to it. He returned to the prow to keep an eye on Kveldulf who was trying to catch the spray whipped up when the prow sawed through the waves. I went to see that my baby Harald and my servant-girl Kirsten were comfortable.

I stayed with them. Harald was trying to walk. Kirsten bounced him on her lap and let him take wobbly little steps on the steering platform but he was restless and wanted to stray further. I could see we were in for a trying time with the energetic toddler on the ship.

Kirsten had approached me about becoming my servant a few days before we were to sail.

'I feel my destiny belongs with you and your children, Sigrid Kveldulfsdaughter. I helped Harald into this world and Olvir became my friend when he stayed with my grandmother and me.'

She was twelve years old with no prospect of a marriage. I liked her direct manner. She was strong and intelligent. Her grandmother had taught her healing so, I decided, she would make a useful addition to the household. I was now grateful for her presence as we held an arm each of the bouncing bundle that was my youngest son.

'Shall you want a daughter next, Sigrid

Kveldulfsdaughter?' She kept her voice low so the helmsman would not hear.

'Ah, well I … I …'

'I think you are, are you not, with child again?'

'But how did you know? I only just began to think so myself?'

She laughed and her light blue eyes gazed at my belly. 'You have looked pale and I heard you retching yesterday morning. I shall be able to deliver your child. The Old One said I'm ready.'

I felt reassured but also reminded of the difficult time when the Valkyries rode the bridge of Bifrost. The girl seemed to understand this for she patted my arm and smiled.

'I'm sure it will be easier this time. The Old One told me it gets easier with each child.'

It was a strange experience being reassured by a girl so young but there was something about Kirsten that belied her years; something in her eyes made me feel I looked at a pool of wisdom gathered by women with special powers over generations since before the time we live in now.

* * *

Thor who rules the wind sped our voyage and gave us good, dry weather. We settled into a peaceful routine. Ragnar taught Olvir and Kveldulf to recognise the different parts of the rigging and their uses. Olvir gained confidence on the ship and on the third day at sea, cheered on by the crew, he made his way from stern to prow leaping from one cross-plank to the next. He spent hours each day playing hnefatafl or just talking with Wulfstan. The Archbishop seemed to enjoy his company and, encouraged by the attention, Olvir was

351

returning to his old, talkative self. At first, I worried that he might annoy the Archbishop with his opinionated chatter but my mind was put at rest when I heard Wulfstan's booming laughter mingle with Olvir's high-pitched giggle. They made an incongruous pair – the ten-year-old, precocious farm-lad and the greying cleric with his rich clothes and warrior bearing.

After four days, we had a lookout posted as we expected to see land very soon. The first signs were gulls and terns gliding on outstretched wings, diving into the green water and sometimes emerging with a silvery fish in their beaks. Then, small patches of seaweed floated past on brown air-filled blisters. That night we rolled ourselves in our blankets and fleeces hoping to see the shoreline of England the next morning.

* * *

I woke in the middle of the night. The rigging whined and groaned. The sail whipped and flapped and made noises like Thor's hammer crashing into the giants' mountain. The men lowered the sail to a third of its size but we still surged forward. Thorfinn, at the helm, had the help of a tall Norwegian but still struggled with the steering-oar. The waves grew so tall that one moment we were lifted high enough to touch the grey clouds and the next we descended into deep valleys surrounded by white crested water-mountains. The wooden hull creaked and shuddered. The waves broke over the sides and water gathered around our feet. My spirits sank as I realised that the gods had neither forgiven nor forgotten my debt. The storm was sent by those whose laws I had broken when I betrayed my brother. I held my Thor's hammer amulet to the wild sky and prayed for mercy if not for me then for my children. I saw Kirsten holding the sleeping Harald in the shelter under the steering platform. Her pale eyes were wide open but she looked calm and unafraid. Kveldulf sat on Olvir's lap by the mast. He thought it was a game and, wild with excitement, cheered when the ship was thrown high on a wave, then he piped a long, shrill note as we slid and crashed into the next trough.

The crew clutched amulets or crosses each according to his preference. Many were sick and their spew mixed with the gathering bilge in the bottom of the ship. The Archbishop was on his knees praying in a loud voice in Latin. In the middle of the ship sat an old, gnarled warrior called Varg the Varangian. He held his Thor's hammer amulet in one hand and a cross in the other as he shouted prayers to Odin, Thor, Niord, Jesus and Jehovah.

Ragnar passed leather buckets and wooden pails and shouted above the roar of the storm that it was time to start bailing. Some were too sick to be of much use, so I took a pail and helped. Next to me, the Archbishop filled and emptied a bucket, his broad back raising and falling in continuous movement. Kveldulf thought this was a new game and used a small wooden bowl to gather the filthy mess. He tried to throw it overboard the way he saw me do but he was, of course, too small and the content of his bowl landed back where it had come from with a fair amount splashing on men, already wet and sick. Olvir, green-faced and trembling, crept to his side and showed him how to tip his bowl into a bucket, which he could then empty over the side of the ship. The child thought this splendid fun. I lashed the pair of them to the mast with a short lead and showed Olvir how to undo the knot with a sharp tug, should the ship break up.

I moved to the stern where I could keep an eye on Harald and Kirsten. I bailed and prayed and listened to the empty retching of the seasick and the fury of the storm. I entered that dreamlike state where the mind watches from a blurred distance as the body labours regardless of pain.

Every seventh wave is larger than the ones before. It was a seventh wave that took the tall Norwegian. He'd been helping Thorfinn keep the rudder steady but, whereas Thorfinn was lashed to the steering-oar, his friend was not and when the vicious wave struck he was washed overboard. Nobody else noticed. I was the only one close enough to hear Thorfinn's frantic call for help. His face was contorted with the effort of holding the rudder steady against the wild water. I crawled across and on to the platform. I pulled myself up and gripped the end of the oar. It tugged and pulled as violent as a wild animal and I braced my body against it to help keep it steady.

'Rope! Tie yourself.' Thorfinn's voice was barely audible in the storm. A length of rope swished like an angry snake from the oar-port. I put it through my belt and tied it. The steering platform was wet and we slipped and struggled. Each time I lost my footing the rope saved me from being washed overboard but my belt tightened like a vice and pushed the breath out of my lungs. The salty water stung my eyes and I kept coughing as I breathed in the heavy spray that soaked every inch of my clothing and every hair on my head. Once, between two waves, I caught a glimpse of Kirsten. She lay half outside the shelter waving her arm.

Her face was white, her eyes wide. She shouted something which was lost in the noise from the storm. I tried to reach her but the rope had swelled and the knot set like iron. The next wave struck. I gripped the oar tighter and groaned with the effort. My feet slipped again and my belt cut into my stomach. I stifled a groan and concentrated on clinging to the steering-oar.

Grey morning-light dawned. The wind and the waves calmed somewhat. *Storm-Wolf* continued to dip and dive but water no longer gushed over the sides. The crew stopped bailing and slumped against whatever support they found. Somebody came up on the platform. An arm held my exhausted, trembling body. In a haze, I heard Ragnar:

'Was she here all night? Were there no men to help? Why didn't you call me?' I didn't hear the reply. My legs gave way. Someone cut the rope from my waist and I slid down on the wet, stinking hull. I clutched my aching belly. Then Kirsten was next to me removing my belt.

'Mistress, you were very foolish. I don't know how ...' The rest of her words floated away in a dark mist.

I woke next to Olvir and Kveldulf. Olvir was awake. He looked at me with hollow eyes. He still clutched the end of the tether in one hand and Kveldulf's harness in the other. I reassured him the storm had passed and helped him loosen his stiff fingers from the leather thongs and untie the knot. Striker came out from under the steering-platform crawling on his belly. Emitting pitiful whines, he licked Kveldulf's face. Kveldulf woke and picked up the dishevelled dog.

'Wasn't that exciting, Striker!'

Olvir closed his eyes and groaned.

The full sail was hoisted but then the wind died altogether and we were left slowly rising and sinking on the swell. The sun hid behind heavy clouds. Thorfinn sat slumped against the side of the ship fast asleep and Ragnar was at the rudder. He had no means of telling where we were. There was no land in sight although it couldn't be far because seaweed and birds appeared again. The crew became more cheerful, discussing which was most urgent: food; water; or a fire to dry themselves out. Olvir and Kveldulf slept for a while then they sat in the prow and had a wager of who would be the first to spot land. Soon they shouted together and pointed to starboard. The clouds were breaking up and the low sun revealed a black shadow on the horizon. Ragnar ordered the oars to be put out. The men were eager and rowed with powerful strokes towards the unknown land.

30

In the dark, nobody saw the blood soaking through my dress and into the sand as I lost my baby. I had been foolish to think about the life growing inside me as a girl. Now, I mourned a daughter, even though Kirsten told me again and again it was too early to tell anything from the bloody mess she cleared up as she washed me and found fresh clothes to dress me in. We nestled in a small depression among the rocks away from prying eyes. Nobody must know that I had been punished by the gods. I was shivering, my whole body covered in a cold sweat.

'You must wipe your tears, Sigrid Kveldulfsdaughter. The men should not see you cry. Come, I need to get you in front of the fire or you'll catch a chill. Women sometimes go down in a fever after what you've been through.' She caught her breath. 'Odin's beard, your poor body is covered in bruises – all round the middle, no wonder …' She continued to mutter to herself while struggling to get me into clothes which were clean but, like everything off the ship, soaking wet. 'Now come here. Let me support you. You can't stay here.'

I trembled and leaned heavily on Kirsten as we walked towards the fire the men had lit in the middle of the beach. Ragnar saw us and came over.

'What kept you?'

Kirsten glared at him and hissed, 'The Mistress is unwell and no wonder, and I don't understand how you could allow …'

'Quiet, Kirsten, you're speaking to my husband.' I staggered and Ragnar caught me and held me steady.

'Sigrid, what is the girl talking about?'

I couldn't answer. I shook my head. My eyes filled with tears again and I bit my lower lip to stop it trembling.

'She lost the child because of having to do the steering all night and …'

She was still speaking when Ragnar turned to me.

'Child! Sigrid, I didn't know. Why do you keep these things from me? How can I protect you if you don't tell me anything?'

Their raised voices attacked my ears. I burst out crying. That silenced both of them. Ragnar held me close and rocked me softly from side to side.

After a while Kirsten said, 'Forgive me, Master, she only just found out herself. Maybe she wasn't sure.' Ragnar dried my tears and Kirsten rubbed my back. 'She's very cold, Master, she should be by the fire.'

Fleeces had been laid out for me, Ragnar and Archbishop Wulfstan. I lay down, grateful for the warmth from the fire and for the flickering light which hid my tear-swollen face.

'Where are the children?'

Ragnar nodded towards a nest of hides and shawls where Olvir and Kveldulf slept surrounded by the crew. The men were all asleep too, except for the handful keeping watch. One other was also awake. Anlaf moved back and forth among his sleeping comrades. He was bent double supporting Harald as he walked on unsteady legs trying to kick sand over the sleeping men.

'See if you can settle Harald, Kirsten. Anlaf must be exhausted.' I watched Kirsten take Harald and sit down next to Olvir and Kveldulf, and I was overcome with love for my children and gratitude for our survival.

I was sore and cold and full of sad thoughts. I didn't expect to be able to sleep. But, many hours later, I was woken by the sun and the noise made by the men as they stretched and cleared their throats, coughing and spitting. I turned over. My body felt covered in bruises, my limbs ached, and my cleft stung and burned. Slowly I sat up and looked around. The sun was rising and the sea and sky merged in a golden glow on the horizon. A slight mist rose from the water's edge and languid waves rolled onto the sand with a soothing murmur. The bay was surrounded by steep cliffs on both sides and a gentle tree-clad slope stretched between them. On the north side of the bay I counted eight ships and a number of smaller vessels moored by three wooden piers or resting in the sand. Smoke rose from behind the trees. Whoever lived here would know that we had arrived.

Ragnar saw that I was awake and brought me fresh water. I managed to smile. We had no time to talk, as the Archbishop came to wish us a good morning.

'I know this land,' he said. 'It's Skarthi's burgh. So we're not too far off course. Jorvik is just two day's ride from here. I could continue by horse. It's as fast, if not faster, than to sail up the Humber and the Ouse. I think you said, Ragnar Sweinson, that you wish to sail for the Irish Sea.'

'Yes, it would suit me to take on water and supplies here and continue north along the coast. But shall you not need an escort? I'm not sure I can spare more than one or two.'

'Oh, I'm sure Ingolf Skarthi will have a few young men kicking their heels and causing trouble. I'll be doing him a favour taking them off his hands for a few days.'

'Who is this Ingolf Skarthi?' I was intrigued by the image of a chieftain with harelip. Usually such children were thought a curse and put out to die.

'He was not born such. His upper lip was slit by a dagger in a fight. His wife sewed it together but it left a mighty scar which gave him the name, a name that carries respect in these parts, I might add.'

I could not let on that I was not fully recovered from my ordeal so I picked up my weapons and joined Ragnar and the Archbishop to pay a visit to Skarthi. We took eighteen men, a number small enough to show peaceful intent but large enough to denote Wulfstan's status. Already of imposing stature, he dressed for the occasion, a large bejewelled cross showed gleaming among the ermine and embroideries of his splendid cloak. He carried his tall crook as behoves an archbishop but under his cloak he wore a mail shirt and his sword was by his side. Ragnar, too, noticed this and raised his eyebrows at me.

Skarthi's burgh was built to withstand attack. Surrounded by a ditch and a palisade on three sides, it nestled at the foot of a forbidding cliff which finished with a steep drop into the sea. The open gate indicated that Skarthi already knew he had nothing to fear from us. Armed housekarls met us and led the way between tightly packed houses to a longhouse built in the Norse fashion with low walls and a tall, steep roof. Smoke seeped out through the openings in the thatch at each end where the ridge finished with two crossed dragons' heads looking in opposite directions keeping watch over the household. Our men were made to wait outside. Ragnar and I were asked to leave our weapons in the wapenhouse before entering the hall. One guard pointed to Wulfstan's sword but faced with the Archbishop's scowl, didn't insist.

Skarthi was a man of importance, judging by his hall. The walls at the top end were covered with woven hangings in brilliant colours showing scenes of hunters and their prey. Skarthi sat leaning against cushions in a seat carved with ravens and wolves' heads, his legs stretched out in front and his hands clasped over the dome of his belly. His large head was dominated by a sprawling moustache so heavy the ends hung below his clean-shaven double chin. He rose hurriedly when he saw us, stepped down from the dais and supported by one of his men bent his knee to Wulfstan.

'Archbishop! I was told to expect visitors but nobody told me such an illustrious traveller had been washed up on my shore.' He kissed the proffered ring and, after the Archbishop had blessed him, Skarthi waved to the servant to help him rise. Panting with the effort, he returned to his seat and made room for Wulfstan to sit next to him. Ragnar and I were introduced, seated on the bench on Skarthi's left side and then ignored.

Wenches brought meat, bread and ale to the table. Realising how hungry I was, I did full justice to everything set in front of me. Ragnar did likewise but Wulfstan turned down the meat.

'It is Friday here as in the rest of the Christian world I assume, Ingolf,' he said.

'Ah, but so it is!' Skarthi dropped his pig's trotter onto the table. 'Those stupid thralls, they ...' he cleared his throat and fumbled at his chest. I smiled when I recognised that he was secreting his Thor's hammer amulet into the folds of his tunic.

'And how is the building of the chapel proceeding, Ingolf?' The Archbishop seemed not to have noticed the discomfiture of our host. 'It must be almost finished. It is, let me think, how many years since King Æthelstan sent me here to baptise you and your household?'

'Ah now, Your Grace, let me think. It can't be more than three, perhaps less.'

'Oh, more than that, surely. Four at least. Oh, and where is the young priest I left behind to help you carry out your religious duties?'

'He ... ahem ... left.'

'Oh really – but the young man was so full of zeal, so eager to serve both King Æthelstan and Our Lord. What made him change his mind? He should have let the King know at the very least.'

Skarthi was seized by a coughing fit and Wulfstan gave him a hearty punch between the shoulder blades. I realised then that the poor priest had met with an untimely death, probably at the hands of Skarthi's people and that Wulfstan was fully aware of this. Skarthi was now sweating and red in the face.

'Your Grace has come a long way to honour your humble servant with a visit. How can I be of service to Your Grace?' he said when he had stopped coughing. Wulfstan explained that he needed men and horses for the journey back to Jorvik and Skarthi agreed with enthusiasm to every request. He beamed with relief and goodwill when Wulfstan declared his intent to leave the same day. His benevolence extended to Ragnar and me in offering supplies and men to help load the ship so we could leave by the next tide.

* * *

The escort for Wulfstan and the supplies for *Storm-Wolf* arrived and Wulfstan decided to leave immediately. Before he left, he gave Olvir a small cross of silver on a chain.

'We never played for money but I think I owe you this all the same. Just don't follow your mother's example and keep bending the top arm back and forth because sooner or later it will break off.' He winked at me. My mouth fell open. I wondered how he knew. Then he mounted his horse, waved the sign of the cross in our direction and rode off.

Some of Skarthi's men arrived with a barrel of fresh water and the carcasses of two sheep and a heifer. They insisted on carrying the supplies out to *Storm-Wolf*. Skarthi had ordered them to give us every assistance, the servant in charge assured me with a smirk.

'They show too much interest in what's on board,' muttered Thorfinn, and Ragnar nodded.

'Get everyone ready,' he said. The men gathered our belongings which had been spread out on the sand to dry. Kirsten and the children were carried out to the ship and told to get in under the steering platform. I went with them and stood in front of their shelter ready for what was to come.

The tide was still out and *Storm-Wolf* rested with her shallow keel embedded in the sand. Some of the crew tried to push her further out and the rest formed a shieldwall at the water's edge. Skarthi had obviously thought to take us by surprise and sent only a handful of warriors. When they saw our strength they turned and ran for the borough. We had some precious moments before they brought reinforcements. But the water was still too shallow to support the hull. The crew heaved and shunted and the ship churned up sand as it moved a few ells further out.

Skarthi's men returned. Now they greatly outnumbered us. Arrows and throwing axes began to find targets among our crew. The shieldwall retreated and put their backs to the ship's sides. *Storm-Wolf* edged into deeper water and was afloat. The men clung to oar-ports and ropes and clambered on board. The extra weight was enough to put us aground again. Skarthi's men advanced through the water towards us. Some carried ladders. Behind them archers added fire to the axes and rocks coming at us through the air. A wave lifted *Storm-Wolf* clear. We cheered. But the wave receded and we were again firmly lodged on the sand.

The steering-oar had not been pulled on board and when the wave hit us, it swung into place. I felt the jolt when the wave left, the ship came down and the rudder dug deep into the sandy bottom of the bay. I rushed over and tried to move it but it was stuck acting as a wedge keeping the *Storm-Wolf* facing the beach. The first of Skarthi's men had reached the side of the ship and were using their ladders to climb on board.

I knew I had caused this attack. Odin and Thor had guided *Storm-Wolf* to Skarthi's borough. I was to be punished and my family and followers with me. I raised my sword to the sky and called to the gods.

'Odin, you refused my sacrifice of a fine horse. You turned away from my remorse, you rejected my plea for forgiveness. But you took my child. A life for a life. I have paid my debt. Save us!' Then I planted my feet firmly in front of the steering platform. Underneath it, Kirsten was hiding with my children. I prepared to defend them.

The attackers struggled through the water to get to us. Many fell trying to get close and climb their ladders to get to us. But they were many more than us and they were fired with greed and the scent of victory. The water coloured red as men fell bleeding among the shallow waves. We had used up spears and throwing axes, our own and the ones aimed at us and returned. We pushed ladders from the sides of the ship and sent men sprawling backwards into the water. We hacked and sliced with our swords and axes. And still they kept coming. Until a cry rang out and they retreated. But they did not pull back in defeat. They looked upwards and cheered. There was a mighty fire on top of the cliff. Rolls of straw had been set alight and came shooting off the edge towards us. Most landed in the water with a furious fizz. But some landed on the deck of *Storm-Wolf*. We used oars to lift them over the sides but more kept coming and fire was taking hold.

I looked up to the sky, hoping for a sign. I felt for my Thor's hammer amulet but my fingers got tangled in my neck-chain. There was my little silver cross, distorted out of all recognition and weakened by my constant bending it. It was easy to twist it off the chain. I threw it in a wide arch towards the sun. It glittered for a moment before falling and disappearing into the water.

There was a rumbling from the clouds behind the village, a flash of lightning and a crash of thunder. Water began to foam around the ship's hull. Thor waited until this our most desperate time before he sent the tidal wave that lifted *Storm-Wolf* free of her fetters. With a triumphant shout the men put out the oars and *Storm-Wolf* rode the foaming water and headed out to sea. I knew we were safe then and I knew we were on our way home.

THE END

Characters in *Shieldmaiden*

<u>King Æthelstan</u> King of Wessex and Mercia 924- 939

Aisgerd <u>Rolfsdaughter,</u> Jarl Swein Hjaltebrand's wife, Ragnar's mother

<u>Old **Ake**</u>, servant at Swanhill

Brother **Ansgar**, monk, scribe at King Æthelstan's court

Anlaf <u>Yngvarson</u>, son of Yngvar and Hrodney of Rannerdale Farm

Bard <u>Beornson</u>, housekarl to Sigrid's father at Becklund then freeman on Swanhill

Beorn <u>the Lame</u>, servant at Buttermere Farm

Bjalke <u>Sigtryggson</u>, Cumbrian chieftain supports Sigrid at the Allthing

Bjarne, son of a servant woman at Buttermere, Olvir's friend

Brita <u>Bjalkesdaughter</u>, Bard Beornson's wife

<u>King **Constantine**</u>, of Scotland

Eahlswith, Steinar's Anglian wife, Sigrid's sister-in-law

Edmund <u>Ætheling</u>, Æthelstan's younger brother, King of Mercia and Wessex 939- 946

Eirik Haraldson (Bloodaxe), son of Harald Finehair, King of Norway c. 930- 935 or 936, challenged for the throne by younger brother Hakon, who gained support of most of the Norwegian chieftains. Eirik was appointed King of Northumbria by Æthelstan after the battle of Brunanburh in 937, deposed by King Edmund in 939

Freydis Helgisdaughter, Thorstein's wife, Sigrid's sister-in-law

Gudrun Haraldsdaughter, Sigrid's mother

Gunnar Sigfusson, owner of the dragonship *Cloudrider* which took Sigrid to Norway

Queen **Gunnhild**, Eirik Bloodaxe's wife, half-sister of King Harald Bluetooth of Denmark

Gyda Sweinsdaughter, Ragnar's sister

King **Hakon** of Norway, took Norway from Eirik Bloodaxe 935 or 936

King **Harald** Finehair, King of Norway c. 872 – c. 930

Hauk Gunnarson, wealthy farmer on Swanhill, Sigrid's first husband

Helgi Thorkilson, Cumbrian chieftain, supports Sigrid at the Allthing

Helgi Biornson, Norwegian Jarl rebelling against King Hakon

Hrodney Rainesdaughter, Yngvar Anlafson's widow, Anlaf's mother, marries Thorfinn

Ingefried Guthfrithdaughter, Gunhild's servant from

Norway, becomes Sigrid's servant

Ketil Thorkelson, thrall at Becklund

Kirsten, Old Kirsten's granddaughter, becomes Sigrid's serving woman

Old **Kirsten**, 'wise woman', healer in Nidaros

Kjeld Gunnarson, Hauk's half-brother

Kveldulf Arnvidson, Sigrid's father

Kveldulf Haukson / Ragnarson, Sigrid's eldest son

Lothar, Ragnar's friend from Neustria

Lydia, Hauk's thrall-woman at Swanhill, mother of Maria, Anna and Jesus

Mord Lambason of Keskadale, Lawman

Olaf Biornson, Norwegian Jarl rebelling against King Hakon

Olaf Guthfrithson, King of the Dublin Danes with claim to be King of Northumbria

Ole the Toothless, thrall at Swanhill

Olvir, young thrall at Becklund, fostered by Sigrid

Ragnar Sweinson, Sigrid's childhood sweetheart, son of Jarl Swein Hjaltebrand from Manx

Rolf Kveldulfson, Sigrid's eldest brother killed aged 12

Sigrid Kveldulfsdaughter, the Shieldmaiden

Skarthi, founder of Scarborough (Skarthi's borough)

Jarl Sigurd of Lade, powerful Norwegian chieftain supporting King Hakon

Steinar Kveldulfson, Sigrid's youngest brother

Jarl Swein Ragnarson Hjaltebrand, chieftain from Manx, Ragnar's father, Kveldulf Arnvidson's blood-brother

Thora Sweinsdaughter, Jarl Swein's daughter, Ragnar's sister

Thorfinn Egilson, Ragnar's father's housekarl.

Thorgunn Ketilsdaughter, Hauk of Swanhill's mother

Thorstein Kveldulfson, Sigrid's eldest surviving brother

Toki, Sigrid's mother's servant in Norway

Ulf Bjalkeson, Anlaf's friend from Kid Crag Farm on Crummockwater

Yngvar Anlafson, Jarl Swein's housekarl, married to Hrodney, father of Anlaf

William Longsword, ruler of Normandy

Archbishop **Wulfstan I** of York

Historical Note on *Shieldmaiden*

Shieldmaiden is a work of fiction based on historical evidence and records. The Battle of Brunanburh is a true event described in the Anglo-Saxon Chronicle and Egil's Saga, where it is called the Battle of Vin Moor. The Raid on Nidaros is fiction but, given that King Hakon's position still wasn't secure, there may well have been such attacks on him and Jarl Sigurd.

Although Sigrid, her family and the other people in Cumbria and Norway are fictional, we know that the Vikings on Manx did flee from King Harald Finehair's revenge and some of them are said to have ended up in Buttermere and Rannerdale but perhaps not at the time or in the manner I describe.

Jarl Sigurd of Lade and the kings Æthelstan, Edmund and Hakon are real people and I have tried to stay true to what is known about them, their whereabouts and their actions at this time. Eirik Bloodaxe is more difficult to pinpoint; the Anglo-Saxon Chronicle doesn't mention him until later but some sources state that he was king of Northumbria, under Æthelstan, after the battle of Brunanburh. I have bought into the bad press given by the saga-writers to his wife, Gunnhild. Archbishop Wulfstan is another true character who appears to have played his own political game in the North of England.

Archaeological and written evidence support traditional Scandinavian legends about warrior women called shieldmaidens.

About the Author

As for me, I was born and grew up in Sweden. I came to England to study for a year, met my husband and remained. We live in Leicestershire but enjoy visiting the old Danelaw, especially Cumbria and Yorkshire. I see it as my duty to challenge the prevailing view of Vikings as mad marauders and remind people that they were also traders, explorers and farmers, in fact they were, as recent DNA surveys in the North of England have shown, our common ancestors.

Marianne Whiting
March 2012

Acknowledgements

I owe great thanks to Leicester Writers' Club, especially Rod Duncan and Chris d'Lacey, for their valuable critique and encouragement. I would also like to thank Jay Rigel-d'Lacey whose enthusiasm for Shieldmaiden kept me going through a difficult patch. Last but not least, a big thank you to my husband Jon for his patience during numerous visits to museums and events.

For more information about
Marianne Whiting

and other **Accent Press** titles

please visit

www.accentpress.co.uk

Lightning Source UK Ltd.
Milton Keynes UK
UKOW03f1433051216
289237UK00002B/11/P